Mark Hill is a London-based full-time writer of novels and scripts. Formerly he was a journalist and a producer at BBC Radio 2 across a range of major daytime shows and projects. He has won two Sony Gold Awards.

Also by Mark Hill

It Was Her

His
First
Lie

MARK HILL

sphere

SPHERE

First published in Great Britain in ebook in 2016 by Sphere
Paperback published in 2017 by Sphere
This edition published in 2018 by Sphere
Originally published as *Two O'Clock Boy*

1 3 5 7 9 10 8 6 4 2

Copyright © Mark Hill 2017

A CIP catalogue record for this book is available from the British Library.

ISBN 978-0-7515-7384-8

Typeset in Adobe Caslon Pro by Palimpsest Book Production Limited,
Falkirk, Stirlingshire
Printed and bound in Great Britain by Clays Ltd, St Ives plc

Papers used by Sphere are from well-managed forests
and other responsible sources.

MIX
Paper from
responsible sources
FSC® C104740

Sphere
An imprint of
Little, Brown Book Group
Carmelite House
50 Victoria Embankment
London
EC4Y 0DZ

An Hachette UK Company
www.hachette.co.uk

www.littlebrown.co.uk

For Fiona & Archie

Time shall unfold what plighted cunning hides;
Who cover faults, at last shame them derides.

WILLIAM SHAKESPEARE

1

The boy loved his parents more than anything on this Earth. And so he had to kill them.

Perched on the edge of the bunk, he listened to them now. To the squeak of their soles on the deck above as they threw recriminations back and forth in voices as vicious as the screeching seagulls wheeling in the sky. He heard the crack of the sail in the wind, the smack of the water against the hull inches from his head, a soothing, hypnotic rhythm.

Slap . . . slap . . . slap . . .

Before everything went wrong, before the boy went away as one person and came back as someone different, they had been full of gentle caresses and soft words for each other. But they argued all the time now, his parents – too stridently, loud enough for him to hear – and the quarrel was always about the same thing: what could be done about their unhappy son?

He understood that they wanted him to know how remorseful they were about what had happened. But their misery only made him feel worse. He couldn't remember the last time he'd been able to speak to them, to utter a single word, and the longer he stayed silent the more his parents fought. The boy plugged his fingers into his ears, closed his eyes, and listened to the dull roar within him.

His love for them was untethering, drifting away on a fierce tide.

Slap . . . slap . . . slap . . .

A muffled voice. 'Darling.'

The boy's hands were pulled gently from his face. His mother crouched before him. Her eyes were rimmed red, and her hair was plastered to her face by sea spray, but she was still startlingly beautiful.

'Why don't you come up top?'

Her cold fingers tucked a loose strand of his hair behind his ear. For a brief moment he felt a familiar tenderness, wanted to clasp her to him and ignore the bitter thoughts that churned in his head. But he didn't, he couldn't. It had been weeks since he'd been able to speak.

A shadow fell across the hatch. His father's voice boomed, 'Is he coming up?'

'Please, let me handle this,' his mother barked over her shoulder, and after a moment of hesitation, the shadow disappeared.

'We're doing the best we can.' She waited for her son to speak. 'But you must tell us how you feel, so that we can help you.'

The boy managed a small nod, and hope flickered in his mother's gaze.

'Your father and I . . . we love you more than anything. If we argue it's because we can never forgive ourselves for what happened to you. You know that, don't you?'

Her eyes filled with tears, and he would do anything to stop her from crying. In a cracked voice, barely more than a whisper, he heard himself say, 'I love you.'

His mother's hand flew to her mouth. She stood, hunched in the cabin.

'We're about to eat sandwiches.' Moving to the steps, she spoke brightly, but her voice trembled. 'Why don't you come up when you're ready?'

He nodded. With a last, eager smile, his mother climbed to the hatch and her body was consumed by sunlight.

The boy's heel thudded against the clasp of the toolbox beneath his berth. He pulled out the metal box and tipped open the lid to reveal his father's tools. Rasps, pliers, a spirit level. Tacks and nails, a chisel slick with grease. Lifting the top tray, the heavier tools were revealed: a saw, a screwdriver, a peen hammer. The varnish on the handle of the hammer was worn away. The wood was rough, its mottled head pounded to a dull grey. He lifted it, felt its weight in his palm.

Clenching the hammer in his fist, he stooped beneath the bulkhead – in the last couple of years he'd grown so much taller – to listen to the clink of plastic plates, his parents' animated voices on the deck.

'Sandwiches are ready!' called his mother.

Every night he had the same dream, like a terrible premonition: his parents passed him on the street without a glance, as if they were total strangers. Sooner or later, he knew, this nightmare would become a reality. The resentment they felt that their child had gone for ever, replaced by somebody else, someone ugly inside, would chip away at their love for him. Until there was nothing left.

And he was afraid that his own fierce love for them was slowly rotting, corroded by blame and bitterness. One day, when it was gone completely, other emotions would fill the desolate space inside him. Fury, rage. A cold, implacable hatred. Already he felt anger swelling like a storm where his love had been. He couldn't bear to hate them, yearned to keep his love for his parents – and his memories of a happy time before he went to that place – uncorrupted, and to carry it with him into an uncertain future.

And so he had to act.

Gripping the hammer, the boy moved towards the hatch. His view filled with the blinding grey of the sky and the blur of the wheeling gulls, which screamed a warning to him that this world would always snatch from him the things he cherished, that life would always be this way.

He stepped onto the windblown deck in the middle of a sea that went on for ever.

Slap . . . slap . . . slap . . .

2

Everybody wanted a piece of Detective Inspector Ray Drake.

He circled the room, accepting handshakes and backslaps until there was no one left to congratulate him. Soon, he hoped, they'd all get too drunk to remember he was there and he'd be able to slip away.

He was being selfish, he knew that, but large social gatherings like this made him uncomfortable, particularly when he was in the spotlight. If she were here, Laura would tell him to leave right away, not to worry about what anybody else thought.

Detective Constable Eddie Upson was already well on the way to getting pissed. Waving his pint around, he cornered Drake to moan about missing out on promotion.

'It's not like I haven't delivered.' Lager slopped belligerently over the lip of his pint. 'You know what I can do.'

'Excuse me a moment, Eddie.'

At the back of the room, clinging to the wall beneath a curled poster of Jimmy Greaves, was Flick Crowley, the only person who looked like she wanted to be in this pub less than he did, and Drake pushed towards her. On his way, he elbowed Frank Wanderly.

'Sorry, Frank.'

5

'That's quite all right.' The duty sergeant clasped his hands together. Tall and gaunt, and with not a single hair on his head, everybody at the nick fondly called him Nosferatu. 'And congratulations once again, DI Drake, it's well deserved.'

A few hours earlier, Drake and his Murder Investigation Team had received a Commendation for outstanding service, commitment and teamwork, after the successful completion of a series of homicide investigations in Haringey. Cops and civilian staff had come from Tottenham Police Station to celebrate beneath a blizzard of Spurs memorabilia – shirts, scarves and photos – on the walls.

Drake smiled his thanks, and kept moving.

'You're looking smart tonight, guv,' Flick said.

Drake was wearing the same clothes he always did, a dark off-the-peg suit, white shirt and a frayed brown tie – which Laura had bought him many years ago and lately he'd taken to wearing again – so he guessed she was being mischievous. He was a restless, wiry man who found it impossible to stop moving for long, and no oil painting either. Drake's craggy face was all unexpected drops and sharp angles, as if carelessly hacked from stone.

'I spoke to Harris earlier.' He placed his glass of orange juice on the ledge against the wall, glad to be shot of it. 'Told him how glad I was that you got the promotion.'

Flick frowned. 'As if you had nothing to do with it.'

Detective Chief Inspector Harris had been adamant that they should bring an experienced pair of hands into the Murder Investigation Team, but Ray Drake had gone to war on Flick's behalf, and she'd been promoted from Detective Constable to Detective Sergeant. He had worked to build her confidence, to make her believe in herself a bit more. She was prone to hide behind procedures and systems, but fundamentally she was a fine copper. In time, when she'd learned more readily to trust her instincts, she'd be a very good detective indeed.

'If anyone deserves the chance, it's you.'

Flick glanced over at Upson, his arms draped over the shoulders of the two young PCs he'd clearly singled out to be his drinking comrades for the evening, regardless of their feelings on the matter. 'Eddie doesn't seem to think so.'

'He'll come round. I want you to lead the next investigation, whenever it comes in.'

'Really?' she asked, surprised.

'I think you're ready, DS Crowley.'

She took a gulp of wine, not knowing what to say. 'I meant to ask, how's April?'

'Good.' Drake stiffened at the mention of his daughter's name. Things hadn't been good between them, not since the funeral, and he hadn't the slightest idea how to make things better. 'She's good.'

'The offer still stands. If you'd like me to talk to her . . .'

'Thank you.' He nodded at Harris. 'The DCI has brought along a couple of suits from Scotland Yard.'

'I didn't mean to—'

'Come on,' he said quickly, 'I'll introduce you.'

'You know what? I think I'll give it a miss.' She drained her glass of red. 'Besides, it looks like Vix has got that area locked down.'

Detective Constable Vix Moore was working the guys from the Yard, nodding gravely, the tips of her long blonde bob bouncing, as they explained the latest Met reorganisation proposals.

'Besides,' said Flick, 'I'm shattered, and I want to get home.'

'Stay a while longer. We're celebrating your good news, as well.'

'To be honest, it's been a crazy couple of months – work's been non-stop – and I fancy an early night.' Drake wondered if there was something else on her mind. Flick's watchful almond eyes gave little away beneath a thick fringe of brown hair. A tall woman, a shade below six foot, she had a tendency to hunch, as if the weight of the world was bearing down on her shoulders. She had been a keen swimmer once upon a time, and a good one, she had told Drake. The top of her arms tapered into a strong, lean body, but her broad shoulders rolled forward apologetically. 'Sorry, guv, but I don't think I could bear it if someone *says a few words*.'

'Fair enough.' Having heard more than one of Harris's interminable speeches, he couldn't blame her. 'But just for the record, I'm proud of you.'

'Thank you.' A hesitant smile played across her face. 'I really appreciate everything you've done.'

Her last words were clipped by the sound of a pen ringing loudly against a glass.

'Attention, everybody!' DCI Harris's stomach strained against a tight Lycra top, and his shins were pale beneath lurid black and yellow cycling shorts.

'Too late,' Drake whispered as conversation died and a respectful space opened around him and Flick.

'I know everyone's having fun, however I really wanted to say a few words about the very deserved commendation given to DI Drake and his team,' said Harris. 'But first, we've a new detective sergeant in our midst, so I want you all to put your hands together for Flick Crowley.'

'Smile for the ladies and gentlemen, DS Crowley,' murmured Drake, behind the grin bolted to his face.

Hanging onto her empty glass, Flick shot him a look that suggested, on balance, she'd rather face a firing squad.

nd le get the scones and... suffer on the floor), murmured Diane, before gie were rolled to the... Diane began her support-eag... ded it to know that juggestion, and I cannot allow more to from heard.

3

Kenny hated going straight. Loathed it.

He'd been a good boy for three years now – three years, eight months and fourteen days, to be exact – and every single minute of every single hour had been excruciating. A few years back, if you'd told him that he'd be strapped onto the dreary treadmill of so-called everyday life, he'd have laughed in your face. Now the joke was on him, having to work nights in a supermarket, stacking shelves and lugging pallets beneath pallid yellow lights that exaggerated every pimple and line on your face.

The night bus groaned away down Tottenham High Road, carrying off the motley collection of night owls who sat obscured like phantoms behind glass thick with condensation, and within minutes Kenny was striding down Scales Road, past the foxes nosing around the bins, to let himself into his little terraced house.

Tonight he'd had another row with his supervisor, a spotty kid with a business degree. He picked fights with Kenny every chance he got just to show who was in charge, stomping up and down the aisles, clip-on tie swinging like a limp dick. Stack those boxes, tidy that display!

On top of that, Kenny had lost his mobile. God knows where. He knew he'd had it when he left home, but when he'd gone to put it in his locker it had disappeared.

10

A floorboard creaked above him, and he spotted Phil's bag nudged beneath the stairs. That girlfriend of his had likely thrown him out again and he was sleeping in the spare room. Kenny loved his sons, honestly he did, but Phil's snore was as loud as a steam train.

He took a glass from a kitchen cabinet and poured a measure of Bell's. This was his nightly ritual, the one part of his day he looked forward to: a modest snifter before bed.

After the first sip the familiar debate began in his head.

He'd been given a second chance, and for that he was grateful. But he missed his old life. This was the truth that always returned in the early hours. He yearned for the thrill of living on the edge. Time was, every decision had consequences. Kenny woke in the morning not knowing how he'd get his hands on money to feed his family, or whether the cops would come knocking. He could be packing a bag for prison or heading out on a five-day bender. Each and every day was different; Kenny had felt *alive*.

Now he was a worker ant, toiling in the early hours alongside students and ethnics. The plan was to buy a cab. He worked nights, slept mornings and went out on his moped in the afternoons to learn The Knowledge. Babs was learning it, too. At weekends they tested each other about roads, cul-de-sacs and byways. In a couple of years they'd have enough in the bank to buy a Hackney Cab. They'd watched a documentary about a cabbie who'd earned so much money he'd bought himself a plot of land on the Costa, a little piece of paradise, complete with a pool and an orchard. That was their dream, their destination. All he had to do was keep turning up for work. It wouldn't be for ever.

Because for reasons he didn't want to examine too carefully, Kenny was desperate to move away.

As far as he could.

That old uneasiness settled on him. His thoughts drifted to those people from the home. It didn't seem possible they were all dead. But it was Jason's death that really got to him. Jason, who'd gone crazy with the stress and strain of it, so they said, and put a shooter to the heads of his nearest and dearest. Jason was a mad sod, everyone knew that, but nobody would convince Kenny that Jason killed his girl and kid and then blew his own brains out.

He drained the glass and placed it in the sink. Blobs of rain pattered across the window. The back door rattled. Checking the handle, he found it unlocked. That was Babs, in and out of the garden all night, smoking, littering the plant pots with fag butts. He turned the key in the door and wearily climbed the stairs.

Kenny took a piss, careful not to splash the seat, and shuffled down the hallway. Christ, it was pitch black. The door to the spare bedroom was open, the room empty. Phil must have changed his mind about staying – or more likely he was still out with mates.

A pungent stink hit him as soon as Kenny opened the door to his bedroom – Babs's muggy exhalations. Kenny loved that smell. He was seconds away from snuggling against her.

But there was another smell he couldn't place – chemical, plastic.

His wife cried out – a toneless, muffled sound.

'Sorry, love.' Kenny stumbled out of his trousers, trying not to disturb her. The stench in his nostrils was bitter, acrid. 'Bloody stinks in here.'

The soles of his socks felt damp. He dabbed anxiously against the wall to find the light switch.

And when he turned it on, when he *saw*, he knew he was lost.

His head was yanked back and a cold blade placed against the loose skin at his throat.

A voice hissed in his ear: 'Hello, Kenny. Long time no see.'

4

Ray Drake walked anxiously towards the crime scene. He was there within minutes; it was barely a few hundred yards from Tottenham Police Station.

Police vans and squad cars were parked along the street. Clots of people gathered in the sweep of the cherry lights to watch the proceedings from the outer cordon. An inner cordon sealed off the middle of the street to all but scene-of-crime officers and authorised personnel. Drake badged the uniform there, and took a pair of polythene shoe-covers from a bag dangling from his clipboard.

Eddie Upson stood on the pavement, making the bins look untidy. His eyes were bloodshot, and his shirt flapped open at the bottom to reveal a wiry tangle of stomach hair. When Drake left the pub last night – after that speech by Harris finally ended – Upson looked settled in for a long session.

'Upstairs, sir.'

Drake nodded up at the bedroom. 'What's it like?'

'Not pleasant.' Upson smothered a yawn. 'It's kind of . . . intense.'

'We keeping you up, Eddie?'

'Bit of a headache.' Upson stretched. 'Thought you'd leave all the crime-scene malarkey to Flick – uh, DS Crowley – now.'

Upson discreetly tucked in his shirt as they walked up the path to the house. Drake knew he shouldn't be there, Flick was the officer in charge and he should just let her get on with it, but Harris would be all over this investigation like a rash. A triple murder just around the corner from a police station – the media would have a field day.

That's what he told himself. But there was something else.

When he was given the name and address of the possible victims, an alarm, a warning signal buried deep inside of him, had gone off, spluttered into life like a candle, dormant for decades, igniting in the depths of a bottomless cave.

He had to be there. He *needed* to be there.

'Talk me through it,' he said.

At the door, they slipped the elasticated bootees onto their shoes, Eddie swaying dangerously as he lifted one leg and then the other.

'The house is rented by a middle-aged couple called Kenny and Barbara Overton.'

'We're sure it's them?'

'Neighbours ID'd their DVLA photos.'

'And the third victim?'

'Kenny and Barbara have two grown-up sons who're always popping in. Phillip and, uh . . .' He squinted at his notebook. 'Ryan.'

'Which one is it?'

'We don't know yet. They're twins – but not identical. Cars are on the way to both addresses.'

They stepped aside to let a pair of scene-of-crime officers carry tubs of equipment into the house. Drake took nitrile gloves from his pocket and shook them out, taking his time about it. There was a faint tremor in his hands when he snapped them over his wrists.

'Coming inside, guv?'

Upson had an expectant look on his face. Drake wondered how long he'd been standing there fiddling with the gloves, unconsciously putting off the moment when he had to step inside . . .

On the landing a large battery-powered arc light was stooped towards the doorway of the front bedroom, its white beam switched off. The bodies inside that room could stay there all day and long into the night, as the CSIs painstakingly recorded the crime scene and a pathologist studied them in situ.

From the room came the whir of a camera. Every detail of the crime scene would be photographed hundreds of times and the images added to an evidence database.

Drake ducked beneath the lamp, stepping carefully across the tread plates that allowed everyone to move around without contaminating evidence on the floor. A crime scene could become a crowded place, with crime scene examiners, coppers, pathologists and medical staff trampling everywhere. On the other side of the room, Flick Crowley frowned at the bodies.

'Who found them?'

'A neighbour gets up early every morning,' said Flick. 'He's out of the house by five thirty, works in the kitchen of a West End hotel. He walks past, sees the front door is wide open. Thinks it's a burglary, so he goes inside to take a look around. Seconds later, he comes out screaming. Runs into a pair of Specials scoffing burgers on the High Road. They come back, call the paramedics and close off the scene.'

'And nobody else saw or heard anything?'

'The neighbour on the left is a young mum. She was up at three a.m. breastfeeding. Said she heard a shout.'

'A shout?'

'A noise, a cry, she couldn't be sure.' Flick pressed against the wall to let the forensics guy leave. 'She didn't think anything of it. Mr and Mrs Overton love a good row, apparently.'

Turned inwards to face each other, the three victims were trussed to kitchen chairs by layer upon layer of plastic film, from toes to nostrils. Their arms were formless lumps pinned to their sides.

The wrapping glinted blue in the stark morning light, except across their torsos, which were slashed and shredded and dripping red. Serrated flesh and chunks of gristle poked from jagged holes in their chests and stomachs. Smooth piping and ruptured veins and organs glistened vividly against glimpses of white ribcage. The gouges were deep and wide and, Drake guessed, made by a long, flat blade. He leaned closer to get a better sense of depth. The fleshy bottom lips of the wounds were angled sharply downwards, like fish mouths.

Their killer had stood over them and brought the knife down again and again. Were they awake, these poor people, Drake wondered, and forced to watch the deaths of their loved ones, knowing they would be next? Were they killed one after the other, in a particular order? Or did the killer stab at them randomly, whirling wildly from one victim to another, until the slaughter was complete?

A sliced arterial vein could spurt blood a good few feet into the air. Spatters of it flecked the walls, the net curtains,

17

the delicate china figurines on the window ledge. The duvet on the bed was soaked, the rug beneath the victims' chairs sodden black. Blood bubbled at the base of the tread plates as Drake stepped across them.

There was a riot of partial footprints in the sticky liquid, left by the special constables who discovered the grisly scene and the paramedics who searched futilely for any faint pulse. Maybe, just maybe, the perpetrator's prints would be among them.

There was no sign of a blade. The killer may have dropped it in panic, in the house or surrounding streets. It could even be lying on the steps of the station round the corner. That would go down well in the press.

'No weapon's been found,' said Flick, as if reading his mind. 'We're hoping to get enough bodies together for a search within twenty minutes. Millie Steiner's on it now.'

A systematic search was difficult at the best of times, let alone in the crowded inner-city streets. The surrounding area was a dense maze. Parts of the High Road would have to be closed off before the rush of Saturday-morning shoppers made the task of finding the weapon all but impossible.

'The King is dead,' intoned a voice behind Drake. 'Long live the King!' Peter Holloway, the crime scene manager, stood in the doorway. 'Just can't keep away, can you, DI Drake?'

'What else am I going to do on a weekend?'

'Practise that golf swing,' he said. 'Or take that lovely daughter of yours somewhere special.'

'I'd rather come and interfere with your crime scene, Peter,' said Drake. 'For old time's sake.'

'My people need to get on,' said Holloway.

'We won't be long,' said Flick.

Holloway was right, of course. His team needed to go about their business. Logging and recording. Videoing, photographing, removing evidence for examination. As CSM, Holloway's job was to coordinate the collection of evidence and protect the integrity of the forensic investigation. Ray Drake always liked to get to the crime scene as soon as possible. The first few hours of any investigation – the so-called Golden Hour – were the most critical, and he and Holloway often exchanged forthright views if the CSM felt he was getting in the way.

Drake had a grudging admiration for the bombastic know-all. A lean, middle-aged man, there was a vanity to his precise movements. When Holloway pulled down the hood of his coveralls, his face was taut and unblemished. Drake often wondered if he'd had some discreet work done.

'You've very big boots to fill, DS Crowley.' A pair of half-moon glasses tipped from his hair onto his nose with a jerk of his head.

'If I didn't know it already,' said Flick, who was looking at the windowsill, 'there's a plenty of people to remind me.'

Holloway gestured with his clipboard. 'You'll never be the investigator that DI Drake is.'

'Thanks,' Flick said quietly. 'I'll try to remember that.'

'No need to be so touchy, DS Crowley. What I mean is, be your own person, do things your own way. If you try to be a mere simulacrum of Ray Drake, you'll fail.'

'I've no idea what a simulacrum is, but thank you anyway.'

'She'll go far, this one,' said Holloway, nodding at her.

Drake didn't look up from the bodies. 'Yes, she will.'

'One's missing,' said Flick.

'Excuse me?'

'The figurines.' She pointed at three porcelain eighteenth-century figures – a woman in a gown and bonnet, men in waistcoats and three-cornered hats – spaced irregularly on the sill. 'There's a space where one's missing.'

'Smashed, maybe,' said Drake.

'Guv . . .?' Vix Moore's head peeked from behind the banister on the landing, her gaze moving quickly from Drake to Flick. 'I mean, guv . . .'

'What is it, Vix?'

'Someone's just turned up at the cordon. Says he's Ryan Overton.'

'I'll come down.' Hesitating in the doorway, Flick looked at the cocooned victims one last time. 'They're like human flies ensnared by a giant spider.'

Holloway followed her to the door. 'I was thinking more along the lines of mouldy wrapped sandwiches at a seaside café.' He turned to Drake. 'Make it quick, please.'

Left alone in the room, Drake forced down the nausea he felt. The stench in the room, of plastic and plasma, was overpowering as he moved from one body to another.

The younger man – in all likelihood Phillip Overton – sat with his head thrown back like a schoolboy laughing at the back of the class, a tight ruffle of plastic shredded around his mouth. His blank eyes were open, and his scalp was sprayed with inky globules of blood.

Barbara Overton's head, partly concealed by the sheets of plastic cut away by the paramedics, lolled on her chest. Her hair, matted with blood and gristle, was pulled back in a lank ponytail, her slack face imprinted with traces of the

20

terror of her final catastrophic moments on Earth.

Drake arrived at Kenny Overton. The tops of his thighs burned when he crouched to get an eye-level view of the dead man's face. Wisps of fine auburn hair congealed against Kenny's scalp. His jowls flopped over the moist plastic around his neck, and his gaping mouth revealed crooked teeth and withered gums stained by vomit and blood.

Horrific death aside, time had not been kind to Kenny Overton.

That sense of foreboding tightened in Drake's stomach. His hand shook when he lifted it. Something hidden, something dangerous and wrong, had been revealed.

A countdown, a slow, inexorable pulse in his gut.

'Kenny,' he whispered. 'It's you.'

5

Ray Drake first met Connor Laird on the hot summer day when Sally Raynor found the new kid at Hackney Wick Police Station.

'Fucking hippy,' an officer muttered as he lifted the wooden counter to allow Sally into the warren of corridors behind the front desk. She swept past in a heavy poncho and long woollen skirt. A battered satchel, its straps curled and frayed, bumped on her hips.

Sergeant Harry Crowley's office was barely larger than a broom cupboard, just big enough to squeeze in Harry and a desk heaped with a mountain of paperwork. The heat hit Sally like a hammer when she walked in, the office was right above the station's boiler. Harry knew where all the bodies were buried in this place, and Sally suspected that someone was trying to sweat him out of the building.

A kid, no older than fourteen or fifteen, was perched on a stool in front of Harry's desk, and she asked, 'Who have you got here?'

Harry scratched his belly. 'A tough guy.'

A fan burred at the edge of his desk, lifting a coil of Brylcreemed hair from Harry's forehead. He looked like

22

Tommy Cooper, that funny magician on the telly, and some joker had given him a red fez, which was forced over the top of a framed photograph of his wife and children.

Harry reached into his tunic to take out a packet of cigarettes, stuck one in the corner of his mouth.

'What's your name?' Sally crouched in front of the boy. A thick helmet of dark hair framed the kid's dirty face, his mouth was an angry smear. 'Where have you come from?'

'Don't waste your breath. He ain't one for talking.' Harry blew out smoke. 'One of my lads found him wandering the streets this afternoon. Dennis knocked his helmet off.'

'Dennis? That's his name?'

'That's what I call him – Dennis the fucking Menace.' Harry poked about on the desk for an ashtray. 'Maybe a slap will loosen his tongue.'

'Don't you dare, Harry.'

The copper's throaty laugh disintegrated into a tangle of coughs. He grabbed his belt, yanked up his sagging trousers. 'That's a bit rich coming from Gordon's girl. Talking of which . . .'

When Harry wiggled his fat fingers, Sally took a battered envelope from her satchel. Inside was a wad of money. He brushed the edges of the notes and dropped the envelope into a drawer.

'I'm going to need a bigger cut from now on; upstairs is getting nervous about our arrangement and it'd be politic to sprinkle more goodwill around the place.'

'Gordon isn't going to like that,' said Sally.

'You tell Tallis he can like it or he can lump it.' The red tip of the cigarette crackled in his mouth.

'You people.' She shook her head. 'Always out for what you can take.'

'If Gordon wants to do business in my borough, he knows the rules.' Harry dabbed at his forehead with a hanky. 'A posh girl like you, maybe you want to pay me some other way.' He came so close she could smell the nicotine and stale sweat lifting from his pores. 'I hear you got a thing for us working-class fellas.'

Sally spoke in a fierce whisper: 'You're scaring the boy, Harry.'

'Scared? Does he look scared to you?' A laugh rattled in Harry's throat. 'Those eyes tell a different story. Go on. Take him away.'

'Take him where?'

He tugged at his belt again. The heavy handcuffs clipped at his waist were forever dragging down his trousers, so he snapped them off, threw them on the desk. 'Gordon runs a children's home, don't he? He can stay there.'

'He may have family, a home.'

'You got somewhere to go back to, Dennis?' Harry cupped an ear, but the boy just stared.

'And what if Gordon won't take him?'

'Drop him down a hole for all I care, but something tells me this one will be useful to him. Come on, get up.'

Grabbing his arm, the sergeant pulled the kid off the stool and swung him against the desk. He made a big show of wiping the vinyl seat with his handkerchief.

'Remember to tell Gordon about the money. And you . . .' Harry jabbed a finger at the kid. 'I don't want to see you again. I got a nose for wrong 'uns, and it tells me that no good is going to come of you.'

* * *

24

When she arrived in the car park with the boy, Sally saw Ray leaning against the bonnet of her Morris Marina, throwing pebbles at a drain.

She sighed. 'I told you to go home.'

'Thought I'd wait for you.' Ray lifted himself off the car. 'To discover what secret thing it was you had to do.'

'Go home, Ray,' said Sally. 'Myra will go spare.'

'She's at some committee meeting with my father, and they'll be there till the evening. So, you know, I've got all day. We can do something.'

'I'm going back to the Longacre.' Sally balanced the satchel on a knee to search for her car key. 'And you can't come.'

'Hi, I'm Ray Drake.' He nodded at the kid who had come out of the station with her – another teenager, roughly the same age as him – but the boy just stared. As soon as Sally opened the driver's door, he clambered into the front passenger seat. Ray frowned at Sally over the roof of the car. 'Not very friendly, is he? What's his name?'

'Don't know yet.'

'Huh. What's wrong with him?'

Sally leaned in, keeping her voice low. 'Not everyone grew up with a silver spoon in their mouth, Ray. Not everyone is taught impeccable manners at expensive public schools. Where do you want me to drop you?'

He grinned. 'The Longacre will do.'

'You know Gordon doesn't want you there.' She placed her hands on the baking metal of the roof. 'He doesn't like you hanging around.'

'And why would that be?'

'Go home, Ray,' she said, and started to climb in – but he made one of his funny faces. All he had to do was go bug-eyed or pucker his lips and she could deny him nothing. It had been the same since he'd been a toddler. When he wanted something, or when she got angry, all he had to do was grin like a maniac or pull his ears, and she would relent. Even now, when he was afraid that all the joy had gone out of her, when it seemed to him that she was a pale shadow of the funny and vivacious Sally he once knew, he could still get round her.

She shook her head. 'Stop it.'

'Stop what?'

'You know what.'

'Tell you what, I'll do you a deal.'

'No deals, Ray.'

'Drop me off outside. I won't come in; I'll make my own way home.'

And before she could reply he had come round the driver's side and lifted the seat to climb into the back.

Sitting behind the wheel in the baking-hot interior, Sally rolled a cigarette, slapped in the dashboard lighter. Ray shifted against the door behind her to make himself unobtrusive, so that he could listen. If there was one thing Ray Drake was good at, it was listening.

'You going to give me the silent treatment all day?' Sally asked the kid beside her.

In the rear-view mirror, Ray saw the make-up caked against her damp cheeks, the rash of angry spots racing down her jaw and neck. Her nails were almost as dirty as those of the mysterious boy next to her.

When the lighter popped, she applied the burning coil to the tip of the roll-up. The stink of tobacco filled the hot car. 'I want to help, but I'm going to need a name.'

'Connor,' said the boy, finally. 'Connor Laird.'

'Where do you live, Connor? Do you have family?'

The boy called Connor turned away to watch shimmering waves of heat slam into the concrete car park. 'Who's Gordon?'

'Now there's a question,' murmured Ray.

Sally's turned angrily. 'Shut up, Ray.'

Removing a fleck of tobacco from her lip, the poncho fell away from the crook of Sally's elbow to reveal livid scars. She quickly flipped it back but Ray saw them, had seen them before. He didn't know if it was the sight of those red tracks or the cloying smoke filling the sweltering compartment that made him feel sick.

'You'll find out soon enough,' Sally told Connor, and started the car.

The Longacre Children's Home butted up against a railway track at the end of a street where once-grand Victorian homes stood derelict. Some of the empty houses had become squats. Colourful banners hung from windows. Wall murals celebrated forgotten revolutions in far-flung places. The car bumped along the pitted road, past abandoned vehicles and dumped furniture.

'How long will I be here?' Connor asked when Sally swung the car to the kerb outside the double-fronted building.

'That depends,' she said. 'Tell me where you live and I'll take you home.'

Connor stabbed a thumb at Ray in the back. 'Isn't he coming in?'

'*He* doesn't live here,' said Sally. 'He's got a home of his own to go to, and he's going there now. Aren't you, Ray?'

'Whatever you say, sis.' Ray sat up, his sopping T-shirt peeling away from the hot plastic of the seat to cling against his spine.

'Why don't you go inside, Connor?' said Sally. 'I'll be a moment.'

The boy looked up the steps to where the door to the home was ajar. The dull roar of children came from somewhere behind the house.

'See you, Connor.' Ray waved, but the boy walked inside without looking back. 'Myra would have a thing or two to say about that boy's manners.'

'I'm not your sister, Ray.'

'You're my big sister.' He angled a foot on the bottom step to look up at the shoddy house, with its rotten window frames and peeling sills. 'And I don't like you hanging around here.'

'I'm your second cousin, the bad girl. Your parents would go crazy if they knew you were with me.' She glanced over her shoulder. 'Here.'

'My parents hate *everyone*.' He grinned. 'Me included, I think. But it's what I think that counts, and you'll always be my sister, the only one I'll ever have.'

'Go away and do something that normal kids do. Go to the pictures, climb a tree. Look up a girl's skirt.' A curtain in the window shivered, and Sally climbed the steps. 'Enjoy your childhood while you can.'

'Myra says I've got a talent for sticking my nose into other people's business. The kids at my school, I know all their secrets.'

'I'm not joking, Ray. I don't want you here.' She spoke quietly. 'And Gordon doesn't want you here.'

28

She jumped in surprise when the door creaked open. A plump kid with red hair stood there.

'Hello, Kenny,' said Ray.

The ginger boy nodded warily and stammered at Sally: 'Gordon says to come in.'

Sally turned back to Ray. 'You don't belong here. Shove off back to school, why don't you?'

'It's months before I go back, the whole summer. I promise you, you'll miss me when I've gone.' When Sally moved to the door, he called, 'I'm not going to let anything happen to my wicked second cousin. Just so she knows.'

'She doesn't need saving. Go and practise your missionary act somewhere else.'

Then she slammed the door behind her, leaving Ray Drake staring up at the house, the smile slipping from his face.

'Who said she needed saving?' he asked.

Inside the home, dust motes danced in the bright hallway. The walls were covered with smeared drawings and dirty fingerprints. Through an open doorway on the left Connor Laird glimpsed an enormous room dominated by two tables, each long enough to seat a dozen kids.

He would later discover there were only two doors left on their hinges in the entire house. One of them closed on a room on the right. When Sally finally came in, she led him through this door into an untidy office where a man with shoulder-length chestnut hair sat with his feet on a desk. His paisley shirt was crushed beneath a scruffy corduroy jacket the colour of strained tea. His forehead and cheeks were pockmarked, and his jaw was hidden behind a sculpted beard. When he saw Connor, the man broke out into a snaggle-toothed smile. Connor quickly pushed the handcuffs he had stolen from the sergeant's desk deeper into his pocket.

'And who's this?' Gordon asked, in a lilting Scottish accent.

'Harry gave him to me.' Sally dropped her satchel onto a sofa, absently scratching her elbow. 'Said he's got nowhere to go.'

'What's your name, son?' Gordon came round the desk to plant his hands on Connor's shoulders.

'Connor.'

'A good Celtic name.'

Sally inspected her nails. 'Connor's the strong, silent type.'

'Keep yourself to yourself, do you? I can understand that. My name is Mr Tallis, but I'd be grateful if you called me Gordon. You're welcome to stay, Connor. Sally will arrange the paperwork, but we needn't worry about that yet.' He smirked at her. 'He's scaring me with those eyes.'

'Harry wants more money.'

'A lad like you will make plenty of mates here, Connor, but I'd be honoured if you considered me your first friend.' When the boy glanced at Sally, Gordon smirked. 'She doesn't count. Sal's only your friend if you've something she wants.' His eyes slid to her. 'Did you give it to him?'

'He wants more, he said—'

Gordon held up a hand. 'Let's get the boy settled in. Then we'll discuss it.'

'The money isn't enough.'

His voice lifted irritably. 'I *said* let's get the boy settled in.' Gordon opened the door to shout into the corridor: 'Kenny!'

Returning to Connor, he said, 'Breakfast is at six thirty

a.m. You'll be expected to have showered and brushed your teeth – there are communal brushes in the bathrooms, we share everything here, Connor – and to have made your bed. Supper is at six. We all muck in with the daily chores. The Dents will add your duties to the rota on the wall. If you're unable to read, one of the other children will explain them to you.'

When Gordon's hand shot out to grab Connor's cheek, the boy snatched at his wrist.

'Ha! You're stronger than you look, and fast. A bit of spunk, too. We're going to be pals, I think, you and me.' Gordon removed his hand from Connor's grip as the red-haired kid reappeared in the doorway. 'Kenny here will show you around. Let's talk again soon, lad.'

The last thing Connor saw as the door closed behind him was Sally – eager, expectant – an arm stretching towards Gordon.

'My name's Kenny,' said the kid, as they walked towards the back of the house, the linoleum crackling beneath their feet. 'Kenny Overton.'

'Connor.'

'I've been here two years.' Kenny spoke like it was a badge of honour. 'But others have been here even longer.'

Every opening revealed more tatty rooms, and scruffy, listless kids. A girl scribbled feverishly in a book, barely looking up as they passed.

'Do you smoke?' asked Kenny, as they arrived in a massive kitchen, a gloomy room despite the midday sun high in the sky. 'You can have one of mine if you promise to be my friend.'

Connor said: 'I'm nobody's friend.'

Kenny blushed. 'Please don't tell Elliot I asked you.'

The room stank of boiled vegetables. Pots and pans hung over a pine table. Outside, a long garden inclined towards a copse of trees. When a train blipped past beyond them, the windows buzzed in their frames.

On the patio a man and a woman were wedged into deckchairs. A can of lager was balanced on the man's belly, which bulged like risen dough over the shiny fabric of his Speedos. The woman, grossly overweight, wore a bikini.

'That's the Dents, Ronnie and Geraldine. They run the place for Gordon. They're all right, as long as you stay out of their way.'

Children swarmed over the faded brown lawn. One boy saw Connor right away. He was tall and broad, a lumbering youth who towered over the other kids.

Connor guessed this was Elliot. His size, the sullen sneer on his face, and the way his mates fanned out on either side of him, marked him out as trouble. Within moments he was pounding up the garden, his gang falling into formation behind him like geese. Sensing the excitement, other kids fell into their slipstream.

Geraldine Dent, who'd seen it all before, called in a bored voice: '*Elliot.*'

Arms pumping like pistons, Elliot pushed Connor into the kitchen, his brow knotted in pantomime menace, shoving him against the table.

'Who's this, then?' He grabbed a fistful of Connor's T-shirt and twisted it. A forest of small heads bobbed in the doorway behind them.

'His name's Connor,' stammered Kenny.

'Shut your face; he can tell me himself!'

One of Elliot's mates pinched Kenny's arm, and he yelped.

'What's your name?' snarled Elliot, shaking the newcomer. 'You wanna live, tell me your name!'

'Connor.'

'Yeah? Well, Connor, around here you do what I say, got it?'

Elliot's mates giggled. One of them – Connor would later learn his name was Jason – jabbed his finger in Connor's ribs. It was typical pack bravado. All his mates crowded close. The tail of Connor's spine throbbed against the table's edge; the stolen handcuffs dug into his leg. Pots and pans bumped against the back of his head.

'I said, have you got it?'

Connor slowly stretched his hands above his head in a display of surrender, and Elliot grinned, sticking out his forefingers like they were six-shooters. 'Stick 'em up!' he said. 'Stick 'em up, pardner!'

All the kids laughed like drains, and they were still laughing when Connor pulled two saucepans from the hooks and swung them hard into either side of Elliot's head with a satisfying bong. The boy crumpled to the floor.

Then Connor stood over Elliot, bringing the pans down on his head, pounding them into his nose – whack, whack, whack – like he was hammering a nail into wood, before the Dents managed to drag him off.

6

'Gav, it's me, open up!'

Elliot Juniper banged on the door with the flat of his hand, still trying to convince himself that it was all a mistake, a big misunderstanding. Everything would straighten itself out soon enough. They'd laugh about it later down the Oak, him and Gavin.

When he cupped his hands against the frosted glass he was sure he could see a figure, barely a smudge at the end of the hallway, and lifted the flap of the letterbox.

'I can see you, Gav. Let me in!'

He didn't want to make a scene on a quiet street like this, all double-fronted homes, big cars in the driveways and trimmed hedges. First sign of trouble and a nervous neighbour, meerkat sticker in the window, would be on the phone to the Old Bill. Elliot hadn't been in trouble for years, but he shouldn't be driving after last night's morose drinking session, didn't want to take any chances.

Thanks to his hangover, the world moved behind a thick membrane. Every molecule above his neck was sore. His brain hurt; his skin and eye sockets too. His nose, bashed flat a long time ago and never right since, throbbed on his face.

Besides, getting breathalysed would be the least of his problems if Rhonda discovered he was driving over the limit.

And it would be even worse – catastrophic didn't seem a strong enough word – if she discovered *why* he was here. Whatever happened, she couldn't know.

Elliot still had his mouth to the flap when the door cracked open. Instinctively, he pushed his way in, expecting to find Gavin. Instead, he saw a small woman in a sweater and leggings.

'Where is he?' Elliot was surprised to discover Gavin had a wife. But when he thought about it – and the realisation made him wince – he hardly knew anything about him. 'Where's Gavin?'

'There's no one called Gavin here.' The woman held the front door open. 'Please leave.'

'Gav!' He grabbed the banister, called upstairs. 'Gavin!'

'This is my house and I'm asking you to—'

'I'm going to leave,' Elliot said, 'when I've spoken to Gavin.'

'And I've told you,' the woman's voice cracked, 'there's no one here with that name.'

Elliot marched into the lounge and saw post stacked on a dining table. He went over and rifled through the envelopes. The same name was on every one. 'Who's Jane McArthur?'

'I am.' The woman stood in the doorway, darting anxious looks up the stairs. 'And this is my house.'

Elliot eyed the photos on the wall: men and women and plenty of a smiling baby, but not a single one of Gavin. He felt the anger deflate inside him, leaving in its place a stinging bewilderment.

And the terrible certainty that his savings were gone.

'I don't understand.' He pulled a hand down his face. 'He said he lived here.'

The woman spoke low. 'Well, he doesn't.'

'I've picked him up here half a dozen times.'

'Not from here you haven't.' She edged towards a phone on a cabinet. 'I'm going to call the police.'

The woman's eyes were wide, her lips pressed tightly together. She was distraught. Any moment now she would burst into tears or scream. Upstairs, a baby began to wail.

For the first time it occurred to Elliot what he had done. A big, burly man – an intimidating sight with his shaved head, tattoo sleeve and smashed nose – and he'd barged into this poor woman's home, was stomping around like he was deranged. For all she knew he was going to rob her, strangle her, take her baby. Burning with shame, he held up his hands in apology, aware that it was too little, too late.

'I'm sorry,' he said. 'There's been a . . . I thought he . . .'

'Please go.' The woman's stricken whisper was almost drowned by the infant cries from upstairs.

Elliot stumbled past her, head down. As soon as he was outside, the door slammed behind him. He hurried down the path without looking back, fumbling in a pocket for his e-cigarette.

Back in the van, he sucked miserably on the vape. He knew it wasn't a good idea to hang around for too long – that poor woman would be calling the police already, he would do the same in her shoes – but Elliot couldn't help but take one last look at the house. It just didn't make sense to him. He'd been here more than once, to wait for Gavin and give him a lift down the pub, had parked in this very spot.

But now he thought about it . . .

He couldn't remember one time when he'd seen Gavin

actually inside the house or stepping outside, closing the door behind him. As far as Elliot could remember, he'd only ever seen Gavin waiting on the step, or bouncing down the path, waggling his fingers in greeting.

Two days ago Gavin had been down the Oak, scheming, planning, selling Elliot a dream of a glorious future in burgers, and now he had vanished with Elliot's money.

All his life's savings. Thirty grand gone, just like that.

Correction.

All of Rhonda's life's savings.

Because, let's face it, she was the only one who ever put money into the account. She was the one who made the effort to put by a little each month. Elliot couldn't save money if his life depended on it. Cash rocketed out of his pocket. Gavin may have run off with it but, unquestionably, it was Elliot's fault the money had gone. He had handed it to him – in cash! He had been an almighty fool, and not for the first time in his miserable life. Elliot was petrified that Rhonda would finally have had enough of his gullibility, his naivety. She might even come to the conclusion – and this made his stomach churn – that he was pulling a fast one and had taken the money himself. After all, people don't change. That's what they say.

She'd get shot of him, and who could blame her?

A little bit of bile slipped up his throat and he swallowed it. He drove home, puffing miserably on the electronic cigarette Rhonda had given him months ago – Elliot still hadn't got used to it, hated the taste, and desperately wanted a proper fag – thinking about how he had sat on the sofa last night phoning Gavin's pay-as-you-go again and again. Leaving hopeful messages, angry messages, pleading messages, and drowning his sorrows when what was called for was a clear head.

His gut told him he would never see Gavin again. All he had was a phone number. That address, the house where he had supposedly lived, was a lie. He didn't even know if Gavin was his real name.

Elliot was glad to get out of Harlow, the Essex town where Gavin had taken him to see the empty shop unit in which they were going to start their burger franchise, or so he had been led to believe. Leaving the sprawl behind, he felt a little better. Dozens of new estates were being built along the M11 corridor, tens of thousands of new homes were eating into this beautiful green space, but Elliot loved the increasing isolation as he drove deeper into the countryside, with its fields and trees, flat open spaces and blue sky. He wound down the window and let the breeze dry his clammy forehead.

He drove into the narrow lane where he lived, beneath the canopy of tree branches folding across the road like clasping hands, and swung the van up the steep, muddy drive, avoiding the crumbling holes, to park up against the dilapidated barn in the barren plot next to his cottage. Cranked the handbrake.

Rhonda would be at work this morning, thank God, and Dylan was God knows where with his mates. It would give Elliot time to work out the best way to tell her what he'd done.

I've lost your money. I gave it to a man down the pub. He's gone.

If it was only about the stolen money he could live with it, just about, but it was the latest in a long succession of

38

dismal Elliot errors of judgement. The thought of losing Rhonda and Dylan made him sick.

The door of the cottage led straight into the living room, which was a mess from all the clothes, papers, bottles and plates that had accumulated during the week. It was his Saturday-morning routine to clean the house while Rhonda was at work. But Elliot couldn't face it this morning. Instead, he dropped onto the sofa without even bothering to clear a space and stared into the ashes of last night's fire.

He sat like that, an Xbox controller digging into a buttock, for several minutes. Despondent, tired, afraid. And then his phone chirruped in his pocket. A text had arrived.

Elliot experienced a brief moment of joy – an adrenalin rush of hope – when he saw it was from Gavin. He'd got worked up for nothing. It had all been a terrible mistake. Gavin was away on business, in some inaccessible place without a signal. He had told Elliot he was in the catering trade and travelled a lot, after all. Thanks to his hangover-addled brain, Elliot had gone to completely the wrong address. That was just like him, jumping to conclusions.

But although the message was simple enough, it took him a few moments to make sense of it:

TURN ON THE NEWS

The TV remote was somewhere on the sofa, beneath the slanket, the layers of cushions and women's mags, Dylan's discarded drink cartons and wrappers. Impatient, nerves shredded, Elliot tipped everything to the floor.

Finding the control wedged into the sofa lining, and pressing up and down the TV channels until he found the

39

right one, or thought he had, he watched live footage of police cars and vans in a London street. Yellow tape snapped in the wind. The camera zoomed to an open door, men and women in white paper suits walking in and out.

The headline threaded across the bottom of the screen: THREE SLAUGHTERED IN NORTH LONDON HOME . . . THREE SLAUGHTERED IN . . .

A reporter's voice spoke of three bodies found inside the house, believed to be Kenneth and Barbara Overton and their son Phillip, although police had as yet made no official statement.

Elliot followed the comings and goings, confused about what he was meant to be looking at, then tried the number. The call rang and rang, and when he tried again, it dropped straight to voicemail. He didn't bother leaving a message. Gavin's voicemail was already full of his angry pleas.

Kenneth Overton, thought Elliot.

Little Kenny from *that* place?

Unease building inside him, he picked up his coat and left the cottage. Unable to face the terrible prospect of her telling him that she'd had enough of him, Elliot didn't want to be there when Rhonda got home.

7

Gripped by nerves, Flick Crowley lingered in her office printing and stapling, putting off the inevitable. But just before lunchtime, she conducted her first team briefing with the North London MIT.

The Incident Room, on the second floor of Tottenham Police Station, was filled with plain-clothed and uniformed officers. She knew many of the people in the room already, and others had been drafted in from the Specialist Crime Directorate.

Drake had appointed her as the lead investigator on the Overton murders, but when she went to the whiteboard where the location and victim details had been written she saw him sitting on the side of a desk, arms folded, deep in thought, and couldn't shake the feeling she was on probation.

'Hello, everybody.' She forced herself to look at the assembled team, not at the floor. 'Sorry to spoil your weekend.'

Most of the people present would hardly have had a chance to settle into their Saturday routines before they were obliged to drop everything – kids' football, shopping trips, lunch and dinner dates – and come into work.

She picked up a marker pen. 'You'll have had time, I hope, to familiarise yourselves with the details. We have three victims, all members of the same family, a stone's throw from here. I don't need to tell you we need to get this solved quickly, and we've been promised the resources to make that happen.'

Detective Sergeant Dudley Kendrick jotted something in the incident logbook. All the details of the case would be recorded in there, along with every development, so that lines of inquiry weren't duplicated.

'The victims have been identified as Kenneth and Barbara Overton, aged forty-eight and fifty-two, and their son Phillip Overton, aged twenty-seven,' said Flick. 'Kenneth and Barbara lived off Scales Road. Between the hours of eleven last night and four o'clock this morning they were bound to chairs and stabbed repeatedly in the chest and stomach. The forensic investigation is continuing, and I'm told we'll get those results in the next day or so, but if you've managed to look at the crime-scene photos you'll know that the attack was brutal and frenzied. It's important that we find the person, or people, responsible. As far as we can tell, no valuables were stolen from the house, and there's no sign of forced entry.'

DC Millie Steiner, a young black officer who had been born and raised in the area, lifted her slight frame in her chair. Flick liked Steiner. She was bright and tenacious and always put in a solid shift, despite attending a bewildering variety of night classes. 'A neighbour told me Barbara Overton used to smoke in the garden, and the door was always unlocked.'

'The perpetrator entered the house with enough plastic film to tightly bind three adults to chairs,' Flick continued, 'and sent texts – purporting to be from their father – to both of the Overtons' sons, Phillip and Ryan. The three victims were found by a neighbour who saw the door was open; this was at,' she checked her notes, 'a quarter to six this morning. The victims were dead by the time paramedics attended the scene.'

Kendrick held up a finger. A veteran of the MIT, he was the only man left this century, it seemed to Flick, who deemed it acceptable to shave his moustache to a thin strip above the lip. 'Three people would be a handful for one person to subdue; you think we're looking for more than one killer?'

'It's possible, but Kenny went to work at seven thirty that night, leaving Barbara alone in the house for a couple of hours at least. Phil Overton's text was sent at 9.39 p.m., and his brother Ryan's around eleven. Kenneth, or Kenny as he was known, didn't get home till after three. The family could have been subdued one at a time. The chairs were arranged in the bedroom to face each other, so perhaps the intention was for them to watch each other die.'

The noisy blast of a jackhammer in the street below disturbed the contemplative moment of silence. Upson fiddled with the height lever on his chair.

'So the sons were lured to the house?' asked Vix Moore sharply.

The young DC had only been on the team for a couple of months but made no bones about her desire to climb to the top of the Homicide and Serious Crime Command greasy pole. Vix wasn't to everyone's taste, but Flick wished she'd had a single ounce of her confidence when she had joined the MIT.

'Kenny Overton's mobile was used to text them both, so we're assuming the murders were premeditated.'

43

Flick pulled the cap off the marker pen with her teeth and wrote on the whiteboard:

COME HOME TONIGHT – V URGENT!!!
LOVE, DAD XXX

'Phil arrived,' said Flick. 'But Ryan didn't pick up the message. Kenny worked nights at the Co-op in Hornsey.'

'Have we run a check on the phone number?' someone asked.

'The messages were sent from Kenny's mobile.' Kendrick clicked his pen top. 'Phillip Overton's phone was found in his pocket when the plastic was cut away from his body. He'd received exactly the same text.'

Flick went on to allocate responsibilities to the team. Friends and family would be interviewed. Ryan was in the building already, along with Phil Overton's on-off girlfriend, and work colleagues from both Kenny's nightshift and Barbara's part-time job. Phil also had a record for minor drugs offences as a teenager, and had popped up on camera during the riots a few years back. They'd compile a list of his known associates.

CCTV footage from the surrounding roads and nearby traffic cameras would be sifted through – a painstaking process that could take days. License plates of vehicles parked nearby would be cross-checked; phone calls made by the family tracked; follow-up house-to-house interviews completed. The morning's sweep of the area had found nothing. No murder weapon, no blood trail or holdall or dumped roll of plastic. Uniformed officers would search again for the weapon and for Kenny's mobile, but with every hour that passed, the chances of finding them became more unlikely.

Flick concluded: 'Kenny Overton has spent his life in and out of prison. Handling stolen goods, shoplifting, dealing, you name it. So let's talk to his former criminal friends. A charge sheet like that, you pick up enemies along the way.'

When Drake nodded absently, Flick felt a delicious thrill of validation. After she'd taken more questions from the room, she tucked her clipboard beneath her arm. She didn't possess a flair for the dramatic, but she would never forget the agonised post-mortem expressions of the Overton family, and felt she had to say something.

'These victims need us to find whoever did this. Because if you've visited the crime scene, or have seen the photos, you'll know that this is an extraordinarily vicious crime, and it is inconceivable that the person, or persons, who committed it be allowed to remain free.'

After the meeting, everyone turned back to their monitors or headed to the coffee machine. Flick went into her new office and shut the door, her heart still clattering in her chest. The desk was bare except for a computer and a framed photo of her nieces and nephew, the shelves empty save for a couple of reference manuals. There was a rap on the door and Drake leaned in, smiling.

'You had them eating out of your hand.'

'You think? I'm not so sure.' Outside, Vix Moore was speaking behind her hand to Kendrick.

'People don't like change, Flick, especially when it upsets the dynamic of a team. But they're a good bunch, they'll get used to it.' He walked to the blinds. 'And you've got a nice view of the car park.'

'You're welcome to it,' she said, knowing full well he had the same depressing view in his office on the floor above. 'Thanks for being there this morning.'

Drake tapped the window with a finger. It was a wonder the panes didn't vibrate when he stood near them. He was a man who seemed to throw a crackling energy into the air around him, like a tuning fork.

She wondered whether something had happened with April. Relations were strained between Drake and his daughter, she knew that much. Flick had met April, along with Myra, Drake's odd, scary mother, at his wife's funeral several months back. The girl had clung to her boyfriend's arm and seemed to go out of her way to avoid her father. Drake was already grieving for his beloved wife. It had saddened Flick to see him so lost.

Now he turned, leaned against the sill. 'Because of the proximity of the murders to the station, and the subsequent media heat, Harris has asked me to keep an eye on the investigation.'

'Of course.' Flick swallowed. 'You're the Senior Investigating Officer.'

'But you're the lead on this. I'm here to help you to run things whichever way you see fit.'

She mustered a smile. 'I appreciate that, guv.'

If she had to pick somebody from upstairs to watch her back, it would be Ray Drake, and she appreciated being able to bounce ideas off him. He was an excellent detective with a wealth of experience, and she owed him her career, no question. In the four years she had worked in the MIT, still an overwhelmingly masculine environment, he'd carefully nurtured her confidence and drive, steadily given her more authority. Yet she couldn't help but be unnerved by the way he'd hung about in the office all morning, couldn't shake the feeling that he expected her to screw up. That he was having second thoughts about her promotion.

That was ridiculous, she told herself, she'd been in the job barely five seconds.

'The killer will be one of Kenny's criminal mates, I'd bet my life on it.' Chances were he was right, but it was an odd thing for Drake to state so early in the investigation. For years, he'd taught her to maintain an objective distance, even when one line of inquiry showed potential. 'I've come across plenty of Kenny Overtons, and they don't change.'

'We'll chase it down,' said Flick.

'He's got himself involved in some illegal enterprise and it's gone sour.' Drake sounded almost indignant. 'Find out what it is and you're home and dry. *That's* your line of inquiry.'

'Okay.' That thought again: *He doesn't trust me.* 'I'd better go see Ryan.'

To her surprise, he stood. 'I'll come with you.'

He thinks I'm going to mess it up.

The interview suite was where the traumatised relatives of the victims of crime were taken. It was decorated in sympathetic pastel colours and filled with soft furnishings. A watercolour hung on the wall. Plastic flowers were arranged on a low table.

Ryan Overton was pacing when they walked in. A family liaison officer, an eternally cheerful detective constable called Sandra Danson, stood at the door.

'Hello again, Ryan, sorry to keep you waiting,' said Flick.

His arms clapped his sides. 'Where am I gonna go on a day like this?'

'Would you like a coffee, Ryan?' Danson was a broad woman who was always experimenting with a new diet. Flick would often get caught behind her in the canteen queue as she interrogated bemused staff about the calories, saturated fats and carbs in each and every dish. She'd often see her again later, raiding the vending machine for chocolate.

'Me and the ex split up a few weeks back.' Ryan slumped in a chair. 'She was always good in situations like this.'

'Would you like us to contact her?' asked Danson.

'She's gone to Tyneside. The relationship didn't end well.'

'Ryan, this is Detective Inspector Drake,' said Flick, and Ryan nodded grimly. 'Can you tell him what you told me about the message you received from your father?'

'From his phone.' Ryan's eyes darted to Drake, leaning against the wall. 'He told me to come round – or someone did – said it was urgent.'

'Ryan was out last night,' Flick told Drake.

'Down the pub.'

'He left his mobile at home.'

'I don't know what I was thinking. I always have it with me. Always. But just this once I left it in the bog when I went out. I didn't see it till I got home at, I dunno, six?'

'Six this morning?' said Drake.

'My local has a lock-in. It can get messy.' Ryan rubbed his eyes with the heel of a hand. 'The landlord won't thank me for telling you.'

Ryan smothered a wince, his emotions still battened down. Sooner or later that anguish would have to come out. Flick had met close relatives of murder victims who buried their feelings in the aftermath. Many of them succumbed to heart attacks or strokes, depression, even suicide.

You had to let the grief out. Get it out, or it would kill you.

'It weren't from the old man. He never, ever texts, you get me?' Ryan's eyes flashed. 'Dad could barely use his phone to make a call, let alone send a message. Besides, he weren't the kind of bloke who'd put loads of kisses.' He grimaced. 'And he ain't going to start now, is he?'

'Is that why you didn't go to the house when you received the text?' asked Flick. 'Because you didn't believe it was your dad?'

'I was off my face; I just wanted some shut-eye. But I couldn't sleep. It was like that message was in my head.' Ryan snorted bitterly. 'And if I went round last night, I would have been dead, wouldn't I?'

'Ryan, I know this is difficult for you, but do you know of anyone who held a grudge towards your parents, bore them any ill will?'

'Ill will?' he snapped. 'I don't know anyone who'd want to slaughter my whole family! Look, the old man weren't no angel. He was into all sorts of dodgy stuff back in the day.'

Opening her notebook, Flick said, 'I've been looking through your father's record. I'm afraid it's a long one. He was convicted—'

'So he *deserves* to be dead, that what you're saying?'

Flick reddened. 'We were wondering if he became involved in any enterprise that could have led to his falling out with someone.'

'I told you earlier, he'd gone straight, he wanted to drive a taxi and live the good life in Spain. When we was kids the old man lied and lied, so I always knew when he was serving up bullshit. If he was involved in something, I'd have known.'

'And what about your brother?' asked Drake.

'Phil weren't no angel. But he didn't have those kind of mates.'

'What kind of mates?'

'The type that would break in and . . . and . . .' Ryan's voice became tiny. 'Butcher his family.' The room fell quiet save for the faint rasp of Ryan's palm scraping across the stubble on his jaw. 'And me neither, before you ask. Dad cleaned up his act after what happened to Jason.'

Drake folded his arms.

'Jason?' asked Flick.

'Dad's best mate, committed suicide years back.' He watched Flick write something. 'He was always round ours when we were kids. Him and Dad went way back. When Jason did himself in it knocked the old man for six.'

'How long ago was this?' asked Flick.

'Three or four years. He shot his girlfriend and their baby daughter, then turned the gun on himself.'

'What was his full name, Ryan?' asked Drake, one shoe tapping on the carpet.

'Burgess. Jason Burgess.'

Flick wrote down the name. She didn't know if it had any relevance, probably not, but she was, and always would be, a thorough note-taker.

'The fire just went out of Dad after that. Mum told him he had to give up the life or sling his hook, and she meant it. Dad didn't have any skills to speak of, so he got it into his head to write a misery memoir.'

'A what?' asked Danson.

'Mum loved those books. *Santa's Secret Kiss. Auntie's Sadistic Cellar.* You know, people cashing in on abusive childhoods. They make a mint, and the old man was always going on about his early days. It was his excuse for everything. *That's why my life's so fucked, Ryan, because my childhood was shit.* Trouble was, he could barely write his own name, let alone a whole book. Didn't stop him trying, though. He even started doing research.' Tears welled in his eyes. '*Ryan,* he says to me, *if you knew what happened at that place, it'd make your hair curl.* He got cold feet about the book. Fact was, he couldn't string a sentence together. He didn't know a comma from his colon. Asked me to stash the notes in my flat, just in case.'

Drake looked up sharply.

'In case of what?' Flick asked.

'I dunno.' Ryan shrugged. 'He seemed to think it was important.'

'We're drifting here,' said Drake.

Flick frowned. Ryan had just lost his mother, father and brother in a shocking act of violence, and Ray Drake was getting impatient.

'Maybe one day I'll write the book myself. As a tribute, like.' Ryan sighed. 'If I'm still alive.'

'You think somebody may still want to kill you?'

He shot her an incredulous look. 'I was meant to be there last night, wasn't I?'

Before Flick could reply, Drake cleared his throat. 'Ryan, you can help us enormously by thinking of all the people your father and brother knew who could do something like this.'

51

'How many times? He was out of it . . . Look, there's one or two names I can give you, but they're small fry, because that's what Dad was. He was a nobody, same as everybody else he knew.'

'Thank you.' Drake's phone rang. 'Sorry, I've got to take this.'

Flick watched him leave, wished he'd never come in the first place. Ryan's head was all over the place. A more gentle approach may have been more productive, certainly more humane. Ray Drake, of all people, should know that. When he'd gone, Ryan placed his head in his hands.

'Am I going to be all right?'

She felt an overwhelming sadness for him. 'You'll be safe, Ryan. You have my word on that.'

8

'Give me a ring, even if you're not coming back. Call when you get this message. I'm not kidding no more, Gav.'

'If that was me,' said Bren, watching Elliot cut the call, 'I would have turned the air blue, called him every name under the sun.'

'Been there, done that.' Elliot shrugged. 'Hasn't made him call back.'

They were sat in the beer garden of the Royal Oak, a stone's throw from Elliot's home. It used to be a sanctuary for him, a quaint little country pub with a thatched roof and whitewashed walls – there had been an inn on this spot since Queen Bess was in pigtails – but it was tainted for him now. Only days ago, he had huddled in one of the snugs with Gavin, who took him carefully through the process of buying a burger franchise. Romancing him, grooming him.

A biting breeze whipped in low across the fields, rattling the table canopies. Elliot was frozen: the landlord didn't turn on the outdoor heaters till evening. Bren shifted his numb buttocks on the narrow plank along the bench. He sat awkwardly, side on from Elliot, chubby legs crossed on the patio. He could probably squeeze his bulk into the narrow gap beneath the bench, just about, but they would need the fire brigade to cut him out again.

'So what are you going to do about it?'

'No idea.'

Elliot wasn't one of those people who coped well with stress, and he certainly wasn't one of life's problem-solvers. Where decisions were concerned he left all the heavy lifting to Rhonda. She always knew the right thing to do. But he wouldn't – he just couldn't – talk to her about this, not if he wanted to hang onto her.

'What did you make of him? Gavin, I mean.'

'He smiled a lot.' Bren, who was the closest thing Elliot had to a friend these days, stroked his cold thighs. 'And he never drank.'

'Yeah.' Bren had nailed it.

'Who sits in a pub and drinks fizzy water? That set off alarm bells.'

Elliot drained his pint. Three beers in, and his hangover was easing, that was something. 'Then why didn't you say so?'

'Ain't against the law not to drink. And, anyway, you were so wrapped up in his get-rich-quick scheme that you wouldn't have listened to me. If it makes you feel any better, I would have fallen for the same scam.' Bren patted his big belly. 'Probably best that I stay away from the burger business, though.'

Elliot appreciated Bren's attempt to cheer him up, but could barely muster a smile. He had fallen hook, line and sinker for Gavin's cheerful bullshit. Gavin had shown him glossy brochures and business plans and paperwork with embossed letterheads; he'd even gone to the trouble of taking him to that empty shop unit. Elliot of all people, who had wasted so much of his own life lying and cheating and stealing, should have known better. Takes one to know one, and all that.

It was karma, that's what it was. All he wanted was a quiet life. Elliot loved his routine, the pub, the long walks. But he had trusted somebody from the outside world. As soon as you let a stranger into your life everything went to shit, it happened every single time.

'She's not going to forgive me,' he said bitterly. 'Not this time.'

'You could always try Owen.'

'Ain't gonna happen,' Elliot said sharply. He had enough problems on his plate without adding Owen Veazey to them.

Bren looked hurt. 'Only trying to help, Ell.'

'Yeah, well . . .' He snatched up his phone and his ridiculous plastic fag, put them in his pocket. 'Keep your ideas to yourself.'

Bren watched him swing his legs from under the bench. 'You going?'

'Better get off.' Elliot felt ashamed of his outburst – Bren was only trying to help, after all – and he clapped him on the shoulder. 'Thanks for listening.'

'Don't dismiss it out of hand, Ell.' Bren's chins quivered against his collar. 'We're not talking a long-term loan. Just to tide you over till you can find this Gavin. You could pop the money back in the bank before Rhonda even notices it's gone. Owen knows you; he'll do you all right.'

'Sure,' said Elliot, who wasn't inclined to touch Owen with a bargepole. 'See you soon, Bren.'

But before he could leave, his phone rang. The screen flashed urgently: Gavin's number.

'You gonna answer it?' asked Bren, watching.

Elliot slowly lifted the mobile to his ear.

And heard a child weep. Juddering sobs. Angry tears.

'Hello?' Elliot asked. 'Gav?'

The sobbing became snivels, and then –

'She'll know the kind of man you are,' said an angry voice.

And it howled: an agonising cry of emotional pain that nearly burst Elliot's eardrum.

He yanked the phone away, cut the call. Stared at the mobile as if it could somehow explain what he'd just heard. Acid churned in his guts.

Elliot was gripped by an odd disconnect. He had the overwhelming feeling that there was something that he really needed to know, something important.

'You know what? I might stay for another pint, after all.' He started walking away. 'You go get them in.'

'Where you off to?' asked Bren.

'To buy some fags.'

9

Lines of inquiry opened up in the investigation by late afternoon.

Flick's team had compiled a list of Kenny's criminal associates, and Upson and Steiner were locating last-known addresses. The response from old mates of Kenny's had been uniform. *Ain't seen Kenny in years. Kenny dropped his old friends. Kenny don't come round here no more. His missus put his head in a noose.* And so on.

Fact was, Kenny's criminal acquaintances didn't have a bad word to say about him. He never grassed, never ripped off his mates, never made enemies.

'So basically . . .' Millie Steiner corrected her posture, as her Alexander Technique teacher had taught her, in a chair borrowed from the Incident Room. 'Kenny was a saint.'

They were sitting in Flick's office. Upson took the edge of Flick's desk, looking down. 'If it weren't for the fact that his record stretches back to flogging used arrows after the Battle of Hastings, I'd have to agree.'

'Ryan's right,' said Flick. 'Kenny was small potatoes, the same goes for Phil. I'm just not seeing it.'

She hadn't seen Ray Drake since he'd walked out of the interview suite earlier. According to Kendrick he'd spent the afternoon with Harris, coordinating a response to the press. The DCI loved his moments in the spotlight, and

Flick imagined him knotting and re-knotting his tie *just so*, and practising authoritative gestures that gave him gravitas in front of the TV people, as Drake advised him on what to say. Drake hated the cameras, hated speaking to the press, and would stay well out of it.

'What about Barbara? Have we missed a trick there?'

'She worked part time at Greggs,' said Steiner. 'Was a hard worker, a bit of a character by all accounts, and loved a chat. Customers liked her.'

'You don't do that to someone . . .' Flick leaned back to examine the ceiling tiles. 'You don't truss up an entire family and stab them to death unless you've a seriously massive grudge.'

'We're working on it, *guv*,' Upson said, picking up the framed photo of Flick's nieces and nephew from her desk. 'Everyone's moving as quickly as they can.'

Flick glared at Upson, but he was too busy frowning at the photo.

'What about the mobile? Someone sent Ryan a message.'

'Kenny complained to a work colleague last night that he'd lost his phone,' Steiner said. 'He swore blind he'd had it on the way to work.'

'Ryan said Kenny took the 41 to Hornsey every night and the night bus back. Someone could have nicked it then.'

Steiner jotted in her notebook. 'I'll get the CCTV footage from London Transport.'

'Wait up.' Upson waved the photo frame, and Flick anxiously expected it to slip from his fingers and shatter on the floor. 'If someone who had reason enough to kill him sat next to Kenny on the bus, wouldn't he recognise him?'

'Perhaps Kenny did recognise him. Perhaps they chatted.

Get someone to dust Kenny's locker at the supermarket. It'll be in a secure area, so get the CCTV as well.'

There was a rap on the window, and Sandra Danson stuck her head in. 'Ryan's finished, Ma'am.'

Flick snatched the frame from Upson and replaced it carefully on her desk. On the way to the interview suite she checked her voicemail messages. They were about work stuff, mostly. Holloway had a query about a departmental charge code. Kendrick wanted to know how far to widen door-to-door inquiries in the surrounding tangle of streets. A friend from college had texted about going for a drink.

It had been a long time since she'd let her hair down – Flick couldn't even remember the last time she'd been on a proper dress-up, cab-home night out. A few months back she'd signed up for one of those internet dating agencies for professionals, had received quite a lot of interest, too, but hadn't done anything about it. She just didn't have the time or, if she was honest, the inclination. She fancied splashing out on some new clothes, getting her hair done. She and Nina could make a day of it, lounging about at some fancy spa, but she worked long hours and weekends, and could never usually muster the energy. She would rather sit around her sister's house where she could relax and chat over a glass of wine while the children ran about making merry hell.

Her thoughts drifted uneasily to Nina and her husband Martin. Flick couldn't shake the feeling that there was something not quite right between them. The last few times she had stayed there she had picked up a tension, a definite atmosphere, but she couldn't put her finger on what it was. Nina and Martin were the happiest couple she knew, no question, and he was as close as a brother to Flick. The idea that their marriage was in trouble – they had three small children, who Flick loved dearly – was too painful to contemplate.

Ryan Overton had spent the afternoon working on a list of Kenny's criminal acquaintances and former friends, anybody who had bad blood with his family, and he'd worked with a furious intensity. Danson said he'd refused any food and drink except a packet of Monster Munch and a can of Red Bull. He looked wretched.

'We'll get you to a hotel, Ryan. Or a police safe house if you prefer.'

Ryan's voice was flat. 'I just wanna go home.'

A squad car was requisitioned to take him back to Finsbury Park where he lived on the twelfth floor of a tower block. Dismissing Danson, Flick climbed in the back of the car. Moving back and forth between the crime scene and the office, tasks multiplying every hour, she hadn't stopped all afternoon, and could do with a few minutes out of the building. Their route took them down the Seven Sisters Road, past the takeaways and convenience stores and the endless shop-to-lease signs. Ryan's head lolled against the headrest as he stared at the shutters rattling down on shops and businesses after a busy trading day.

'They were giving it a real go, you know? Dad had finally got his life on track. Thanks to Jason, in a weird way.'

Kenny and Jason: two lifelong friends who died violently with their families, Jason by his own hand, Kenny at the hands of a murderer. Flick had checked the suicide on the database and found no reason to question the coroner's verdict. Jason Burgess had killed his partner and their infant daughter. He'd had well-documented mental health issues, a history of violent crime. It had never been established where he'd purchased the firearm, but he'd have known plenty of people who'd supply one for the right price. There was just one nagging question: a gun would cost hundreds, perhaps thousands of pounds – how could Burgess, living from hand to mouth, afford something like that?

'At the station you said your dad didn't believe Jason killed himself,' Flick said.

'Stubborn old git wouldn't let it go, but Dad had a blind spot about Jason.'

'Do you think Jason did it?'

'Course. He was a nutcase, he had serious anger issues. Mum couldn't stand him.' Ryan eyed a couple of women emerging from a Turkish café. 'She hated the way he was in and out of our house, stinking up the sofa, drinking all the old man's booze, moaning about his life. Get Kenny and Jason together and they'd break your fucking heart. If anyone was going to turn a gun on himself it was Uncle Jase. One day, when I was about twelve, me, Phil and Mum came home to find him sitting in the kitchen, a bloody great knife on the table.' He spread his hands apart: *this* big. 'He wasn't allowed in the house for a while after that.'

He leaned forward to the driver to indicate a turning. 'Next left, mate. Anyway, when Jason died, Dad was cut up about it. Mum told him to get his act together or he'd be out on his arse. That was when he said he was going to write the book.' Ryan laughed bitterly. 'As if! My old man, the author – never going to happen, was it?'

'Why'd he change his mind about it, do you think?'

'Dad would come out in a cold sweat just holding a pencil.

Besides, in his heart of hearts I don't think he wanted to look back.' A muscle in his jaw ticked. 'He told me that he'd found some people from his past, from a children's home he was at called the Longacre, but you could see something about it had rattled him.'

Flick turned to face him. 'What?'

'He never said, kept it all bottled up. That's when he gave me his notes in a file.' Ryan tapped the side of his nose. '*Keep 'em safe, son.*'

'What was in the file?'

'Mouldy bits of paper, as far as I could tell, old newspapers. My eyes glazed over, to be honest.'

'Can you find it for me, Ryan?'

'I'll try, but don't hold your breath. Don't know if I've even got it any more.'

The car pulled up onto the forecourt of a tower block. A group of kids booted a football against a wall. They gestured at the car and made siren sounds. *Nee naw nee naw.*

'He was finally getting himself together.' Ryan watched the kids kicking the ball about. 'He was really trying, you know?'

'We can talk again tomorrow,' said Flick.

'What if they come for me?' He turned to her. 'What if whoever killed them wants to finish the job?'

'We're not going to leave you alone, Ryan. There'll be an armed officer outside your door round the clock, for as long as it takes.'

Ryan snorted, reaching for his seat belt release. 'No offence, but I've seen that movie, and it *never* works.'

At dusk, when Ray Drake arrived beneath the black mass of Ryan Overton's tower block, a few determined kids were still kicking a football.

Work had kept him from coming earlier. Drake wanted to keep an eye on Flick's investigation, but DCI Harris had insisted he coordinate the police response to the frenzied media coverage. A meeting with a Met communication officer had dragged on. The press office was inundated with inquiries, and a briefing was hastily organised, had gone reasonably well despite there being little to report. As usual, Drake positioned himself well away from the nest of cameras and microphones while Harris enjoyed the limelight.

He stared up at the tower, a rectangle against the night sky. Drake hadn't given a thought to Kenny Overton for many years. The idea that he had been living so close to the nick was disconcerting. It had been a long time since they'd last seen each other, decades, and they probably wouldn't have given each other a second glance if they'd passed on the street. But Drake's instinct was that Kenny's murder, so near to his place of work, wasn't just a coincidence. Ryan Overton's remark about Kenny's childhood, and *that* research, had nagged at him all afternoon.

He tried to concentrate on his wife's recital of a Prokofiev concerto – Laura had been a professional musician and

Drake played all her acclaimed cello recordings on repeat on the music system – but the music did nothing to temper his anxiety. Taking out his mobile, he scrolled again to that familiar number.

It rang and rang and rang, and then his daughter's voice said: 'Hi, this is April. I can't get to the phone right now, but you're clever, and know what to do!'

The tone beeped in his ear. She hadn't come home last night. He'd phoned her five, maybe six times already today, and hadn't left a message, but he was determined to say something this time, to ask how she was, and when he would see her. Staring at the parked cars ahead, Ray Drake took a deep breath, opened his mouth and—

A body plummeted out of the sky and smashed onto the roof of the car in front with an almighty bang and crack of glass.

The car's suspension bounced. The alarm screeched, wing lights flashed crazily. A broken arm flopped from the dented roof to hang across the shattered windscreen. The kids raced off across the forecourt screaming in terror, melting into the muddle of subways and passages.

Drake flung open his door and crunched across the glass towards the body. Ryan Overton's ragdoll limbs were flung every which way, the two ends of his torso at right angles. A woman screamed nearby. A dog barked at the pulsing wail of the alarm. Running to the tower block entrance, Drake stabbed random intercom buttons. When the door unlocked with a hornet buzz, he ran inside.

Two lifts, a fire door to a stairwell.

There was little chance the killer could have left the building in the scant seconds since Overton's body fell twelve storeys. An LED indicator showed a lift dropping towards the lobby: five . . . four . . . three . . . two . . . one . . .

The pneumatic machinery wheezed. The lift settled. The doors trundled open. Drake lurched forward, and a woman screamed, pulling her toddler close. He held up his hands, *don't be afraid*, and backed away. He flung open the door to the stairwell, and his soles slapped on the concrete as he took two steps at a time, sticking close to the banister, darting glances up the central shaft.

By the time he pulled open the door to the twelfth floor his knees were buckling. He could barely get his breath. Drake doubled over, heart pumping, shirt clinging to his back, propped his hands on his knees and waited for air to fill his lungs. Time was, momentum would have kept him moving, but he was a middle-aged man now. A few yards over, the lift clanked into life. Just as he reached it, the small square window in the door disappeared into the floor, obscuring whoever was inside.

A fire door dissected the long corridor and Drake ran through it. The copper outside Overton's flat was startled when he pulled out his badge. 'Open it up!'

The officer fumbled a door key beneath the sallow ceiling lights. The car alarm squealed faintly on the other side of the building. Curious residents emerged from flats. Drake shouted: 'Get back inside!'

They slipped into the flat, through a stubby hallway into the living room. Wild applause thundered from the television. The balcony window was open. Heavy curtains moved in the wind. Drake saw a small crowd gathering around Ryan Overton's broken body splayed across the roof of the car. The alarm screaming, lights flashing. A slim figure in a red hoodie peeled from the group, walking casually towards the entrance of the estate. Stepping onto the street, the figure paused to salute Drake, then disappeared into the dark.

'Oh my . . .' The officer stared down at the body, dumbfounded.

'With me.'

Slipping gloves from his pocket, Drake led the way back down the corridor and through the fire door. It was solid metal, another square of reinforced glass in the centre. When it was shut, the copper at Overton's door wouldn't have seen anything on the other side.

Drake pushed at the doors of the flats on the same side of the corridor as Ryan's. The third door swung open at his touch, the lock was broken. He stepped into the dark flat to find the balcony window open. Ryan's flat was four windows along. The balconies in between were placed evenly apart. With a bit of dexterity it would have been possible to jump from one to the other, and into Overton's flat.

'What's your name?'

'Gill.'

'Officer Gill, I need you to get downstairs,' said Drake. 'Move those people away from the body. Don't let anybody use the lifts, or enter or leave the building.'

Gill swallowed. 'I was outside . . . nobody came . . .'

'Did you leave the door at any time?' The uniform shook his head. 'Did you fall asleep?' Gill flinched, shocked. 'Then you did your job. Go downstairs.'

Back in the corridor, Drake watched Gill disappear into the stairwell. Sirens emerged faintly from the city din. He hadn't much time.

When he returned to Overton's flat, it was filled with explosions and gunfire – a movie on the television. The flat reeked of booze and stale smoke. An open pack of B&H lay on a low table, an ashtray cradled the ash skeleton of a cigarette. An empty Bacardi bottle lay on the floor beside an upturned chair. The intruder must have come in through the window as Overton faced the TV, clamped a hand over his mouth, or a knife to his throat, and dragged him to the balcony to tip him over.

Along the back wall was a shelf of storage boxes. Drake peered inside. There was a cupboard containing DVDs, a torn carton of cigarettes, a stash of mucky mags.

No box of research.

The bedroom off the hallway was tiny, barely big enough for a queen-sized bed and a pine wardrobe. Drake rifled through a chest of drawers and found underwear, balled-up T-shirts, belts.

The wardrobe door listed to the side when he pulled it open. A single suit hung inside, reeking of mothballs. Jeans, shirts, a denim jacket. Pristine white trainers were lined up at the bottom, a pair of leather shoes in a box. He ran his fingers along the duvet lining. There was nothing under the bed except for a lone sock, furred by lint and dust.

The sirens were louder now, converging. No box file, no notes.

The kitchen was barely more than an alcove. He flung open cupboards full of glasses and broken devices. A pair of scales, stacked plates and bowls, a toaster missing a plug shoved at the back.

Outside, the siren of an ambulance whooped as it entered the estate. The living-room walls pulsed blue. Drake heard raised voices in the corridor. He was running out of time.

Switching on the light in the bathroom, he saw a shower cubicle and toilet, a sink smeared with dried toothpaste. The space smelled of damp towels and talc.

High on a wall was a shelf for towels. Drake pressed his hand between the rough cotton – and felt paper, a couple of dumped tabloids. But underneath the bottom towel was a shoebox. Drake took the box into the living room and opened it, ignoring the shouts and clanging doors in the corridor. Inside was a pile of clear plastic folders containing newspaper cuttings. Headlines leapt out at him as he flicked quickly through the brown and curled cuttings: CRASH A TRAGIC . . . SUICIDE SAYS COURT . . . TWINS KILLED . . .

Footsteps, voices, outside the door of the flat.

His heart lurched when he saw the cutting, yellow with age, at the bottom.

The headline read: JUDGE VISITS LOCAL CHILDREN'S HOME.

Below it was a black-and-white photograph, the forced smiles of a grim line of adults and children.

Tallis, Kenny, Toby, Jason, the judge and his wife, Elliot, Amelia.

Connor Laird, slipping into the shadows at the edge of the photo.

Disappearing before his eyes.

Her hand, hot and clammy.

Fetid breath. Fingers clawing.

The crackle of flame.

Drake was about to slip the photo out and pocket it, when a voice said: 'Sir?'

Flick Crowley stood at the door. She stared at the upturned chair, the curtains swaying in the breeze. The clipping in his gloved hands. 'I don't understand.'

'Someone climbed over the balcony.' Drake eased the clipping back into the pile, replaced the lid on the box, as uniforms poured into the room. 'From a neighbouring flat.'

'Is that the file Ryan was talking about?' When Drake nodded, she said: 'I'll get it bagged up and taken away.' She stared, looking sick. 'I promised Ryan we'd keep him safe.'

'I can handle this if you—'

'*No.*' She shook her head. 'I'll be fine.' Then she gave him a curious look, as if it had only just occurred to her that he was already here in Ryan Overton's flat. 'Show me where they got in.'

Drake moved to the door, glancing back uneasily at the shoebox.

11

Spending all day down the pub probably wasn't the best way to get a grip on the situation, but it was the only way Elliot knew how to absorb the increasingly disconcerting turn of events.

It was bad enough that Gavin had taken his money, but to bring to his attention a triple murder and then to cry down the phone like a baby, to hurl angry insults . . . Perhaps Gavin was a headcase and was having some kind of breakdown. Or perhaps Elliot was.

Truth was, he was putting off for as long as possible having to explain to Rhonda about the money – how he had lost tens of thousands of pounds of her savings. The idea that she would throw him out gnawed at him. After umpteen pints, and too many fags, he badly needed forty winks. Maybe then he could muster up the courage to come clean.

I gave it away, all of it.

Gavin, that weird voice on the phone, had hit a nerve.

She'll know the kind of man you are.

And then there was that business with poor Kenny . . .

But when he walked up the lane, the sky thickening with dark, and heard raised voices, he knew he wouldn't be able to skulk upstairs for a nap.

Elliot lingered at the front door, getting his shit together. He pinched the metal tendrils of the wind chime hanging above the door so that they didn't jangle in his ear, threw the cigarette he had been smoking down the drive. Straightening his collar, he cupped his hand over his mouth to check his own stinking breath.

'We're in here,' called Rhonda from the kitchen, when he let himself inside. The living room was spotless, the surfaces dusted and the carpet vacuumed, and Elliot felt even worse. Rhonda had come home, after working all Saturday, and cleaned up.

He walked into the kitchen to see Dylan flinging his arms around, and saying: 'I ain't gonna do that!'

The kid stuffed his hands into the pockets of his leather jacket. He was tall and skinny with big eyes, olive skin and a swirl of curly hair gelled across his forehead into an enormous fringe. His mouth pouted in disgust as Rhonda, still dressed in her blue dental assistant's smock, moved around the room spraying cleaner on every surface.

'I'm not asking you.' She rubbed the kitchen table with a cloth. 'That's not how this works.'

'You mean,' Dylan made an incredulous face, 'this is a dictatorship.'

'If you like.' Rhonda blew a spiral of hair out of her eyes. 'You live in my house, you follow my rules.'

'Well, I'm sorry, Kim Jong-un, you don't have the right to tell me who I can and can't see.'

'I'm your mum, and the last time I looked, that gives me every right.'

Conscious of the stink of booze on him, Elliot loitered at the door. 'You're going to have to bring me up to speed.'

'He rules North Korea,' Dylan said, smirking.

'Very good, I see what you did there.'

71

Rhonda threw the cloth in the sink and regarded her son, hands on hips. She had the same olive skin, and the same curly hair, which was permed into tight, shivering corkscrews, but none of her son's height. She couldn't have been more than five foot five. 'A couple of Dylan's so-called mates have got done for shoplifting.'

Dylan shoved his hands into his pockets. 'What's that got to do with me? The answer, in case you're wondering, is nothing!'

'They were caught stealing sweets from the shop down the road, the one by the GP.' Rhonda shook her head as if she couldn't quite get her brain around it. 'Another boy – leather jacket, skinny jeans, ridiculous fringe – was seen legging it.'

Dylan slapped his forehead. 'Which could describe literally thousands of other kids. *Thousands*. All this goes to show is what a low opinion you have of me, your own son.'

Rhonda appealed to Elliot. 'Tell him.'

'It's a pretty silly fringe,' he said.

'Okay, we'll give you the benefit of the doubt.' Rhonda pulled kitchen towel off the holder to rub at the fridge handle. 'Let's just suppose, for the sake of a quiet life, it's not you. But you're not seeing those boys again for a while.'

'Yeah?' Dylan snorted. 'And how are you going to stop me?'

'By taking away your phone.'

'But you won't.' Dylan flashed a smile, a nasty, triumphant thing. 'Because then you'd have no idea where I was, I could be arrested or run over, I could be lying on the road dead, and then you'd be sorry.'

Dylan was a sweet kid most of the time. They used to

be good pals, Elliot and the boy. But these days, consumed by turbulent teenage hormones, he probed boundaries constantly, tested limits, flew off the handle at the slightest thing. His mother struggled to cope with his moods. Christ, they both did.

It didn't help that Rhonda worked every hour available to put food on the table and, he winced, put a little money aside each month. Or that Elliot, who worked cash-in-hand on building sites, never knew what hours he would be working from one day to the next – times being what they were, sometimes he didn't work at all. Dylan resented living at the end of a potholed lane in the country – the 'arse end of the arse end of nowhere', he called it – and spent a lot of time staring at his phone or cocooned in enormous headphones. That's when he wasn't off with his mates, getting up to who knows what.

The kid didn't know he was born. Elliot wanted to tell Dylan where he was at his age, in that shithole home, and what he did there. How he had nightmares, even now, about what went on at the Longacre. That place had made him the man he was. A ne'er-do-well, a jailbird. A failure.

And look what happened to Kenny.

When he thought of that TV footage, an unexpected feeling veered close. That information, the vital, connective fact he needed to make sense of what had been happening to him, bobbed tantalisingly near, like a piece of driftwood on the tide. For a moment he felt like a tremendous truth was about to be revealed to him . . .

But then Rhonda said to Elliot: 'Please, you have a go.'

'The last thing your mum needs is for you to get involved in any—'

'In any what?' The boy's eyes flashed.

'Just stay away from trouble. Once you get sucked into—'

'You're a fine one to talk. You being in prison for most of your life.'

'That's enough!' snapped Rhonda.

'Then you should listen to me,' Elliot said calmly. Getting into a shouting match wasn't going to help, he had learned that much. 'Because you don't want to end up like I did.'

'A burglar.' Dylan counted on his fingers. 'A thief, a *thug*.'

'Yeah.' Elliot swallowed. 'And a few more besides.'

Rhonda ripped off another square of kitchen towel and blew her nose.

'I got off to the wrong start in life,' continued Elliot, and Dylan played an imaginary violin. 'I didn't have your advantages. A home, a mum who loves me; I had to learn the hard way. But I did learn, eventually.' He reddened, thinking of the money he had lost. 'I learned from my mistakes.'

'Fell on your feet, didn't you?'

'I don't understand.'

'Mum took you in off the street, gave you a home.'

'I wasn't on the street. But, if you like, yeah, I owe everything to your mum. She believed in me.'

'*Believes*,' said Rhonda, squeezing his hand.

'And when are you going to pay her back what you owe?'

Elliot sucked in a breath. 'Excuse me?'

'When are you going to pay her back for all this beautiful trust by getting a proper job, one you can actually stick at for more than five minutes? When are *you* going to make something of yourself, instead of pissing off down the pub all day?'

'I like to think,' Elliot ploughed on, 'that we're a family, the three of us. We support each other, and trust—'

74

'But we're not, though, are we?' Dylan's voice cracked with emotion. 'Me and Mum are family, but you're not, you're some passing bloke.'

'Dylan!' Rhonda strode forward. 'Take that back.'

'You can't take back a *fact*.'

'Go to your room!'

'I'm not five years old! I'm going out.' He stormed past Elliot.

A moment later, they heard the front door slam. The old sash windows rattled.

'He makes me so angry.'

Elliot bunched kitchen towel and gave it to Rhonda. 'He can't help it. At his age, he's got all these hormones flying about. He doesn't know if he's coming or going half the time.'

'He shouldn't talk to you that way.'

'He'll calm down. And later he'll get into a state about something else. Look, he's left his phone.' Dylan's beloved android device sat on the table. 'So he won't have gone far.'

He pulled Rhonda to him. Her tears dampened his shirt.

'I just don't know what's going on in his head right now.' Her voice was muffled against his chest.

'He'll come good; he's not a bad kid.'

'Yeah.' She folded the tissue to dab at her eyes. 'You came good, after all. It was touch and go, but you're a good boy now.'

'I am.'

She'll know the kind of man you are.

He pressed her head to his chest so she couldn't see his bleary eyes. But she pushed away from him. 'I'd better get back to the cleaning. Somebody didn't do it this morning.'

'Sorry, I—'

'Went down the pub.'

'Bren had something he wanted to talk about.'

'And you stink of smoke.'

He held up his palms. 'I've had a couple.'

'Whatever it was, I'm sure it must have been important for you to spend all day there.' Rhonda sighed. 'Maybe what we need is a holiday.'

Elliot's chest tightened. 'We could go see your mum in the valleys.'

'I was thinking somewhere more exotic. Palm trees, cocktails, white sand. We could do with some sun. Mauritius, maybe. Let's splurge.'

'Sure,' he said. 'We can talk about it.'

'I'll look on the internet tonight.'

'There's no rush.'

Moments later she was dragging the vacuum cleaner up the stairs. He was about to take out his phone when the front door opened. Dylan came into the kitchen, snatched up his own mobile.

'I can't be sure,' said Elliot, 'but I think your mum is angry.'

'You think?' Dylan smirked. 'You're an idiot, Elliot.'

'That's me.' Elliot was glad he could still dredge a smile of sorts from the boy. Every week brought some painful change in Dylan's personality, some complicated new reaction to the world. Perhaps in a few months he wouldn't smile at all. But Elliot, like a prospector clinging to a mountainside, would continue to dig deep for them. 'Elliot the idiot.'

'I'm going out.' Dylan headed towards the door.

'So,' Elliot said, 'if you were going to steal from that shop, what would you have taken? Hypothetically, I mean.'

Dylan made a big show of taking a container of mints from his pocket, shaking one into his hand and popping it onto his tongue.

'Don't do it again,' said Elliot, serious.

And then the boy was gone. Elliot heard the thud of the hoover against the skirting upstairs. He took out his phone and called Bren.

'Ell, what gives?'

'I've been thinking about what you said this morning. Let's set up a meet with Owen. Just for a chat.'

'Sure thing. When do you want to see him?'

'Soon,' said Elliot hoarsely. 'As soon as possible.'

12

Convinced that he kept seeing the same vehicle hanging back in the distance, Drake pulled his car to the kerb and killed the engine. In the rear-view mirror, clubbers staggered down the Pentonville Road towards King's Cross and the Tube. At a bus stop, a man's head rested facedown on a briefcase hugged to his chest.

It had been a long night at the tower block. A tent had been erected around the shattered body of Ryan Overton, its white walls rippling and cracking in the wind whistling through the estate. Access to the block was restricted so that the lifts, stairwell and twelfth-floor corridor could be dusted for prints.

Flick Crowley, shell-shocked, had kept herself busy. The shoebox of cuttings was barcoded and removed by Holloway's team.

Drake had joined the MIT at the section house for a couple of hours, fielded an anxious call from Harris, and then left. Traffic was thin at this early hour – an occasional vehicle climbed the road – but he had a nagging sense, barely more than that, of the same car in the distance.

A silver open-top roared up the hill towards the Angel, a scream in the stillness. Drake was reaching for the ignition when his phone rang. His immediate hope was that it was April, but the caller's number was blocked. He touched the screen.

'DI Drake,' he said, listening to the purr of an engine at the other end.

Nobody spoke, so he cut the call. It rang again. With a fluttering sense of unease, he put it to his ear and listened. A long way behind, just beyond the junction at the Angel, a car slowed to a stop and killed its lights.

Down the phone he heard a handbrake crank, the jangle of keys.

'Who is this?' said Drake. 'You've got the wrong number.'

The seat belt whipped across his chest when he unclicked it. He had a vague idea about walking towards the car, was reaching for the driver's door when he heard a sound in his ear.

Faint, barely more than a breath . . .

The angry sobbing of a boy.

Drake snatched at the door release and stepped onto the road – just as a car blipped by inches from him, its horn blaring angrily. He threw himself against the Mercedes. When he returned the phone to his ear, the call had been cut.

Trotting towards the junction, picking up speed, he saw the full beams of the car flash on. An Audi, he thought, but couldn't be sure. The engine fired, and when Drake ran, the vehicle turned in a screeching swerve and accelerated away. Drake watched it disappear down the City Road. Then went back to his car to continue his journey home.

Ray Drake lived in a five-storey townhouse in an expensive Islington square. Technically, it was still Myra Drake's house; she'd been born there, and insisted she had every intention of dying in it. But she now lived in a flat in the basement with internal access to the main house. Myra sneered at the

79

stair lift Laura had fitted to the basement stairs and refused to use it. She sourly observed all the improvements Ray's wife had made to the house down the years. For so long a musty Victorian pile, Laura had painstakingly modernised and refurbished it. Walls were knocked down, creating a sense of light and space, ancient wiring and fittings ripped out and much of Myra's dark and fusty furniture banished to her flat. The old woman had put up stiff resistance, but with velvet stubbornness Laura had got her way. A few short months ago all Drake's family had lived there, but his wife was gone now and April was barely there.

Water spattered noisily into the gleaming stainless-steel sink when Drake ran the cold tap in the kitchen. He drank a glass of water and pulled out a stool to scroll down his logged calls to April. So far she'd ignored every single one.

Drake squinted when the light went on. Myra shuffled into the kitchen, a clawed hand holding her dressing gown tight at the neck. The old woman had never been much of a sleeper, and often drifted around the house in the early hours. More than once she'd scared the wits out of them all by floating past in the dead of night, like a wraith.

'Why are you sitting in the dark?' she asked sharply.

'I just got in.'

'You look shattered, Raymond. Go to bed.'

'I will, in a minute.'

Waving dismissively, the old woman edged to the fridge to pour a glass of milk. Without her glasses she was long-sighted, and hooked a crooked forefinger over the top of the glass so that she didn't overfill it. When she returned the jug to the fridge, she stood with her aged, bony hands, as thin and sharp as the talons of a bird of prey, flat on the counter. At eighty-seven, age had evaporated the round lines of her face, leaving her gaunt and skeletal. High cheekbones curved into triangular shadow beneath her pallid eyes. Her hair, once fashioned into a muscular perm, was thinning against her skull. But she was still an imposing figure, despite a stoop, and her mind was as sharp as ever.

'Where's April?'

Myra looked at him grimly over the glass. 'She's gone, Raymond.'

'What are you talking about?'

The old woman's voice was brittle. 'She's packed her things and left.'

'When did this happen?' he asked, shocked.

'Yesterday.' He bit down on his annoyance. God forbid the old woman actually rang him to tell him. 'The boy came to pick her up.'

The *boy*. Myra could never bring herself to utter Jordan's name. Something like this had been on the cards for a while, but he hadn't wanted to admit it to himself.

'The girl has always had too little structure in her life. You have given her too much rope.'

'She's old enough to make her own choices.'

'She needs her father, now of all times. That boy is . . .' Myra's thin lips curled in distaste. 'What we used to call a Flash Harry.'

Jordan never stood a chance with Myra. His father was a self-made businessman, a cockney market trader made good. Myra's family was old money, as was her late husband's. Notions of class and entitlement gnawed at Myra.

'She'll come back; she just needs time.'

A thin band of milk glistened in the down of her top lip.

81

'She's a selfish child, always has been. You must bring her home.'

He sighed. 'Myra . . .'

'I don't like to see you unhappy, Raymond.' Those eyes, yellowed and spotted by broken blood vessels, studied him. 'You do not cope well. And there's something else, I can see it in your eyes. Something is troubling you. Is it that case I heard on the news? The triple murder.'

'There's been a fourth killing. A mother, a father and their two sons are dead. One of the victims . . . his name was Kenny Overton.'

'And what's the significance of this person?'

'He was at the home,' he said.

'*That* place.' She pushed away the glass. 'Well, these things happen.'

'There've been other deaths. People from the Longacre.'

Myra's long fingers absently rubbed the locket she always wore around her neck. 'You've been under enormous strain recently.'

'Something's *happening*, Myra.' Picking up on his anxiety, she waited for him to continue. 'There's a photograph . . . from a newspaper cutting.'

'And these murders, do they have anything to do with what . . . happened?'

'Yes,' he said, meeting her eyes. 'I think so.'

'I shall retire to bed. I'll wash up in the morning.' The rough towelling of her dressing gown brushed against his thigh as she passed him, stopping at the door. 'I'm sure you are perfectly capable of handling it. You must do whatever is necessary, as you always have, to protect your daughter.'

His eyes lifted to hers. 'Yes.'

'You're in charge of the investigation?'

'I'm SIO.'

'Well, then.' The old woman plucked a speck of lint from the arm of her gown and placed it in a pocket. 'It gives me no pleasure to say it, Raymond, but—'

'Not now, Myra.' He rinsed the glass at the sink, placed it on the draining board.

'She made you soft, that wife of yours.'

'Myra . . .'

'I know you don't like to hear these things, but you must act before it's too late. Before you lose your daughter for ever.'

'You've made your point.' He snatched up his keys.

'Where are you going?'

'There's something I've got to do.'

When he slammed out of the front door, she switched off the light and stood, absently rubbing the locket, thinking about her beloved son.

13

A heavy metal door stuttered beneath a harsh yellow light, the image frozen on a computer screen.

'The bad news is there's only one camera on the estate.' Eddie Upson pressed a button on the keypad and the image moved. 'Good news is it's just above the entrance.'

Numbers at the top of the screen – a time stamp – began to hurl forward, the milliseconds a blur of movement. The image showed the entrance to Ryan Overton's tower block taken from a high angle in the dank lobby. The light was gloomy, the exterior beyond the heavy metal doors pitch black.

'The video is low resolution so don't expect terrific quality.'

He moved the jogging mechanism on the player to reveal a family, a man and a woman, a small boy, moving into the frame from the direction of the elevator. The frame rate on the image was so poor that the figures jerked forward with every step, cheating time and space. With a final tug of his arm, the boy was pulled out the door, which snapped closed.

'We've yet to identify everyone who came in and out around the time of Ryan's death. That's fourteen people. I'd imagine most, if not all, live on the estate.'

The rooftops outside the window were swollen with the imminent dawn. A pile of printouts littered the desk, images of everybody who had entered and exited the building an hour each side of the murder. Men and women in winter coats, carrying shopping bags, pushing buggies, kids surging inside with bikes and skateboards.

'This guy looks like our best bet. He entered the building fifteen minutes before Ryan took the express elevator.'

'No jokes, please, Eddie.' Flick wasn't in the mood.

Cranking the jogging wheel on the playback equipment, Upson pointed at the screen. A dark shadow could be glimpsed on the window of the entrance. The image jumped. The door was ajar. A figure stepped inside – face buried in a red hoodie – to move at the extreme edge of the screen. Flick saw a shoulder and an elbow, the fingers of a gloved hand, the soft point of the hood.

'You'd have to be clinging to the wall to skirt the lens like that.' Millie Steiner leaned forward. 'They're avoiding the camera.'

Moments later the figure was gone.

'Show me again,' said Flick. She made Upson replay the image several times. He jogged the sequence back and forth. A dark figure. The door swung open. Tip of the hood. A gloved hand. Gone, repeat.

'How tall would you say?'

'Five foot eight or nine,' said Steiner.

'Man or woman?'

Upson sipped from a can of coke. 'It's difficult to say. That hooded top is baggy. Whoever it was had to be powerful enough to tip a strong lad like Ryan Overton over the balcony. A bloke, if I had to guess.'

Maybe not, thought Flick. They'd have to wait for the autopsy report, but if the empty Bacardi bottle in the flat was anything to go by, Ryan had been drowning his sorrows.

Taken by surprise, unsteady on his feet, and with the right momentum, it wouldn't have taken much effort to tip him over that balcony.

'Now run it on.'

Upson jogged the image forwards. The screen became an explosion of undulating lines. The time stamp went crazy. Slowing the image, he touched the screen.

'There's the guv.'

Drake crashed through the door and disappeared immediately. A moment later a mother and toddler left the building. Flick was gripped by the image of empty space. The numbers hurtled onwards. A couple of minutes later the hooded figure, face still hidden, ran from the elevator side of the frame to press the exit button and lunge through the entrance. It was barely onscreen for a second.

'The DI had a choice: take the stairs or stay in reception. Unfortunately, he chose wrong.'

'I probably would have done the same.' Steiner stifled a yawn.

'It's been a long day,' said Flick, looking with surprise at the time on her phone. 'Go home and sleep. Come back in refreshed tomorrow.'

Upson didn't need telling twice. 'Don't mind if I do.' Flick heard his bones pop when he stood and stretched, tugged his jacket from the back of the chair. 'You coming, Fli . . . boss?'

'I've a couple of things to finish up,' she said, but Upson had already left the glassed-in office, barely bigger than a cubicle, where they kept the video equipment.

Crushed cans were lined up on the desk. Millie Steiner picked up a bin and swept them into it. 'Whatever you're thinking, don't.' When Flick didn't respond, she added: 'He was protected.'

'Not well enough.'

Flick hadn't eaten anything since a sandwich at lunchtime, God knows how many hours ago. She was shattered, her blood sugar was bumping along the bottom, and she couldn't shake the feeling that she was responsible for Ryan Overton's death, despite everyone's reassurances. If she'd insisted he stayed in a Met safe house, he'd still be alive.

'I shouldn't have let him go home, it—'

A lump formed in her throat and she stopped. Steiner was a sweet and empathetic girl, and Flick knew she could speak in confidence, but she wasn't about to get emotional in front of her.

'Why don't you go home? It'll look better in the morning.'

'I will.'

When Millie had gone, Flick turned off the lights and walked through the empty Incident Room. Met Police badge screensavers bounced across computer screens. Her first day as lead officer on an investigation, and it had all been a bit of a mess. In her office, she collapsed into the chair.

It was a surprise to Flick that Ray Drake had seen fit to go to Ryan Overton's flat last night, almost stumbling upon Ryan's killer in the process. The DI said he'd decided on the spur of the moment to look in on Ryan, but the fact that he had even gone there without informing her didn't seem like a huge vote of confidence. Did he trust her to lead the investigation? The murder of a family was going to heap pressure on everyone to get a quick result, she understood that, but if he had concerns she wished he'd raised them with her directly.

'Bollocks to it,' she muttered. She logged out of the computer, picked up her bag.

In his office, the duty sergeant was sat among a nest of monitors showing various parts of the building.

'Heck of a day, DI Crowley.' Frank Wanderly grinned. 'I take a few days off and as soon as I get back all hell breaks loose.'

'Go anywhere nice?' asked Flick.

'Just pottered about in the garden.'

Most people would jet off somewhere warm to soak up some rays, but Flick could just imagine Nosferatu, who liked to work the late shift, walking around his garden in the dead of night with a watering can, moonlight gleaming off that shiny skull.

'You have a good morning, Frank,' she said, buzzing herself out to the car park.

After the heat blasting from the station radiators, the cold winter air made her shudder. Flick would get a couple of hours' sleep and take a shower, then grab breakfast on the way back in.

In the car, she slumped against the driver's seat, fatigue washing over her. Within moments she felt herself being dragged down towards sleep – and jerked out of her stupor. Forcing herself to sit up, limbs as heavy as lead, Flick vigorously rubbed a hand up and down her face, lifted the key to the ignition – just as the automatic gate to the car park rattled open, and Ray Drake's Mercedes swung in, its headlights sweeping across the concrete. Drake climbed out of the vehicle. Its lights winked as it locked.

If Flick had left five minutes earlier, she'd be on her way home. He couldn't see her, she could just slip away, but she was anxious about his close scrutiny of the investigation. At the tower block and in the office there'd been little time to talk. She felt a responsibility, felt compelled, to give him an update. Maybe, at the same time, she could fish for a few crumbs of reassurance about the job she was doing.

With a sigh, Flick slipped the key from the ignition, pulled her bag over her shoulder and slipped from the car.

14

Frank Wanderly peered at the clock above the door when he saw Ray Drake. 'Another early one, Detective Inspector?'

'Busy day ahead, Frank.'

The sergeant jammed paper from his desk into a recycling bin. 'You wait for one homicide and four come along at once.'

'DS Crowley has certainly got her hands full,' said Drake, impatient to get on.

'Got to give her credit, though, she's working flat out. She only left five minutes ago.'

The years Wanderly had spent working till dawn beneath electric light hung on his pale face like a shroud. But he was an amiable man, who never seemed to resent the endless parade of drunks and derelicts that washed up at the station in the early hours.

'How's your daughter, Ray?'

'Pretty good, thanks.'

The phone rang. The sergeant's hand hovered over it. Drake said quickly, 'By the way, Frank, I forgot to put something in the Property Room earlier, can I borrow the key?'

'Of course.' Wanderly lifted a finger, *one moment*, and answered the call, 'Sergeant Frank Wanderly. Who's speaking, please?' As he began his conversation, he spun his chair to a shallow metal cabinet on the wall. Inside were dozens of keys. He rifled through them, took one out and lobbed it at Drake. 'I'm afraid they need to speak to CID on that particular issue . . .'

His office was on the second floor, the MIT Incident Room was on the first, but Ray Drake took the stairs to the basement. Access to the Property Room was restricted. Once evidence had been logged, it was tagged and kept secure until it could be examined. Items from hundreds of investigations were kept there: seized drugs, stolen goods, weapons such as decommissioned firearms.

The black bulb of a CCTV camera squatted above the door, but there was nothing Drake could do about that. No one was likely to check the recording. If they did, he'd repeat his earlier lie to Wanderly.

The air conditioning chilled him as soon as he let himself through the heavy door. Fluorescents buzzed into noisy life to reveal a massive room with long freestanding steel shelves bolted to the concrete floor, every inch piled with evidence. Larger items were placed against the bare brick walls: a damaged safe, a fish tank, a cash register. A set of hub caps was wedged behind an acetylene cylinder.

Snapping on gloves, Drake headed to the first aisle where the most recent evidence was placed. His fingers brushed over the plastic wrapping and boxes as he checked dates and barcodes.

With a growing sense of unease, Drake moved methodically down the length of the shelving. Several minutes later he still hadn't found the shoebox. For all he knew, the cuttings were still in the office upstairs, strewn across a desk. He couldn't remain down here much longer – the camera would record the time he spent inside.

And then he saw it. The box had fallen behind a pile of boxes. The plastic wrapping wasn't sealed, which suggested not everything inside had been logged. Maybe no one had looked at it yet. Removing the lid, he saw the transparent plastic folders. Inside each of those, a cutting.

He scanned each one, flicking through the flopping plastic, skimming the headlines and first paragraphs: SUICIDE . . . BLAZE . . . JUDGE . . . CRASH . . .

What he saw of each article, piecing together names and dates and stories, only increased his disquiet. It was no wonder Kenny Overton had abandoned his research, no wonder he had yearned to go abroad, far away. And yet, Drake suspected, it wouldn't have made the slightest bit of difference. Moving to the ends of the Earth wouldn't have saved him. Familiar names, people he hadn't thought about in decades – now erased from the world, and long forgotten – detonated dread memories . . .

Of Tallis, of Sally – he hadn't thought about Sally in a long time, and felt a pang of guilt – and of all the doomed kids at that home.

Drake found what he was looking for, the oldest cutting in the file. Slipping it from the plastic, he eyed the photograph that could be enough to end his career and destroy his relationship with his daughter if Flick's investigation swung in the wrong direction. His eyes lingered on the kid on the edge of the dismal group of people who posed on that fateful day.

A boy from a lifetime ago.

Connor Laird, slipping into the shadows. Cringing from the camera's flash, half turned, one pale eye glaring.

There was a barcode at the top of the plastic sheet. The

clipping had been logged. He couldn't just walk away with it.

'Guv?'

The metal door boomed shut. Drake's heart leapt.

'Just a moment!' His voice was a throaty croak. 'Give me a second!'

'Guv? Where are you?'

A woman's voice. Footsteps approaching on the concrete. He stepped back to see Flick Crowley at the end of the aisle.

'Flick!' he said, in as cheery a voice as he could muster. 'Let me just put this back!'

Drake stepped close to the shelving, smothering her view of the clipping. He quickly folded the paper below the photograph and tore, coughing to cover the sound of the dry paper splitting apart along the crease.

'Just one . . .' Stuffing the photo inside his breast pocket, he replaced the rest of the cutting in the plastic and shoved it into the box. Pushed the box back into the wrapping. '. . . moment!'

When he looked up, Flick was at his side. He had no idea how much she had seen.

She frowned, looking at him, then down at the box.

'Frank told me you'd gone home,' he said, gulping down his agitation. 'I was just reading this stuff.'

She blinked at him. 'I thought you were at home, sir.'

'I've been in my office all night.'

She gazed at him curiously. Her eyes dropped to his gloves, and he peeled them off as casually as he could.

'That's the research Kenny gave Ryan.' She nodded at the box in his hands. 'Anything interesting?'

'Ancient history,' he said. 'Old newspaper cuttings, mainly.'

She reached out for it. 'I'll take a look.'

'Leave it till morning.' He struggled to keep the annoyance from his voice. 'You look done in, Flick, why are you still here?'

'To tell the truth, I don't think I'd be able to sleep.' She took the box off the shelf, shivering in the chill of the air conditioning.

'I'm not asking you. Go home and sleep. You're not going to get anything done by running yourself into the ground.'

He reached for the box, but Flick held it tightly. 'I'm here now, I'll just take a quick look.' When he stared, she said: 'Shall we go? It's freezing down here.'

The heavy door to the Property Room clanged shut.

'Do you think this is the end of it? Now the Overtons are dead?'

'It's a contract job,' Drake said. 'Kenny, Phil, maybe even Ryan, was involved in some criminal enterprise that backfired.' He dropped the gloves in a waste bin. 'So, yes, I think it's over. Don't over-complicate things, Flick.'

She hesitated, her fingers drumming a question on the wrapping around the box, but when he held open the door to the stairwell, she walked through. Drake wondered how much she'd seen in the Property Room. Flick Crowley was a copper who rarely deviated from well-trodden systems of investigation. That could buy him time to discover what was going on. But he also knew she was a clever and stubborn investigator, and it would be foolish to underestimate her.

His skin prickled with foreboding. Something was set in motion all those years ago. An evil from that home had been revived, he was certain of that. And if he didn't take measures, it would be the end of him.

On his way home he pulled the car to the kerb, and dropped the newspaper photograph down a drain. Watched the faces of the kids – Amelia, Connor, Elliot and the others – soak into the dank water and tear apart.

15

1984

Elliot listened to Gordon's heavy steps pound on the stairs.

Bang, bang, bang.

Hands trembling, he pulled the thin blanket over him. In the darkness, he could barely make out the silhouettes of the other kids. They lay unmoving in their beds, frozen with fear. Usually Elliot would sleep like a log. But this time he knew – his guts churned at the thought of it – that Gordon was coming for him.

His smashed nose hurt like hell. He wished it had been fixed properly, at a hospital. After Connor's attack, Gerry Dent had laughed and said he should get it seen by a doctor or it would look like an exploded tomato for the rest of his life. But Gordon refused point blank, so the Dents patched it up as best they could. For days, the dressings on Elliot's face were a sodden mess of mucus and snot. When the bandages finally came off, his nose didn't look right.

'We all get the face we deserve eventually, Elliot,' Gordon smirked. 'You just got yours early.'

Elliot clenched his jaw, determined not to cry. The one thing he wanted from life was a family, lots of kids, which he'd bring up right – not that he'd ever admit it, wild horses wouldn't make him tell anyone – but there was little chance of that happening now, not with this nose.

If the pain made his eyes water, the embarrassment was even worse. At least none of the kids had the nerve to laugh at him to his face.

Since Connor arrived, everything had gone wrong. Gordon had taken a shine to the new kid, chose him now to make his special deliveries, and Elliot was out of favour. And that meant he was fair game if Gordon was drunk or in a bad-tempered mood, which was nearly all the time, these days.

He gave Connor the evils at every opportunity, but Elliot's so-called mates, turncoats like Ricky and Jason, didn't have the stomach for a fight. They saw something in the new kid's eyes, a coldness, an unpredictability, that made them keep their distance.

If the business in the kitchen was anything to go by, Connor was sneaky. Elliot's left eyelid fluttered every time he heard the pots and pans jangle on their hooks. But the day would come when he would get his revenge, he just had to bide his time. Keeping his temper in check wasn't easy. He was a chip off the old block. His old man had been lightning quick with his fists, Elliot had learned that the hard way, right up to the moment his father dropped dead from a heart attack, leaving him to rot in this dump.

If Elliot had learned one thing from his dad, it was to use his size and strength to get what he wanted. As a result, it had always been him who had been Gordon's eyes and ears about the place, who got to lounge about the office, reading comics. That was where you wanted to be – at Gordon's side, not shoved in with the rest of the kids –

because it meant you didn't have to fear the heavy tread of his shoes on the stairs in the dead of night.

Bang, bang, bang.

'He gave you a bloody good hiding, Elliot,' Gordon said that morning, chuckling. 'He messed you up good, boy.'

'He took me by surprise.' Elliot glared at Connor. It still hurt when he spoke, and there was a persistent ringing in his ears.

The manager sat with his feet on his desk. The door to the small room behind him, with its dirty mattress and ribbed green radiator, was closed. Elliot guessed Sally was in there, asleep, or off her face. When she first arrived, Sally had acted as a kind of buffer between Gordon and the children, shielding them, taking the edge off his temper, but now she seemed to spend most of the time in that room, sleeping so deeply and for so long you'd think she was never going to wake up.

'Connor's got brains and balls.' Gordon tossed the desk paperweight. It made a smacking sound in his palm when he caught it. 'So you're going to show him where to make deliveries around town.'

All Elliot had to do was grab that paperweight, a glass globe speckled with bubbles, and swing it into the kid's face. Then they'd see who had the brains; then they'd see who had the balls.

Gordon jumped to his feet to spin the dial on the office safe. When the door chunked open, he took out packets of brown paper, sealed with shiny zigzags of sticky tape, and heaped them into an Adidas sports bag.

'I want you to show Connor the ropes,' he said. 'The addresses, the routes, introduce him to the customers. And then you're done.'

Elliot whined. 'Gordon—'

'And then you're done, boy.'

'I can find them myself,' Connor said.

'No. My customers don't talk to just anyone. Elliot will make the necessary introductions.'

A tornado of resentment twisted inside of Elliot. He would be the same as all the other kids now, and that was a bad place to be.

Bang, bang, bang.

The manager crouched in front of him. 'I understand what you're feeling. Your nose has been put out of joint in more ways than one. But look on the bright side, lad – no more walking to the ends of the earth. You'll be able to relax, get to know the other boys and girls.' He squeezed Elliot's shoulder. 'We'll always be mates. But Connor . . . he's got that little extra something.'

That afternoon, Elliot and Connor walked across the borough, sticking to the least populated byways. They passed abandoned factories and railway sidings, squeezing through fenced-off gaps on streets bombed forty years before. They looked like a couple of restless teenagers aimlessly roaming across the city, except that Connor carried the sports bag containing the brown packets. They made deliveries to houses and estates, underpasses, squats and even business premises. Elliot begrudgingly introduced Connor to twitching men and women who could barely look them in the eye. Connor studied them carefully, memorising faces, routes and meeting points, taking it all in.

The two boys barely said a word to each other all day. Elliot was sulking and Connor kept himself to himself, and anyway spent most of the time looking over his shoulder.

Because they were being followed.

Sure enough, there was a figure hanging back in the distance, hiding around corners. Elliot was terrified they were going to get arrested, slung in prison, and it was with relief he saw it was only that posh kid who was always hanging around the home waiting for Sally, the one called Ray.

'What does he want?' asked Elliot.

Connor didn't answer. He watched the kid carefully but kept moving, and by the end of the afternoon, nearing their last delivery at a snooker hall down by the marshes, it looked like the boy had drifted away. By then Elliot was hot and itchy and tired, and when his nose throbbed, which was basically *all the time*, it reminded him of what Connor had done to it. He'd had enough. He hurled himself onto a park bench beside the canal, unable to keep his mouth shut any longer.

'Why you hanging about here, anyway?'

Connor stared. 'You're the one who's stopped.'

'I mean, why are you at the home? You don't belong. Nobody knows you're there. You could piss off any time.'

Wasps buzzed around the rusted frame of a shopping trolley poking from the brown water. Connor dropped the bag and stood on the edge of the canal path. Elliot was gripped by the urge to shove him into the water, but something told him he'd live to regret it.

'I don't want to go anywhere else.'

'Why not?' Elliot couldn't believe his ears. No one in their right mind would want to be at that place, with the casual cruelty of the Dents and Gordon's beatings, and what happened late at night when he was drunk and his heavy steps echoed on the wooden stairs. 'It don't make no sense. I'd be off like a shot!'

'Because . . .' Staring at his own elongated reflection on the surface of the stagnant water, Connor's reply trailed off. He was a weird one, all right.

Perhaps it was the fact that he didn't even bother to answer that enraged Elliot, but all the frustration he felt – his busted nose, the ringing in his ears, the way Gordon treated the new kid – boiled up inside of him. He jumped off the bench and picked up the bag. He swung it high, meaning to lob it in the water – but at the last moment he came to his senses and dropped it to the ground.

'I could have got you in trouble,' he told Connor. 'I could have told Gordon you lost it.'

'I don't care what he thinks.'

The kid was full of it. 'Sure you do. He'd kill us!'

Connor picked up the bag by its strap and Elliot thought he was going to continue on his way, but instead he spun on his heels like an Olympic discus thrower, and let go of the bag. It flew over their heads and landed in the water. They watched it turn in a lazy circle on the surface and then sink, the last package of drugs inside. Elliot groaned in disbelief. This kid was a maniac.

'We don't tell him!' Elliot said in a panic 'We'll say we made the delivery.' Connor's lack of concern only made him more frantic. 'Say you won't tell him!'

But Connor just walked off.

When they got back to the home, one of the kids, a sullen girl called Amelia, was sitting outside. She watched them warily, ready to run.

'What you doing here?' snapped Elliot.

Amelia wore a pink T-shirt, a cracked silver star embossed on the front, and flared jeans. Her hair was tied back in a scruffy ponytail. Ignoring him, she hugged her notebook and tensely watched Connor. Elliot didn't usually pay much attention to this kid. Amelia was one of the quiet ones, the ones with dull eyes who stepped aside when he approached – there were loads of those in this place. But this one loved to draw. Meek as a lamb she was, but always getting in trouble for scrawling on the walls and furniture, on every smooth surface she could find. Gordon got angry about it, she'd been on the end of a series of slaps, but it didn't stop her. In the end, Gerry Dent had bought her a sketchbook, which she'd lovingly covered with stickers, glitter and crepe paper.

As soon as they stepped inside, they understood why she was hovering. Shouts and screams came from behind the closed office door. Usually, you walked into the house and heard the thrum of the kids in your head, like a swarm of bees. But on days like this, when Gordon had been drinking, everyone scattered to the bottom of the garden or the far corners of the house. They knew what was coming and they did their best to make themselves invisible. The manager drank every night, but some days he started drinking first thing in the morning and didn't stop – those were the days you feared.

'How long's it been going on?' Connor asked Amelia.

'What does it matter?' said Elliot. 'If they—'

'I'm not talking to you,' Connor snapped.

Elliot was getting sick of the way the new kid treated him.

'Hours,' Amelia said.

'Drinking,' said Elliot, who knew how the rows always started, and how they ended. 'And . . . other stuff.'

Connor stood at the office door and listened to Gordon and Sally screaming obscenities.

'She's crying,' he said.

Connor rattled the knob, and the thought of the door flying open to reveal Gordon terrified Elliot, who sloped away quickly, thinking about that last package slipping beneath the water in a foam of bubbles.

Maybe they'd get away with it – some of the people they delivered to couldn't tell you what day of the week it was, perhaps they wouldn't notice. But Elliot had no doubt that Connor would lie and say he had done it, that he would really drop him in the shit. He considered getting his attack in first and telling Gordon that Connor had lost the package. But he knew that wouldn't work, Gordon wouldn't believe him, not in a million years.

At dinner, Elliot's chest and stomach were knotted so tightly that he could barely breathe, let alone eat. The food tasted like ashes in his mouth. He didn't hear any of the conversation at the table, didn't even join in when Jason and Kenny and David started flinging food. For the first time since he'd been at the Longacre, he considered legging it. Nothing happened that evening, though. Gordon didn't emerge from his office, and Elliot dared to hope they'd got away with it.

But that night, tossing and turning in bed in the early hours, he heard the muffled ring of a phone downstairs, and knew his luck had run out.

Bang, bang, bang.

That small room behind Gordon's desk terrified him.

He'd never been inside, but the kids who had been taken there were never the same again. They lost something – he couldn't explain what it was, exactly: a spark, a fragment of themselves. You could see it in their eyes, in the way they looked at you but didn't see you.

There were six of them in the bedroom. Connor was below the bay window, with Amelia on a mattress beside him. Kenny was in the room, too, and Karen and Debs. Elliot's bed was nearest the door. Everyone was supposed to be asleep, but he could hear quick, panicked breaths. A train clattered along the track behind the house, sending patterns of light jerking across the ceiling. Elliot glimpsed Connor, turned away.

Minutes later, the office door opened. A whimper came from one of the other beds. Elliot's shattered nose throbbed, as if in warning.

Bang, bang, bang.

Gordon's footsteps, slow and heavy. The rasp of his palm on the banister.

Elliot pressed his eyes shut, pretending to sleep, but when Gordon reached the doorway, he couldn't resist looking. The manager stood so close to the end of his bed that he could smell his body odour, the alcohol lashing off him. Gordon dabbed at the wall, trying to find the light. He gave up – it didn't work anyway – and slapped at the crumbling plaster.

'Is there something you want to tell me, lad?' he slurred into the darkness. 'Because you've put me in a very awkward situation.'

Elliot shook. This wasn't how things were meant to be.

'I got a call,' Gordon continued. 'A friend of mine didn't receive his goods. To say he's not happy is an understatement.

And if he's not happy – well, you can imagine how unhappy I am.'

'Don't know what you're talking about,' said Elliot. 'Go away.'

'Let's go; we'll talk it through downstairs. Come along, boy.' The noise in Elliot's head was unbearable. Lurching forward, Gordon's knees bumped against the frame and the bed shuddered. Elliot forced himself not to cry out. 'I'll not tell you again.'

'Leave him alone,' said a voice, and Elliot tensed. He could just make out the silhouette of Connor standing in the middle of the room.

Gordon's neck craned forward. 'That you, Connor?'

'Go away.'

'Don't be like that, lad. I don't know what Elliot did with the produce, but it's very expensive, so it is, and either he gives it back or he accepts the consequences.'

'I lost it.' Connor's shadow darted across the floor so quickly that Gordon stumbled backwards in surprise. 'I threw the bag in the canal.'

Gordon swayed, his ragged breath catching in his throat. 'Well, you are a brave lad, I was right about you.' He wagged a finger. 'Perhaps you did it, perhaps you didn't. But tonight, I think, you have me at a disadvantage. I'll be honest, I'm not feeling hunky-dory. That Sally has sapped me dry. None of you appreciate what I have to put up with where that girl is concerned. So I'm going to let it go, just this one time.' Elliot heard the dry snap of his whiskers as the manager ran a hand down his beard. He shuffled to the door. 'You kids have a good night's sleep, and I'll see you in the morning.'

Then they heard his slow heavy steps on the stairs.

Bang, bang, bang.

Far below, the door to the office opened and closed.

Connor had slipped back into bed. Elliot could just about make him out, the pillow pressed over his head beneath a sliver of moonlight.

'Connor!' he whispered. 'Connor!'

But Connor never answered. Elliot lay down, his earlier terror turning to guilt and shame. Connor had stood up to Gordon – something that Elliot would never dare to do – when it would have been easier to make Elliot's life a living hell.

He had challenged him, embarrassed him in front of the other kids, and that was something Gordon would never – could never – forget. Connor was a nutcase. It was the only explanation.

And if they ever went to war, those two, Elliot didn't want to be there, because he had no idea how far they would go, the adult and the boy, to destroy the other.

16

Back at her desk, weary and starving, Flick considered taking Ray Drake's advice about going home. But she was there now, wedged into her chair with her coat on, the shoebox in front of her. The first grey threads of morning bloated the horizon. Delivery vans and lorries rumbled along the High Road below.

She didn't think she had the energy to return the box to the basement, let alone drive home, so she took out the cuttings that Ray Drake had found in Ryan Overton's flat. Articles from old newspapers and photocopies on curling paper. The clippings were torn and dog-eared, many were littered with Post-it notes covered in an illegible scrawl.

An A4 sheet of yellow lined paper had been slipped into one of the plastic sheaves. Flick could barely make out the scribbled blizzard of spidery writing and crossings-out. At first she thought it was a code, but then she realised that Kenny, a man who had spent much of his childhood institutionalised, could barely write. If necessary, there were graphologists they could employ, but she was reluctant. Cutbacks being what they were, the MIT was expected to justify the cost of everything.

The one thing she could read, because it was printed in clumsy block capitals, was a list of crossed-out names.

~~DAVID HORNER~~
~~KAREN SMITH~~
~~REGINA BERMAN~~
~~RICKY HANCOCK~~
~~JASON BURGESS~~

At the bottom were other names:

ELLIOT JUNIPER
AMELIA TROY
DEBORAH WILLETTS
CONNOR LAIRD???!!!

Flick laid the list to one side and picked up the clippings. The first was a single column, glued to a sheet of A4. It was taken from the *Sheffield Star*, and dated 20 October 1991.

Mother and Twins Killed in Fire

A single mother and her infant twins were last night killed in a blaze that ripped through a sheltered housing complex.

Firemen were unable to save Regina Berman (17) and her one-year-old daughters, Annabel and Darcey, who died from smoke inhalation in an upstairs bedroom of their flat.

Residents and staff were evacuated to a nearby leisure centre when the blaze ripped through Colney Court in the early hours of the morning.

Miss Berman had joined the Colney Assisted Housing scheme after being made homeless. Neighbours described her as a good mother who made an impression on everyone she met.

'Her little girls had so much to live for,' neighbour, Hilary Frost (43), said. 'They were poor, but always had a smile for everybody.'

The cause of the blaze, which is thought to have started in the family's flat, is still unknown.

Flapping her arms out of her coat, Flick picked up the next article. The *South London Guardian and Gazette*, 23 January 1998.

Local Couple Tragedy – Suicide Says Court

A local couple killed themselves in a suicide pact, a court heard.

Jeff Moore and Karen Smith, both 30, of Sweepers Road, Bermondsey, attached a rubber hose to the exhaust of their car on 12 November last year and died of carbon monoxide poisoning.

A neighbour alerted police when he spotted smoke coming from beneath a garage door. When police and ambulance crews gained access, they found Mr Moore and Miss Smith in the back seat of the vehicle.

The court heard Mr Moore, a refuse collector for Lambeth Council, and Miss Smith, who worked in the Clean 'N' Tidy Launderette in New Cross, had both been depressed about not being able to adopt because of Miss Smith's history of drink and drug dependency.

A friend of the couple, Benedict Donaldson, was ejected from the court when he interrupted proceedings. Speaking to the *South London Guardian*, he angrily refuted the Coroner's assertion that the couple had killed themselves.

'I spoke to Karen and Jeff nearly every day and they were happy, and looking forward to the future.'

The Coroner recorded a verdict of suicide.

Flick placed the article face down on top of the first. Her mouth was dry – a coke from the vending machine would give her a sugar kick – but she wanted to finish reading. The next cutting was printed on greasy paper that looked like it had curled through a fax machine. It was from the *Canberra Star*, dated 5 September 2001.

A stable mate at a local stud farm has died in a barn fire that also claimed the lives of six horses.

David Horner (27) was bedded down at the Appletree Stud Farm to nurse a sick mare when the blaze ripped through the barn during the night. A workmate who spotted the flames pulled Mr Horner from the blaze, but he later died in hospital.

Several horses were saved, but a number had to be put down as a result of their injuries.

English-born Mr Horner had worked at the ranch for several years.

Owner Wayne Garry told the Canberra Star that Mr Horner had a special bond with the animals. 'Davey was a shy guy, and awkward with people. Those horses meant everything to him. We're all sick here; it's a senseless waste of a life.'

Authorities suspect a dropped cigarette could have been

the cause of the fire, but stressed that they didn't want to preempt any inquiry.

Flick made a note to find out if David Horner had any family in the UK, and reached for the next clipping. From the *St Albans Examiner*, dated 14 March 2008:

Crash A Tragic Accident
A family of five were killed when their car left the road and sank in the River Ver.
Local man Ricky Hancock (38), unemployed —

Flick blinked. Another family. She took a breath, and read on.

Local man Ricky Hancock (38), unemployed, his wife Jennifer (34) and their three children, Nathan (12), Fleming (8) and Tiffany (4), all drowned.
Mr Justice Egan told St Albans Coroner's Court that Mr Hancock was four times over the limit when the Peugeot sank into the freezing river in a matter of seconds. The family had been returning from a party outside St Albans.
Partygoer Sheila Fisher told the court that she had seen another man climb into the car with the family. No one else at the party confirmed the sighting, and Mrs Fisher admitted she had consumed a lot of alcohol and could be mistaken.

Flick rubbed her eyes. She double-checked the articles against the list of crossed-out names. There weren't any clippings about the death of Jason Burgess, but Kenny knew those facts all too well. Jason shot dead his partner and daughter, then turned the gun on himself.

Another family dead.

Neither were there articles about the death of anyone called Elliot Juniper, Deborah Willetts, Amelia Troy – that last name was familiar to her somehow – or Connor Laird, whose name had been underlined. There was nothing to suggest that they'd died in a fire or drowned or committed suicide. Everyone else on the list, the ones with their names scored through by Kenny's uncertain hand, were dead. Their families, if they had families, were dead.

And now Kenny Overton and his own family had been murdered.

According to Ryan, all these people had been at the same children's home – the Longacre – a long time ago. If that were true, nobody would ever make a connection between the victims, who had scattered across the country, across continents, decades ago. And these were only the people Kenny had managed to locate.

What had become of all the others from the home?

Perhaps it was the tentative fingers of dawn light pressing into her eyes, or the fact that she'd hardly eaten a thing, but a wave of nausea washed over her. The implication of what she'd read still sinking in, she took out the last two clippings. Both were stiff with age. The first was taken from the *Hackney Express*. An edition dated 31 July 1984. The short article was headlined: JUDGE VISITS LOCAL CHILDREN'S HOME.

Noted High Court judge Leonard Drake dropped in to meet the kids at the Longacre Children's Home this week.

Mr Drake and his wife Myra visited in his role as Chairman of the Hackney Children's Protection League to meet manager Gordon Tallis and his dedicated staff.

The eminent judge, who has presided over some of the country's biggest court cases, told the *Express* he was impressed with what he'd seen of the home, a refuge for many kids in the borough without a family.

'The children seem happy here. I've communicated my delight to Mr Tallis.'

Mr Tallis said the children in the home, who range in age from eight to sixteen years, were over the moon to have such an important person visit.

'Sometimes,' he told our reporter, 'the children can feel forgotten by the outside world, so it was a boost to everyone's morale that Mr and Mrs Drake took the time to visit us. We're all very grateful!'

There was a caption above the article, but the accompanying photo was missing. The top edge of the paper was serrated roughly where it had been torn. The caption said: *A happy visit: (From left to right) Mr Gordon Tallis, Kenny Overton, Toby Turrell, Jason Burgess, Mr Leonard Drake and Mrs Myra Drake, Elliot Juniper, Amelia Troy, Connor Laird.*

Flick blinked. Leonard and Myra Drake. Ray Drake's parents. His father, if she remembered correctly, had been a High Court judge, and Flick had seen his sour old mother at Laura Drake's funeral. If Ray had read these clippings earlier, why hadn't he mentioned it?

The door to her office swung open and a cleaner walked in with a sack. The Incident Room was filled with the drone of vacuum cleaners.

113

'I'm sorry.' Flick held up a finger. 'I'll get out of your way in a few moments.'

The last newspaper clipping was dated 6 August 1984. An entire page this time, folded in the middle. The *Hackney Express* masthead was at the top. The front-page headline, in large black capitals, read: LOCAL HERO KILLED IN CHILDREN'S HOME BLAZE.

A children's home manager died a hero when a blaze ripped through the building to which he had devoted his life.

Gordon Tallis (44) made the fatal decision to return one last time to the burning building and was overwhelmed by flames.

Firefighters arrived at the scene late on Wednesday night and battled the blaze into the morning, but the building was gutted by fire.

Sergeant Harry Crowley of Hackney Police told the *Express*: 'Gordon was a respected figure in the local community. He loved those kids, and it was absolutely typical that he went back inside – he was a man who cared too much.'

'Fuck!' Flick slapped the desktop angrily. When she looked up, the cleaner had returned and she blushed. 'I'm sorry. Just one more minute.'

Of all the people, it had to be *him*.

Another body was discovered in the blaze, but has yet to be identified. Police are concerned for the safety of 14-year-old Connor Laird.

'Connor is a vulnerable lad,' said Sgt Crowley. 'He panicked during this awful tragedy, and we ask him to come

114

forward – if only to let us know he's safe and well.'

Hours earlier, Mr Tallis had welcomed High Court judge Leonard Drake and his wife Myra to the home on a special visit, as reported in the Hackney Express last week. The blaze destroyed the building in the early hours, as last week's *Express* went to press.

Him. She was still annoyed at seeing her father's name. 'Get a grip, Flick,' she muttered.

A photograph below the article showed the aftermath of the blaze. A double-fronted three-storey house was gutted, its windows blown out, the broken timber of its roof protruding into the sky like the ribcage of a vast animal. A fire engine was parked in the foreground of the photo and two police cars. Figures pointed up at the smoking husk.

It all seemed so long ago, so irrelevant. Except that it wasn't. Flick had never been one of those coppers who put her faith in instinct. She trusted the process, and liked to build cases slowly and methodically, accumulating layer upon layer of evidence. But she sensed that this photo, these clippings, held the key to the deaths of Kenny Overton and his family.

Flick called Eddie Upson's number. The clock on the wall said: 6.34 a.m. He'd only gone home a few short hours ago. She realised she was being selfish, and was about to hang up, when he answered.

'Yeah, guv.' His voice was groggy.

She picked up a pen and a scrap of paper. 'Sorry to wake you, Eddie.'

'It's all right.' He yawned. 'I like to take a freezing shower first thing, then read the Bible for an hour. What can I do you for?'

115

'Does the name Connor Laird ring any bells to you?'

'Connor what?'

'Connor Laird.' She spelled it. 'L–A–I–R–D.'

'Uh.' She heard the rustle of his duvet. 'Nope, should it?'

'What about Elliot Juniper?'

'Juniper?'

'Like the berry.'

'Doesn't ring any bells.'

'Deborah Willetts.'

He grunted, *no*.

'What about Amelia Troy?'

'Like the artist, you mean?'

The penny dropped. 'Thanks, Eddie. Get back to sleep.'

'I'll be in as soon as I can, boss.'

She put down her pen. 'There's no hurry.'

Gathering up the cuttings – not noticing a Post-it note flutter to the floor – Flick rested the pile on her lap and closed her eyes. Another wave of tiredness washed over her and she felt her weight slide towards her feet, as if she were melting into the floor. A plinking noise next door jerked her awake.

The cleaners had gone. The lights in the Incident Room flickered on, and Dudley Kendrick walked in. He waved through the glass as he turned on his computer, taking out a coffee and a croissant from a paper bag. The smell of it made Flick's stomach rumble.

Looking at her phone, she remembered that her sister had rung a couple of times yesterday. In the chaos of events she hadn't had the chance to call her back. Flick had no business phoning anybody at this time on a Sunday morning, but Nina's kids would already be rampaging around the house, and her sister would be up with them, so no harm done. But when Flick rang the number it was Martin, her brother-in-law, who answered.

'Flick,' he said, in that Aussie drawl of his.

Hearing Angel and Hugo screaming in the background, the burble of the radio and the flatulent sizzle of something on the pan, Flick had half a mind to head straight there. Martin's fry-ups were legendary, and she could do with some cuddles from the kids, maybe grab some sleep. Flick was at their house so often she kept a change of clothes in the spare bedroom, her own toothbrush in the bathroom. Nobody could begrudge her a few hours after working through the night.

'I know it's early,' she said.

Usually, Martin would give her an earful of good-natured abuse for calling so early. But all he said this morning was an awkward, 'yeah', and she worried again that something was wrong between him and her sister.

'Nina's in bed. Coral was up half the night with a tummy bug.'

'Is she okay?' she asked, concerned.

'She's fine, but mother and child are sleeping off a shit night.'

'It's just, Nina called me. Do you know what about?'

'You know what?' She sensed that he was choosing his words carefully. 'I think she should probably talk to you herself.'

'Is everything okay there, Martin?'

'Do I need a lawyer, Flick?' He laughed. 'Look, we're all great here, but it's not a good time. Angel – don't hit your brother!'

'I'll speak to her later,' she said. 'If you think—'

'I've got to go. The eggs are burning and Angel's war with Hugo has just gone to Defcon One. It's just another day in paradise, Flick.'

'Yeah,' she said. 'Lucky you.'

She waited for a reply, but he'd already rung off. Flick dropped the phone onto her desk and stretched. A walk round the block and breakfast in a local café would be sensible.

But there was one more thing she wanted to do. Switching on her computer, Flick waited for it to boot up, then clicked on a search engine and typed in: *Amelia Troy.*

17

Elliot burned with guilt and shame when he saw Owen Veazey at his usual table in a tatty pub clinging to the edge of an estate in Harlow. Owen had been a regular for donkey's years. Elliot remembered seeing him there a decade ago, when he was still knocking about on the edges of the local criminal element, and the place had looked rundown even then.

Low and squat, and built with the same bleak functionality as the maisonettes that surrounded it, the pub was hunched at the end of a paved precinct where half a dozen anorexic trees were planted in squares of mud and dog shit. The pub's entrance and its windows were topped by half-closed shutters, like metal eyelids, which protected it from vandalism when it was shut, and its customers, a shabby swarm of derelicts and old fellas, from the attention of the local constabulary during its highly irregular opening hours.

If you were unfortunate enough to be wandering in this part of town before breakfast on a Sunday morning, you'd be hard pressed to know it was even a pub. The sign had fallen off years back, and it was in nobody's interest to put it back on again.

Wall lamps threw sour brown light over the scruffy interior, despite the hard winter glare outside, so that Elliot felt like he was trudging along the bottom of a muddy pond.

A few Sunday-morning diehards sat at the bar watching girls twerk and grind on a music video. A fruit machine burbled against a pillar, bursting occasionally into a noisy instrumental version of 'U Can't Touch This' as lights raced up and down its panels.

'Sit yourself down, Elliot.' Owen rose in greeting. 'It's good to see you.'

He was an older man, with a tanned, wrinkled face and neat short back and sides, pressed trousers, comfortable loafers, and a mustard golfing sweater. He owned a number of these jumpers, Elliot remembered, in a variety of colours. When Owen sat, he carefully lifted the creases of his trousers, a proper pair of slacks, between thumb and forefinger. He was an incongruous sight in this grubby pub, dressed in his Pro-Celebrity tournament clobber, while everyone else pitched up in shapeless grey joggers and football shirts.

'It's been too long, Elliot.' Owen's soft voice was often lost against the whirl of the fruit machine. 'You're looking well.'

'You too, Owen.'

A wiry, sharp-faced man with a harelip came to the table, four pints wedged between his stretched hands.

'This is Perry,' Owen gestured at the man, 'an associate of mine. We saw you coming and took the liberty of getting you a drink. It's cooking lager, I'm afraid, not much demand for microbreweries around here.'

'Cheers, Owen.' Bren slurped his pint.

Elliot didn't recognise Perry, and didn't care for the way the man barely acknowledged them. Instead, the newcomer licked a finger to turn the sports pages on a tabloid.

Owen sipped his pint. 'We don't see you around any more.'

The way he talked, it was like they were close friends who had drifted apart. But the truth was Elliot could count on one hand the number of occasions he had met Owen. The last time had been when he had just met Rhonda and was spending every moment he could with her, when it was a revelation to him that he might live an honest life. But everyone around here knew about Owen Veazey: his reputation, the kind of activities he was mixed up in. Lending money wasn't the half of it. Elliot had for once used some common sense and kept his distance.

In fact, now that he was here with Owen and his charming friend Perry, Elliot was fast coming to the conclusion that he was on the verge of making a terrible mistake and hardened his resolve. Owen's terms, he decided, would have to be bloody good. Elliot would take a lot of convincing about the loan. If he didn't like what he heard, he would get up and walk out.

'Life takes you in different directions,' he told Owen.

'Ain't that the truth?'

The old man clocked Elliot smearing his sweaty palms on his jeans. 'I appreciate how difficult it is for you to come to me. Nobody in their right mind, let's face it, would approach Owen Veazey for money. You'd have to be mad or desperate. Which are you, Elliott, mad or desperate?'

'A little bit of both, probably.'

Owen nodded. 'Tell me what it is you're after.'

The fruit machine whirled excitedly as a couple of blokes fed coins into its slot, and Bren turned to watch them play.

'A short-term loan.'

'How much are we talking?'

'Thirty grand.'

The old man raised his eyes to the ceiling, as if working out the numbers. 'That's a lot of money at short notice, even for me.'

There was still time for Elliot to go home and fall on Rhonda's mercy. Tell her how he'd lost the money. The only thing Elliot was guilty of was being a fool – if being a fool was a crime, Elliot would be serving life – but he clenched his fists, certain she would never believe him.

'I'm not going to ask why you need it.' Owen flicked a look at Bren, who was mesmerised by the machine's spinning reels. 'It's none of my business. But there would be consequences for you and for your family if you borrow money from me. Do you understand?'

'I do,' Elliot croaked.

'Have a drink.' Owen gestured to his glass. 'Bren tells me you've a wife and kid.'

'We're not married.' Elliot sipped the pint, but the lager didn't shift the frog in his throat. 'He's not my boy.'

'Do you love them?'

'Very much.' he said. 'They're . . .'

Truth was Elliot didn't want to diminish his devotion to Rhonda, and to Dylan, by describing it to Owen. The old man seemed to sense his reluctance, and smiled.

'I'm glad to hear it, Elliot. I've had three – no . . .' He frowned at Perry. 'How many wives have I had?'

'Four.' Perry's eyes never lifted from the paper. 'Last time I counted.'

'That's right, four.' Owen grinned. 'Lovely ladies, all, except the second one. She was a fucking nightmare, to be honest. But as you can imagine, I'm no angel either. Point is, I know how difficult it is to keep a relationship together.

So I'm going to put my cards on the table, Elliot, because I like you. We don't know each other very well, but Bren speaks very highly of you, and that's good enough for me.'

Steeling himself for the conditions of the loan, Elliot resolved again not to agree to Owen's terms straight away, not to make any rash decisions. He didn't want to be paying him back till the end of days.

'I could lend you money.' Owen clicked his fingers. 'I could lend it to you just like that. But you know how I operate. You've probably heard the horror stories. Because if I lend you money, Elliot, you'll be paying me back for years, decades even. There'd be so much interest on the loan you'd never get the monkey off your back. I'd be on you, and Perry would be all over you, like a second skin. Your relationship with . . .'

'Rhonda,' said Bren.

'Your relationship with Rhonda will deteriorate. I've seen how this goes, Elliot, many times, and it's not pretty. I don't want that to happen to you. Which is why I'm not going to lend you the money.'

Dumbfounded, Elliot gazed at the bubbles popping on his pint.

'Where most people are concerned, I don't give a toss,' continued Owen. 'I hope you understand my thinking on this.'

'It's just a short-term loan.' The machine behind him burst into song and coins clattered into its tray. 'Until I can find the man who—'

'There is no such thing as a short-term loan. Not in my world.'

'Bren said you—'

123

'Bren made a mistake. I appreciate his bringing you along, it's always good to catch up with old pals, but I'm not going to be able to help you.'

Elliot felt sick. He didn't want to be in this pub, with its nicotine-stained walls and creaking furniture and tired clientele, the noise from the fruit machine so loud that he could hardly hear himself think. But he couldn't go home empty handed.

'When Rhonda sees the money is gone, she's going to leave me.'

Owen raised the pint to his lips. 'But at least you won't be up to your neck in debt.'

Elliot scraped back his chair and dropped his head into his hands. He was out of options, and would have to fall on Rhonda's mercy.

He had no idea how long he was slumped like that when he heard Owen say: 'Bren, give us a moment.'

'Sure thing.'

Elliot heard Bren's grunt of effort as he climbed to his feet, felt a quick, reassuring squeeze on his shoulder. When Elliot sat up, the blood drained from his skull, making him light-headed.

'Tell you what,' said Owen, 'I've a suggestion. I'm a man down on a job I've got coming up. A little bit of breaking and entering.'

'No.' Elliot physically recoiled.

'Hear me out before you say no.' Owen moved his glass out of the way, to lean forward. 'It's at the house of a retired couple. In your neck of the woods, as a matter of fact. He was a banker, a broker, something like that.'

'No.' Elliot shook his head.

Perry threw down the paper. Started probing his gums with a finger.

'I know for a fact, and don't ask me how, that this couple keep a lot of cash at home,' continued Owen. 'We're talking thousands, tens of thousands. And they're away right now. So what I'm proposing is—'

'No,' Elliot said.

'Bren tells me you did some time for burglary back in the day. I need someone with experience, a bit of know-how, to accompany a friend of mine,' he nodded at Perry, 'into the house within forty-eight hours, before they come back from holiday.'

'I've got to go.' Elliot stood. 'That's not me; I haven't done that for—'

'I understand. Please, don't feel insulted.' Owen raised his palms. 'You've a problem and I saw an opportunity. It seemed a way to kill two birds with one stone, so to speak.'

Elliot just wanted out of there. 'Thanks for the offer, but—'

'Don't mention it.' The old man rose and clasped his hand tightly. Elliot felt a corner of card stab into the flesh of his thumb. 'A short-term loan. No interest, no hassle. Could be in your account by tomorrow.' When Elliot stared, Owen let go. 'Point taken.'

Perry nodded. 'Bye, then.'

Sunlight burned into Elliot's eyes when he got outside. He squinted at the business card with Owen's number on it. He didn't want it, would tear it up as soon as he got home, that's what he'd do. Striding across the estate, a flimsy supermarket bag dancing around his ankles, he lit a B&H. Halfway to the van he heard a voice behind him.

'Wait, Ell! Hold up!' Bren waddled towards him, wheezing.

In his agitation, Elliot had almost left him behind. He turned angrily. 'What else did you tell Owen about me?'

Bren caught his breath before he answered. 'What do you mean?'

'He knew I'd done time.'

'He asked about you.' Bren looked confused. 'He wanted to know the kind of man you are.'

The kind of man you are.

'He asked me to do a job.' Elliot's cheeks pinched as he sucked bitterly on the cigarette. 'A one-off, he said, and he'd lend me the money, interest free, in return.'

Bren didn't seem outraged by what Owen had suggested or, it seemed to Elliot, particularly surprised.

'That's Owen all over.' Bren shrugged. 'He don't mean anything by it. He's just trying to help.'

'Trying to help!' Elliot lurched forward. 'Hell will freeze over before I do that again, do you understand?'

'Okay, then.' Bren stepped back. 'We all know where we stand. No harm done.'

Elliot walked quickly to his van, wanting to be out of that dismal place. Didn't care, right at that moment, if Bren came with him or not.

18

'It's a waste of time and resources.' Ray Drake folded his arms. 'And I'm surprised we're even talking about it.'

First thing on Sunday morning, and Flick was struggling. She'd lined up the cuttings on her desk, but Drake barely gave them a glance.

'Kenny Overton researched these—'

'You're making basic mistakes.' He spoke over her. 'Concentrate on your gaps analysis – working out what we know and what we don't. The movements of the victims, compiling phone data, interviewing—'

'With respect, sir,' she said, 'we're doing all that.'

The Incident Room was full. Flick could see her team bashing the phones, chasing up reports. She held out the list of names, but Drake went to the window. It was as if he didn't want to look at it. Flick could understand his scepticism, but she had never seen him so agitated. She wondered how much grief Harris had given him in the aftermath of Ryan Overton's death. She couldn't get the memory of his prowling about in the Property Room out of her mind . . .

A cough – a sound – he stepped forward.

Now wasn't the time to mention it. She felt that the Sword of Damocles was poised above her head, and that her promotion would be rescinded before she'd even had time to get her feet under the desk. The irony wasn't lost on her. Flick had a reputation as a plodder; Drake himself had urged her to work more instinctively. Now she was, and he was slapping her down.

'Kenny researched all these people because they went to the children's home Ryan mentioned. Look.' She held up one of the clippings, but Drake made no move to take it. 'He tried to find the kids he'd known at the Longacre in the eighties and discovered many had died.'

'How many?' Drake asked.

'Five.'

'So, in actual fact, very few.'

'There could have been fifty kids at that home, or just nine.'

'Kids who have been institutionalised for any length of time can be damaged. Many become addicts, criminals. They form self-destructive habits and their lives spiral out of control. The death rate will naturally be higher.'

'Did you read the cuttings?' Last night he'd said he had, but now she wasn't so sure. If he'd read them, he'd understand what she was trying to say. 'Most of these people were killed in unexplained circumstances.'

'Jason Burgess committed suicide. As did Karen Smith and her partner.' Drake propped himself against the sill. 'There's nothing in there that has any significance to this investigation.'

She spaced all the cuttings apart on the desk. 'David Horner was burned—'

'Listen to me, Flick.' Drake's voice lifted irritably. 'Kenny Overton was a fantasist, a dreamer – Ryan admitted it himself – who spent his life trying to figure out where it all went wrong. Trying to find some kind of meaning to every bad choice he made.' He gestured at the plastic slips. 'What about all the other cuttings he threw away because they simply didn't fit with the idea he'd formed in his head that he was a victim? Besides, there's no evidence to suggest he knew any of these people. These could be articles torn randomly from old newspapers.'

'That'll be easy enough to check,' said Flick.

Drake looked away. 'I wouldn't be so sure.'

'Their families, sir.' She counted on her fingers. 'Karen Smith, Jason Burgess, Ricky Hancock – they all died with their loved ones, everyone except David Horner, who didn't have any. And now Kenny is murdered . . . along with *his* family.'

Drake watched all the activity in the Incident Room, as if there were far more important things that they should be doing. 'What did I tell you last night? Don't overcomplicate things. You know as well as I do that there's a tight window of opportunity in any investigation. Don't get dragged off on some ludicrous flight of fancy.'

He was closing her down in every direction. There was a good reason why Drake didn't want to follow this line of inquiry further, and they both knew what it was. She'd avoided mentioning it till now. She picked up the cutting with the photograph torn away.

'We know Kenny went to the Longacre. The photograph is missing.' She showed him the torn edge above the caption. 'But his name is here, along with some others, including . . .' She placed a finger beneath the names of Leonard and Myra Drake.

'I saw it.' Drake's left hand ticked impatiently against his leg. 'Leonard . . . my father was involved in a number of children's charities back then. It was a long time ago.'

'Perhaps your mother would remember something . . .'

'Myra can barely remember the day before yesterday.'

Flick's impression of the old woman was that she was still as sharp as a blade. 'That's not—'

'Flick.' Drake pinched the bridge of his nose. 'I'm going to be honest with you. Harris is spitting feathers. He wants to know why Ryan was allowed to go home.'

'Ryan insisted,' she said quickly. 'And we had an armed—'

'He knows all that,' said Drake, not unkindly. 'But he's thinking that right now this investigation, because of its profile, needs a more experienced lead officer.' He looked annoyed when her mobile buzzed. She placed it in her top drawer. 'I told him you deserve this chance because I have faith in your abilities. But the pressure to get motoring on this is intense. What we absolutely don't need right now is to waste time flying off on a fantastical tangent.'

She swallowed. 'Yes, guv.'

When he opened the door, the burble of the Incident Room, the chunter of printers and the ringing phones, poured into her office. For the first time he glanced at the cuttings. 'Let's talk later.'

The best thing Flick could have done right then was to knuckle down to work, God knows there was plenty piling up, but she was convinced she'd be replaced sooner or later, come what may. And besides, she'd already made the call . . .

'One more thing, guv.' She snatched a sheet off the printer. 'Those other names on the list – the ones that aren't crossed out – appear in the caption of the missing photograph. Elliot

Juniper has a criminal file. Theft, burglary, handling stolen goods; a list as long as your arm.' With a sigh, Drake closed the door. 'Someone called Connor Laird is mentioned, and Deborah Willetts, I can't find either of them in the system, but look.' She placed the printout on the edge of her desk, as if she was trying to tempt a feral cat with a treat.

Drake looked exasperated. 'Where's this going, Flick?'

'There's only a single mention of the Longacre children's home anywhere on the internet,' she said quickly. 'It burned down just hours after your mother and father visited it, in nineteen eighty-four. But Amelia Troy's name rang a bell. A few years ago she was the biggest thing to hit British Art. She won the Turner Prize, her paintings sold for tens of thousands. Troy and her husband Ned Binns were this golden couple of the art world.'

Drake reluctantly picked up the sheet.

'That's a newspaper interview she did years ago,' continued Flick. 'She mentions being in a children's home in Hackney called the Longacre.'

A photo below the interview showed Amelia Troy and Ned Binns on a sofa, dressed identically from head to toe in black denim and Doc Martens. Their legs were entwined so you couldn't tell where one of them ended and the other began, their heads leaned together in a single massive explosion of bird's-nest hair. They looked lazily at the camera from beneath heavy lids. Amelia wore thick make-up and blood-red lipstick. Ned's face was hidden behind a riotous red beard. Burning cigarettes drooped languidly in their fingers.

'And she's still alive,' said Drake.

'Yes, but about seven years ago she almost died in a

suspected overdose that killed her husband.' She waited for a moment while Ray Drake scanned the interview. 'It was all over the papers.'

Drake dropped the sheet. 'So what are you saying?'

'Point is, he died, she nearly died. Another kid from the Longacre, another accident. I just think it's worth talking to her.' When Drake laughed shortly, Flick gestured to the Incident Room. 'Everyone's hard at work. Amelia Troy still lives at the same address in Bethnal Green.'

Drake shook his head. 'You haven't been listening to me, Flick.'

She blurted out: 'I've already arranged to see her.'

Flick did her best not to shrink from his grim stare.

'We'll take my car,' he said finally.

19

A whipping cluster of colourful balloons taped to a battered steel door wasn't what Ray Drake was expecting.

He thought he knew all about Amelia Troy – had made it his business to know. There was a time when you couldn't turn on the TV or open a magazine without seeing her unfocused gaze, or hearing her throaty, self-regarding laugh as she ranted about life, politics, art. There wasn't a subject under the sun about which she didn't have an opinion. When the papers required outrageous state-of-the-nation analysis or a provocative quote to spice up a tired news story, Amelia was happy to oblige.

It was that period when Art was as big as rock 'n' roll and enormous amounts of money were being made by a new generation of hungry, media-savvy young artists. Amelia Troy was right at the vanguard of it. She was never slow to regale interviewers with her traumatic rags-to-riches story. Chain-smoking, sipping from a hip flask, she'd explain how she bounced from institution to institution as a child, hinting darkly of brutal abuse, a life of terror.

The only way to cope, she said, was to harness the creativity within her. She drew her bleak, dangerous world on walls and windows using crayons, felt tips, chalk or boot polish, whatever she could get her hands on. One day she shoplifted a 99p painting set from a corner shop. That set, she said, changed her life. With the help of a couple of well-heeled benefactors, and the vaguest suggestion of sexual favours along the way, Troy got into one of the country's top art colleges. From that moment, she proclaimed arrogantly, Art would never be the same.

Critics lapped it up. Troy's work, they said, was a 'tumorous clot of catastrophic energy, as treacherous and implacable as cancer'. She painted kinetic and intoxicating canvases of blood reds and sinister blacks, which almost, but not quite, obliterated the carefully detailed figures beneath. Instead of a signature, each painting was signed with a trademark Amelia kiss. A powerful clique of art dealers paid obscene amounts for it. Troy's shows sold out. And her nihilistic lifestyle added a more dangerous context to her anguished body of work.

When she married another *enfant terrible* of the art world, a self-proclaimed conceptual terrorist called Ned Binns, her work and appearance began to deteriorate. Her uniform of shapeless Clash T-shirts and jeans only accentuated her dramatic weight loss. Commentators drily noted the way her mass of hair was knotted and uncombed, and her thick make-up more sloppily applied.

When a whisper campaign implied a dependency to heroin, Troy's increasingly irrational behaviour did nothing to dispel the rumours. No society party was complete without the newly-weds hurling abuse at each other. Binns had his own demons, but despite his well-documented adultery and his controversial works, which involved sending threatening letters to politicians and celebrities and compiling a multi-media exhibition out of the tangled legal paper trail, Amelia Troy stood by her man.

But the moment she became forever known as a burnout – a totem of the wicked, hedonistic art scene – came when she showed up drunk for an awards ceremony and showered the attendees with a string of obscenities live on television.

Troy fell off the radar. She shuffled in and out of rehab, so they said, battling addiction and mental health problems. And by the time Troy and Binns were discovered naked and overdosed on the bed in their apartment, the fickle art world had moved on.

By all accounts Troy had a lucky escape. She was at death's door, and her body would have lain undiscovered for weeks, perhaps months, if her husband hadn't managed to rouse himself long enough from his terminal stupor to call 999. When the paramedics arrived, Binns was dead – and Amelia barely alive.

A comeback exhibition at a fringe gallery of work promising a more positive outlook on life was poorly received. The world, it appeared, only wanted to know Amelia Troy as an artistic fuck-up.

It had been a relief to Drake when she'd drifted back into obscurity. He couldn't even remember the last time he'd read anything about her, but he certainly remembered the precocious girl from the Longacre and her sketchbook filled with uncanny life drawings. There'd never been anything in her personality back then to suggest she'd become a gobby firebrand and, for a short while, the most famous artist in Britain. Amelia had been like the other children – quiet, anxious, someone who instinctively withdrew from the dangerous gaze of adults.

It was a risk to come to her warehouse. The danger was

that she'd remember him. But something, someone, was circling, and he needed all the information he could get. He clung to a quote from the single interview she'd given following her overdose. A reporter had asked her why she barely painted any more.

'Because I can't remember any of it,' she'd replied, 'it's gone.' Asked what it was she couldn't remember, she'd said: '*Everything*.'

Huddled against the wall.
Her hand hot and clammy in his.
Flecks of spittle arcing high.
Threats, obscenities.

Flick stared at the balloons whipping in the breeze. 'Looks like a party.'

The journey to Amelia's apartment had been tense. Flick had spent most of the time on the phone to the office, furiously scribbling notes, eager to show that she wasn't abandoning her other responsibilities. Approaching Bethnal Green, they drove down a winding road past industrial units – the prefab businesses, scrapyards and lock-ups shuttered this Sunday lunchtime – alongside a rail track. At the end was a hulking redbrick Victorian warehouse isolated on scrubland. The meshed windows on the ground floor were intact, but the building looked abandoned. There was a gravel area big enough to park a couple of cars. The steel entrance, with its jostling balloons, was wedged open.

'She said to go to the top floor.'

The small lobby was cold and damp, but the elevator was still an impressive piece of machinery. When Flick hit the button its gears detonated into life in the depths of the building. A box trundled down towards them, cables grinding.

136

The panelled elevator was lit by a bare bulb. Closing the cage, they ascended past sealed-off stumps of corridor. Halfway up, Drake and Flick heard something unexpected in that gloomy place: the sound of happy children.

When the elevator shunted to a halt, and Drake pulled back the lattice, they emerged into the centre of a vast space saturated with blinding light from the surrounding tall windows. The floor was spattered with speckled blobs of dried paint, which made the surface uneven. Sitting at a long trestle table were a dozen kids, painting and drawing and filling the enormous space with chat and laughter. Other children bolted like unstable atoms, paint dripping from the brushes in their hands, despite the best efforts of a small group of adults to get them under control.

Flick frowned at the sole of one of her shoes, and the sticky yellow splodge of paint smeared there, as a woman walked towards them.

'DS Flick Crowley.' Flick held out her hand. 'We're looking for—'

'Thank God.' The woman threw up her arms. 'I thought you didn't look like parents. The last thing we need is for one of the kids to walk off with a stranger!'

It took a moment for Ray Drake to realise that this amiable woman, casually dressed in a splattered T-shirt and jeans ripped at the knees, dark hair pulled back in a loose ponytail, was Amelia Troy. She looked healthy and tanned and happy. Younger than he remembered from newspaper cuttings ten, fifteen years back, when she had seemed prematurely aged. And happier, by far, than the miserable, timid child he remembered from the home.

'This is Detective Inspector Raymond Drake,' said Flick.

Amelia took his hand. Her shake was strong, and despite the chill in the vast space, warm. Drake held her look, searching for any hint of recognition, but sensed no response.

'You're having a party,' he said.

'I see why you're a policeman, absolutely nothing escapes your attention. I hold an open house for local kids every weekend, God help me. There aren't many places in this world where they can come and have creative fun and make a mess.' She gestured to a kid who was splashing orange paint on a roll of paper. 'Every week I think, Never again! But they love it so much.' She laughed. 'They can lark about, get themselves filthy and express themselves. This is a working space – or it was.'

'This is your studio?' asked Flick.

'This is my home.'

Drake turned to see that the other end of the massive warehouse, past the central elevator, was furnished as a living area, with sofas, lamps, a television on a stool; beyond that, separated by a long stretch of concrete, was an enormous double bed, a kitchen area. Everything was open plan, the areas separated by narrow paths of space like the floor of a department store.

'It must cost a fortune to warm up.'

'I may as well just chuck fifty-pound notes out the windows. Strategically placed heaters make it bearable, just about.' She smiled at Drake. 'And my beloved electric blanket, of course.'

'It's like something out of a movie,' said Flick, incredulous.

'I've lived here for nearly twenty years now and I'm too lazy to move.' A toddler crashed into Amelia's legs and fell

138

over. 'Blooming heck, Darnell, you can run fast!' For a split second the boy looked like he was going to cry, but Amelia placed a hand against his cheek, and he calmed immediately. Plonked back on his feet, he ran off, screaming with delight. 'I can't hear myself think in here, why don't we go upstairs?'

Taking a packet of cigarettes and a lighter from a ribbed radiator hidden behind a painting, she led them to a fire door. Canvases were leaned beneath the windows. Chaotic patterns, which, if you looked closer, began to take on the outlines of people. Some appeared finished but most were abandoned, or ruined by obliterating brushstrokes. In the bottom right-hand corner of each, the red imprint of her lips.

'The kids look like they've been making their own improvements to your work.'

'A few years back those paintings would have cost you an arm and a leg.' Amelia shrugged. 'These days I can't give them away.'

Their feet clanged up the steps of an iron fire escape clinging to the outside of the building.

'You don't seem worried about it.'

'I still paint for pleasure, but these days I don't feel my entire life is ruined because my work isn't hanging in the reception of some scumbag corporation.'

The tarpaper on the roof of the building was covered with fag butts, which skittered like insects in the breeze. A deckchair, its canvas middle flapping, sat by a chimney mount, a mug filled with rainwater beside it. East London lay below them, squat and grey, beneath an armada of charging cloud.

'You're not what I was expecting,' said Flick, stepping onto the roof.

'You're wondering what I've done with the tragic druggie.' The tip of Amelia's cigarette fizzed when she lit it. 'Everyone's a bit surprised, but I suppose that's my own fault, you can never escape your past. Truth is, these days I live a dull and inconsequential life. Bog standard.'

'Nothing more bog standard than living in a warehouse,' said Drake.

She laughed. 'So why is it you're here?'

Flick handed her a photograph. Pressing the cigarette between her lips, Amelia studied it. 'And who is this?'

'His name is Kenny Overton,' said Flick. 'Do you recognise him?'

Amelia tucked a loose strand of hair behind her ear. Drake watched the way the tendons and veins bulged just beneath the skin of her hand, in sharp contrast to her face, which was smooth and angular and, even now in middle age, very striking. There were faint lines splaying from her eyes. Considering the life she had lived – an abusive childhood, years of drug dependency – she had aged extraordinarily well.

'This poor man's family was killed; it was in the papers,' she said. 'But what has it got to do with me?'

'We understand Mr Overton was at the Longacre children's home with you in the nineteen eighties,' said Flick.

Amelia blew out smoke thoughtfully. 'Was he now?'

'We're investigating a possible link between the home and the murder of Mr Overton and his family.'

Amelia gently fanned the photo, as if it were a Polaroid developing in her hand, then gave it back to Flick. 'I'm afraid I can't help you.'

'You don't remember him?'

140

'I'm sorry, I'm not trying to be difficult . . . I don't remember anything about that place.' Her eyes drifted to Drake. 'I've a bit of a block.'

'A block?' asked Flick.

'For many years I carried that home around in here.' She tapped her temple. 'I was obsessed, I never stopped going on about it, it nearly destroyed me – well, you only have to look at my work. The horror of that place poured onto the canvas, my demons fuelled my art. I would have given anything to rid myself of those memories, even though I made millions from them. But the amazing thing is they're gone.' She sighed. 'Something happened to me a few years back . . . I don't know if you know this, but my husband died.'

'Ned,' said Flick.

'The very one.' Her gaze drifted over Flick's shoulder to a phone mast glittering atop a tower block. 'And you probably know we overdosed. He died and I . . . I was in a coma for weeks. It was touch and go; the doctors thought I was a goner. And when I awoke all my memories of that place were gone, every detail.'

The sun began to poke through a tear in the clouds. Amelia shaded her eyes. It was the middle of winter but her tan was deep and even. She may have given up painting, Drake thought, but she still clearly had rich friends across the world, and more than enough money to travel whenever and wherever she desired.

'The anger I had for that place energised my work and made me very successful.' She puffed on her cigarette. 'When those memories went, so did my urge, my obsession, let's say, to create. I've tried, really I have, darling, but everything

141

I've painted since has been toss. *C'est la vie*. After Ned's death I was done with the business, really.'

'Can that just happen, losing your memory like that?'

'A couple of therapists told me I'm in a fugue state – do you know what that is? I don't, really. I've . . .' Her voice became an officious monotone. '*Escaped from reality, taken on a new persona.* They said it was only temporary. Well, it's been years now. They're still inside me, those memories, and I've been warned they'll emerge sooner or later, to mess up my life all over again, lucky old me.'

'Isn't that unhealthy?' asked Flick. 'Keeping all that stuff buried?'

Amelia pinched the smoking tip off the cigarette and flicked the dead butt across the roof. 'Oh, I imagine so! I should be a quivering jelly of neuroses. I have my moments. I miss Ned very much . . .' She watched a train click past on the track below. 'But not as much as I thought I would. We loved each other, but we also made each other very miserable. Ned wasn't a happy man, and sometimes he could be . . . difficult. These last seven years, though, I've been content. For the first time in my life I don't feel the awful pain of that place. One day it may come back, I can't do anything about that, but until it does, I'm going to enjoy life.' Her eyes widened. 'Christ, listen to me go on.'

'It's a far cry from the life you lived with your husband,' said Flick. 'The children's parties and everything.'

'Yes, it is.' Amelia kicked at a clump of gravel with her foot. 'Ned would have hated the life I have now, *hated* it, we both would have. Back then, we shared one ambition.'

'What was that?'

'We wanted to die.' She smiled ruefully. 'He managed to

142

achieve it. I didn't, and I'm glad I didn't. But the life I have now would have been a living hell to Ned.' She frowned at her watch. 'Look, a few years ago I would have loved nothing more than to discuss my problems until sundown; you'd get tears, smashed furniture, the lot. But there's ice cream to dish out, so maybe you could tell me why you're talking to me about a man I apparently knew a hundred years ago.' When Flick glanced at Drake, Amelia frowned. 'Am I in danger?'

'It's only one avenue of investigation,' Drake said, 'and not a very promising one; we don't want to alarm you.'

'That bloody place.' The colour drained from her face. 'For years it made me cut myself and pump my veins full of shit. It nearly finished me. And now you're telling me it's not done with me yet?'

'It's most likely nothing,' said Flick. 'But has anything unusual happened recently?'

'Such as?'

'Has anybody spoken to you about the Longacre? Have you received any odd calls?'

Amelia hugged her chest. A cloud raced across the sun, sending the temperature plummeting. 'You're making me very anxious.'

'As I say,' Drake shot Flick a warning look, 'it's only one line of investigation.'

'What did you say your name was again?'

'Detective Inspector Ray Drake.' He took out a card. Flick reached into her bag and found one of her own.

'There's absolutely no reason to be alarmed,' Flick touched Amelia's arm, 'but feel free to phone me any time you want.'

When they moved towards the fire escape, Amelia paused

143

to gaze sadly at the city stretched across the horizon. 'That place, I can't remember anything about it, but I still can't escape from it.'

When they arrived back in the car park, Drake pointed a fob at his car, which unlocked with a whoop. He leaned across the roof to Flick, who stood on the passenger side.

'It was a waste of time,' he said. 'All we've done is frighten a woman for no good reason. I want an update on the investigation on my desk by the end of the day.'

Flick nodded, a blush sizzling up her neck, and climbed inside.

Pulling his seat belt around him, Drake recalled that last, uncertain smile Amelia Troy had given him as the cage of the elevator slammed shut and he descended into the depths of the building, and realised how grateful he was to see her again after all these years.

20

1984

Ray was never much into sports at school. He was too slight for rugby, and didn't care for getting slammed face down into the mud by the bigger boys. Rowing, with its freezing early mornings, was a struggle.

But he had always been agile and never shied away from a challenge, attributes that came in handy when he decided, just for the fun of it, to climb up the side of the Longacre and into a first-floor window. Well, partly for the fun of it. He wouldn't be going to the trouble if Sally had phoned him, as she normally made the effort to do. If she wasn't going to let him know that she was okay, he would just have to bloody well find out for himself.

Part of him enjoyed all the cloak-and-dagger stuff. Perhaps, when he was older, he could become a spy rather than the boring barrister his parents expected him to be. You can be anything you want in life, Ray sensed that instinctively – whether he could convince Myra and Leonard of the fact was another story.

Sally's car was outside the home when he arrived, and he heard the children inside, but nobody was answering the door. So Ray jumped at the drainpipe, scrambling for a foothold on the brackets that fixed the pipe to the brick.

There was a tricky moment when bolts shifted and the pipe jerked away from the wall, and he hung on for dear life, but then he managed to get a hand to the nearest sash window and lift it. Heaving himself over the sill, swinging his legs inside, he collapsed on the worn carpet, laid staring up at a stain on a ceiling tile, getting his breath back.

Then a voice asked: 'Who are you?'

Ray sat up to see a young girl sitting on a mattress against the wall opposite. Her knees were bunched in front of her, pencil poised over a notebook covered in crepe and glitter.

'Me and Jason have got a game going on,' Ray said. 'Hide-and-seek.'

The key to getting by at school, he had discovered, was to walk about as if you owned it, as if you had the brazen right to be there as much as any of the house masters, captains or the senior boys who fancied themselves as judge, jury and executioner. Ray was quick-witted and personable, people liked him, and he had discovered that more often than not he could talk himself out of – and sometimes into – difficult situations.

But the girl said, 'You're not from here.'

'I am.' He climbed to his feet. 'You just don't see me because I'm really, *really* good at hide-and-seek.'

He could see she didn't believe a word of it. Most kids would have screamed the place down if they saw a stranger falling through an upstairs window. Instead, she went back to her book, totally absorbed. The top of her pencil twirled and danced over the page.

Ray's interest was piqued. 'What are you doing?'

'Drawing.'

'Oh, yeah?' He threaded his way through the clutter of

146

furniture, careful not to bang his shins on the corners of the beds that jutted into the room like an invading fleet. 'Can I have a look?'

She didn't say yes, but she didn't say no either, and Ray gently tugged the book from her grasp. He turned the pages, expecting to see the usual childish stick figures and bulging girlish hearts, and was surprised by the detailed, painfully intricate images. The girl had drawn various kids he vaguely recognised from the home – Kenny, Regina, Connor – and he found himself drawn ever deeper into the winding swirls and whorls curling around the page. The gentle strokes would crackle suddenly, like a surge of electricity, and the detail of a face emerged out of the disturbance. Some of the children were smiling, some of them were laughing, but they all had unbearably sad eyes, expressive beyond their years.

He was seriously impressed.

'Did you do these all by yourself?' The girl nodded, eyes clamped on the sketchbook in case he tried to run off with it. 'I'm Ray. What's your name?'

'Amelia Troy.'

He held out his hand, as he had been taught to do since he was barely able to walk. She stared, but he kept it there until her fingers tentatively reached out, and they shook.

'You're a real talent,' he said, and a smile ghosted across Amelia's face. 'Maybe you could draw me one day. Do you want to be an artist when you grow up?'

Her eyes widened, as if he had asked her if she was planning to travel to the moon. You can be anybody you want to be, that's what he told himself, but maybe not if you're a child like Amelia, living in a dump like this, with its damp

147

and draughts and peeling wallpaper, and its festering atmosphere of dread.

'You know what?' he said. 'Myra – my mother – sits on the board of an art gallery, and it's quite a famous one. When you're older, if you do me some drawings, I can arrange for them to see them. Maybe they could recommend a college you could go to. Would you like that?'

The girl looked down, embarrassed. Ray realised Amelia had probably been made many promises in her short life, and not a single one of them had happened.

'I'll do it for you,' he said, and meant it. Ray never said anything without meaning it. 'Because I've a feeling we're going to be friends.'

The girl rolled her eyes. 'We've only just met.'

'Doesn't matter,' he said. 'I'm never wrong about stuff like that.'

He looked around the dismal room, with its clutter of beds and mattress and clothes strewn all over the floor, the windows smeared with a thousand and one fingerprints, and wondered what had led Sally to this place. How she could tolerate the stink of filth and unhappiness. She had grown up in a home where she had everything she could possibly want: a loving family life and a good education. She had come here originally because she wanted to make a difference to the lives of these kids. Now it seemed to him that something had gone terribly wrong. She had fallen under the spell of Gordon Tallis, that much was clear to Ray, and was as much as prisoner of this place as the children.

Ray wanted her out of there, and all the children, too. But there was nothing he could do – he was just a kid. One day, when he was older, people would listen to him. He would have the authority of an adult and would set about making a difference, a *real* difference, to the lives of people. One day, he knew, he would do some good in the world.

His parents expected him to become a barrister, not because of any sense of social justice on their part, but because it was what Leonard had done, and Leonard's father before him, and his father before that. Well, Ray would see about that. To defy his parents would be unthinkable. But Ray had inherited Myra Drake's iron will, her indestructible self-belief, and they knew it. One day he would force them to understand that what they demanded of him wasn't what he wanted for himself.

'Do you know Sally?' Ray asked Amelia. 'Do you know where I can find her?'

'She'll be in the office,' said the girl. 'Where she always is.'

He returned the book. 'It was lovely to meet you, Amelia. We're going to meet again.'

'Are we?'

'I made you a promise.' He stood. 'And I keep my promises.'

On the landing he heard the low thrum of the children's voices in the garden – Sally said they were encouraged to stay outside during the summer – and banging from the kitchen. Ray crept over the bare floorboards, and down the stairs.

The closed door of the office was on the left. When he yanked on the handle, it didn't budge, so he knocked.

'Sal! Are you in there?' He kept an eye on the long hallway and the kitchen, where the shadows of Gordon's staff, the Dents, lumbered across the black-and-white tiles.

'Sal!' When he put his ear to the office door, he heard the roar of air. 'Sally!'

'So this is a nice surprise,' said a voice, and Ray turned to see the manager sat on the bottom stair, hands flopping forward over his knees. 'Particularly as I don't remember anyone letting you in.'

Ray blurted out: 'One of the children.'

'If you say so, lad.' Gordon lifted a hand, unconvinced. 'Maybe next time you could let us know when you intend to drop in, so we can polish our best silver, perhaps dish up a few canapés.'

'Where's Sally?'

'She's asleep. She works very long hours, Raymond – that's your name, yes? – and she's all tired out.'

From the doorway opposite appeared the new kid, Connor, and another boy, a brute called Elliot. The last time Ray had seen him, he'd had a bandage around his face. But it was gone now, and his nose was misshapen and purple.

Ray felt uneasy. 'I'd like to see her.'

'Another time, perhaps. Let me give her a message for you.'

'Maybe we could wake her up.'

'Disturbing a young lady's beauty sleep, breaking and entering? And here's me thinking you were a young gentleman.'

'If you don't mind, I've come all this way.'

Gordon laughed. 'You are by far the most polite housebreaker I've ever met, but I'm afraid our children are unsettled by strangers, so I'm going to have to ask you to leave.'

'And I'm going to have to insist,' said Ray, praying that his voice didn't crack, 'that I see her.'

'Why don't we just call the police?'

150

Ray stood his ground when Gordon approached, but his hands trembled behind his back. 'I can't see you doing that.'

'You're a bright and clever boy. A credit, no doubt, to your very expensive education.' Gordon's smile vanished. 'But you're not welcome, lad. I cannot allow people to let themselves in and walk about the place.'

'My parents are very involved in children's charities.'

'Good for them,' said Gordon. 'Public-spirited people, so they are.'

'Maybe they could come and see the work you do here.' Ray swallowed. 'They would be very interested.'

'They're welcome,' Gordon spread his arms wide, 'any time.'

'I just want to see—'

'I'm not going to ask you again,' said Gordon.

But Ray didn't want to go. He wanted to see Sally, and he didn't understand why he wasn't allowed. When he was small, Ray had depended more than he liked to admit on her affection. Goodness knows he got little enough from his parents. They loved him, he was sure of that, but just weren't wired to show it. The environment he grew up in was stifling, prohibitive. From an early age he attended a series of expensive prep schools where he was taught to be – expected to behave as – a young adult. Sally had spent a lot of time with him. With her he could behave how he wanted, just be a small kid, she had no expectations of him. The thought of losing her to this place . . . sickened him.

But he had no choice, and he had to go.

Nodding at Connor, he said, 'How are you enjoying it here?'

But the boy didn't answer. There was a frightening intensity in his eyes. Ray had met lots of bullies, there were plenty of them at school – you learned quickly who to avoid, and

Ray had always been a good judge of character – but he didn't understand this kid at all. There was a truculence to Connor, a wilfulness. It was insecurity or malice . . . or maybe something worse.

Ray nodded at Amelia, who stood on the stairs, and was about to go when the office door opened.

'What are you doing here?' Sally asked sleepily. She was dressed, but her hair pressed against her cheeks, twisting around the sunglasses she wore.

'You never called me,' Ray said, with relief. 'I was worried!'

'This is a wonderful, heart-warming moment,' Gordon growled. 'But please, Sal, take the boy out of here. Now.'

Sally pushed Ray outside, and they sat on the steps, looking down on the street and the train track. Reggae music pumped lazily from one of the squats.

'I asked you not to come here,' she said.

'You didn't call.' All the tension of his encounter with Gordon whipping loose inside him, he struggled to keep a whine from his voice.

'Sometimes I don't get the chance,' she said. 'I've responsibilities, things to do.'

'I need to know that you're okay.'

'You don't have to worry about me.'

'But I do. This place . . .' He darted a look over his shoulder. 'It's wrong.'

'I asked you not to come here. I expressly asked you.'

'You're not the same person.'

'No, I'm not. Because I'm not a child any more, Ray, I'm an adult, and being an adult isn't a whole lot of fun sometimes, as you'll find out.'

'Not around here it isn't – or being a kid, for that matter.'

He nodded at the sunglasses. 'Take them off.'

'Don't tell me what to do.'

'Why not?' He couldn't help himself, and tried to grab at the glasses, but Sally jumped up, holding them to her face.

'Because I'm not going to be ordered around by you!' She went to lean on the railings, out of his reach, and they stayed there like that, both of them upset, until she said: 'If you want to meet we can do that, every couple of weeks or so, but not here. I promise to ring, but I don't want you to come here. I mean it this time, Ray.'

That was fine with him. He didn't want to come back anyway. There was stuff about this home that he didn't want to know about – those deliveries he saw Connor and Elliot making around the borough, for a start – and if he did ask her about it, she might well refuse to see him again, and he couldn't bear that. Sally was right: this was no place for him. He'd be going back to school in a couple of months, would be gone for the best part of the year, and schoolwork would consume all his time and energy. When he came back to the city, with a bit of luck she would have moved on, and they'd both be able to forget about this wretched place for good.

'I'll stay away, but you have to call me,' he said. 'Twice a week.'

'It's a deal.' She placed a finger beneath the glasses to rub an eye and when they lifted momentarily he thought he saw a tinge of yellow beneath an eyelid, which made him feel sick. 'Just because I'm here, with Gordon, doesn't mean I'm going to stop caring about you.'

Maybe that's what this was all about. He wasn't worried about Sally at all, just about himself. Maybe he couldn't face the fact that she was free to make her own mistakes, had her own life to live, her own life to ruin. She was able to go where she wanted, could drift to the ends of the earth and never come back if that's what she wanted. Myra and Leonard allowed him no such uncertainty. He would go back to school, and then to Oxford, and he would become a barrister, end of story. His whole life was mapped out for him, and there was nothing he could do about it, unless something drastic happened, unless something cataclysmic occurred to completely alter his destiny. That was why he felt so emotional – she was free and he was trapped.

Ray wondered whether, in the years to come, when they were both adults and he had his own life and family and responsibilities, they would still be friends. He prayed that they would.

'It's a deal,' he repeated under his breath.

Sensing his misery, Sally sat down, putting an arm around him. To his relief, she changed the subject. Reminded him of an afternoon in the park when he was small and fell in a pond – the look on Myra's face was a picture! He laughed at that, and they started talking about the days they spent together when he was barely taller than her knees – forgetting about Gordon and the Longacre – until dusk, a good three hours later, when she told him she had to go back in.

Ray stood and noticed his hands were covered in glitter from Amelia's notebook. He wiped his them down his legs as Sally opened the door to go back inside and when he looked up he saw, or thought he saw, Connor Laird standing in the gloom of the hallway, like a mirror image, his expression hidden in shadow.

When he trotted down the steps to go home, Ray was relieved he didn't have to go back to that place ever again.

21

Flick worked into the evening, only nipping out of the office to pick up a Happy Meal, which she devoured at her desk as she trawled through the automatic number plate recognition data Steiner had compiled. Chewing on the burger, her thoughts drifted back to those cuttings Kenny Overton had painstakingly collected. The people he believed had been at the same children's home decades ago, and who had since died.

Despite the fruitless meeting with Amelia Troy, and Ray Drake's displeasure at her wasting time on what he insisted was a dead end, something nagged at her about the cuttings, but she knew she'd be walking on thin ice if she diverted resources into looking into the deaths of those people. The fact that Drake's parents had visited the Longacre must have rattled him more than he was letting on, and she couldn't shake the memory of him in the Property Room. Flick would never be one of life's maverick coppers – she'd spent her whole career slavishly playing by the rules, not exploiting them as her dad had done – but she absolutely hated loose ends. She needed to be satisfied in her own mind about those articles, and it was a bitter irony that the one person who could probably provide details about the Longacre was the last person in the world she wanted to see: her father.

The fries made her feel queasy, so she threw the greasy

pocket in the bin and read interview reports. A couple of names kept cropping up in the investigation. According to one of his mates, Phillip Overton had owed money to a loan shark. He'd kept the debt quiet, hadn't even told his brother. The money, a couple of grand, was eventually paid back at the usual astronomic rate of interest, but not before a couple of nasty encounters with the street lender.

Flick called Eddie Upson into the office.

'How long ago are we talking?'

'About six months,' he said. 'Phil played football at a local leisure centre. A couple of his teammates saw him have beer chucked in his face by the guy in a pub.'

After grabbing a few hours' sleep, Upson was chipper this afternoon. It was Flick, who'd worked through the night, who felt – and probably looked – like something from a horror show.

'Got a name?'

'The Golden Eagle.'

'The loan shark, Eddie.'

'Dave Flynn,' said Upson. 'Sounds a dashing kind of guy. Vix is chasing up an address now.'

Door-to-door interviews at the two crime scenes hadn't turned up any new leads. At Ryan Overton's estate, where a distrust of the police was endemic, it was especially tough to get information. The pensioner who lived in the flat that had been used to gain access to Ryan's balcony was in Gdansk, and not due to return until the following week.

There was a stack of other interviews and evidence reports for Flick to plough through. Peter Holloway's scene-of-crime analysis was pending. Pathology results weren't due for another twenty-four hours, and she'd been warned not to expect any results that would smash the investigation wide open.

At the end of the day, Holloway sat in her office, legs crossed neatly at the knees. 'Nothing so far,' he said.

'You're telling me that the perpetrator went in and out of the Overton house, and in and out of Ryan's flat, without leaving any trace evidence?'

Holloway's glasses dropped to his chest. 'Don't shoot the messenger, DI Crowley. The intruder or intruders took considerable care.'

Flick was incredulous. 'No prints, no hairs or flakes of skin.'

'It'll all be in the report,' Holloway said. 'Our perpetrator was in Ryan Overton's flat for a matter of seconds rather than minutes, and knew what they were doing. This is a person who has prepared meticulously, and who, I suggest, has a more than passing knowledge of forensic procedure. That's not necessarily to say they have professional insight. Television crime dramas feature forensic techniques; texts are freely available on the internet and shared on social media. Pay attention to the basics and it's relatively simple to cover your tracks.'

She struggled to keep the disappointment from her voice. 'Thanks, Peter.'

Holloway stood. 'One day into the investigation and you look awful.'

'I have an underactive thyroid,' she said defensively.

'Remember to eat occasionally, DS Crowley.' He eyed the remains of her fast food in the bin. 'Something nutritious.'

'I will.' She cracked a window, conscious of the greasy burger smell. 'I think that's everything for now.'

In the evening, with the Incident Room emptying, Flick was shutting down her computer when she noticed a Post-it note curled beneath the wheel of her chair. Printed in Kenny Overton's clumsy capitals was the name RONNIE DENT, and an address in Euston. Curious, she typed in Dent's name and to her surprise found that a string of his previous convictions – assault, shoplifting, drink driving and drug offences – had been Back Record Converted, transferred from paper files to the Holmes 2 computer database, along with his employment history. There, right at the top, was a mention of the Longacre home.

With the investigation stalling and few leads showing promise, she'd put off going to see Drake for as long as possible. But when she finally mustered the courage to go upstairs, just before eight, his office was empty.

Tiredness washed over her as she drove home. Pulling up at traffic lights to turn left towards her flat, the indicator ticked heavily in her head. She really needed a good night's sleep. But Nina hadn't phoned and Flick couldn't rid herself of the suspicion that there was something her sister was keeping from her. Besides, the bed in Nina's spare room was much more comfortable than her own knackered futon. A horn blared behind her – the lights had turned green.

Flick cranked the indicator right, and swung the car in the opposite direction.

22

Something was approaching.

He felt it pulsing, no more than a fleeting movement at the corner of his eye, edging out of the shadows. This phantom, this reckoning, almost upon him.

The past was crashing into the present. Decades ago, something had been set in motion, a terrible force gaining momentum. Feeding, becoming stronger. All the while Ray Drake had been building something precious. He was a son, a father – and a husband who had been forced to watch his wife fade away before his eyes, her cells eviscerated by disease. And now he sensed a greater catastrophe – with the slaughter of a family just yards from his own police station.

A curtain had been lifted to reveal an evil design. He had to be ready.

Drake pulled up outside Jordan Bolsover's luxury Docklands apartment building and killed the engine, listened to the end of one of Laura's Bach suites, letting her music flood through him and calm his jangling nerves. When the last note faded, the distant burble of traffic and churning river barely penetrated the quiet of the car.

Nestled behind cubes of shrubbery, the building was bathed in a blue light, which danced and rippled across the surface of the Thames. It was typical of City-boy Jordan to have a swanky riverside pad. Drake made a point of doing his homework on every man who came into his daughter's orbit, and didn't like what he found in his credit rating. Jordan spent money hand over fist. There was the apartment, the sports car, the exotic holidays, the membership of the exclusive gym where celebrities pounded the treadmill safely removed from the Great Unwashed. Jordon's expensive bespoke suits were tailored to accentuate each of the muscle groups in the torso he'd sculpted with the aid of a personal trainer. Back when they still spoke, April told Drake that Jordan was buying into a syndicate to own a thoroughbred. The low six-digit salary that Jordan earned would barely cover all these outgoings.

The money wasn't an issue, but Drake didn't like Jordan, who was arrogant and narcissistic. It drove him crazy to think that his little girl could fall in love with such a man. But Drake also knew that was exactly *why* she'd fallen for Jordan – because it sent him nuts. The more April knew Drake despised her boyfriend, the more her bond with Jordan strengthened.

Laura hadn't liked Jordan either, but she'd told Drake to back off and let the relationship cool of its own accord. Laura knew how to let problems burn themselves out. Drake loved his wife and trusted her instincts absolutely, but she was gone now, and he needed to keep his daughter close.

His mobile rang. The screen flashed: CALLER UNKNOWN. This was the sixth call. Each time he picked it up he heard a child's weeping.

But the electronically altered voice was too low, too stylised for it to be a child, and this time when he connected the call – and said, 'Ray Drake' – it spoke.

'I don't want to speak to you, put the other one on.'

160

'You're talking to—'

'I said put him on!' barked the voice.

'Who is this?' Drake listened to the electronic squall, his heart racing. 'Tell me who—'

The line went dead. A moment later, Drake scrolled down his contacts list until he found the number he needed. After several rings, the call was answered.

'Lewis,' he said. 'How goes it?'

'Ray,' said Lewis Allen. 'This is out of the blue. What's the time?'

Drake could hear conversation in the background, the clink of cutlery. 'It's late, Lewis, I'm sorry.'

'You're doing me a favour,' said Allen, voice low. 'We've got neighbours round. Hold on a sec.' Drake heard the laughter fade as Allen moved into another room and closed the door. 'That's better, I can hear you now. It's been a long time, Ray, and you were never one for social calls.'

'Amelia Troy,' said Drake. 'Remember her?'

Lewis Allen whistled. 'How could I forget? It was a big deal at the time. Her husband was some big artist or something. Well,' he snorted, 'I say artist, but I use the term loosely.'

Drake and Allen went way back, had walked the beat together as young PCs, and joined CID at about the same time. Then Allen moved to the nick at Bethnal Green, where he'd investigated the circumstances of the overdose of Troy and Binns.

'Remind me how they were found, she and her husband,' said Drake.

'Why are you asking after all these years, Ray? Got new evidence or something?'

161

'It's April,' said Drake. 'She's doing an essay, some evening college thing. I said I'd ask you. It escaped my mind and she's got to have it done by tomorrow.'

'No problem,' said Allen, playing along with the lie. 'The emergency dispatcher got a call.'

'From who?'

'Binns. He and the wife took an overdose, and the last thing he did before he fell unconscious was to call 999. You listen to the call, he was incoherent, could barely speak. The signal was traced to a warehouse they lived in, him and Troy. The paramedics found 'em laying on a bed, surrounded by junkie paraphernalia, syringes everywhere.'

'And Binns was dead.'

'He was done for when they arrived. Troy was barely alive, and was raced to hospital. Just in time, by all accounts. She was one lucky lady.'

Ned Binns was a troubled soul who took vast quantities of drugs. His wealth and marriage to Troy had opened up whole new opportunities for self-destruction. Allen and the other coppers who attended the scene concluded it was just another tragic overdose, and their decision was subsequently supported by the coroner's verdict.

But Drake had to be sure.

'Was Amelia Troy ever charged?'

'A file was sent to the CPS. Binns was a loose cannon, a bipolar smackhead. The rumour was he used to knock her around.'

'I didn't know that,' said Drake.

'It was decided she needed psychiatric help, not prison. If he hadn't made that call, she'd be dead.'

'Binns was at death's door, but he managed to call 999?'

'I've seen druggies do some seriously unexpected things,' Allen said. 'Journalists tried to sniff out all the salacious details, but there was nothing fishy about it. They overdosed, Ray, simple as that.'

'Thanks, Lewis, I appreciate it.' The blast of a tugboat horn as it chugged up river penetrated the quiet of the car.

'Hell of an essay your daughter's writing. Things have moved on from Van Gogh's ear, I suppose. I was really sorry to hear about Laura, Ray. She was a lovely lady.'

'I owe you, Lewis.'

Drake killed the connection and walked to reception. A shimmering blue light gave the walls a poolside glimmer. The porter, an old guy frowning over a puzzle book, looked up as Drake strode to the elevator.

'Can I help you, sir?'

'I'll see myself up.' Drake pressed the button for the eighth floor.

'I have to buzz you—'

The porter moved around the side of his desk too quickly, clipping his knee. His exclamation was cut off as the lift door closed.

Don't come on strong, Ray. She's scared and confused. Drake's fingers curled as he imagined Laura's hand slipping into it. *Don't argue. Don't get angry. You'll lose her.*

'I'll try,' he said, out loud.

The eighth-floor corridor smelled of pine freshener. A vase of flowers decorated an alcove. Drake could hear the thud of music and muffled laughter coming from Jordan's apartment. He rang the doorbell, and when the laughter continued, put his thumb on it and kept it there.

The door finally swung open. 'I've turned it down already!'

Jordan's tracksuit bottoms were worn low to expose his taut stomach and jutting abs, a bottle of Japanese beer was tucked into the elastic waist like a holstered gun. An unbuttoned pale cream shirt revealed a fine gold chain across his hairless chest. Since Drake had seen him last, Jordan's cropped hair had turned platinum.

'Mr Drake! How's it going?'

Music and laughter continued behind the closed living-room door. Despite the young man's apparent surprise, Drake had a feeling he was expected.

'Can I come in?'

'Course!'

Jordan bowed gravely. Drake saw his pupils were large and round, and wondered what he'd discover on the other side of that closed door.

Stay calm.

He led Drake into a dark bedroom. 'We've some mates over. Why don't you wait here and I'll get April?'

The unmade duvet on the bed was coiled like a scoop of ice cream. There was a built-in wardrobe along the length of one wall, an en-suite bathroom. The walls were covered with arty monochromes of snaking naked torsos. April's trolley case stood at the end of a king-sized bed. He picked it up, easily: empty.

Balcony doors were flung open to the cold evening and the sparkling city lights at dusk. A boat puttered down the river, leaving a frothy wake. On the balcony was a metal table with two chairs. Drake prodded the mashed butts in an ashtray. Several were marked with lipstick.

'What are you doing here?'

The bedside lamp clicked on, and Drake barely recognised

164

his own daughter. Her blonde hair flamed red in the glow of the lamp, and her skin, so pale and porcelain in the sunlight, was almost translucent. There were shadows beneath her eyes. For the first time, Drake saw just how much weight she'd lost. Her feet were bare. Arcing across the top of her left foot was a tattoo he'd never seen before, an orchid.

His first instinct was to go to her, but he checked himself. These days, any attempt at affection antagonised her. Instead, he nodded to the balcony. 'You're smoking now?'

'I'm old enough.' Once it had been a joke between them, *when I'm old enough*, then a threat. Now it was a dismissal. 'I asked you why you're here.'

He nodded at the case. 'I don't know what you're trying to prove. Come home.'

'This is my home now.' She gestured around her. 'Mine and Jordan's.'

Drake enjoyed the battle of wills that often took place with suspects across a metal table in an interview room, and invariably got what he wanted. What was left unspoken, he knew, often screamed more loudly than any confession. Ray Drake had forgotten more secrets than most people had ever learned. But here, in this bedroom, the unspoken fact of their mutual grief – April for her mother, Drake for his wife – stood between them, and he couldn't find the words that would make everything good again.

Jordan slipped into the room to take her hand. April towered over him.

'I had to learn from Myra that you'd left home.'

'And I bet Gran loved telling you I'd gone. I bet she couldn't wait.' April snorted. 'You should be happy for me, Ray.'

165

To his irritation, she'd begun to address him by his first name, the same way he addressed the old woman.

'Please don't—'

'I didn't even think you'd notice. You're always so busy at work.'

'It wasn't my—'

She spat out the words: 'Mum was dying.'

And there it was, out loud. This was the conversation they should have had months ago, just the two of them, at home; their home, not in a strange room clinging to the cold river.

'We're engaged now.' She held up a hand, a ring glinting on a finger in the soft light. 'Aren't you going to congratulate us, Ray?'

'Don't call me that.' *Don't get angry.* 'I'm your dad.'

'Look, Mr Drake – Ray.' Jordan stepped forward. 'Thing is, I love April, and she loves me. You've got it into your head that I'm a bit down market, I accept that, but I have to pinch myself to believe that your daughter would honour someone like me with her love.' He took April's hand. 'I intend to make her happy.'

Drake didn't take his eyes of his daughter. 'Come home.'

'Fact is, Ray, you two ain't been getting on. Maybe you can both get a bit of distance now April lives with me, get things into perspective. It'd be heartbreaking if the two of you fell out – permanent, like.'

Ignoring him, Drake said: 'You don't know what you're doing.'

She laughed bitterly. 'Of course I don't – I'm in love. But then you wouldn't understand a little thing like *feelings*.'

She turned and ran from the room.

'Well.' Jordan made a face. 'That could have gone better.'

As Drake moved past, Jordan grabbed his arm. When Drake reeled angrily towards him, he held his hands up.

'Leave her be, Ray.' His voice was soft. 'She's upset.'

'I'm going to talk to my daughter.'

'I'd rather you didn't. We've got company.'

'What will I find next door?' asked Drake.

'It's a mess. There's drunk people, empty bottles and smelly takeaway food. You know how it is.'

'Drugs?'

'Of course not, Ray . . . Mr Drake.' Jordan made a big show of looking offended. 'What do you take me for?'

'Some spliff, maybe, or cocaine? Because you know how I'd react, don't you?'

Jordan grinned. 'You'd go mental.'

'As a police officer, I'd find myself in a very difficult position. There'd be shouting and recrimination, and April would have another reason to hate me. Is that what you're banking on, Jordan? That I'll barge my way in next door?'

'This anger you've got inside of you, Ray, it's not healthy. Get to the gym and onto a punchbag, let it all out.'

Drake rubbed the silk of Jordan's shirt collar between his fingers.

'Careful with that.' Jordan shifted uneasily. 'That's expensive.'

'If I discover my daughter is taking drugs, we're going to have a talk, you and me.'

Jordan forced a smile. 'Look forward to it, Mr Drake.'

Drake pushed past him and out the front door. He marched to the lift without looking back, stomach clenched like a fist.

167

'Tell you what,' Jordan called from the door, 'just to show there's no hard feelings, you're still invited to the wedding. Leave it with me, I'll talk April round.' Drake stabbed at the lift button and finally the doors trundled open. 'You take care, Ray!'

The porter was hovering by the lift when he arrived back in reception. 'If you're visiting, you're supposed to sign in!'

Drake stormed into the car park. The river lapped angrily against the embankment. In the car he fumbled with the music system. Shut his eyes and listened to Mozart's Requiem, let the music pour through him.

Laura had taught him how to let it soak the anger from every muscle and tendon, from the marrow in his bones, to cool the blood boiling in his veins. The engine purred below him, barely more than a soft vibration.

A faint trace of Laura's perfume lingered in the compartment. He imagined he heard, as the last mournful notes of the mass faded, the steady rhythm of her breath beside him.

Ray Drake missed his wife so much.

23

Nina and Martin lived in a big, comfortable house in Green Lanes, which smelled of pot-pourri. Giant sofas covered in exotic throws and cushions nestled against colourful walls. Lamps threw soft light through stained-glass doors. Objects d'art – mementoes they had brought home from their world travels – were placed on ever higher shelves so that they wouldn't end up in small hands and used as weapons.

It was a home from home for Flick, who hated her own cramped one-bedroom flat, and she stayed there frequently. She could relax, even amid the explosive tantrums and rows that broke out every five minutes among the children. Nina and Martin never minded her being there, or so they said, and her nieces and nephew clearly adored having her about the place. It was the kind of loving, nurturing environment that Flick could never imagine having for herself, so the idea that Nina and Martin's long marriage could be in trouble filled her with consternation.

She had her own key, but didn't like to use it – didn't want to give anyone the impression that she was taking their hospitality for granted – and when she rang the bell Martin opened the door immediately.

'Hi,' she said. 'Off out?'

'Yeah.' He plunged one arm into a North Face jacket as he searched the pockets of another coat on the banister.

169

Martin was an architect who worked on local government building projects. Flick had known him for nearly two decades now, since her sister came home months early from her gap-year world tour to drop the bombshell that she had married an Aussie she met in Goa just three weeks previously. Nobody had expected it to last five minutes, let alone nineteen years, but Nina and Martin's marriage had always appeared rock solid, not that Flick claimed to be any kind of expert on the subject. Martin was a charming husband, and a kind and thoughtful father who spent hours playing with his kids, and Flick loved him to bits, but he had been evasive on the phone that morning, and she was convinced he was avoiding her eye as he stomped towards the kitchen, calling: 'Nina, where's my keys?'

'I haven't seen them,' she heard her sister shout, and then their voices dropped to an irritable whisper. Flick didn't want to eavesdrop, but couldn't help herself, and was kind of relieved when all she could hear was the *tap, tap, tap* of claws on the floorboards. An old Labrador shambled towards her, tail thumping against the wall. Flick stroked its smooth head, pulling her face clear of its slathering tongue, and tried to pretend Nina and Martin weren't rowing. 'Hey, Lulu, nice breath.'

Moments later, Martin rushed back down the hallway, keys in his grasp. 'Got a poker game,' he said, and left.

'I'm in here,' called Nina.

Flick found her sister in the kitchen. A long counter swung in a gentle curve towards a dining table spotted with lumps of candle wax from the numerous evenings Nina and Martin entertained friends. On summer nights the entire rear glass wall opened so that all the shrubs and plants and flowers in the garden appeared to pour inside. The room was personable and tasteful and tidy – all the more remarkable, thought Flick, because Nina and Martin had three exuberant and messy under-tens.

'Since when did your husband play poker?'

'He plays occasionally.' Nina crouched at the dishwasher prodding buttons. 'He's under the mistaken impression it gives him a tough cowboy vibe. Have you eaten?'

'I'm not hungry.'

'Auntie Flick!' called Coral, the seven-year-old, from upstairs. 'Come and see me.'

'I'll be right up,' Flick shouted, and turned to her sister. 'I thought they'd all be asleep by now.'

'She's wearing her princess outfit in bed. Honestly, the pink is an obscenity, but she won't take it off, she's desperate to show you.' Nina slammed shut the dishwasher door and pressed a folded pair of glasses to her nose to read a label on a bottle of red.

'I'm not in the mood for a drink,' said Flick, 'I'm dead on my feet.'

'You're going to want a glass of this.'

Nina padded in her bare feet to a drawer. She was dressed in a loose top and yoga pants, and her strawberry-blonde hair was piled high on her head by an artfully placed pencil. Slim and toned, she was as tall as Flick, but there was no crick in her posture, no apology for her height or her place in the world. She took out a corkscrew.

'This is the real deal.' Nina posed mock seductively with the bottle, as if she were a hostess stroking the top prize on a game show. 'It's from Martin's *special* stash of very expensive wines. The idea was to drink them on momentous occasions.

171

Each case costs hundreds of your English pounds. Trust me, you're going to want this.'

'I am honoured,' said Flick warily. 'What's the celebration?'

Nina took two long-stem glasses from a cupboard. 'I told him that if I was going to have this conversation with you alone, because Martin couldn't get away fast enough, then he would have to pay a forfeit.' She twisted the corkscrew pensively. The cork eased out with a soft plop.

'If you're trying to terrify me, you're going about it the right way. What's going on?'

Nina poured the ruby-red liquid and pushed a glass across the table. 'Tell me what you think.'

'I don't care about the wine. Is there something wrong between you and Martin? If I've been overstaying my welcome I promise not to stay over again, unless expressly invited.'

'Don't be ridiculous,' said Nina. 'We love you being here, which makes what I have to say all the more hideous.'

'Are you splitting up?' Panic surged in Flick. 'Oh God, you are.'

'No, of course not!' Nina burst into tears.

'Auntie Flick!' shouted Coral.

'Up in a minute!' Flick held her sister. 'Please, just tell me.'

Nina lifted the hem of her top to dab at her eyes. 'It's good news, really it is, but it feels . . . it feels . . .'

What was really upsetting about this whole situation was that it was Flick's older sister who was usually so composed. She was the strong one, the rock, the anchor. When their father left home it was Nina who pulled the young Flick and their mother through the trauma; and when Daniel vanished into thin air, and the weeks and months passed and they heard nothing, she was the one who pressed for the investigation into their brother's disappearance to be kept open. It was Nina who organised their mother's care when she became sick. She dragged the Crowleys kicking and screaming through every family crisis and out the other side.

Flick took her sister's face in her hands. 'Tell me.'

'You haven't even tasted this.' Nina lifted her glass, miserably. 'It's Argentinian.'

'Tell me,' said Flick gently. 'Please.'

'We're going away,' said Nina.

'I see.' Flick was stunned, yes, but she had always expected something like this to happen sooner or later. London was no place for a growing family. She immediately began to do the calculations. Thinking about the best way to see her nieces and nephew if they moved out of the city. It would be a wrench not being able to turn up when she liked, and it would be difficult to see them every weekend because of her unpredictable working hours, but it wouldn't be so bad.

'To Sydney,' said Nina. 'We're going to Australia.'

Flick stared. 'When?'

'Okay, so . . .' Nina turned away to find things to tidy. 'Martin's been offered a job, and school places for the kids have been arranged. It wasn't planned, I swear, it all happened out of the blue. His parents are elderly now, and he's their only child . . . You know he always wanted to go back eventually.'

'I'm happy for you,' said Flick quietly.

Nina's bottom lip quivered. 'I don't know what I'm even saying right now. I'm so sorry, darling.'

Flick picked up her glass. 'You've nothing to be sorry about. The kids will love it out there. The sun, the outdoor life. You'll have a pool, probably, and you'll go to the beach and have barbies and all that. You're going to be so happy, and I'm glad.'

'Then why do I feel so terrible about it?'

'Because you love your sister and don't want to upset her, but you don't have to worry because she's absolutely fine about it.'

'You're not fine about it, but thanks for lying.' Nina gazed at her. 'When I'm not here, maybe you and Dad—'

'That's not going to happen,' said Flick, smiling flatly.

'Someone has to keep an eye on him. You'll have something in common now; you can get together to badmouth me for leaving.' Nina stared at her. 'Please, Flick, I'm struggling for a silver lining here.'

'Don't worry.' Flick did her best to sound happy. 'What an adventure you're going to have.'

She opened her arms and Nina walked into them. They stood like that, holding each other. Flick didn't want to let go of Nina, or any of them. Her sister, thousands of miles away . . .

'You're going to keep a room ready so that I can come and see you.'

'It'll be the very best room, with a view of the opera house or a kangaroo park. We'll get you a koala, a real one. It'll sit on your bed and wait for you.'

'Auntie Flick!' screamed Coral. 'I can't get to sleep!'

'I'd better go up.' Flick stepped away, the tiredness making her light-headed. She was shattered – emotionally, physically – and knew she wouldn't be able to stay on her feet for long, but it didn't stop her gulping the wine down in one mouthful.

She pointed to the glass as she headed out of the room. 'Refill, please.'

24

All the way home, that feeling he was being followed. Drake swung the car into the dark square outside his house. The engine shuddered and died.

On the passenger seat, the phone rang. The caller's name and number was blocked. He put it to his ear, ready this time. 'Yes.'

The electronic voice was aggressive. 'You thought you could hide from me?'

'Who is this?'

'You thought I wouldn't *know* where to find you?'

Drake twisted in his seat to scan the square. 'Why should I speak to you, if you won't identify yourself?'

'Because you're to blame!' The static exploded angrily, the words becoming discordant. 'You're guilty and you're going to pay the price. Don't think for one moment, *one moment*, you won't. You made it happen, *you* made it happen, and you will pay, just like those others.'

'Tell me your name.' Drake swung open the car door, stepping into the cold night to look beyond the yellow spray of the streetlamps.

'I'm many people now, so many people,' said the voice, speaking urgently. 'One, two, twelve, twenty, so many it's difficult to keep count.' Digital glitches gave every word, each vowel, an abrupt glottal slap. 'So don't try to find me, because I'm all around you. I'm close, I'm everywhere.'

'We knew each other.' Turning in a slow circle, Drake's feet crunched on the frost clinging to the road. 'I met you at the home.'

'You can't hide from me,' said the voice bitterly. 'I found you, like I found the others.'

Drake tried to sound calm, reasonable. 'Why don't we meet?'

'Oh, we're going to meet,' the voice screeched. 'You think I don't know where you are, and how to get to you? I know who you are.'

On the other side of the square an indistinct figure approached, phone clamped to its ear, and Drake moved towards it, his feet clipping noisily on the road.

The voice was shouting, smothered by clicks and loops as the connection warped and distorted. 'I – ember – you did – I – saw – fire!'

'I don't know what you think you—'

'You're to bla – and like the oth – you will pay the con–quences!'

The figure – he saw a raincoat, a cap pulled low – increased its stride as Drake accelerated towards it, but then it turned quickly into a gate and fumbled a key at a door. Drake stopped dead on the pavement, recognising his neighbour. The door thudded shut.

'Do you think it's right that everyone should carry on with their lives as if nothing happened?' screamed the voice, the connection stabilising. 'I was alone in that place!'

'Tell me your name.'

'You're going to pay!'

'Tell me who you are,' repeated Drake.

176

'You think you don't have to face the consequences of your actions. You're wrong and you will pay, you will all pay.'

Moving back towards his own house, Drake saw a slanted shadow across the alley that led to the garden. The side door was ajar. 'You killed them all?'

'Not all, but soon.'

'Then let's meet, let's talk about it.'

'Oh, we'll meet soon enough.' Static flared in Drake's ear. 'Sooner than you think.'

Drake pushed open the side door, peered down the unlit path. 'When?'

'You people, with your happy lives, with your loving families, have no idea. You think you can carry on like nothing happened!'

'Are you here now?' Drake squinted into the blackness of the side alley. 'Are you at my home?'

'Just remember I know who you are, and where you are,' the voice said. 'The wife is already dead, I would have liked to have killed her myself, but the daughter . . .'

'No!' Drake's heart clenched.

'You remember me,' the voice screamed, 'and I know you. The Two O'Clock Boy is coming!'

A car sped past, the heavy thud of bass thumping from its window, making Drake flinch. When he replaced the phone to his ear, the call had been disconnected. He slipped it into his pocket.

The path at the side of the house was usually lit by a security light activated by a motion detector, but when Drake waved a hand beneath the sensor it didn't work. He walked slowly along the narrow corridor, one hand against the cold brick, the light diminishing with every step.

177

At the edge of the garden, foliage shivered in the wind. Fallen leaves crunched beneath his feet. Then—

Footsteps ran along the alley. Pain detonated in his head, a starburst of light and colour obliterated his vision. His legs crumpled beneath him. Drake had a fleeting sense of someone in front and also behind, and he let the forward momentum barrel him into the waist of his attacker, heaving them against the wall.

Grappling for a hold, Drake lashed out with a fist, but there was no power behind his punch, and another jolting pain in his kidneys took his breath away. He dropped to his knees and slid onto his back beneath a hail of blows. Curled up, covering his head as best he could against kicks and punches. Thudding into his hands, his face and stomach, sending jolting pain along his ribs and spine.

It was all he could do to breathe. A boot stung his cheek. A rib clicked in his chest. With one final fierce kick into his side, the attack stopped. Drake rolled onto his back, groaning, vision spinning. Two figures towered above him, their features obliterated by darting shapes behind his eyes.

One of them crouched. Breath bloomed in Drake's face. 'Cockroach! You're a cockroach!' A finger was pushed hard into his temple, forcing his head to the paving. 'Mind your own fucking business!'

Someone spat on his shirt, and then he heard footsteps clatter away. Craning his neck, he saw the silhouettes of his burly attackers high-fiving, heard the smack of their palms, as they leapt, laughing, exhilarated, on the tilted paving.

When they had gone, Drake lay on the stone patio, letting the pounding in his head subside, watching the stars trail across the sky like meteorites, until the world shifted itself the right way up. His phone vibrated in his breast pocket. Even the gentle buzz of it, the flutter of the slim sliver of metal, was a hammer against his chest. Gingerly, he lifted his arm, gritting his teeth against the jolting shocks crackling down his body, and took it out. Its blue screen flashed in his face.

He didn't want to answer it, just wanted to lie there for a while, let the frost dampen his hair – but knew he had to.

His voice was a croak. 'Ray Drake.'

'DI Drake?' Amelia Troy's voice was tense. 'There's somebody here. I think there's somebody outside my building.'

25

The boy was bright eyed and bushy tailed, and as soon as he saw him, Elliot wanted to smash his face in.

'Who's this, then?' he asked.

'I'm Toby!'

He was the kind of kid you saw on telly shows. A mop of blond hair, a button nose and a big smile – off for adventures all day and back home for tea, the Secret Seven and all that crap. He even dressed like it. He wore a tank top patterned with purple diamonds that looked like someone's blind granny had knitted it. The leather tongue on his sandals curled with age, and his trousers didn't quite reach down to his ankles – he'd grown out of them – revealing ridiculous red woollen socks.

Elliot smirked. 'Where's he been evacuated from?'

A muscle tweaked in Gordon's jaw. 'Shake the boy's hand, lads, like proper gentlemen.'

Connor and Elliot reluctantly took his hand and he shook energetically. But when Gordon turned away, Elliot scowled.

Toby beamed as if he didn't see it. 'I'm on holiday!'

There was something off about him, Elliot decided. He was too tidy, too spirited. He didn't belong here, not in this place.

180

There was something different about Gordon, too. Recently, he'd been looking increasingly unkempt; his pock-marked face had become blotchy, and he wore the same clothes every day. But this morning he'd made an effort, changed his shirt, pulled on a tie, and for the first morning in a long time didn't stink of spirits. To go and meet the boy's parents, Gordon said, and bring him back here.

'Toby's going to be staying with us, just for a week or two.'

'Yes, sir!' The boy spoke as if being there was the most exciting thing ever. Elliot almost felt sorry for the kid. He was clever, you could tell by his bright eyes, by the way he spoke, but he knew *nothing* about the world.

'I want you two to look after him, and ensure he settles in.' Gordon locked eyes with Elliot. 'Do you hear me? The boy is to be made welcome.' He ruffled Toby's hair. 'He's a happy chappy.'

Elliot favoured the kid with an angry grin. He slapped Toby on the back so hard that the boy staggered forward. 'I'll show you around.'

When the two boys left the office, Gordon pulled down the tie and collapsed into his chair.

'Toby's the son of a couple of old friends.' Taking a bottle from a drawer, his hand trembled as he poured Scotch into a dirty glass. 'I knew his father a long time ago, back when I was still something vaguely respectable in the community. They're good people, Connor. Better than you or I will ever be.' The tendons in his neck snapped taut like rope when he drank. 'The lad's grandma is unwell and lives in Singapore. Do you have any idea where that is, boy?'

'Asia,' said Connor.

'Aye, a world away. Toby's parents have gone to care for her, and Bernard has asked me to look after his son while they're gone because he thinks I'm a good man. What do you think of that? The fool thinks I'm the man to care for his boy.' He rubbed a hand across his bewildered face. 'And like an idiot I said yes, because for one moment I forgot who I really was, I forgot I'm the kind of creature who swims with sharks. Always moving, always looking to feed.' He moved his hand through the air like a fin through the ocean, eyeing Connor. 'You're a little like that, too, I'd say . . . or perhaps you think you're better than me.'

When Connor didn't reply, Gordon jumped up to pace. 'Truth of the matter is, Connor, I've debts. You know what debts are?'

'You owe people money.'

'Big debts, lad. I owe money to some very bad people, and on top of that I've a dirty pig demanding cash I don't have. I could do without having some snotty kid hanging around the place. Because we both know, don't we, that I'm not a good man.' He stopped at the desk to refill the glass. 'Perhaps a long time ago I had the potential to be one, but I made the wrong choices. As you will, too. The last thing I need is for him to run back home telling tales about this place to Ma and Pa. So I'm relying on you and Elliot to keep him happy. If I hear he's sad, if I see tears bulging in his angelic little eyes, I'm going to hold you responsible.'

When Connor turned to leave, Gordon put down the glass and said: 'And do you know another thing about sharks, Connor?'

'No.'

'Sharks never forget, boy. So don't be thinking you got

away with our little confrontation the other night.'

In the kitchen, Connor heard Toby's voice lifting from the bottom of the garden as he animatedly explained something about a bug on a leaf to Kenny and Debs and several others.

'Who does he think he is? He shook everyone's hand.' Elliot put on a posh voice when Connor arrived at his side. *'I'm Toby! How do yew do! How do yew do!'* His foot tapped impatiently, as if eager to stamp the insect into the mud and the new kid along with it. 'If he tries to explain stuff to me, I'll give him something to think about!'

'You'll do nothing.'

Elliot bit down on his response; he owed Connor now.

Ronnie and Gerry were sat fully dressed in the sun with a Monopoly board between them, and no sign of the tins of lager that usually littered the floor beneath their deckchairs. The Dents playing a board game – the world had gone mad.

If Toby Turrell was surprised by the squalor of the house, or the listless behaviour of the children, he didn't show it. Over the next week he was like a ray of sunshine at the Longacre. His delighted singing could be heard all over the house. It was high and reedy like a choirboy's, and even Connor found it soothing, particularly at night when his voice drifted down from the bedroom above. Toby organised games in the garden, and if Connor didn't take part himself, he made a point of rounding up some of the other kids to join in.

Gordon kept mostly to his office. But on the occasions when he did emerge, he would laugh and joke. If there was a spill in the kitchen, or a child broke one of the rules, he wouldn't scream or lash out. He wouldn't lock them for hours in the small room behind the office. At night nobody listened anxiously for the thud of his footsteps on the stairs.

Everyone's mood lifted, even Elliot had to admit that. Nobody understood why it had changed with the arrival of this boy – they were just going to enjoy the freedom while it lasted. The kids hoped Toby would stay there for ever, but he told everyone in his sing-song voice that he was on holiday. His parents would be coming soon to take him home.

Even that Ray kid had stopped hanging around. Connor didn't see him when he was trudging alone around the borough with the brown packages hidden in a bag, and the handcuffs he always kept hidden in his pocket. Alone all day, his mind whirled with painful thoughts and feelings. Sometimes he felt like he was going to snap, like he was going to explode. He didn't understand how he had ended up at that place, or why he stayed. It would be the easiest thing in the world to slip away. The city was big, the country vast, and Gordon couldn't find him in a million years, wouldn't even bother. But at the end of each day, when the bag was empty, something made him go back there – a weird sense of responsibility – even though the other kids avoided him. Sometimes the situation would become too much and would stop him in his tracks. It came out of nowhere, always when he was alone, when nobody could see. An angry loneliness would blast through him like a shockwave, making him dizzy, and he would drop to his knees and wait for it to pass.

Connor wanted to cry, but he couldn't.

When his parents were delayed in Singapore, Toby's stay was extended. A week became two, became three. The strain of having to keep his temper in check was getting to Gordon. Connor could see that. The manager did his best to stay out of the way, but the funk of booze and body odour in his office was almost unbearable on the occasions Connor went in there. Total strangers, mostly Gordon's business associates, trooped in and out as usual, and there was often laughing and music behind the door into the early hours. Once, the copper from the nick, the one whose handcuffs he had stolen, came out without giving him a second glance. When he did emerge from his office, Gordon was snappy and irritable, and didn't care whether Toby saw it or not.

One night, it was Elliot's turn to help Gerry Dent make dinner, sausages and packet mash. Connor was sat between Ricky and Regina at one of the two dining tables. Chatter tumbled anxiously from Toby Turrell, opposite. The novelty of his presence had worn off. Most of the kids had become tired of his incessant stream of conversation and his knowledge about everything under the sun, and stayed out of his way.

And despite the increasingly bored efforts of Ronnie and Gerry to keep order, Toby had seen more than enough of the bullying and tension rife in the home, and spent a lot of time alone reading the books he'd brought with him. He was smiling as he babbled to Kenny, but Connor could sense his puzzlement about still being there.

'My parents are going to come for me, soon. They're coming to take me home. Shall we play a game after this, Kenny?'

'Don't feel like it,' mumbled Kenny, and turned away.

185

Connor hadn't seen Gordon. Usually, at about teatime, he strode from his office to bark instructions to the Dents, but tonight he was nowhere to be seen. Toby's voice soared above the other conversations at the table, grating on everybody's nerves.

'Daddy builds things.' His attention turned hopefully to Connor. 'And I help.'

Connor watched the kitchen doorway, suspicious. Elliot was walking around with a satisfied look on his face. Something was going on, something was definitely up.

'He likes to teach me things. Carpentry, pottery. Honest work, he calls it. When I'm older, when I'm grown up, I shall make the most beautiful things. Daddy says I will be a very useful chap.'

When Elliot brought the food in, softly placing the plates in front of the kids, there was an angelic expression on his face that had no business being there. Usually, he enjoyed dropping the plates of lumpy mash and gristly sausage hard on the table so that the gravy splashed everywhere. But there was a gentleness about his movements that hardened Connor's suspicions.

Connor was starving, as he always was on his delivery days. He was usually out of the door before breakfast, and back in the afternoon after walking miles. But looking down at the yellow splodge of mash in its puddle of thin gravy, he lost his appetite. He'd eat as much as he could stomach. The other children hungrily forked up their food as soon as it was put in front of them – everyone except Toby who, too busy talking, hadn't realised his plate hadn't arrived yet. Elliot came out of the kitchen with it, his thumb carelessly slipped into the mash.

186

Placing the plate down, he winked at Connor. 'Here you go.'

Toby didn't notice the food. 'You must be very careful near a lathe, and follow the safety instructions, or you will lose a hand.'

Finally, he picked up his fork and looked down.

The sound of his chair screeching on the linoleum cut through the conversation. Elliot guffawed, and the kids crowded around Toby to look. Scrabbling around the mound of mash, its legs flicking in the gravy, was a cockroach. Everyone giggled, including Connor. It was funny to see the little creature, shiny brown shell glistening with tiny globules of food, antennas jerking and twitching, as it stumbled around.

'Everybody back to your seats.' There were tears of laughter in Elliot's eyes, but his voice was firm. 'So Toby can eat.'

'But there's a . . .'

Debs reached for the plate. 'I'll take it back.'

'Leave it!' Elliot slammed his hand on the table. 'Nobody leaves here until their food is eaten. That's the rules.'

Connor had wondered when something like this was going to happen. Elliot had been spoiling for a fight with the kid since he'd arrived.

Toby gazed bleakly around the table. 'I can't!'

Nobody could take their eyes off the creature leaving trembling indentations in the mash. Elliot raised the plate to Toby's face.

'Eat it!'

'You ain't in charge, Elliot,' said Connor, leaping to his feet.

Sensing his best hope lay with him, Toby edged behind Connor.

'He's going to eat it.' Elliot's eyes flashed with anger. 'Or I'll stuff it down his throat myself! Shouldn't be a problem, his gob's always open!'

Meeting in the middle of the room, their foreheads bumped together hard. This wasn't about the new kid, Connor knew, he was just the excuse. Elliot had been boiling with resentment since he'd given him a hiding.

'You got me by surprise last time,' Elliot said hoarsely. 'But everyone knows I can take you, any time I want!'

'Gordon said we look after the kid,' Connor said.

'He don't get no special treatment!'

Elliot's forehead burned against his own. Connor was ready to teach him another lesson. This time he'd make sure Elliot stayed on the floor. He fancied giving him a hiding.

'What's going on here?'

When Gordon staggered into the room, Connor knew things were going to get worse. A wailing Toby raced to him, burying his head against the manager's chest. Gordon's hand stroked the boy's hair. Toby said something but his voice was muffled against Gordon's shirt, which was wet with his tears. The manager gently pulled back his head.

'Someone . . . put a cockroach . . . in my food!'

Out of the corner of his eye, unwilling to turn his face from Elliot, Connor glimpsed Sally in the doorway.

'Who did this?' Gordon slurred. His eyes moved slowly around the table, from Ricky to David to Debs and Cliff and Amelia. His gaze lingered on Jason. 'Was it you?'

When the boy's eyes nearly popped out of his head in terror, Gordon turned to Elliot.

188

'No, this smells like you.' Elliot stared back, defiant. 'I distinctly remember asking you to play nice.'

Connor moved towards the knives and forks on the table, but Elliot caught his eye. *Stay out of this.*

Gordon's smile twisted into a spiteful leer. 'I'm going to ask you one more time.'

'Yeah.' Tears welled in Elliot's eyes. He couldn't hide behind Connor, not this time. 'I did.'

'You can't find it in your shrivelled little heart to be kind to a new boy for five minutes? At least you're true to yourself, lad.'

The manager swiped him across the face with the back of his hand. Elliot flew backwards, crashing across the table. Plates and glasses smashed around his head when he hit the floor.

'Gordon!' Sally stumbled forwards.

'Poor Elliot's upset, so he is. He's not getting enough respect around here, isn't that right? So just this one time we're all going to do as King Elliot says.' He grabbed Toby. 'Come here, boy.'

'Gordon, that's enough.'

'Shut up!'

Sally flinched. Toby was crying harder now, his sobs unbearably loud as Gordon picked up the plate. When the kid squirmed, Gordon gripped his neck and forced his head to the food.

'Eat it,' said Gordon softly. The kids watched with a sick fascination as Toby picked up a lump of mash and put it in his quivering mouth. Tears and snot poured down his lips. The cockroach turned exhaustedly on the plate. 'All of it.'

Toby wailed. 'I'm not hungry!'

189

'Look at you.' The manager's voice was all cheery reason and encouragement, but his sweating, scarlet face told a different story. 'You're all skin and bones. Look how wee you are. What you need is protein. Eat it up.'

'I'm not hungry.'

'Look, I'll help you.' The manager picked up the cockroach, the creature's antennae rotating furiously in his fingers. 'Open wide.' Gordon forced open Toby's mouth and shoved the insect in. 'Now chew.'

The boy closed his mouth. Connor was sickened by the gagging sounds he made, the soft crunching in the heavy silence of the room. He saw Debs staring at him, a pleading look in her eyes, as if he could do something to make it stop. But Connor did nothing. These kids, they didn't care about him. Nobody wanted him there, they hated him – so he didn't lift a finger.

Ronnie Dent exploded with laughter, and Gerry smirked. Karen retched on the floor as Amelia ran from the room.

'That's good, now open your mouth,' Gordon said, forcing open his jaw. Toby's teeth and gums were smeared with brown juice, pulpy flecks of flesh and shell. 'Here's a good boy who does what he's told. The rest of you could learn a lesson from him.'

The plate of food dropped from Gordon's hand and clattered to the floor. He gripped the boy's neck. 'Now, me and Toby are going to my office. You boys and girls eat your dinners.'

Toby wasn't seen again that night.

26

Thistles scratched at Ray Drake's trousers as he stumbled along the side of Amelia Troy's warehouse. Something scampered away in the weeds. Drake pointed the torchlight at a rusted coke can, stepping carefully in the thick tangle. In this kind of place – remote, even in the heart of the city – there could be used syringes on the ground.

On the far side of the building, where scrub and thicket swept towards the train track, he switched off the torch and propped himself against the wall to listen for anything out of the ordinary, ignoring the shooting pains in his ribs. All he heard was the pounding in his own head, the dull ambient hum of the city at night.

After his attackers had fled, Drake had let himself into his house – the old woman was asleep downstairs, thankfully – to swallow pain-relief tablets. Livid bruises were already deepening across his chest and stomach. Pain crackled along his ribs, but he didn't think any were broken. He changed his suit and shirt and splashed water on his face, gingerly avoiding the swelling beneath his eyes.

A train clicked in the distance, a gentle rhythmic cascade. Drake continued along the wall and the tide of rubbish and rusted metal. The ground-floor windows were shuttered and protected by mesh. Steel plates were bolted across disused loading bays. If anyone had been here, stalking around the building, they were probably gone by now. If they *were* still here, the state he was in, he wasn't sure what he'd be able to do about it.

Amelia was standing at the door, silhouetted against the bare bulb, while he placed the torch in the boot of his car.

'Anything?' she called. 'There was definitely someone here, keeping close to the wall.'

Slamming the boot shut, pain knifed down his shoulder and he winced. 'Did you see them?'

'I saw their shadow on the ground.' When Drake approached, her hand flew to her face. 'Christ! What happened to you?'

'Somebody resisting arrest,' he said. 'It happens.'

Amelia stepped aside to let him inside. The heavy door clanged shut. She snapped two deadlocks, turned keys at the top and bottom of the door. Ascending in the wooden lift, Drake saw grey stubs of corridor flicker briefly in the wan bulb's light. This was a grim and foreboding place for anyone to live in, let alone a single woman.

'The other floors are alarmed,' she said, as if reading his mind. 'And the elevator is switched off every night. Nobody can get upstairs.' Her eyes flicked uncertainly to his. 'That's the idea, anyway.'

'I'm not sure you could live in a more insecure environment if you tried,' he said.

Following her out onto the concrete expanse of her floor, he saw the enormous space was lit by a dozen standing lamps, which didn't quite obliterate the pools of darkness in between. Nests of plug boxes snaked across the concrete. The long trestle table in the studio space had been cleared. Isolated in a soft puddle of light, Amelia's living space looked like a theatre set, a weird Pinteresque fever dream. The edges of the sofas were eaten away by shadow, the faceless torso of a wooden tailor's dummy listed on a pole at the edge of light. Somewhere, lost in the darkness, was her bed. Where her husband had died; where Amelia had nearly died.

'Very moody,' he said.

She tugged a cigarette from a packet on the sill. 'I know it's a bit eighties rock video, but it's all I've got left of Ned. I love it here most of the time . . . but maybe not tonight.' She lit the cigarette. 'I'm sorry, would you like a drink?'

'No, thanks,' he said, eyeing the bottle of beer on a coffee table beside a paperback biography of an artist he'd never heard of.

Amelia peered at him through a cloud of smoke. 'Of course, you're on duty. Or is that a myth about drinking on duty?'

'I just don't want to,' he said.

The paintings leaned against radiators looked ominous, the deep reds turned jet black in the gloom. When Amelia lifted the cigarette to her mouth, Drake saw her hand tremble.

'Tell me again,' he said.

She let out a deep breath and pointed down at his car. 'He ran across the gravel towards the door. He was moving fast, but I saw his shadow stretch along the ground. There's no reason to come down this end of the road unless you're here to visit any of the businesses on the way and they're shut, obviously. Occasionally kids hang about, but never this late.'

Drake shoved his hands in his pockets. 'You think it was a man.'

'In my experience, crazy stalkers tend to be men.'

'What time was this?'

'Uh.' She picked at the label on the bottle. 'It was about eleven o'clock. I haven't been . . . Well, earlier, I wasn't altogether truthful to you and your colleague. You gave me something of a shock, and I didn't say anything because I suppose I was feeling a bit defensive, but . . . I think someone's been watching me. It's nothing I can put my finger on. A strange feeling when I'm out, sometimes, or an odd miscall.'

'What kind of miscall?'

'When I answer, the caller hangs up. I've had three or four in the last few days. I can count on one hand the number of people who have my number. It could be some robot trying to sell insurance, of course.'

'Does the caller say anything?' Amelia shook her head. 'For your own piece of mind it might be a good idea to move out for a couple of days. Is there anybody you could stay with?'

'There's no one.'

'A hotel.'

'No, I want to stay here.' Her eyes flashed angrily, and she folded her arms across her chest. 'I'm sorry; I'm a bit on edge.'

'Of course.' Drake turned away. There were so many shadows you could hide a whole army of intruders. 'Do you mind if I look around?'

'Be my guest.' Smoke poured from her nostrils as she mashed the cigarette in an ashtray. 'By the way, I have something for you.'

Amelia looked through a pile of papers on a sill, and he walked around the windows, checking they were secure, and that the exit to the roof was locked. Eight floors up, it was

194

unlikely anybody could get in, but after what happened to Ryan Overton . . .

'What does your wife feel about your working all hours of the night?' Amelia was standing behind him. Her gaze dropped to his wedding band, and he put his hand in his pocket. 'I'm sorry, there's probably some strict rule about asking policemen personal questions.'

'There's no rule about asking,' Drake said. 'But I've got one about answering.'

'DI Drake, have we . . . met before?' she asked. 'When you came this afternoon I had an overpowering sense that I knew you. You seem so . . . familiar to me.'

He began to move. 'Not as far as I know.'

'Were you one of the policemen who found Ned and me, perhaps? My memory of that time is a touch unreliable on account of my mostly, you know, being in a coma. And let's not forget the dissociative amnesia.' He sensed her keeping pace behind him. 'But maybe you came to the hospital.'

'No,' he said. 'We've never met.'

'That's a shame.' She swung round in front of him, touched his arm.

Her hand, hot and clammy, in his.
Head pulsing.
Fingers clawing at him.

'Because I don't get this feeling often, Detective Inspector.'

He nodded at the windows. 'Everything seems secure.'

'Good.' She let out a dramatic breath. 'I feel much better now that you've discharged your duty to your satisfaction. You'll probably be relieved to get away from the mad woman and home to the wife.'

'She died.' It was the last thing he should have said, but

the words slipped out unbidden. He was sickened by the urge he had to tell her.

'That explains why I feel I know you. You're another lost soul doomed to carry your dead spouse around with you. We're two peas in a pod.' When he looked away, she winced. 'Sorry, my morbid small talk isn't quite hitting the mark tonight. The truth is I'm scared.'

'You have no reason to be.'

'Don't I?' she said quickly. 'Every time I think everything's going to be okay . . . I thought my husband would keep me safe, but he used to . . . Ned was . . .' She smiled sadly. 'Well, I imagine you know all about Ned.'

Drake nodded. 'Yes.'

'That's past now, my husband will never touch me again, but I can't seem to be able to leave everything behind. And the worst thing is I don't even know what it is, who it is, that I should be scared of.'

They stood there for a long moment, and then she took his hand.

'Thank you for coming,' she said.

Smoke bulging beneath the door.

Threats, obscenities, in his ear.

Her hand, hot, in his.

She withdrew her hand and rubbed her calloused fingertips self-consciously. 'One of the problems of being an artist, I'm afraid. Paints and detergents play havoc with your skin.'

'If you feel safer now . . .'

'Time for bed,' she said. 'I'll take something to knock myself out.' Amelia held up her hands quickly, smiling. 'Oh, don't worry, DI Drake, these days it's strictly prescription.'

'Then I'll go.'

'Wait,' she said. 'The last time you were here you and your colleague asked if I had been in contact with anyone from the home. I remembered today that someone wrote to me.' She gave him a slip of paper with a name on it, Deborah Yildiz, and an address in South London. 'This woman has written to me several times saying that she was at the Longacre and asking to meet. I never replied. I get a lot of mail from people and, well, they often ask for money . . . and you know how I feel about that place.'

On the way down, they stood beneath the yellow wash of the elevator bulb.

'If you hear anything else, or if anything else occurs to you,' he said, 'call me.'

'And I've DS Crowley's number.'

'Call me,' he said, and she smiled.

On the ground floor Amelia unlocked the steel door and pulled back the deadbolts. When he stepped outside she gave him a curious look.

'You don't seem like the kind of man who shares information about himself very often, DI Drake. I'm sorry, I've already embarrassed you, so, in for a penny . . . You look like a man with a lot of stuff packed down tightly. I just wanted to say . . . it doesn't work. Take it from somebody who knows.' In the gloom, Drake thought he saw tears glisten in her eyes. 'Just let go of whatever it is or you will never be free.'

He stared as she closed the door on him.

Outside, listening to the locks snap into place, Drake took out the slip of paper and read the name and address.

The name Deborah only registered very dimly. There

197

were so many kids in that place, so many faces. But Kenny's cuttings included the name Deborah Willetts. It would very difficult for Flick to trace her if Yildiz was her married name.

He only hoped the man who called himself the Two O'Clock Boy hadn't found her first.

27

Rusting appliances were stacked against a metal fence outside the scruffy ground-floor maisonette on an estate in Somers Town. Rubbish spewed from the gaping mouth of a wheelie bin. Flick stepped over the carcass of a cooked chicken, heard the rasping thump of heavy bass coming from an upstairs window.

Despite a good night's sleep at her sister's – not even the three young children screaming up and down the hallway at the crack of dawn could wake her – she felt drained. When her phone alarm went off she took a shower, dressed and slipped out of the house while everyone was having breakfast. The kids chattered, and she heard Nina's patient voice trying to keep some semblance of order – *move your chair so others can sit down, Coral; who wants juice?* – while a cheerful pop song played on the radio. The smell of eggs and coffee made Flick hesitate at the door, but she couldn't face a repeat of the previous night's conversation. She'd managed to avoid bursting into tears then, but more apologies from Nina would only her upset her again. And her sister would bring up Harry, insisting Flick should let bygones be bygones with their father. Flick wasn't in the mood for a repeat of that conversation.

She rang the bell, and the door was opened by a woman wearing a tartan onesie and flip-flops. Her thin, under-nourished hair was feathered around her face, and her bottled tan, which looked positively terracotta in the morning sun, streaked at the nape of her neck.

The woman's eyes flashed with expectation beneath long false lashes. 'You from social services?'

'Police.' Flick took out her ID. 'Detective Sergeant Flick Crowley.'

The woman threw her head back, exasperated. 'I thought we'd got all this sorted. Either take him away or leave us alone.'

'I don't know what you think this is about, but I was hoping to talk to Mr Ronnie Dent.'

'Is that right? Whatever it is you think he's done, you're wrong. Because he ain't left the house for three godawful years.'

'I wanted to talk to him about somewhere he worked years ago. He may be able to provide information.'

'A cold case!' The woman's eyebrows shot up. 'Like on the television.'

'Yes,' said Flick. 'That's exactly it.'

'You ain't come to take him away, then? Because it won't take me long to pack his stuff. He don't have much to his name; anything he owned was sold years ago.'

'Not today.'

The woman's sour attitude returned. 'Better come in.'

The hallway was crowded with cardboard boxes and supermarket bags, and smelled of old socks and pork chops. The pounding bass made the light shade sway. She led Flick upstairs, a cigarette packet outlined in a pocket against one buttock and a mobile phone in the other.

'I'm his granddaughter, by the way. Julie. I've been going on about getting him moved to a home for years. I told the social workers but it's murder getting them to listen. The

200

way Grandad is now,' she whispered fiercely, 'he's driving us mental.'

'Us?' asked Flick.

'Me and that brother of mine.' At the top of the stairs, Julie Dent rapped on a door with the edge of a bulky ring. 'Turn that bloody music down!' A voice returned fire inside, but the volume edged down. 'We're only kids, really. It ain't fair that we have to put up with it.'

Flick had presumed Julie was approaching middle age, but looking closer, saw that she was a lot younger, in her mid-twenties, perhaps.

'Gran died years ago. Gerry went out in a blaze of glory, downed three bottles of Duty Free.' She nodded appreciatively. 'He don't leave his room no more, except to piss. His lungs have almost packed in. There must be somewhere they can take him; he finds it a strain here, poor soul. We do our best, course we do, but he does our heads in most of the time.'

The walls of Ronnie Dent's bedroom were painted a depressing beige colour and stained with damp, the worn carpet moth-eaten. The smell was diabolical. Julie cracked a window.

'Jesus, Grandad, it's like someone died in here.'

An old man lay in bed, his emaciated body outlined beneath a single sheet. He was peering up at a portable television atop a wardrobe. His granddaughter quickly pulled the sheet over his arms. 'Look at you, you exhibitionist, showing off all your saggy bits. You got a visitor.'

Thud, thud, thud. The bass throbbed next door.

The old man ignored them both.

'Mr Dent, I'm Detective Sergeant Flick Crowley. I was wondering if I could ask you a few questions.'

201

Perching on the end of the bed, she tried not to look at the twisting brown nails on his yellow feet, which poked from beneath the sheet like jagged shards of broken pottery. Dent was watching a children's show, all primary colours, baby voices and trilling xylophones. 'It's about the Longacre home in Hackney. You worked there in the nineteen eighties, I understand.'

'Probably don't remember, do you, Grandad?' Julie returned Flick's look. 'He can barely remember what day it is, or his grandson's name.'

'It's Liam, you silly cow,' Dent snarled. 'And it's Tuesday.'

'But it ain't, is it?' Julie surged forward, teeth bared. 'It ain't Tuesday! See what I mean? He winds me right up!'

The old man scowled. 'Get me a tea! Four sugars.'

'I'll get you something in a minute!' Julie spat, and shot a crafty glance at Flick. 'We like a bit of banter, don't we, Grandad?'

Flick noticed discolouration at the top of the old man's arms. Pulling the sheet down, she saw cloudy bruises.

'How did you get those, Ronnie?'

'He falls over. His balance ain't good,' Julie said. 'Is it, Grandad?'

'My balance ain't good.'

'We do our best, but we're busy people, I got a part-time job. And him next door is useless, well, he's only a kid. I've said it once, I've said it a thousand times, Grandad should be in a home. We love him, of course we do, but it's not like we're close or anything.'

Thud, thud, thud. The music was so loud Flick could barely hear herself think.

'The Longacre . . .' The deep creases in the old man's

202

forehead crinkled. 'Yeah, I worked there. Me and Gerry.'

'You never told me you worked at a children's home?' said Julie. 'What the fuck do you know about kiddies?'

Ronnie Dent narrowed his eyes. 'There's plenty you don't know about me.'

'I bet there fucking is!' Julie erupted. 'No secret money stashed away, though, aye? No pot of gold! You're a drain on the house, you eat my food, use my electricity!' Her voice was shrill. 'Soil your clothes!'

'You're a hateful person!'

Thud, thud, thud, through the walls.

'I got cause! You're a vampire sucking the life out of me. They should put you down!'

'Get away from me!' *Thud, thud, thud.*

Flick stood. 'Julie, would you do me a favour and ask . . . ?'

'His name is Liam.'

'Would you ask Liam to turn down the music?'

Julie sucked air through her teeth. 'I'll see what I can do, but I ain't promising anything. He don't listen to me, nobody does in this house.'

Flip-flops slapping on the carpet, she left. Flick sat back down on the bed. The old man's eyes were clamped on the television.

'You worked at the Longacre, Mr Dent . . .'

'Did I?' His eyes narrowed. 'Maybe. I don't remember.'

Flick grabbed her notebook. 'You said you and your wife worked there, Mr Dent.'

He sighed. 'I miss her.'

'I bet the pair of you had some happy times.' Both the Dents had recorded offences going back years, including ABH, fraud, various drugs, shoplifting and a few motoring misdemeanours. Happy times, indeed. I'm going to read out the names of children at the home to see if you remember them . . . Deborah Willetts.'

His attention drifting back to the TV, Dent shook his head vaguely. The bass next door was joined by the growl of a furious argument between Julie and Liam.

'David Horner,' Flick said, watching him closely. 'Karen Smith.'

Thud, thud, thud. Thud, thud, thud.

Snatching up the remote, Dent lifted it at the television. The volume went up, competing against the bass and the argument.

'Toby Turrell,' Flick said loudly. 'Ricky Hancock . . . Jason Burgess . . .'

This was no good. She was getting nowhere.

'Kenny Overton . . . Elliot Juniper . . . Amelia Troy . . .'

The old man stared at the television.

'Connor Laird,' she said.

His Adam's apple jerked. His hand shot out to grab at her wrist.

'Connor Laird,' Dent whispered. His tongue darted between his teeth. His grip was feeble but his papery touch was repulsive.

Leaning close to hear him better, she asked: 'Do you remember him, Ronnie?'

And then he bellowed in her face, a bovine wail that drowned out the TV, the music and voices. Flick lurched back.

The thin sheet covering the old man dropped from his bony chest as he jerked upright to let out another scream. Within a moment, Julie Dent was back in the room, along with an acne-scarred kid in a baseball cap, who laughed. 'He's off again!'

'Now look!' shouted Julie, over the old man's wail. 'I knew this would happen!'

'Connor Laird,' said Flick. 'Do you remember him?'

The old man's distress increased. The boy doubled over. 'Go on, Grandad,' he jeered. 'Let it all out!'

Julie grabbed Flick by the shoulders. 'Look what you've done!'

'He recognises the name,' said Flick. The hairs on the back of her neck stood up.

The missing kid: Connor Laird. Dent was terrified of him.

'He don't know fuck all about anything.' Julie's face twitched with anger. 'He's a senile old fool and I've had it with him.' She reeled towards the old man, holding a hand above her head. 'Up to here!'

The kid in the cutting: Connor Laird.

Thud, thud, thud.

'Having a bad trip, Grandad, yeah?' The boy walked out, laughing.

Something about that cutting.

Ronnie Dent screamed: 'Don't let him near me!'

Flick moved closer. 'Who, Ronnie? Connor Laird?'

The old man's pigeon chest heaved. 'Don't let him near!'

'I think you'd better leave!' said Julie Dent.

'Keep him away!'

Flick needed to get out of there. Without looking back – the music and wailing in her ears, the boy's cruel laughter – she clattered down the stairs, cracking her shin on a side table at the bottom.

Julie followed her down, shouting as Flick heaved open the door. The knocker juddered. 'You tell the social services to come and get him! Or I'll dump him on the motorway, you see if I don't!'

When the door slammed behind her, and she'd made it all the way down the path in one piece, Flick placed her hands on her hips and breathed out slowly to calm herself.

That name repeating in her head. Connor Laird.

The kid from the missing photograph.

The torn cutting.

The boy in that cutting.

Connor Laird.

Something about that cutting.

28

He'd barely pulled past Loughborough Junction, with its railway bridges cutting across the roofs in every direction, when he saw water pour from a turning and gush into the drain, thick black smoke tumbling above it. And he knew he was already too late.

Drake rolled his Mercedes past the turning, stopping on Coldharbour Lane, just past the junction, to watch the fire engines, patrol cars and ambulances blocking off a street. Evacuated residents stood watching in slippers and dressing gowns as firefighters dragged hoses back and forth beneath the black smoke rolling from the first-floor window of a mansion block.

There was no point in staying. He sensed already what had happened in this South London street. The body of Deborah Yildiz, formerly Willetts, would be found in that building – and her family, if she had any.

The last thing he needed was local police asking awkward questions and making a note of his car and registration. So he quickly scanned the openings to the crooked alleys sliced into the junction, with their walkways and shuttered businesses – the auto repair shops and joineries and design companies wedged into the narrow spaces – and decided to leave. Reaching for the ignition, his eyes whipped past the side mirror –

And caught sight of the figure by the entrance of the overground train station.

It wore dark clothes and a woollen hat pulled low, and the instant Drake saw it, it started moving.

Drake accelerated into the next turning to circle back, past the grinding pumps and the shouts of the firemen, towards the station. Adrenalin spiked in his veins, washing away the pain. He gunned the engine beneath the bridge, turning into the road he thought the figure had disappeared along.

And he thought: What next?

What would he do when he caught the Two O'Clock Boy?

He didn't want to contemplate what had to be done, and was almost relieved when he lost sight of the tall man. Drake cruised slowly along the road, tower blocks looming beyond a green space on the left, twisting in his seat to find him. But the pavements on either side were empty. The figure could have doubled backed behind the station, or vanished into the maze of surrounding streets.

But then he saw a flicker of movement in the rear-view, saw the top of the woollen hat bobbing behind a row of cars in the narrow alley beneath the arches of a railway bridge. Drake pumped the brakes. Reversed back, swerving with a screech so that the nose of his car was pointed down the alley.

And there was the guy, the so-called Two O'Clock Boy, running down the middle towards a dead end. Drake saw a flash of pale flesh as the figure darted a look over his shoulder.

And then he put his foot down.

The car surged forwards. A high chain-link fence blocked off the far end. The row of cars on the park side were bumper to bumper. Drake would be on him in less than a minute. He saw the figure thicken in his vision, saw it dart another look over its shoulder, its features hidden beneath the hat. The road was empty of people. Drake debated what to do. He could injure the guy, knock him over the roof of the car, and then tip him into the boot . . .

Or he could finish it.

The shuttered businesses built into the arches flew past – Drake swerved to miss a concrete block in the road – keeping pace with the loping figure, still deciding what to do. The answer came to him, and it was obvious.

End it now. Here on this long, empty lane.

He accelerated, gaining ground quickly, and the figure loomed closer, its arms and legs pumping ineffectually. The man panicked, tried to jump over a car bonnet, but misjudged the leap and bounced off its door, going down in the road. And Drake pressed his foot hard on the pedal, the engine roaring in his ears, bearing down on him.

He'd drive into him, send him flying into the air so that he fell to the floor in a heap of broken bones. He'd dump the body somewhere. The whole nightmare would be over. April would be safe.

It was the only way.

The figure scrambled to its feet as Drake's car hurtled at him, and spun. Drake glimpsed a pale whirl of face just as one of the wheels bumped over a brick. The car's suspension lifted, and when it dropped—

The figure was gone.

Drake slammed his foot on the brake, gripping the wheel

209

as the Mercedes drifted, tyre rubber burning, and came to a screeching halt. He jumped from the car.

Door alarm pulsing: *ping ping ping*.

There was nothing in front of the car – nobody.

He kicked the door shut and moved stiffly to the pavement. The businesses were padlocked, the man nowhere to be seen. A few yards further along one arch hadn't been developed, providing a cut-through beneath the bridge. Light poured in from the other side. Drake ducked beneath the curling corner of wire mesh that covered the opening. He moved quickly over the accumulation of stinking rubbish, and out the other side into another set of arches. The space on this side was much wider and the bridge opposite soared higher. At the far end, a group of men loaded planks of wood onto a lorry.

When Drake heard a noise coming from behind a protruding wall to his left, he plucked a brick from the floor and swung round the other side, his arm up, ready to fight. Saw a group of young men – two white, two black. Money changing hands – some kind of drug deal. They stared at Drake and the brick.

'What the—?' The kids stepped back in shock.

'Where is he?' said Drake.

'Who the fuck are you?' one of them stammered.

A couple edged away, a couple moved forward. Drake didn't have time for this. 'The man who came through here.'

One of the kids stomped towards him, and Drake drew back his arm, ready to pound the brick into his face, in no mood to take another beating. The kid thought better of it, and fled. Spooked, the others followed, bolting towards the entrance of the road.

Drake dropped the brick, slapped the dust from his fingers, walking into the wide, open space filled with diggers and skips of scrap metal. The Two O'Clock Boy was gone, if he had even come this way in the first place. Drake made his way back beneath the arch. The brickwork roared around him as a train trundled above. His head was filled with sound, and a sudden, unwelcome memory of the track that ran behind the Longacre.

He climbed into his car and sat behind the wheel, thinking he had lost the last, best chance to get the man he had briefly known decades ago, and whose fragile emotional state had tipped into a murderous psychosis. Taking out his phone, Ray Drake thought briefly about trying to speak to April again, but immediately pocketed it. And then he smelled the tang of something in the compartment.

Petrol.

Before he could react, a hand whipped from behind to pull his head back, and a blade was placed against his throat. Drake sucked down a breath, fully expecting to never get the chance to let it out again. Expecting to see his own hot blood spurt across the dash and windscreen. When the blade slashed his jugular he would bleed to death in a matter of minutes. Even quicker, if the carotid artery was sliced open.

His quick, shallow breaths masked the excited, rasping exhalations of the man hidden in the back. Drake's eyes lifted to the rear-view mirror, but his assailant was safely hidden out of sight.

'So this is it,' said Drake. 'You're going to kill me.'

What he felt, more than anything, was anger at a wasted opportunity. If he had pressed his foot on the accelerator earlier, he would have killed the man who called himself the Two O'Clock Boy. He should have finished the job. Instead, he was going to die and the realisation sickened him . . . April would be next.

The blade tightened against his throat. He felt it nick into his skin.

'Like you killed those others.' Drake's heart clattered against his chest. His eyes lifted to the empty mirror. 'Tell me about them.'

He felt hot breath in his ear, smelled the trace of a familiar scent. But nobody spoke.

A horn blasted, he heard an engine. A van pulled up behind his own car, a voice calling: 'Move it!'

'Kill me and this is finished. You leave everybody else alone. I'm the one you want, right? I saved your life, I kept you alive, I'm responsible. Nobody else needs to get hurt.'

The gloved hand tightened around his forehead. His head was yanked back hard. The tip of the blade probed the flesh at his throat. Drake imagined the torn meat of his trachea suddenly flopping onto his chest, followed by a deluge of his blood. He closed his eyes, and thought of how much he loved his daughter and how much he loved his wife.

'Kill me, but leave my daughter. *Please*, leave my daughter. All you have to do is say yes.'

The breath pumped, quick and eager.

'Come on, mate,' called the voice in the van, 'move!' The horn blasted again.

'Let me hear you say it. *Yes*.' But the man in the back didn't speak, he didn't want to be identified, and it gave Drake a glimmer of hope. 'You'd better finish the job now, or I will come for you and I will kill you. Do you understand me?'

He heard a smack of lips, and the blade was pressed so hard against his Adam's apple that he could barely swallow.

'Don't be shy,' said Drake. 'Just say yes.'

Then a door slammed on the van, and footsteps approached. Drake's head was released. The knife glinted past his eyes as it whipped away. The back door opened, and Drake hit his door release to stumble into the alley. But the van driver was already in front of him, remonstrating. 'Come on, fella, shift the car, some of us have work to do.'

Legs shaking, Drake slumped against the door to watch the Two O'Clock Boy, face hidden by the woollen hat, escape across the park.

29

When she arrived in the Incident Room, Flick was morti-
fied to see Eddie Upson at the whiteboard. She'd phoned
to warn her team that she'd be late, but he had already taken
the daily meeting, held first thing every morning, in her
absence. Vix Moore eyed her walking past and murmured
something to Kendrick. In contrast, Millie Steiner, bless her
heart, gave Flick an encouraging nod.

'Sorry I'm late,' Flick told Eddie, who followed her into
her office. 'I had someone to go and see on the way in.'

'No problem,' he said, 'but we may need a new
whiteboard.'

Flick slapped the space bar on her keyboard to awaken
the screen. 'Why?'

Eddie held up a marker pen. 'I thought this was a magic
marker, but it's permanent ink.'

'You need alcohol.'

Upson rolled his eyes. 'Tell me about it.'

'To clean the whiteboard,' she said.

'Yeah, that's what I meant.'

'Do me a favour, Eddie,' said Flick, as he turned to go.
'I need an address.'

'I'll get Vix to do it. Wait, I'll *try* to get Vix to do it.'

'No,' said Flick. The last thing she needed was DC Moore
asking awkward questions. 'I'd rather you did it. It's Elliot—'

But then Ray Drake walked in and she blinked, astonished, at the livid yellow bruises beneath one eye, the red nick across his throat.

'Juniper?' Eddie was unaware of Drake behind him. 'The name you mentioned yesterday, do you still want it?'

'Please,' she said, but she must have looked a picture because Eddie followed her gaze, seeing the DI's terse expression, closing the door behind him.

'What on earth happened?'

'It was nothing.' Drake lowered himself stiffly into a chair. 'Some kids attempted to relieve me of my wallet last night, shoved me the ground. They got in a couple of kicks and ran.'

'Did you report it?'

'No point, it was too dark to get a good look at them. Anyway . . .' Drake seemed agitated to Flick. 'Where are we on the investigation?'

Several of the plastic pockets containing the newspaper articles were peeking from a drawer of her desk. She'd not put them back in the Property Room, but had closed the drawer when she'd left yesterday.

'Has anybody been working in here?'

'The cleaners were in my office, so I used your desk earlier,' said Drake. 'I trust that's okay.'

Drake in the basement, stepping forward.

A cough – another sound.

Tucking the plastic inside, she closed the drawer. 'Of course.'

'Holloway's people need to get a move on with the forensic reports,' he said. 'And there's plenty of CCTV still to get through. Steiner's doing her best, but she's snowed under.'

215

'I'll get someone to help her.'

'Ryan Overton had links with some people who steal scrap metal and sell it on, did you know that?'

'I'll get up to date as soon as I get my email working.'

Drake stood to go, but then turned irritably. 'Why do you want Elliot Juniper's address?'

She prodded at her mouse. 'Is your email down?'

'Flick,' Drake said quietly, 'tell me you've dropped the other stuff, this children's home nonsense.'

'Why?' She struggled to keep the shrillness out of her voice. 'All these years you've told me to trust my instincts, told me to think less like a bureaucrat and more like a detective. Now I am, and you're annoyed.'

Drake came around the desk. There was a splash of mud on one of his shoes. He wasn't the kind of man who wore dirty shoes. But then, the whole world seemed to be turning on its head, these days.

'Amelia Troy was a dead end. She knew nothing about this home you've become obsessed with.'

'Because she can't remember a thing!'

'What have you been doing?'

'Connor Laird,' she barked at him, and Drake flinched, as if she'd shot him in the chest. 'The boy named in the caption of the missing—'

'I recognise the name.'

'There's an old man called—'

'Flick—' Drake pinched the bridge of his nose in exasperation.

'Just hear me out.' Her heart was pumping. 'There's an old guy called Ronnie Dent who worked at the Longacre home. When I mentioned Connor Laird's name he became

216

hysterical. He was ranting and raving, and terrified of the boy even after all these years. I've tried to look him up, guv, but there's no record of a Connor Laird anywhere. No convictions, no social security or national insurance, no driving license, nothing. The boy disappeared into thin air.'

'So he's dead, or emigrated.' Drake folded his arms. 'It's been three decades.'

'Maybe.' She took the cutting with the photo torn from it out of the drawer, and slipped it across the desk. 'Or maybe not. All I know is that all the other children in that caption are dead.'

'Except Amelia Troy.'

'Yes.'

'And, as far as we know, Deborah Willetts.' He plunged his hands into his pockets, turned to the window. 'She's probably married now, living out her life in quiet obscurity.'

'But everybody else . . .' she said quickly. 'I'd like to speak to your—'

'I've told you, absolutely not. She's a frail old lady.'

'Then I'll speak to Elliot Juniper.'

'Right now, DS Crowley,' he said, 'the best thing you could do is concentrate on your job while you still have one. Because, to be honest, I'm running out of patience with this . . . farce.'

'I'll go in my free time.'

'You're investigating four murders, you have *no* free time.'

As he strode to the door, Flick jumped up so quickly that her chair rolled into the radiator behind. 'What were you doing in the Property Room?'

A muscle ticked in Drake's jaw. 'I'm going to forget you spoke to me like that.'

Then he left, slamming the door behind him.

Flick's face burned. She had the terrifying, and oddly liberating, feeling that she had gone too far. The sensible thing to do would be to go next door to rally the troops, get up to speed on the morning's developments. If need be, she'd hold the meeting all over again, just to show who was in charge. For the moment, at least, she was still leading this damned investigation.

But instead she picked up the article about the visit of the Drakes to the home, let the plastic sheet flap gently in her fingers.

There was something about this particular cutting that gnawed at her.

A cough, another sound, Drake stepped forward.

A cough, a *tearing* sound.

The surprise on his face – no, the *shock* – when he saw her.

Flick fumbled the half-page back into the pocket, put it in a drawer. She took a small key from the shallow plastic tray where she kept staples and paperclips, and locked it.

Just as the office door flew openly so violently that it bounced against the wall and shuddered. Drake stood there.

'Come on,' he said.

'Where are we going?'

'To finish this once and for all.'

30

The journey out of London took far too long because of endless northbound roadworks. By the time the motorway snarl cleared, Drake had twenty minutes of hard, fast cruising before he eased his Mercedes off the M11.

Once again Flick spent most of the journey on her phone, keeping on top of things in the office and filling Drake in on developments – if you could even call them that. In particular, Kendrick and Moore had tried to link the Overton murders with a series of burglaries that had recently plagued the borough. But the modus operandi was completely different, and that line of inquiry stalled quickly. It didn't stop Vix from speaking at great length about all the work she had put in.

Ray Drake had come to keep an eye on Flick, and also to put to bed once and for all her obsession with the Longacre. But there was another reason. He wanted to get the measure of Elliot after all these years. Wanted to see him, but not be seen.

After all, Elliot had been one of Gordon's Two O'Clock Boys.

In between calls, Flick gazed tensely out of the window, and Drake thought of that journey from the police station to the Longacre in Sally's car – the stifling heat, the stench of tobacco smoke – all those decades ago.

Following the navigation system's instructions, they drove

past a war memorial on a village green the size of a billiard table, and along a series of winding lanes, past woods and fields. Drake kept an eye on the rear-view mirror, half expecting a murderous face to pop up in the back.

'Not long now,' he said, turning into a lane that was almost hidden from the main road. The car's suspension bounced on the uneven surface. Drake eased past Elliot Juniper's cottage, alongside a listing barn set back from the road, and reversed up the drive, cranked the handbrake on the steep slope. Smoke billowed from the chimney of the cottage.

When Flick opened her door, he said, 'I'll stay here.'

'Aren't you coming in?' she asked, surprised.

'I've some calls to make,' he lied. 'You go ahead.'

She hesitated a moment, then climbed out. Drake adjusted the side mirror to get a better view of the cottage door, watched her climb the drive and knock.

It had been a long time since Drake had seen Elliot Juniper, but he hadn't changed, not really. Much of his bulk had slid down his torso in middle age: a bulging stomach drooped over the belt of his jeans. His hair was shaved, perhaps because there wasn't much left to grow. From this distance, Elliot's flattened nose appeared to spiral on his face, like an optical effect.

Drake cracked the window, but Flick and Elliot were too far away for him to hear anything above the shiver of the leaves on the wall of trees in the lane.

Inside. Drake watched them linger on the doorstep. *Go inside.*

But instead Elliot left the door ajar behind him and walked with Flick halfway down the slope. Drake heard her voice, but not her words. Shoulders slumped, the big man crossed his arms and listened, that same anxious expression etched into his face all these years later.

Don't mention my name, Drake thought.

Flick nodded at the car. Elliot glanced towards the Mercedes. Ray Drake was safely hidden behind his head-rest, but Elliot stooped as he tried to see inside. *Not my name.* She said something, and Elliot responded. His eyes widened and he bent his knees, once again trying to see inside.

'Damn it,' said Drake, annoyed that he couldn't hear a thing. He pushed open the car door, crunched across the stony ground towards them. As he approached, Flick was saying: '. . . to know if you have seen Connor Laird.'

Looking from Flick to Drake, Elliot laughed in astonishment. 'Is this some kind of joke?'

Drake took out his ID and held it up, kept it suspended in front of Elliot's face to let the name and the photo fully sink in. 'DI Ray Drake.'

'Is that right?' Elliot gaped at the contusions and bruises on his face, the angry red dash at his throat. 'You look like you've been through the wars, if you don't mind me saying.'

'Answer the question, please,' said Drake. 'Have you lately seen a man called . . .' he turned to Flick. 'What is he called again? Connor . . .'

'Laird,' she said.

Elliot shook his head, bewildered. 'I don't . . .'

'Have you?' Drake asked tersely.

'No,' said Elliot, staring at Drake.

'Or anybody else from the Longacre?' Flick said.

'Ain't been in touch with any of that lot for years. It's all ancient history.' He turned finally to her. 'And as I told you, I haven't been in trouble with the law for donkey's.'

'Nobody's suggesting you have, sir.'

Elliot's gaze kept returning to Drake. 'You said this was to do with Kenny Overton's death?'

'So you haven't heard from Kenny?' asked Flick.

Hesitating, the big man turned his phone in his fingers. But standing out of Flick's sightline, Drake shook his head slowly, emphatically. The answer is: *no.*

'I only know what I saw on television, about him and his family. A terrible business. But what's it got to do with me?'

'Nothing. It's a routine visit,' said Drake. 'We're speaking to anybody who may have known Kenny.'

'You're going a hell of a way back.'

'What was he like?' asked Flick.

'Who? Kenny?'

'Connor Laird.'

Elliot crossed his arms. 'As I say, it was a long time ago. We was kids.'

'What do you remember about him?'

'I remember he did this to my nose.' Elliot held a finger up to his face and laughed, bleakly. 'Everyone was scared of good old Connor. He was cold, unpredictable. You never knew what he would do next.'

'Would you recognise him if you saw him?' asked Flick.

Elliot looked at her in surprise, but before he could answer, a teenager came up the slope, a pair of bulky headphones folded over his head. He walked backwards, admiring the Mercedes unexpectedly parked there. When he saw Elliot with two strangers, he pulled the phones to his shoulders. Music ticked from the earpads.

222

'This is my boy,' said Elliot bashfully. 'Dylan.'

How do you do, Dylan?' Flick held out her hand. 'Detective Sergeant Flick Crowley.'

'Police,' said Dylan flatly.

'A clever boy, takes after his old man.' Elliot winked at Dylan. 'It ain't nothing to worry about. They're asking about stuff that happened a long time ago, when I was your age. I'll see you inside.'

Dylan looked uncertainly at them and then trudged to the house.

'Nice kid,' said Flick.

'Couldn't ask for better,' said Elliot. 'Was there anything else?'

Flick was about to speak, but Drake said impatiently, 'No, we'll leave you alone. Thank you for your cooperation.'

He held out his hand. Elliot considered it doubtfully, then shook, and Drake walked to the car to wait for Flick to follow him back.

'He's lying,' said Flick, pulling her seat belt around her. 'You can tell.'

'About what?' Drake reached for the ignition.

'I don't know exactly,' she said. 'But he was as pale as a ghost.'

'He's a man with a criminal record who's just received an unexpected visit from two Met police officers,' said Drake. 'That fear of the law never goes away.'

He flung open the door suddenly. Flick asked, 'Where are you going?'

'Forgot to give him a card.' Drake reached into his jacket. 'Won't be a moment.'

He walked back to the cottage, beneath the swaying trees.

A gust of wind sent a spurt of leaves flying around his head like demented bats.

Before he even knocked on the door, it opened. There was an edge of panic in Elliot's voice: 'All these years later and imagine my surprise at who comes knocking. What the fuck is going on?'

'Step inside,' said Drake. 'We don't have much time.'

A fire crackled in the room, which was small and tidy. Smoke tumbled against the blackened brick and pulled into the chimney.

When Drake started to speak, Elliot put a finger to his lips, nodded upstairs. 'The walls in this house are as thin as a fag paper.'

'Where were you this morning? At about six a.m.?'

'Where do you think? I was in bed.' Elliot looked annoyed, but also afraid, and Drake believed him. Elliot's conviction sheet didn't exactly scream *criminal genius*.

'We're in trouble.'

Elliot laughed bleakly. 'I figured you'd grow up to be many things, but a copper wasn't one of them.'

'I've got a certain skill at it.'

'I bet you have at that.'

'Listen to me.' Drake stepped forward. 'People we knew from the Longacre are being killed. Kenny and his wife and sons are just the latest.'

'One son.' Elliot blinked. 'The news said one son.'

'The second was murdered last night. Thrown off a tower block.'

Elliot blinked. 'Who else, then?'

'People from the home.'

'*Which* people from the home?'

224

'Most of them.' Elliot's eyes bulged in horror. Drake lifted the net curtain in the window to peer down the drive. 'Jason, David, Regina, Karen, Ricky. Debs was killed this morning. They're just the ones I know about.'

'And who do you figure for this?'

Drake dropped the curtain. 'He calls himself the Two O'Clock Boy.'

'Fuck, fuck, fuck.' Elliot dragged his hands down his face. 'You are fucking kidding me.'

'I think we're next.' There was a movement on the floorboards above, and Drake lowered his voice. 'I think he's coming after us.'

'I *know* him.' Elliot groaned. 'Calls himself Gavin.'

'He calls himself a lot of things these days.'

'He told me about Kenny. I gave him money.'

'Money?'

'Lots of money. Is that what this is about, money? If that's what he wants, he can keep it.'

'What does he look like, this Gavin?'

'I don't know, like some bloke.' Elliot grimaced, thinking. 'Uh, tall.'

'He had a clear opportunity to kill me this morning, but he didn't.' Lifting the curtain again, Drake saw Flick climb from the car and look up at the cottage. 'I think he's left us last for a reason.'

'And why's that?' Elliot snatched a packet of cigarettes off the arm of a sofa, fumbled one from the packet.

'Because he hates us, because he blames us for what happened to him,' said Drake, 'because he's insane. He's methodical, patient and very angry. He's killed those people and their families over a long period of time. Found them,

225

murdered them, left no trace – until now. He wants us to know what he's doing.'

'Us?'

'He's got something special planned for you and me, I think.'

'He was a basket case back then, no question. But a murderer?'

Drake watched Elliot light the cigarette and take quick, nervous puffs. 'You married, Elliot?'

'I've a partner. Dylan's my stepson.'

'He'll kill them, too. It's what he does.'

Elliot tried to keep the panic from his voice. 'What am I going to say to Rhonda? What am I going to tell her?'

'You don't tell her anything. You all go away for a while, don't tell anybody where, till I can get to him.'

'I told you, I've got *no* money, he took it all, and I just happen to be all out of magic fucking beans.'

'I need a gun,' said Drake. 'Do you have one?'

'Me? No!' Elliot grimaced. 'What would I do with one of those? What are you going to do, shoot him?'

'Yes.'

Cigarette smoke danced in front of Elliot's face as he lifted his hand to rub his eyes. 'I could do without all this right now, to be honest.'

'You smoking?' called Dylan at the top of the stairs.

Elliot jumped at the sound of his voice. 'Sorry, I'm putting it out now.'

He opened the door and threw out the cigarette, which bounced and sparked on the stony drive. Drake saw Flick waiting impatiently by the car and turned to go, but Elliot grabbed his arm.

'That place, I'll never get it out of my system, I've always known that. It's like a bullet embedded near my heart, slowly working its way in. I've always known that one day it'll be the end of me. It's going to kill me stone dead. But right now I've got a good life, a family, something I never thought would be for the likes of me. And just as I start to feel a little peace, a little . . . normality, you come back into my life, you along with that, that . . .' He shook his head bitterly. 'I don't believe it, after all this time . . .' Elliot snorted miserably. 'Connor Laird.'

'Remember what he told you the last time you saw him.' Drake leaned close. 'Connor Laird is *gone*. Let's keep it that way.'

And then he turned, strode down the drive without looking back. Flick watched him approach over the top of the car.

'You were a long time,' she said.

'You'll have to forgive an old man's prostate.' Drake climbed in, placed his hands on the wheel. 'This is finished, yes – it's over?'

'Yes,' said Flick, looking away. 'It's over.'

He started the car, and glancing in the rear-view, saw the curtains twitch in Elliot's cottage.

31

As they dropped back onto the North Circular, the pips beeped on the radio at the top of the hour. A newscaster said: 'Police in South London are investigating the deaths of a couple in their home this morning. Mehmet and Deb—'

Drake switched off the radio, and when Flick looked at him, said: 'Do you mind? We've enough murders on our hands. I don't particularly want to hear about any more.'

The traffic ahead thickened. Drake eased up behind an estate car to wait for the tailback to get moving. Hands clasped in her lap, Flick made a face. 'This is going to sound like a really crass question.'

'Let's hear it, then.'

'What's the thing you miss most about Laura?'

Drake blew out his cheeks. 'I don't even know how to start answering that question. It's too big.'

She shifted in her seat towards him. 'A small thing, then.'

Drake thought about it. 'She kept me sane.'

'That sounds like a pretty big thing.'

'She kept me from – how would April put it? – from losing my shit.'

'You don't seem a particularly mad person.'

'That,' he said, the edges of his mouth curling into a tight smile, 'is because I am a very good actor.'

The traffic crawled forward and he nosed the car into

the stream of traffic in the left-hand lane, ready for the Tottenham turn-off.

'So what stops you now?' she asked eventually. 'Going mad, I mean?'

'I've April to worry about.' His fingers drummed on the top of the wheel. 'She's still angry about her mother dying, she's . . . vulnerable. I'm not her favourite person right now. I don't like it, but I understand why, because I'm a useful punchbag. But she'll come round. Sooner or later she's going to need me, and I've got to be there for her.' He glanced at her. 'Something on your mind, Flick?'

'It's not the same, and I'm certainly not comparing it to . . . your loss. But my sister's going away with her family, to Australia. We're close, and I know I can visit once a year, or twice maybe, but without them here . . .'

She shook her head, wished she'd never started the conversation. But right now, despite everything, Drake was the only person she felt able to talk to. This murder investigation had driven a wedge between them for reasons she didn't fully understand, but when all was said and done, he had supported her so much more than her own father. Drake's family was important to him, she knew, and he would understand.

'I think I've relied on her too much, taken for granted that Nina would always be there when I needed her, and nothing would ever change.'

'It's tough.'

'If I'm being honest,' she said, and felt a hard lump in her throat, 'I've turned thirty and they're all I've got.'

'There's your father.'

'We don't get on.' She shrugged. 'The usual torturous

229

family stuff. He left Mum for another woman when I was young and we hardly saw him. A lot of things happened after that. My older brother walked out of the house one day and we never saw him again, you know about that, it hit us all very hard. Then when Mum got dementia Dad didn't lift a finger. He infuriates me, always has. I don't know how long it's been since I saw him last. But Nina has made the effort.' She frowned. 'He's in a home now, a good one, and she pays for it, would you believe.'

'And how do you feel about that?'

'It's none of my business what she does with her money.' She hesitated. 'I told you Dad was a copper.'

Drake nodded. He knew all about Harry Crowley. Let's face it, mostly everyone at the station did.

They didn't speak again until they were cruising past White Hart Lane, just a few minutes from the station. 'Do you miss your own dad?' she asked.

'Leonard . . . my father died when I was eighteen. I didn't know him very well, not really. I wish I'd got to know him better; I have a lot to thank him for. Look, it's none of my business, but maybe you should go and see your father. Make peace. Before, you know . . .'

'Before it's too late.'

'I didn't want to say that,' Drake said. 'But one day he won't be there and . . . well, you know the rest.'

'Sorry to bring it up.' Flick felt guilty about talking about death, not when he had so recently lost his wife. 'Your mother is still going strong!'

'Oh, Myra will outlive us all.' He threw her a sideways glance. 'She tells me she has no intention whatsoever of dying, and I believe her.'

Flick watched the shops and cafés flash by on the High Road. 'Perhaps I will go to see him. There's stuff we need to talk about.'

'There you go.'

But you won't like it, she thought, if you knew what I want to talk to him about: the Longacre, the night it burned down, and the boy called Connor Laird.

She thought, once again, about Drake down in the Property Room. She wanted to know what he was doing there in the dead of night. The noise she heard.

A cough, and then something else – another sound, like—

'What?' Drake asked her, and she realised she had been staring at him.

As soon as she got into her office, Flick unlocked the desk drawer and took out the article about the visit of Leonard and Myra Drake to the Longacre, slipped it from the plastic sheaf. She turned it over in her fingers. Checked the date, reread the names.

She reached into her bag for a pair of nitrile gloves. Snapping them over her wrists, she gently teased the clipping onto the desk. Despite the sun streaming in behind her, Flick clicked on the anglepoise lamp and positioned it above the sheet. Something about this cutting . . .

The next thing she heard was her office door open. When she looked up, Vix Moore was stood there.

'I want to make a complaint about DC Upson.'

Flick stared. 'What kind of a complaint?'

'Detective Constable Upson has a very unfortunate manner. We're the same rank, but he's always telling me what to do. He asks me for an update on my work every five – no, every two minutes – and is frankly very rude.' Vix stepped forward. 'Furthermore, I don't feel that the work I'm being given is helping me progress as a detective.'

'What have you been doing?'

'Leafleting,' she said bitterly.

Half a page from a local newspaper, dated 31 July 1984. The photograph was torn away.

Flick tried to keep the impatience out of her voice. 'I'll speak to DS Upson, you leave it with me.'

A cough, another sound, the look of shock on Drake's face in the Property Room.

A cough, another sound.

But DC Moore didn't move, and she asked: 'Was there something else?'

'I'd like some media training. One day I'm going to be interviewed – by the papers or by television – and I want to be prepared. I think I'd be very good on the media communications side of things, an asset.'

'Good idea, we'll look into it. Thanks, Vix.'

Flick put her head down. A few moments later, she heard the door slam. The fibre of the old newspaper was stiff and brown. Examining the torn edge, she saw it had wisps of pulp along it, very fine, almost translucent against the dark veneer of the desk. This half-page of newspaper was over thirty years old. The edges on three sides were worn, blunted. Yet the torn edge had tiny shreds of paper still attached. That didn't make sense after thirty years. It would have worn smooth long ago.

Which meant it had been torn recently.

Drake in the basement. As she'd moved into the aisle she'd heard a noise. His cough, yes, but something else as he'd stepped quickly to the shelf to smother her view. Her pulse quickened.

Her office door swung open again and Eddie Upson stormed into the room. 'What was Vix saying about me?'

A cough, another sound, Drake stepped forward.

A cough, a *tearing* sound.

He tore it.

Ray Drake tore the photo away, and took it.

'Get your coat.' Flick stood quickly. 'We're going out.'

32

Sick of the secrets multiplying in his head, exhausted after a sleepless night, Elliot resolved to come clean and tell Rhonda he'd lost their savings.

He had spent the hours before dawn watching the black night dissolve into tepid daylight, trying to work out the best way to do it, and decided to fall on her mercy. And since the shocking visit of a man he'd known briefly a long time ago and had never imagined he'd see again, who was now a *cop*, he was petrified.

Kids from the Longacre killed, and their loved ones slaughtered, by someone calling himself the Two O'Clock Boy. If the copper was right, he would as sure as hell come after Elliot. They had to get away. He had to convince Rhonda and Dylan to take a long holiday, just till this whole fucked-up situation blew over. But even if by some miracle she said, *Sure, let's drop everything, I'll call work to say I'll be back in a few weeks or months, whatever,* she'd find out they had no savings left. The only way he could convince her to come away with him was to come clean about the money.

So Elliot went the whole hog. He kneeled before her like a penitent knight while she sat on the sofa, her small hands in his.

'There was a guy, down the pub.' He winced, the whole thing sounded like the beginning of a bad joke. 'We were going to start a business together, selling burgers. He said we needed to pay a deposit and then I'd get the money back. I didn't ask you because I thought you would say no.'

He waited for her to get angry or upset, but she just frowned at him.

'So, yeah.' He swallowed.' I handed it over to him.'

'All of it?'

He nodded. 'Every penny.'

She untangled her hands from his, placed them in her lap, a small gesture that made him feel wretched.

'Why would you do that?'

'Because I'm Elliot the idiot, and I've a special kind of talent for messing up.' He grimaced. 'Always have had, always will.'

'And who did you give it to?'

'A bloke called Gavin.'

'A bloke called Gavin,' she repeated.

'Well, he said his name was Gavin.' The last thing he could tell her was that he may have given all their hard-earned cash – *Rhonda's* hard-earned cash – to a multiple murderer. He didn't want to terrify her, not on top of everything else. 'I wanted to prove I could make a go of my own business. I wanted to surprise you.'

'Well.' Rhonda smiled bitterly. 'Mission accomplished.'

'I wanted you to know that I can . . .' His voice trailed away. What was the point in telling her what she already knew, that he couldn't be trusted That no matter how much he tried to kid himself, he would always make a mess of any given situation, nailed on?

'Tell me you didn't spend the money on drugs or gambling, or prostitutes—'

235

'No!' It sickened him that she could think that. 'I'd never –'

'You would never what?' she spat. 'Because you seem to get up to an awful lot without my knowledge, Elliot.'

'Why don't we go away?' he said. 'Take that holiday?'

'You just lost all our money,' she said, and stood suddenly.

'Where are you going?'

'To get a glass of water,' she said. 'If that's okay with you?'

'I'll get it.'

'No.' She waved him off. 'I'll go. I have to do everything else around here.'

When she was gone, he thrust his hands in his pockets and stood at the window, looking miserably at the abandoned barn next door.

That barn was the first thing he saw every morning, on the days he managed to get out of bed before midday – if he had no work to go to, he often didn't – and every day it was a little bit nearer to collapsing. Insects munched on the timber day and night and weeds forced themselves further into the grain of the dry, brittle planks. Every day, without anyone really noticing, the edifice was weakened a little bit more.

That was what his memories of the Longacre were doing to Elliot, eating away at him. Other kids from the home, they could probably handle their memories. But they hadn't seen half of what Elliot had, and he didn't know how to cope with his thoughts, so he did his best to bury them.

So many memories . . . Of Tallis's heavy tread on the stairs, and the time he made Turrell eat the cockroach, and what happened to Sally, and Connor Laird's cold, implacable anger in those final, harrowing hours at the home, a night that would be forever imprinted into Elliot's DNA like a white-hot iron seared into flesh. Those were the memories that ate away at him, as surely as the weeds and insects that patiently consumed that dilapidated barn.

And what was worse, they weren't just memories any more. The terror of the Longacre, a place he thought was done with him, had re-emerged to torment him once more. People he never thought he would see again, never *cared* to see again, had resurfaced, and one of them wanted to kill him. And kill Rhonda and kill Dylan.

The tap gushed in the kitchen. He heard water splash into a glass.

This was his moment to get it all off his chest. The time was right to tell Rhonda everything: about the violence and the abuse, and the crimes he committed when he was too young to know any better. When he was manipulated and bullied by Tallis. When he was a child – a frightened, terrified boy. And then he would tell her about Connor and Sally and Turrell, and about Ray Drake – about what happened all those years ago – and about the terrible danger they were in now, decades later.

Finally he would get it all out. All those other kids, they were dead, or so he was told. But Elliot was alive and he had to move forward, and the only way to do that was to tell Rhonda. Let it all come tumbling into the daylight where it couldn't do any more damage, and where they could examine it. Rhonda would know what to do, how to put him back together. Elliot pressed a hand to his face and decided to take that chance.

The time was now. He took a deep breath.
But.

This scared him, terrified him – she might leave him when she found out about the cold-blooded murders. He hadn't done them, they weren't his fault, but he had been there, and had said nothing about them. Not to anyone, ever. Because he was still the same scared little kid. If what he had done was wrong, then he was sorry, but he had only been a kid and he wasn't to blame for what went on in that place.

She'll know the kind of man you are.

Don't burden her with all your selfish shit. Just suck it up.

So when she came back into the room, instead of telling her the truth, what he said was: 'I can get it back.'

'What?' she asked warily. 'What can you get back?'

'The money. I can get it back.'

And it was a lie, another one to add to all the other lies he had told in his lifetime. Elliot was good with lies, always had been. He wasn't good at much, but he was a natural born liar.

She sipped the water. 'You said this man, this Gavin, has gone.'

'I think . . . I think I know where I can find him.' He held her gaze. 'It just occurred to me. Tell you what, why don't you and Dylan get away for a few days, and let me get everything sorted?'

'What's going on, Elliot? Why are you so keen for us to go away?'

There's this man, he's a psychopath and he's killed before. Kenny, Jason, Karen, so many others. He's trying to kill me – and you, too. But, oh yeah, I can't tell you about that, can't tell you the truth, because I'm gutless, I'm a coward.

And if you . . . *oh God, if you leave me . . .*

238

'Nothing's going on.' He sounded unconvincing, even to himself. 'It was just, you know, a suggestion. You haven't seen your mum for – how long is it now, nearly a year?'

'We're not going anywhere.'

'I can get the money, and then when you come back—'

'I *work*,' she snapped. 'I bring in money so that you can give it away to complete strangers. Dylan is at school. We can't just drop everything.'

His face burned with shame at her words. 'Right.'

Rhonda put on her coat. 'I've got one child, Elliot, and I really don't need another one. There's something you're not telling me, and I want to know what it is. I thought we had got past this kind of behaviour.'

'We have, but—'

'I'm late for work; we'll talk when I get home.' She picked up her bag. 'I don't know, I'm going to have to think about a few things.'

'What things?' he asked, in alarm.

'But, Elliot . . .' She opened the front door. 'Get that money back.'

'Yes,' he said quickly.

As soon as she drove off in her Ford Focus, he took out the business card he still had in his jeans pocket with a heavy heart, and pressed a number into his phone.

'It's Elliot Juniper,' he said, when Owen Veazey answered.

'Elliot, how nice.' That damned fruit machine hooted and bleeped in the background. Owen was at his usual table.

'That job . . . is the offer still open?'

'It is, as a matter of fact. You've left it a bit late, but . . . why not?'

'And the money—'

'Will be paid into your account as soon as it's done. Interest free, for as long as you need it.' Owen paused. 'Within reason, of course.'

Elliot closed his eyes. 'When?'

'Perry will pick you up later,' said Owen.

Lies upon lies upon lies.

240

33

1984

Screams and shouts and the sound of crashing furniture came from behind the door to Gordon's office. The children melted into the furthest parts of the house. Ricky and Cliff pulled up weeds in the garden and flung them at each other. Amelia disappeared into the eaves. Some of the others, Kenny and Jason among them, flew from room to room, playing tag.

Elliot was warned by Connor to stay away from Toby, who sat against a tree, head bowed, knees pulled up to his face. Elliot resented being told what to do by Connor, but knew he'd gone too far. Since the cockroach incident several days ago, and since Gordon had started taking him into the small room behind his office of a night, Toby had become withdrawn, distant. He stayed as far from the other children as he could. It was wrong that he was here in the first place. His parents were idiots for not seeing the kind of man Gordon was.

'He got what was coming to him,' Elliot insisted, as they stood looking down the garden at him. 'He deserves everything he gets.'

Connor didn't care what happened to any of them. 'I'm out of here.'

Elliot turned to Connor, incredulous. 'You can't.'

'You don't tell me what I can do.'

But then he saw Elliot thinking about what would happen next. Things would go back to the way they used to be. He would get his delivery job back, be at Gordon's side again. Good luck to him. Connor had stayed for too long, for no good reason. Everybody was scared of him, they'd be happy to see him go. Anyway, Gordon was losing the plot. Something bad was going to happen, Connor sensed that very clearly.

'See ya, then.' Elliot poked a finger into Connor's chest. 'Shame you won't be around to see that fart get what's coming to him.'

'Think about it.' Connor resisted the urge to snap off Elliot's finger. 'Toby ain't like us, he's got family. What do you think he's going to say when he gets out of this place? What do you think he's going to say about what happened?'

Brain cranking into gear, Elliot's eyes snapped wide.

'That's right.' Connor lowered his voice as Karen squeezed past them. 'And then they're gonna look at what else goes on here. They'll find out about your deliveries for Gordon.'

'And yours!'

'I ain't going to be here.' He would just disappear. It was the one thing he had learned to do in his short life. Vanish into the world; keep moving from place to place. Nobody would see him; nobody would know him. 'I'll be gone, and they'll never find me.'

Elliot swallowed. 'And then what'll happen?'

'They'll close this place down and you'll get sent to prison or borstal. You ain't gonna live the good life there, not from what I've heard. You got to make sure Gordon stays away from the kid.'

'How am I gonna do that?' said Elliot, panicking. 'I don't want to go to those places. I definitely don't.'

Now he'd made the decision, Connor just wanted to go. 'Not my problem.'

Down the hallway, the front door opened. Ronnie Dent came in carrying a bag clinking with bottles and knocked on the office door, disappearing inside.

'Gordon ain't gonna listen to me, he never does.' Elliot stared. 'But he'll listen to you.'

Connor shook his head. 'I'm out of here.'

If Elliot or those other kids wanted help they could get that do-gooding Ray kid to come and give them a big hug. Good riddance to the lot of them.

'If you tell him, he'll leave the kid alone.' When Connor turned to go, Elliot grabbed him. 'You gotta help me out. Tell him what you told me. Make him realise, get him to apologise.'

Connor remembered the trouble Elliot had made for him, and for Toby, and angrily slapped his hand away. 'Don't touch me.'

'You're a mate.' Elliot's voice cracked. 'The only one I got.'

When Connor thought about it, he realised he had nothing to lose. He'd made up his mind to go. He would speak to Gordon, and if the manager lost his temper he'd walk out the door and never look back.

'All right,' he said finally, 'I'll do it. But you're coming with me.'

Gordon barked something when they knocked on the door of the office. On his way out, Ronnie Dent stepped aside to let them into the gloomy room. The curtains in the bay window were closed. A sickly stench hung in the air. Slumped on the sofa, Sally barely lifted her head when they walked in, but Gordon jumped up from behind his desk.

'What can I do for you, lads?'

Elliot nudged Connor forward. 'We wanted . . . a word.'

'Have as many as you like.'

Connor said: 'You gotta leave the kid alone.'

Gordon frowned. 'Sorry, son. I'm not with you.'

'Toby.'

'Ah, young Master Turrell.'

'The kid's parents . . .'

'What about them?'

'They ain't gonna like it if you . . .'

'If I what, Connor?'

Gordon's voice was calm, reasonable, but Connor knew to tread carefully. Behind him, Elliot stared at the floor.

'You've got to leave him alone.'

The manager leaned against the desk, feet crossed at the ankles.

'And what do I care about those people? They handed their precious boy to me without considering the consequences.'

'Don't listen to him.' Sally slurred from the sofa. 'He's a drunken fool. He's losing his mind.'

'Be quiet, dear Sal, this doesn't concern you.'

Hauling herself off the sofa, Sally jabbed a dirty fingernail at Gordon. 'Just you be careful, or I'll go – and then you'll be sorry.'

'How will I be sorry, exactly?' Gordon laughed. 'Will I be sorry that you're not here to use all my merchandise? Will I be sorry that you're not sucking me dry?'

Sally shot him a ghastly smile. 'You'll be surprised.'

Gordon's hand shot out to grab her neck. 'So surprise me, Sal.'

'Let her go.' Connor moved forward, the hairs on his arms standing on end, his skin crackling. Part of him was thinking: it doesn't matter, *just go*. But part of him had wanted this moment for a long time. Gordon needed teaching a lesson, needed taking down a peg, and nobody else was going to do it.

'So, finally, the wee man makes his big move.' Gordon pushed Sally away. 'You know, Connor, I've been waiting for this moment. We've been doing this dance for too long now, you and me.' He clicked his fingers, swayed his hips. 'And what about you, Elliot, care to join in? Perhaps together you'll give old Gordon a hiding. Let's find out. Come on, lad, the more the merrier.'

Sally slapped him hard across the face. 'I know people.'

Gordon blinked in surprise. Touching at his cheek, he spoke softly: 'And who is it, you know, Sal, to make me scared? That weakling cousin of yours?'

'His father, he's a judge. I'm going to tell him.'

'Tell him what?'

'Things.'

Gordon's voice lifted angrily. 'Tell him what? Be clear, woman!'

'I'll tell him everything.'

'What's everything?'

'About this place, about what goes on here.'

'I forget sometimes how far you have fallen in life, Sal.' Gordon picked up the glass paperweight from the desk and tossed it from one hand to the other. 'You have to watch

Sally, boys. Watch her carefully or she'll sting you like a scorpion.'

She threw an imploring look at Connor: *get out*, and he turned. He'd done what he came to do, he'd done his best for Elliot, and for the Toby kid, but when he left none of this would mean anything to him. He was going somewhere far away – he wasn't the kind of person, he decided, who was going to spend his life in one place – he'd keep moving, to different cities, different countries, where he didn't have to answer to anybody.

As he stepped to the door, Elliot looked stricken.

'Bye then, lad,' called Gordon.

All Connor had to do was fling open the door and he'd be gone, but his hand froze on the handle. Before he left he wanted more than anything to pound Gordon into the dust, to make him suffer. When he turned back to the room, Gordon smirked.

'Now look, he's staying. He fancies his chances against me. What do we think? Connor's a strong lad, but how far is he willing to go?' He looked at Sally, at Elliot. 'What are his limits, I wonder? I fancy myself a great judge of character.'

Gordon propped his hands on his knees to look deeply into Connor's eyes, as if he was gazing into his very soul. 'I see anger and resentment and confusion, and so much pain . . . and yes, there it is . . . I see the potential for great cruelty.'

He walked away, smacking the paperweight between his palms. 'But what do you think, Connor? Do you think you can match me?'

Connor's nerves, his muscles, screamed. Wanting to leap at Gordon and smash his fists into him. Destroy him.

'Do you think, for example,' he asked, 'that you could kill someone? I have, lad, and I'm comfortable with the fact.'

Sally stepped forward. 'Gordon—'

'Are you willing to kill? I want to hear it.'

But Connor didn't answer, couldn't think straight. An unbearable pressure built in his head, and he stood on the balls of his feet, ready to fly at Gordon.

The manager leered. 'Do you think, boy, that you could do *this*?'

Then Gordon lifted the paperweight high above his head, and in a swift motion, he dashed it down onto the crown of Sally's head. Her legs crumpled like pipe cleaners and she collapsed onto the rug.

Connor and Elliot stared, stunned. Sally laid face down, hair fanned around her head.

'Now look what you've made me do,' Gordon said, with a sick smile.

Get on your feet, thought Connor. *That's enough, now.*

But Sally didn't move. Gordon retreated behind his desk to pour a drink with a shaking hand. Liquid spilled down his chin when he drank. The paperweight slid from his grip, rolled across the desk and off the edge.

'Come on, Sal,' he said, over his shoulder. 'You've made your point.'

But Sally didn't move. Gordon squatted beside her, lifted one of her wrists to feel for a pulse.

'What's wrong with her?' Elliot's face was drenched in sweat. 'Is she gonna be all right?'

'No, she isn't going to be all right.' Gordon climbed to his feet, smiling bitterly. 'She very much isn't going to be all right.'

Right at that moment the door opened and Toby Turrell came in, hands pressed to his face, which was wet with tears. He had barely begun to beg to be able to call his parents, to be allowed to go home, when he saw the pale, shocked expressions of the two boys in the room, and of Gordon.

Only then did he see Sally's body at his feet, blood pumping from the hole in her shattered skull and sliding down her long hair, to curve around the sole of his sandal.

34

Eddie Upson's car was a pigsty. The back seat was a shelf for old tabloids and tossed chocolate wrappers and coffee cups. The atmosphere was a smelly funk of soured milk, and Flick felt queasy all the way to Islington. She cracked the passenger window, while Upson complained to her about Vix Moore.

'I ask her to do something, I ask nicely, and she huffs and puffs.'

'All I'm saying—'

'I'm on eggshells around her. She treats me like a bad smell.'

Sometimes, when Eddie had dodged the deodorant in the morning, there *was* a bad smell in the room. She wound the window lower. 'Apologise and that'll be the end of it.'

Eddie lifted his hands from the wheel in exasperation. 'I've done nothing wrong!'

'Pull over here,' she said.

'Fine, I'll apologise, but it won't do any good.' He swung the car to the kerb in the Islington Square. 'What are we doing here?'

'Never you mind. I'll be five minutes.'

The wind was picking up, shivering the spindly, leafless trees on the pavement, as she climbed the steps to Ray Drake's door. She'd rather not have brought Upson, but she

249

didn't want Drake to think she was pursuing her own investigations again.

Flick had encountered many vicious criminals in her job, had sat in rooms with people who would tear your ears off if you glanced away, but she was terrified at the prospect of speaking to this one old lady. Laura Drake's funeral was a heartfelt occasion, held at a pretty church packed with flowers and wreaths. Every pew was crammed with musician friends of Laura's – a string quartet played – but Flick had found Myra Drake a cold and forbidding woman who sat with her nose in the air as her granddaughter fell to pieces and Ray Drake stared, ashen-faced, at the coffin. She had seemed a chilling and ambivalent presence.

And right now she was the only person who could provide Flick with any information about the Longacre. The consequences of this visit would be severe when Drake found out. But if the DI was, as she suspected, tampering with evidence – it was possible a remorseless killer was at large, and yet Drake was seemingly covering the murderer's tracks – she wanted to know why.

Myra Drake opened the door as soon as Flick rang the bell. Even in her eighties, she was still a tall and imposing figure, with a crook in her spine that made her look like a vulture in a cardigan.

'Mrs Drake, we met briefly at—'

'I know who you are.' The old woman's gaze was steady. 'My son isn't here.'

'I'm not here to see DI Drake; I wanted to talk to you.'

'That won't be possible,' she said, and was about to close the door, but Flick placed her hand on the frame.

'It's about the Longacre. You and your husband visited the home in—'

'I'm perfectly aware of what I have and haven't done. Does my son know you're here, Miss . . .?'

'Crowley. No, he doesn't.' Flick sensed her opportunity slipping away. 'May I come in?'

'Please remove your hand.'

She said quickly: 'Do you remember a boy at the home called Connor Laird?'

Flick saw surprise, and something else – something like *fear* – drop momentarily down the old woman's face, like a glitch on a television screen.

'Connor Laird,' she repeated. 'A boy called Connor Laird?'

Myra Drake tugged at a locket around her neck with a gnarled hand. 'My son will sack you when he discovers you are here.'

'He can't sack me, Myra.' She didn't care for the way the old woman had behaved in the church, refusing to comfort her son or granddaughter. She didn't care if she was reprimanded or even dismissed, because for the first time in a long time Flick felt the excitement of police work coursing through her veins, and annoying this condescending old woman was the icing on the cake. 'You remember him, don't you?'

'I don't care for your attitude or your questions about that boy.'

'Did you know him? Connor Laird.' Every time she said his name, Myra seemed to shrink a little bit more.

'Take your hand off my door.'

'Connor Laird, Myra.'

Myra's shoulders slumped and she looked confused. Flick

251

remembered how old she was, how frail and vulnerable. She had the awful feeling she was bullying this old woman and removed her hand from the door.

And with a triumphant smile, Myra Drake slammed it in her face.

Annoyed that she had been played for a fool, Flick wanted to jam her finger on the bell and keep it there, but the stubborn old mare, she knew, wouldn't open the door. She imagined Myra was already dialling her precious son. From her reaction to Connor Laird's name, she clearly remembered the boy. In all likelihood she had already discussed him with Ray Drake.

Upson was slapping his hands on the wheel to a song on the radio when Flick climbed back in the car. He turned the ignition.

'That was quick.' He drove out of the square. 'Heading back now?'

'No,' she snapped.

The indicator ticked at a junction, a tense metronome in the interior, and Upson clicked it off. A car beeped behind them as he cranked the handbrake.

'Eddie, please,' she said. 'Just drive.'

He lifted his hands in exasperation. 'I don't know where we're going.'

'Hackney,' she said, blushing. 'We're going to Hackney.'

Upson sighed. 'Have I got *punchbag* written on my forehead today?'

An empty can in the footwell tumbled over her shoes whenever he took a corner and she threw it over her shoulder. Embarrassed by her outburst, Flick persisted with questions about his family, and by the time they reached Mare Street she had even managed to squeeze some terse conversation from him.

When they arrived Flick was relieved to leave the car's cloying atmosphere of curdled dairy and resentment. 'Get yourself a coffee,' she told him.

The weekly *Hackney Express* had closed fifteen years ago, a casualty of the declining fortunes of the local newspaper industry. For a while its name lived on in the tangerine masthead of a free sheet called the *Hackney Argent and Express*, but a mouthful in a diminishing market, the title was shortened to the *Hackney Argent*.

The reception, with its stacks of newspapers and cardboard cutouts of grinning celebrities, managed to be both sparse and untidy. A sales team spoke on headsets behind the counter. When Flick asked about the *Express*, the teenage receptionist was dismissive.

'This is the *Argent*,' she said.

'But it used to be the *Express*.'

The girl's expression hardened. 'What's it about?'

'I'm looking for a report from nineteen eighty-four.'

Flick may as well have asked her about Tudor England. 'That was *way* before I was born.'

'I was hoping there'd be copies of the *Express* on computer or microfiche.'

Please not microfiche, thought Flick. It was cumbersome to use. The Met had long ago transferred its microfiche files onto a computer database. But she needn't have worried, the girl clearly didn't have the faintest idea what she was talking about.

'Micro . . . ?'

'Fiche,' Flick told her, growing impatient.

'Micro . . . fish.'

'It's like camera film, which you run through a machine and read off a screen.'

The girl's face was incredulous. 'I got all my photos on my phone.'

'We don't have anything as sophisticated as that, I'm afraid.' A middle-aged woman came bustling to the counter, a mug of tea swinging carelessly in her fist. Her glossy black hair was cut into a bulbous helmet around her plump face. Beneath a long sweater, leggings as thick and straight as artillery shells disappeared into Ugg boots. 'What is it that you're looking for?'

'I'm investigating four murders,' said Flick, showing her ID.

The young girl leaned forward, interested now. 'Wow.'

'You can be my assistant,' Flick said, but the girl favoured her with a look that suggested she didn't care to be anybody's assistant.

'Do you have an exact date?'

'July thirty-first, nineteen eighty-four.'

The woman, who said her name was Diane, wrote down the date and gave Flick an appraising look. 'It's just as well you've got long legs.'

Ushering her behind the counter, Diane led Flick downstairs to an ill-lit corridor, which smelled of bleach.

'This is where we keep all the old binders.' Diane opened a door and pressed a switch. Fluorescent lights buzzed into life. 'Good luck in getting to them.'

The entire room was filled with office furniture and equipment dumped every way up. Tables and desks, filing cabinets, a photocopier, beige computer drives and monitors, all gathering dust. It was impossible to step in any direction without having to clamber over something.

'Over there.' The entire length of the wall was lined with shelves full of tall volumes. Diane pointed to the far corner.

Tossing clutter out of her way, Flick hesitantly moved forwards. Nearly twisting her ankle while straddling a fax machine, she saw the embossed gold lettering on the spines of the leather books, archives of a host of long-defunct newspapers. Halfway across the room, her phone buzzed. She saw a text from April Drake. Biting down her excitement, she tucked away the phone.

Finally reaching the back of the room, Flick climbed on upturned drawers to reach the highest shelf. Each of the *Hackney Express* volumes contained six months' worth of newspapers. The *Jul–Dec 1984* binder was against the wall. The drawers wobbled precariously beneath her as, balancing like a surfer riding a wave, she plucked at the lip of the binding. The volume was squeezed tight. It wouldn't shift. The drawers teetered. Locking her knees, she tried again. The cheap leather of the book shifted with a dry snap, separating from the wall and the adjacent volume. Flick prised the heavy book from the space.

Climbing carefully off the drawers, she opened the cover, as heavy as the lid of a box, and turned the dry, brittle pages.

'Found what you wanted?' called Diane from the doorway.

'Yes, thank you!' said Flick.

Anticipation rose in her. After about ten minutes, she found it. The newspaper was dated 6 August 1984. The front-page headline said: LOCAL HERO KILLED IN CHILDREN'S HOME BLAZE.

A children's home manager died a hero when a blaze ripped through the building to which he had devoted his life.

Gordon Tallis (44) made the fatal decision to return one last time to the burning building and was overwhelmed by flames.

This was the article in Kenny Overton's clippings, with the photograph of the blackened remains of the home below. A caption beneath it, missing from Kenny's file, credited the photograph to Trevor Sutherland.

Flick turned to the previous week's edition, 31 July 1984. The front-page headline was about an outbreak of graffiti in the borough. She carefully scanned each page in the news section, then the features section, the classifieds, the sports pages at the back.

And that was it.

Somehow she'd managed to miss the story of the Drakes' visit to the home and the accompanying photograph, so she flipped back to the front of the paper and started again, counting the page numbers.

One sheet, pages seven and eight, was missing. It had been removed. A thin strip of paper raced down the spine, straight and sharp to the touch.

Another dead end.

'You will put it back where you found it, won't you?' called Diane.

Flick slammed the volume shut. Dust exploded into the air, and she sneezed. Balancing precariously on the drawers again, she replaced it on the shelf and made her way carefully back across the room, as if negotiating a minefield.

'Has anyone else been down here recently?'

'Not as far as I recall,' said Diane. 'I've always thought it pointless keeping those silly volumes, but it's a kind of heritage, isn't it?'

'Nobody has asked to do research for a book or a university paper?'

Someone sliced out that page, covering their tracks, someone who didn't want to be identified.

'In my time here nobody has shown any interest in anything to do with the *Express*. Tell me what you're after, and I'll ask in editorial.'

Flick told her about the article detailing Leonard and Myra Drake's visit to the Longacre home. Diane wrote down the date and page number of the edition in a pad and tore it out. The sound made Flick shudder. It was the noise she'd heard down in the Property Room when she interrupted Ray Drake.

When he tore the photograph from the cutting.

Tampering with evidence, hiding something.

Connected somehow, implicated in a way she didn't understand, to the deaths of an untold number of people.

35

Ray Drake stayed away from pubs if he could help it. He was forced to go to them occasionally for work functions, like the celebration bash the other night. But alcohol was for other people. He'd never smoked, never taken drugs, avoided caffeine. He and Laura often ate out and dined with her friends, but there was nothing in this cave of wood and mirror, imbued with a sharp vinegar tang, to make him a good man, a better man. And that's all he had ever wanted to be.

His instincts had pulled him towards police work, but his home life had given him balance. It was quiet and loving, ordered and nourishing, Laura had blessed him with that. But she was gone now, and he was forced to face this situation alone. His vivid memories of his wife were fading, swept away by the recent storm of events, and now he was in danger of losing April. It was unthinkable; it would be catastrophic. If something happened to his daughter, he sensed he would unravel. He had to keep his daughter safe, his life on track. The Two O'Clock Boy could strike at any time. Drake had to stop him.

Easier said than done, but Drake didn't have the luxury of doing nothing. All it took was for Flick Crowley to voice her suspicions about the Longacre in the office and the investigation could swing in that direction.

Getting a gun from the station was out of the question. He didn't have the authorisation to access the firearms locker. Ray Drake knew plenty of criminals who would supply one for the right price, but most of those people could cheerfully hold you to account for it later.

His repeated attempts to call April came to nothing. Her phone was switched off, or went to voicemail. So Drake pocketed his mobile and took a table in the pub in Bethnal Green to wait for Amelia Troy. She'd texted him this morning, and when he phoned back, she asked to meet.

Somewhere public, she said. Somewhere busy.

A pair of regulars chatted at the bar. A boisterous group of builders in overalls flopped noisily at a nearby table.

Shading his eyes against the low winter sun, he saw Amelia Troy approach along the high street. Hair pulled back, wearing sunglasses, a yellow hoodie beneath a battered leather jacket; hands thrust into the pockets of her jeans, which tapered into dirty white plimsolls. Something was clamped beneath an arm. When she slumped into the seat opposite, a curled book covered in crepe paper fell to the table, specks of glitter working into the grain of the wood. Drake couldn't take his eyes off it.

'Drink?'

She ignored the question, nodded towards the swelling on his face: 'You never really explained how you got that.'

'I thought I did. Somebody resisting arrest, a fellow we needed to talk to about some robberies.'

'You investigate robberies as well as murders?'

'If necessary,' he said. 'Is everything okay?'

'I had another call last night. Five, maybe ten minutes, after you'd left.'

Drake placed his juice to the side. 'Why didn't you—'

'The voice was electronically altered. You know, like a robot's.'

He nodded, wary. 'What did it say?'

'It said that I had to remember where I had come from, and then I would know why I must . . . why I must die. It said I was to blame.' She laughed, a skittering sound that filled Drake with foreboding. 'But like I told you, I *can't* remember, it the one thing I can't do. So I asked what I had to remember, and you know what it told me?' She watched him carefully. 'It told me to ask you.' Drake shifted in his seat. 'Do you have any idea what it was talking about, DI Drake?'

He forced his gaze from the sketchbook. 'No. How could I?'

'So, as we know, I've no idea what happened back then. But I've always recorded my experiences. I've dozens of books like this, though not quite as old.' More specks of glitter drifted to the table when she tapped the cover. 'All through my shitty life, the drugs, the suicide attempts, the husband who hurt me, I've worked hard. Last night I searched for any drawings I did as a kid. I hire storage, one of those places with twenty-four-hour access. I keep all my preliminary sketches there.'

Her fingers scratched across the crepe.

'I spent the rest of the night there, going through my sketchbooks. The truth is, I didn't feel safe at home and I was too embarrassed to ask you to return. At this storage place, I didn't feel so alone. I found many projects I started and abandoned. Perhaps I'll pick up a few of them again, see if the old magic is still there.'

'It's an idea,' said Drake.

'You look tense, Ray. Can I call you Ray? I feel I know you, I said that last night, didn't I, that your face is familiar to me.' She picked up the sketchbook, the kind of cheap stationery found in any newsagent, her name in neat bubble writing on the cover, and turned the pages with a thumb. 'This is one of the sketchbooks I had as a kid. I don't remember it, but it's very old, as you can see. I was amazed when I saw some of the illustrations. I was pretty good even back then, if I say so myself.' She slid it towards him. 'Take a look.'

'Amelia—'

'Look at it, please.'

Drake opened it to see the drawings and patterns she had done as a child. He remembered her, the book against her knees, a pencil dancing in her hand, lost in her own world. On every page the designs became more elaborate. Sketches of people appeared. There was Gerry Dent. The likeness was clumsy, Amelia still had much to learn about life drawing, but she had caught the essence of the woman: her slovenliness, her dull, predatory gaze.

'I've no idea who she is.' Amelia swiped through the pages. 'Or any of these other people.'

Other kids from the Longacre. She'd captured them playing, laughing, crying. He recognised a boy called Cliff who had a compulsion to eat dirt, and Lena, a girl whose mattress was lumpy from the stolen toys she hid underneath it.

'I wonder where those children are now. Are they getting on with their lives somewhere or, like Kenny, are they . . . ?'

Her voice trailed away when he turned a page – and saw

a drawing of himself, sitting on the steps outside the home. She had captured his sad, troubled expression. The unruly hair, the jagged plummet of his cheeks.

'That's you, yes?' Her voice cracked. 'I'd say that's definitely you.'

'Amelia.' He pushed the book away.

'Explain why I drew you in one of my sketchbooks thirty years ago.'

'It's just a kid, your mind—'

'Please don't tell me I'm paranoid. These days I know the difference between illusion and reality.' She looked stricken. 'I have nightmares. I see a room on fire. I see children, and a crazed man with a beard. I see him shouting and pulling at me, I feel his breath on my face. He hates me and wants to kill me, wants to kill us all. I wake up drenched in sweat, my sheets sopping. So if that's you,' she tapped the image, 'I really would like to know why you've been lying to me.'

The door to the street burst open and more builders swaggered in, laughing.

Drake swallowed. 'That's me.'

Amelia giggled nervously. 'I don't understand.'

Drake leaned forward. 'It's complicated but, yes, I—'

'I have to go.'

'Amelia, please.'

Her thighs banged against the underside of the table when she stood, and Drake's glass shattered on the floor. Someone at the bar cheered. 'Why have I been scared since I saw that drawing? Is it because when I turned on the radio this morning I discovered a woman called Deborah Yildiz was burned to death just hours after I gave you her address?'

'It's not what you think.'

He reached out, but she yanked her hand away. 'Stay away from me!'

'Everything all right over here?' A group of builders came over and crowded behind Drake's chair.

'We're fine, thanks,' he said, without looking up.

'Yeah?' One of the men, hair coated with plaster dust, nodded at Amelia. 'Cos the lady looks like she wants to leave.'

Amelia flew out of the door. Drake watched her throw the hood over her head and melt into the crowd.

'You might want to get that deposit back, chum,' the guy said. 'From the charm school!'

The men turned away, laughing. Drake looked again at his own glowering portrait, then slipped the sketchbook into his pocket.

Minutes later, he sat in his car, which was parked in a quiet residential street, and thought about playing one of Laura's concertos. But he knew it wouldn't do any good. He wouldn't hear her music. That silent roar inside of him, those troubled memories, would drown it out.

He felt anger spiking inside him with every hour that passed, like the agitated head of a seismograph jumping on paper. Felt it rising ever more strongly, filling the empty space his wife left inside him the day she died.

36

'They're next door listening to the Cornetto man,' said the receptionist at Valleywell Retirement Village. 'Pop on in, he's used to all the comings and goings.'

Flick headed towards the baritone rendition of 'O Sole Mio' blasting from the lounge, slipping inside to see the singer belting out the song to a room of elderly men and women. He was an incongruous sight on a weekday in Finchley, in his dinner jacket, bow tie and scarlet cummerbund, hair slicked back in the Mafioso style. Flick scanned the room for Harry, but it wasn't easy when all she could see was an ocean of grey hair. The receptionist had been certain he would be there – 'the ladies and gentlemen love their opera' – but her father's appreciation of music, Flick remembered, went as far as a bit of Dolly.

As soon as he saw her, the singer picked up a red rose from a pile next to the CD player providing his orchestral backing tracks, and threaded his way through the clutter of sofas and chairs to drop to one knee in front of Flick and serenade her. *'Ma n'atu sole, Cchiù bello, oje ne', O sole mio, Sta 'nfronte a te!'*

Dying a little inside, Flick politely accepted the rose. She was relieved to spot Harry at a patio table in the garden, and quickly skirted around the edge of the room. If her father was pleased that his youngest daughter had unexpectedly walked back into his life, he didn't show it.

'Ladies,' Harry vaguely gestured to two women at the table, 'this is my daughter.'

Flick was surprised to see how much weight he had lost. Harry's wavy silver hair still curdled over his head, but his skin sucked in sharply below the cheeks, and a trembling fin of skin hung beneath his jaw. He wore a lurid Hawaiian shirt, long shorts and desert boots. A trilby was placed on the table in front of him.

'Sit yourself down.' He gestured to a chair. 'Becca, Claire, meet Felicity.'

Inside, the backing track changed to a jolly tune Flick recognised from a million TV ads. The baritone pumped his arms as he sang.

'That's not your daughter,' said one of the women.

'You're thinking of my eldest. I got two daughters. This is Felicity, she's followed in her old man's footsteps. She's a constable, a Murder Detective!'

'I'm a DS now,' corrected Flick, but he would have known that, Nina would have told him.

'The single one,' said Claire. 'Can't keep a man.'

'She'd have more success with men if she smiled,' said Becca.

'Can we talk?' Flick asked her father, impatient.

'Perhaps she's not interested in men. Perhaps she's one of those.'

'What have I told you about reading those magazines?' Harry wagged a finger at Becca. 'Putting ideas into your head!' He tilted the hat quickly onto his head as if trapping a mouse beneath it. 'Now, ladies, I expect Felicity won't be staying long, so perhaps you could excuse us.'

The two women took an age pulling on their cardigans

and gathering up their things – Flick had cleared crime scenes more quickly – and clung to each other as they made the treacherous journey inside.

'My harem.' Harry laughed, as Flick took in the view of the landscaped garden and new-build bungalows on either side. 'Don't pay no mind. At their age, they get the wrong end of the stick. You're still with that Alex, of course.'

'We broke up,' said Flick. Years ago, as he well knew.

'Play the field while you can, girl, but remember the clock's ticking. You don't want to end up on your own.'

'I'm not here to talk about that,' she said quickly. 'When you were based at Hackney nick in the eighties there was a children's home.' She took out her notebook and pen. 'Run by a man called Gordon . . .'

'Tallis.' Harry sipped from a mug. 'That's a name that takes me back.'

'What can you tell me about him?'

'He was a squalid little man who ran a squalid little home on a squalid little street. It would have been closed down in a heartbeat these days. The whole area was bulldozed and redeveloped a long time ago. It's all swanky apartments now, and vegan restaurants.'

'He was abusive?'

'Not only that, but he used the kids to shift heroin around North London.'

'How do you know that?'

'Everyone knew. Well, certain people did.' Harry took off the hat to pat his hair, tipped it back in place. 'You hate me because I've never lived up to standards you consider acceptable, but you have to remember it was a different world back then. Yes, I was on the take, but I wasn't the only one.

266

Tallis paid money to keep certain officers off his back. I was the conduit, the channel, if you will. He delivered cash to me and I distributed it to cops, councillors and numerous petty officials, who would turn a blind eye to his using the home to move drugs. A clever little operation, nobody would suspect a children's home, not back then. A vulnerable young woman called Sally Raynor came to make the payment. She was upper class but preferred the gutter, and you couldn't get more lowlife than Gordon Tallis. Nice girl but a mess, an addict. She disappeared off the face of the earth.'

'You think Tallis had something to do with it.'

'He was a combustible chap.' He drilled a finger into his temple. 'Not right upstairs. A creepy fellow with a smile that made your skin crawl.'

'And he died in a fire at the home.'

'The Longacre burned to the ground, with him inside. Not a great loss to society. I imagine the kids did a jig for joy.'

'Was it started on purpose?'

'Word is, Gordon's friends in the drugs business were becoming very unhappy with the way he was running things. When his body was found inside it was handcuffed to a radiator.'

Flick sat bolt upright. 'Handcuffed?'

'Yeah.' Harry winced. 'My handcuffs, as it happens.' When she stared, he said, 'Don't look at me like that, they were stolen.'

'By whom?' asked Flick.

'By a nasty little shit called Connor Laird.'

Flick felt the blood accelerate around her veins. Inside, the baritone threw his hands up at the climax to the song, and his audience clapped.

'Connor Laird. Do you know what became of him?'

'Oh, yeah.' Harry smiled at her eager question. 'He also burned to death in that fire.'

Inside, the backing track on the opera singer's CD player changed, and the singer's baritone soared over the first notes of 'Nessun Dorma'.

'What a racket.' Harry shook his head. 'We have to listen to that every week. It's terrible what they do to pensioners. Take my advice, Felicity, don't get old.' He sighed at his daughter's obvious impatience. 'Look, we didn't have the fancy forensics you people rely on these days. An unidentified body was found next to Tallis, and Connor Laird was the only kid not to come out of that home. All the others, every single one of them, were accounted for.'

'You're absolutely sure it was him?'

'As sure as we could be.'

'But how do you *know*?'

'Because,' said Harry patiently, 'Tallis and Connor had got into some kind of conflict that escalated out of control, and it looks like he took the kid with him.'

'And this fire, these deaths, were never investigated; why?'

'There would be a few coppers, my love, with prosperous retirements to look forward to, who would have to answer some very difficult questions if their relationship with Gordon Tallis was put under a microscope. There was no paperwork connected to Connor, no birth certificate, no family or dependents. He came out of nowhere and he died.' He tugged at the pouch of skin beneath his jaw. 'And nobody cared, because it was in a lot of people's interests, mine included, that they didn't.'

'And what if he wasn't dead?'

268

'He's dead.'

'Hypothetically, what would become of him?'

He thought about it. 'Connor Laird was a bad seed. I met him once, I looked into his eyes and they were – what's the word? – *feral*. He was full of contempt for the world, and everyone in it. Nothing good would come of him. If he grew up . . . well, woe betide anybody who got in his way.' Harry narrowed his eyes. 'I remember the fire occurred just after that judge and his wife visited the place.'

Flick gripped her pen. 'Leonard Drake?'

'That was him. One of our detectives went to his house for a statement and the old boy told him in no uncertain terms to sling his hook.'

'I've got to go.'

'Already?' asked Harry. 'Got what you wanted and now you're going?'

'Yes.'

'Listen to that.' Harry smiled at the baritone, whose hands were clasped to his chest as he serenaded an old couple on a sofa. 'He's singing something slow and sad and lonesome. Must be for us, Felicity.'

So Nina had already told him she was going to Australia.

'I'm too old for all this nonsense,' he said. 'I don't want to go on fighting this war, can't we call a truce? It makes me sad that Nina can find it in her heart to forgive and you can't.'

'I'm going.'

'I'm holding out an olive branch here,' he said, exasperated.

'You couldn't even be bothered to see mum.' Flick threw the notebook and pen in her bag. 'I asked and asked, but you didn't go. You took no interest in us,' Flick said bitterly, 'in me or Nina or Daniel.'

'Look,' Harry said softly, 'the affairs, leaving your mum, not taking an interest when she was ill, and, of course, my misadventures in uniform – I've never lived up to your lofty standards and never will. But let's be honest. What you really hate me for is the one thing that I could do nothing about. Dan.'

'That's not true,' she said, and her phone went off in her bag. By the time she snatched it up, it had rung off.

'Well, let me tell you something.' His expression darkened. 'He was your brother, but he was my *son*, my only son, and you will never know what it's like to lose a child. To spend every day wondering whether he's out there somewhere or buried in a shallow grave.'

'I'm not listening to this.'

It had always been like this between them, they couldn't spend more than twenty minutes in each other's company without the usual resentments rising to the surface.

'Nina, who is a loving and caring person, has always known how much his disappearance hit me, *here*.' Harry thumped his chest. 'So don't for one second believe you've got a monopoly in suffering. And I'll tell you something else: she deserves a life away from me and from *you*.'

Flick flinched. 'That's not true, she loves—'

'Me and you, we're parasites, Felicity.' He always knew how to play on her anxieties. 'And as far as I'm concerned, she and that family of hers deserve every happiness.' Harry looked at the residents and staff enraptured by the singer's performance. 'And one last thing, Flick—'

'Don't call me that.'

'When you get all twisted up about how much you dislike me, just remember, I got people around me night and day. I sometimes have to go and sit in my room to get away from the hectic social whirl. So, yeah, I'll regret not seeing you if that's the way it has to be, but I will never be lonely. Can you honestly say the same?'

Right at that moment, the singer reached the big climax of 'Nessun Dorma', and there was a smattering of applause. He bowed low and moved around the room giving out roses. The patio doors opened and a female staff member stood at the door. 'Everything okay, Harry?'

'Grand, love.' A big smile lit up his face. 'Got a visitor.'

Flick waited for him to say, *my daughter*. But he didn't.

'You missed the performance,' said the woman.

'I'll catch it next week, or maybe the week after that.' He winked. 'I'm just coming in now.'

When the woman left, Harry sidled up to his daughter. 'Pop in again if you're in the neighbourhood. Make it a longer visit next time.'

Before he'd taken two steps inside he was grinning and laughing, the life and soul, surrounded by a group of residents. Flick was wondering if there was another way she could get to reception when her phone rang again.

37

Ray Drake rubbed his eyes wearily. 'You're being unreasonable.'

Myra perched on the edge of a frayed and tatty sofa that had been in the house since before she was born. When Laura refurbished, Myra insisted it stayed. It was good for her spine, she said, but everyone knew she was just being bloody-minded. She folded the *Telegraph* she had been reading and dropped it beside her.

'Remind me again why I should leave my home?'

'The matter we spoke about the other night.'

'The killings,' she said. 'Children from *that* place.'

'We're looking into it, but—'

'I trust you are.' She watched him pace restlessly over the top of her reading glasses. 'That policewoman came to see me today.'

Drake stopped dead. 'Flick Crowley.'

'You invited her to the funeral, I recall, although goodness knows how it was any of her business.'

Flick was proving stubborn in her determination to look into the Longacre. He'd speak to Harris about getting her removed from the investigation, but knew that if Amelia Troy had already contacted her, his life would spiral out of control very quickly.

'What did she say?'

272

'She asked me about the home. I sent her away with a flea in her ear. My advice to you, Raymond, is to sack her immediately.'

'You haven't answered me. Will you go away, just for a short while? I'm not going to be able to be here all the time.'

Myra took off the glasses. 'And what does that matter to me?'

She was forcing him to say it out loud. 'You may be in danger, Myra.'

The old woman rubbed the scuffed metal of the oval locket around her neck. 'But where would I go?'

'Out of town,' he said. 'To family. Take a holiday.'

'I'm eighty-seven years old. A holiday would finish me off.'

'There must be people you can . . .' He racked his brains, annoyed that he still knew so little about this infuriating and intensely private woman. Many years ago, after what happened at the home, she'd cut herself off from family – or, at least, the few family members she had been on speaking terms with. Most of those had, presumably, died of old age.

'I'll take my chances here.'

'I'd rather you—'

'Stop. You're talking to me now, Raymond, not some idiot colleague.' When she heaved herself from the sofa, Drake went to help but she waved him off. 'Is that why you look like you've been dragged through a bush backwards? Did someone attack you?'

'It's just . . . a precaution.'

'Now you listen to me. When Leonard and I became involved with the fallout from that damned home, we understood the consequences of what we were doing. I'm not

273

going to leave everything behind because some pipsqueak is threatening me.'

She'd never given an inch. Never compromised, never backed down.

'He's killed many times, Myra. He's dangerous.'

'And I have great faith in your ability to stop him.'

'At least let me get someone to stay with you.' It wouldn't be impossible to hire some discreet muscle. He knew people who could ensure her safety. 'Just until I can sort out this problem.'

'I will not have strangers in my home.'

'He's coming for me and he'll come for you, too.'

'And how do you know that?'

'Because he told me,' he snapped. 'I'm begging you, be reasonable.'

'I didn't bring you up to be the kind of man to beg,' she hissed.

She touched the edges of her hair. Once upon a time it was a fierce helmet, a towering Thatcheresque construction. Now there were large patches where Drake could see her scalp, plastered with scurf.

'My grandparents lived in this house,' she said quietly. 'I've lived here all my life, and I hope you will remain here when I am gone, even though I know you've been unhappy here lately.' That, he knew, was the nearest she'd get to mentioning Laura. 'I will not run away, it is simply not in my nature.'

He nodded at the locket. 'May I see?'

After a moment's consideration, she said: 'If you wish.'

She lifted the wisps of fine hair drifting down the back of her neck and Drake stepped behind her to undo the tiny

274

clasp. Myra opened the locket. Inside was a small photograph, its edges clipped in a rough hexagonal. He'd never seen it before and she'd never offered to show it. Her crooked finger trembled over the photo, as if she were afraid to touch it, afraid the image would fade beneath her touch.

'I've never thanked you,' he said. 'For everything you've done for me.'

A look that he'd never seen before, the faintest suggestion of vulnerability, passed across Myra's face, and she turned away.

'You were not the easiest boy, but Leonard was very fond of you. He may not have shown it, but be sure of it. And I have . . . loved you, I hope, in my own way.' She snapped the locket shut and her voice hardened. 'The most important thing now is that you protect your daughter. April needs you, even if the selfish child doesn't realise it. She must be your only responsibility.'

'All my life,' he bit down on his annoyance, 'I've done what you said.'

Her mouth twitched in distaste. 'You're embarrassing yourself, Raymond.'

'And now I want you to do as I tell you.'

'This is my—'

'You'll do as I say!'

She considered him, coldly.

'There's a nephew,' she said finally. 'He lives in Kent. I shall telephone to inform him he shall have the pleasure of my company for a few days. I can only imagine his surprise. Does that suit?' Drake nodded, but a part of him wasn't convinced of her intentions. 'In the meantime, I've something that you may find useful.'

She went to a drawer and took out a folded piece of cloth, carefully unwrapped the fabric . . .

To reveal a small handgun.

He stepped forward. 'Where on earth did you get that?'

'We've had it many years. Leonard brought it back from the war.'

Drake removed the magazine from the grip, which was full. Snapped it back in.

'It's a Beretta, I believe,' said Myra, watching him weigh the pistol in his hand. 'It should work; he took very good care of it. I hope for your sake it does.'

'Myra, you're a marvel.' He shook his head in amazement. 'Why didn't you tell me about this before?'

'It would not have been very wise to let you play with such an object when you were younger.' She fixed her gaze on his. 'Do what you have to do, Raymond, so that we can get back to normal.'

38

Perry drove two wheels onto the verge and cranked the handbrake. A necklace of light moved across the darkness at the top of the field opposite, traffic snaking along the M11.

He reached across to the glove compartment, digging his elbow into Elliot's ribs, to take out two balaclavas and then something that made Elliot nearly shit himself with fear.

'Why the hell did you bring a gun?' Ignoring him, Perry slapped the dash shut and palmed the weapon, a squat, ugly thing, into his pocket. 'I asked why—'

'What does it matter?' Perry swung round, nostrils flaring. He had barely spoken on the way, not that Elliot was clamouring for conversation, but his surly silence had frayed Elliot's nerves.

'What does it *matter*?' Elliot tried to keep the rising panic from his voice. 'You said nobody would be here, you said they were on holiday!'

'I didn't say anything like that,' Perry sneered. 'If Owen wants to spin you a line it's his call. And, anyway, it's just two old people; try not to wet your knickers.'

'I'm not coming in.' Breaking and entering, burglary, that was bad enough, but this was a home invasion, aggravated assault with a deadly weapon, and Elliot wasn't going to cross that line. That's not the kind of man he was. Not now, not ever.

'You're coming in,' insisted Perry, pulling the balaclava over his head, 'or Owen will have something to say about it.'

No way, no fucking way was Elliot going inside. He spoke very slowly, so there was no misunderstanding him: 'You're on your own.'

Perry leaned in close to intimidate, his eyes small, hard pellets inside the black fabric of the balaclava. 'Fine, you can drive. Just make sure you're ready as soon as I come out.' He snatched a rucksack from the back seat and winked. 'Back in a mo.'

Elliot watched anxiously as Perry walked up the lane towards the big house, half hidden by swaying pampas grass, at the top of a long, curving drive. No good was going to come of this, he knew that much. When Owen found out Elliot had refused go in with Perry he would withhold the money. Elliot hadn't held up his end of the bargain, he'd say, hadn't played his part. Elliot would be back to square one. He'd promised Rhonda he would get the money. They needed it to get away.

On top of that, Perry's body language, the casual way he sauntered up the drive, told him everything he needed to know about what was going to happen inside.

Minutes later, Elliot thought he heard a scream.

He slammed his hand on the dashboard – this couldn't be happening! – and yanked the balaclava over his head. The wool pricked his scalp. He could barely breathe.

Elliot ran up the drive, the front of the house jumping in his eyeholes, and saw the front door was ajar. There wasn't another home in sight, but – he heard raised voices, a moan – it was stupid to take such a chance. In the hallway he rushed towards the sitting room, but getting the angles wrong inside the mask, he ill-judged the turn, cracking his shoulder on the doorframe.

An elderly man in a cardigan cringed in a chair. Seen through the narrow eyeholes of Elliot's balaclava, the room swerving all over the place, the man looked as if he was clinging to the armrests as the chair was swept about on a turbulent sea.

'No!' pleaded the man. 'My wife!'

Elliot's heart leapt into his mouth when he saw Perry standing over an old woman. The scene swung up and down, visible only in fragments. The woman on her knees, arms lifted protectively above her head, long hair spilling from a clip onto a shoulder. Perry, jabbing the weapon, screaming: 'Open it!'

'No,' she moaned. 'I don't know what you're—'

'Open – the – fucking – safe!' Perry grabbed her neck. Pressed her to the floor, stuck the gun at the back of her head.

Elliot turned, fleetingly seeing the old man's pale, rigid face whip past the eyeholes. And when he spun back, sweating beneath the hot, itchy fabric, panic rising in his chest, he couldn't find Perry and the old woman. He could only hear Perry screaming: 'Open it, open it, open—'

And then, from behind Elliot: 'Please! Don't hurt my wife!'

'Open the safe, or I'm going to—'

Eyes flashing with anger, Perry pressed the weapon into the woman's neck. Her moans were lost in the thick carpet. Elliot couldn't see a safe, couldn't see a thing, couldn't breathe, had to do something.

'You! Move it!' Perry jerked the gun towards a cabinet, and Elliot realised that he was screaming at him. He stumbled forward, catching his foot on the tasseled edge of a rug. His chest was about to burst. There wasn't enough air in the room, not enough oxygen in the world, to fill his lungs. He pushed the cabinet along the shagpile to reveal a safe set into the wall.

'We've got a problem here,' said Perry to the old man, who rocked backwards and forwards on the chair, 'because I'm going to need a code, we ain't got a code—'

'Then let's go,' said Elliot urgently.

'We ain't going till we've got the code.' Perry's head snapped up. 'Or these two old farts are dead!'

He wrenched at the woman's shoulder, dragging her head off the floor, the weapon's barrel swinging carelessly in his other hand. 'I'm going to count from five and if that safe isn't open when I get to zero you're going to die.'

The man wept, tears pouring down the hands covering his face, wetting the cuffs of his shirt and glistening on the plain gold wedding band he had worn for thirty, forty, fifty years or more.

'Ain't no time for tears, fella,' snarled Perry, 'just numbers.'

'Perry,' Elliot stepped forward, 'don't.'

Perry's eyes burned with rage at Elliot's use of his name. 'Five!'

'Don't do this!'

'Four!'

The old man pressed his hands together as if in prayer, as Perry traced the gun barrel along his wife's hairline and down her temple, resting it in the hollow of her wet eye socket.

And the woman said something, but Elliot couldn't hear what it was. Burning up, he pulled the balaclava off his head. They could see him now and he didn't care.

'Put it back on!' screamed Perry.

But it was too late, because the old man, white with fear, with dread, looked Elliot full in the face. And Elliot wondered how long they had been married, this couple. A lifetime, judging by the framed photos of kids and grandkids around the room, by the numerous mementoes of a marriage, a union cemented more strongly with every minute, month, decade.

'Three!'

And Elliot, angry now – enraged by the old fool's stubbornness, his willingness to get himself and his wife killed for cash and stupid trinkets that don't mean a thing if you're lucky enough to possess the love and companionship of another person, just one person, to help you through this terrible, shitty life, to pick you up when you fell – surged forward. 'For fuck's sake, tell him! Tell him the code!'

'Two!'

Then the old man squeezed his eyes shut, and his mouth opened and closed – but nothing came out. A mewling sound came from the carpet. Elliot lurched to Perry. 'She's trying to tell us, she's trying to—'

But Perry, insensible with rage, was leaning over the woman. 'You are this close, *this* close, from getting your brains blown out!' And then he straightened his gun arm, execution-style.

Elliot shouted: 'No!'

And the old man tipped forward, slammed face down into the rug, a stuttering moan coming from his mouth, a

281

froth of spittle arcing across his cheek. His arms and legs thrashed, his body was wracked by spasms.

'Please,' wailed the woman. 'He's having a fit.'

Elliot kneeled to take her trembling, anguished face in his hands, looking her in the eyes, almost in tears himself.

'Please,' he whispered desperately, the smell of petrol, of soil, filling his nostrils. 'Tell us and we'll go.'

And she told him – seven eight four nine seven one, seven eight four nine seven one – between juddering sobs, before crawling on her hands and knees to the jerking body of her husband.

And Perry flew to the safe.

39

1984

In the dead of night they carried Sally's body to the bottom of the garden, along the narrow path beneath the copse of trees. Gordon held the front of the rug and Elliot and Connor struggled with the other end. Toby walked behind, snivelling. The moon and stars disappeared as they stumbled with the heavy load beneath the canopy of leaves and reappeared above the wall at the bottom. A petrol canister was propped there, a pair of spades.

Gordon had earlier locked the three boys in the office with the body while he went to fetch the equipment, and to tell the Dents to get the other kids to bed early. Connor, Elliot and Toby couldn't help but stare at the body and the fingers of blood probing every crack in the floorboards. Toby didn't stop weeping. Finally, Elliot gave up telling him to pack it in.

Taking a torch from his pocket, Gordon ran a beam of light along the length of the rolled-up rug. Sally's feet hung limply out the bottom, the chipped varnish on her toes catching the light. He threw the torch down and sat on the rug, slipping off a shoe to rub his foot, emitting little smacking noises of satisfaction.

'You lads are doing me a mighty favour, and I appreciate

it.' Gordon took out a flask. 'The thing is, Sally wanted it both ways. She wanted everything I had, but she wanted me to change, she expected me to be something I'm not. I'm not excusing what I did, but it's the truth. When you boys are older you'll realise that you'll always be stuck with yourself.'

Connor asked: 'What do we do now?'

'You're going to dig a bloody great hole is what you're going to do, against that wall.' He clapped his hands together. 'Come on, chop-chop.'

Connor and Elliot dug at the dry earth, which crumbled easily beneath the spades. They worked in silence as Gordon sat and watched, drinking steadily.

'You boys have been good friends to me. You don't know how difficult it can be, the burden I carry.' His fingers absently stroked the rug. 'I loved that girl, but she had a mouth on her. I'm a patient man, but she pushed me too far.'

Below the topsoil the ground was damp, and they lifted great chunks of it. Elliot tore ferociously into the earth. His shoulders ached as he dug the spade into the earth. Lifted a clump of mud, dropped it onto the pile. Dug the spade into the earth, lifted the soil, placed it on the heap.

'I won't forget this.' Planting his legs apart, Gordon lowered his head into his hands. 'This is a special moment, so it is. We're bonding, the four of us, because we're in this together now, for all time. You're my late-night buddies,' he glanced at his watch, 'you're my Two O'Clock Boys. That's what we are, we're pals for life, the Two O'Clock Boys.'

Then Elliot became lost in robot labour – digging the spade into the earth and tipping it to the side, the smell of soil filling his nostrils – and it was a while before he realised Connor had stopped digging, and was listening to Gordon's snores.

'Come on, let's get this done.'

There was a cold gleam in Connor's eye that Elliot understood immediately. 'We'll do it now, while he's asleep, and then we'll go.'

'You can't!' said Elliot.

'We do it now.'

'What about the kid?' Elliot stammered. 'He'll tell his parents and then what?'

But Connor climbed from the hole and stood over Gordon.

'Connor!' Elliot lunged forward. 'You can't just—'

'Shut up!' Connor hefted the spade, turned it in his hands so that the dull metal edge would cleave Gordon's skull into two. 'We'll never have a better time.'

'You can't!'

Elliot grabbed at him, but Connor pushed him off. Gordon's chest heaved with each guttural snore. Connor lifted the spade above his head, his arms shaking violently, damp palms slick on the wooden shaft.

And he still hadn't swung it down when Gordon's head snapped up to leer at Connor and the spade trembling above his head.

'Finally, let's see what you're made of,' he said quietly. 'I believed you had it in you to go the whole way, lad, but you're just like those others. Weak, like Elliot. A victim, like our friend Toby. I thought I saw something in those cold eyes of yours, Connor; I really thought you would be different.'

Gordon lifted himself from the rug, taking a moment to

brush down his trousers before taking the spade from Connor. 'You want to see how it's done again, do you, boy? Let me show you.'

He walked to Toby and threw him into the trench, then picked up the canister to slop petrol all over the boy. The stench of the liquid lifted into the air, making Elliot's eyes sting. He stumbled back, blinking. Toby screamed, scrabbling around on the mud like the cockroach on his plate. Gordon poured the petrol until the boy's hair, skin and clothes were drenched.

'Watch me.' Gordon pulled a lighter from his pocket, flicking open the lid to spark the flint. A long, flickering flame whipped in the night air. '*This* is how to do it.'

'Don't,' said Connor.

Toby screeched. Elliot shook violently. Connor stepped forward. 'He's got family, Gordon, people who love him and who are waiting for him!'

Gordon swayed above the trench. A shelf of mud gave way beneath his feet and he almost toppled forward. There was a deafening rush of noise and a mail train hurtled past a few feet away, shaking the trees. Elliot saw, but couldn't hear, Toby's frenzied shriek. The flame danced violently in Gordon's hand.

'He can't go home, Connor,' said Gordon, when it had passed. 'Not now.'

'Yeah,' said Connor quickly. 'You're right, but we'll talk about it tomorrow, when you're . . . when you've got a clear head.'

Elliot heard the bones in Gordon's neck crack. Then the lid of the lighter snapped shut, and he threw it at Connor. When the boy caught it, it was hot to the touch.

'Get him out of there.' Gordon stared at Sally's body.

286

'Burn her and then fill in the hole. Cover it with leaves and branches. When I come back tomorrow, I don't want to be able to see it. I'll make sure the kids stay out of the garden for a few days.'

Then he stumbled back through the trees to the house, and Elliot scrambled into the hole to pull Toby out. 'Get back to the house and wash, and stop crying.'

'Leave your clothes,' said Connor.

The boy undressed, shivering with cold and fear. They threw his clothes into the trench and Toby went whimpering up the path. Elliot and Connor dragged the rug containing Sally's body into the hole, splashed petrol onto it and set it alight.

Smoke and sparks lifted into the air between them. Connor pulled his T-shirt over his nose against the smell of burning flesh.

'You gonna have a family, Connor?' asked Elliot, as they slumped against the wall listening to the crack and fizz of the fire. Entranced by the flames leaping off the rug, Connor didn't answer.

'I'm gonna have a wife,' continued Elliot. 'And loads of kids. I'll bring them up right; they ain't ever gonna be afraid of nothing. I'll be a dad, a proper dad . . .' He threw a stick into the flames. 'Just got to get out of this place first.'

Neither of them spoke for the rest of the night. They dozed. By the time the sky began to swell, and the stars faded in the sky, the flames had dwindled. They shovelled mud back into the trench, smothering the last embers, avoided looking at the smouldering corpse. When the hole was filled, they covered the fresh soil with leaves, branches and large stones as best they could.

At dawn, shouts drifted down from the house – the other kids were awake – and Gordon came along the garden with a bucket of hot water so they could wash. He stared at the disturbed earth, made the sign of the cross on his chest, and left without saying a word.

Exhausted, the two boys walked up the path beneath the trees towards the house, in the cloudy grey wash of the morning.

40

They accelerated up the narrow lane, flew along it, headlight beams carving out the way beneath the thick canopy of trees. Too fast along a road barely wide enough for a single vehicle.

Elliot braced himself against the dash as Perry wrestled with the tight turns, wanting to be as far away from the house as quickly as possible. He felt sickened. This wasn't who he was. How could he have been so stupid? Now he could never look Rhonda or Dylan in the face again.

But he didn't want to die, and they were taking the bends too fast, the wheels shuddering off the green verges, Perry barely paying attention to the road as he screamed at Elliot.

'They saw you! You used my name!' His face was scrunched tight with anger, the cords in his neck snapped taut. Flecks of his spittle spotted Elliot's cheek. 'She saw your face! You said my name! You said my—'

He gunned the engine harder, and the car swerved. The sharp fingers of an overhanging tree tore at the roof. Elliot, filled with terror, shouted: 'Watch the road, watch the—'

And on a bend he had a split second – no more than that – to register a vehicle coming the other way. 'Car! Car!'

Perry swore, jerking the wheel to the left, the angry blare of a horn bearing down on them, and the car careened up the verge. Elliot was thrown against Perry's shoulder as the passenger side lifted. Perry's hands clenched the wheel, wrestled to regain control as it jerked left and right and left. Foot scrabbling frantically for the brake pedal, finding the accelerator instead.

The engine moaned. Shrubs and bushes hurtled towards them, sticks and branches cracked against the windscreen, obscuring their view as the car plunged over the verge and into the undergrowth. Perry found the brake – and pressed hard.

Both men were propelled forward. Elliot's head flew into the dash. His neck whiplashed. Perry's chest smashed against the wheel.

The car spun on the soft earth and careened to a halt.

Elliot stared into the gloom, through the mess of leaves and twigs heaped across the windscreen, a swirl of shapes and colours dancing in his eyes. Stunned, unsure of where he was, or even for a few short moments, who he was. Perry moaned. When Elliot turned his head, an electric jolt of pain crackled down his neck. He pressed his weight against the door, fumbling for the release, and tipped onto the damp, muddy earth. He stood, hands propped on his knees. A wall of trees hemmed them in on the slope, it was a miracle the car hadn't smashed into any of the ancient trunks. Elliot, not wearing his seat belt, would have gone through the windscreen. Would be dead, for sure.

'We . . . got . . . back.' A voice behind him.

Tremors of shock vibrated up his spine when Elliot stood. 'What?'

'We got to go back.' Perry slumped against the car.

'Why?' Elliot wanted to laugh at the insanity of the suggestion.

'Because . . .' Perry clutched his chest, grimacing. 'They saw your face and you used my name.'

He had taken a knock to the head. That was the only explanation.

'The police will be there.' Elliot felt his anger swell. He'd taken part in an armed robbery, and there was nobody to blame but himself. Rhonda was never going to forgive him – he could barely believe it himself. He thought of the old man wrenching on the carpet, flapping like a fish on dry land, his wife kneeling beside him, pleading in his ear. *It'll be okay, it's all going to be okay.* Just thinking of her husband despite the terror she must have felt, as Perry slid the contents of the safe, money and valuables, into the rucksack.

'They saw your face, you said my name.' Perry's voice dripped with contempt. 'They can identify us.'

'The house will be crawling with police.' Elliot couldn't believe what he was hearing. If he was going to go back, it would be to return the money and fall on the mercy of the cops. Not to, not to—

'We're in the shit if we don't.' Perry pressed the heel of his hand against his bleeding forehead.

'You were going to kill her!'

'Didn't, though, did I?' Perry took the gun from his pocket. 'But it ain't too late. We've no choice now.'

'I'm not going back.' Elliot reeled forward on the uneven ground, twigs snapping beneath his feet. 'And you ain't either!'

'This is all because of you.' Perry lifted the gun to Elliot's head. 'Perhaps I should shoot you.'

'You were going to kill her,' repeated Elliot. Blood gushed in his head, like rapids through a rock fissure, a deafening roar in his ears. When he turned his neck, his nerves shrieked.

'Get in the car.'

'Let's just get home.' Elliot clapped his hands down his sides.

Rhonda would tell him the right thing to do. He didn't know any more, he couldn't be trusted. 'I just want to go home!'

'Get in the car, or I'll do you here,' snapped Perry.

Elliot laughed bitterly. 'Then you'll just have to do it.'

Hesitation rippled down Perry's face, then he squeezed the trigger.

And Elliot flinched.

They stood there for a moment, both of them wondering why nothing had happened, and then Perry fumbled with the safety catch on the weapon. And Elliot realised that he had to do something, or in a few, short seconds he'd be dead. Perry was going to shoot him and his body would rot here in the middle of the woods.

So he ran forward, his pumping legs creating a chain reaction of screaming muscle, and went in low. Head down, charging like a rhino, piling into Perry's chest. Pain exploded inside his head, whipping like naked electric cables down his body as Perry smashed the butt of the gun on his shoulder.

And they went down, rolling along the ground, leaves and clumps of mud spinning off them as they scrabbled at each other's arms and legs, trying to get a grip, trying to get the upper hand. Elliot felt the gun fly from Perry's fingers, and a fist swipe across his cheek. But Elliot was bigger and heavier than Perry. Rolling onto him, he spread his weight and pinned him to the floor. Struggling, Perry's mouth twisted in a rictus of impotent rage.

Elliot lifted his fist—

Saw the old woman crawling along the floor towards her husband, her face contorted by anguish.

And drove it down into Perry's face. Lifted it high again—

And saw Dylan popping a mint onto his tongue, felt

Rhonda's head against his chest, her hair tangled in his thick fingers.

Smashed the fist down into Perry's face – blood exploded from his nose, but Elliot didn't care – raised his fist high—

He knew he would lose her, because he had let everybody down, because he hadn't changed, not really. He was just the same man, the same pathetic Elliot, and always would be.

The fist came down.

He would never change. He would lose her, and he would lose Dylan, and he would be alone, because his old man was right, he was nothing, he was shit, he was scum. Tallis was right, he deserved nothing from this life. He had watched Sally Raynor die, had burned her corpse in an unmarked grave, and she was lost long ago, and he deserved nothing, not happiness, not peace and not love.

She'll know the kind of man you are.

A bully, a thief, a lowlife.

Screaming with fury, he smashed his fist down into Perry's face again and again. But Perry was gone and instead it was Gordon beneath him, who laughed and laughed in his face.

They were better off without him. Because no matter how hard he tried he could never change, when all he wanted was a quiet life with the woman he loved and her boy – *his* boy, *his* family.

And Elliot drove his fist into Gordon again and again and again, his nostrils filled with the stench of soil and petrol and burning flesh, until he could barely see who it was, the face was so covered with blood and mud and mucus and phlegm.

He lifted his fist one final time high above his head—

Bully, bully, bully.

And it trembled there, because he saw Gordon was gone. Instead Perry's head slumped to the side, eyes slits in his bloody, swollen cheeks. With a growing sense of horror, Elliot realised that Perry wasn't moving. He lowered his fist. Slumped against the man's chest, and sobbed.

I've killed him, he thought.

Elliot rolled off Perry's body onto the cold ground. Birdsong trilled as he stared up at the trees swaying high above, leaves spinning down towards him. After a moment he stood, cleared the mulch and mud off him as best he could. There was no going back from this, no leading a normal life, no playing happy families.

I've killed him.

A vehicle blipped past on the road, only yards away.

Elliot staggered to the car and popped the boot. He grabbed Perry's ankles and dragged him to the rear of the vehicle, twigs and berries and leaves gathering in the dead man's armpits. Pain lashing down his neck, Elliot wrapped his arms around Perry's chest and tipped him into the boot. Slammed it shut.

The faint sound of a siren on the wind made him freeze. Then he picked up the gun, muddy and slippery, and stuffed it into the rucksack, which he pulled from behind the front seat of the car. Hefted it over his shoulder, ignoring the shooting pains, and set off through the woods.

The voice of the Two O'Clock Boy – the only man in the world who knew that Elliot could never change – going round and round in his head.

She'll know the kind of man you are.

41

If Drake knew what she was doing, he'd go ballistic. Doorstepping the old woman was one thing; secretly pressing his beloved daughter for information was taking Flick's betrayal to a whole new level. But there was something Drake wasn't telling her, something that involved him and Myra and that home, and it was important enough to make him steal evidence. While she was still clinging to the investigation by her fingertips, she was determined to discover what it was.

And besides, she was only fulfilling a promise she'd made to the girl. At Laura's funeral Flick had told April that she would be a shoulder to cry on any time she wanted – she remembered Ray Drake had been grateful for the offer. Now she was making good on her word. When Flick had returned her call, still shaken from her meeting with Harry, April had sounded upset – she didn't know who to talk to, she said – and they arranged to meet immediately.

When she arrived at the Pret in Camden Town, grateful to peel away from the army of tourists marching towards the Lock, April was already there, looking very pretty and very miserable in an expensive cashmere coat, and clutching in her lap the kind of bag Flick could only dream of affording. All this designer stuff, she presumed, a perk of being with that City boy of hers.

Flick leaned in for an awkward hug, feeling the treachery lift off her like vapour, and asked April if she wanted coffee. The girl shook her head. Flick bought them both sparkling water.

'I hear you've moved out,' she said, cracking the cap on her bottle.

The girl mumbled. 'Yes, to Jordan's.'

'You know I'm a detective sergeant now?'

'How's it going?'

'Let's just say it's a learning curve.' Flick smiled. 'Your dad is worried about you.'

'I'm sure he is.'

'You don't sound like you believe it.'

'He probably is in his own way but . . .' April shrugged. 'Well, everyone thinks they know him, but they don't.'

'I'm not going to go running back to him; this is strictly between you and me.'

'He's so controlling, suffocating. Secretive, you know?'

Flick took a casual sip of water. 'In what way?'

'He came to Jordan's apartment and he keeps calling and calling. It's like he won't let me have my own life.'

Controlling, suffocating. That didn't sound like the Ray Drake she knew, but then the memory of him in the Property Room popped into her head. Taking that photo, stealing evidence.

'Has he hit you or . . . hurt you in any way?'

'Hit me?' April looked shocked. 'Of course he hasn't!'

'I'm sorry.' Flick held up her hands. 'I was just trying to—'

'He's just not an easy man to know, he keeps everything . . . in.'

'A lot of men do.'

'Sometimes I think he's going to, I don't know . . . explode. He went off the rails when he was younger; I bet you didn't know that.'

'Oh?'

'Gran took him out of school.'

'Why?'

'I don't know, something happened, raging teenage hormones. I asked Gran about it and she said he was challenging, whatever that means. Getting Gran to talk about anything is *challenging*.'

'Your father sounds like a chip off the old block.'

'You can say that again. I think he's turning into Gran. She scares the shit out of me sometimes.' April laughed, but there was no humour in it. 'That's not right, is it, being scared of your own gran?'

'It's probably not as unusual as you think.'

'She's the coldest person you ever met. He's turning into her and maybe one day I'll turn into him, and on it goes . . .' Tears bulged in the girl's eyes, and Flick went to the counter to get a napkin. The girl wept quietly for a minute, turning her engagement ring on her finger. 'Jordan hates him – and now he hates me.'

'Is that why you wanted to see me, April?'

The girl dabbed at her eyes. 'He asked me to move in, but now he says he's never loved me, never wanted to be with me. He told me to get out.'

Flick squeezed April's hand, which tightened around the soggy balled napkin. 'Why don't you go home? Your dad just wants you back.'

April shook her head. 'I can't!'

'Why not?'

She took a deep, shuddering breath. 'Because I've been awful to him.'

'He doesn't care about that. He just wants you to be happy. Your mum's death knocked you both for six, and you're finding it difficult to talk. You're both hurting, both grieving, and you need each other. Whatever you do, don't . . .' She felt her chest tighten. 'Don't fall out with your dad.'

'I don't understand it. When Mum was still . . . Jordan loved me. He was there for me. I love him.'

'Is he at home now?' asked Flick.

'He's at work. He'll be home later . . . maybe. He usually goes out after work, to pubs and clubs – who knows where else? – and gets in at all hours.' She met Flick's eyes, reproachfully. 'Or not at all.'

'You're welcome to stay with me.'

'I've a friend I can go to.'

'Give your friend a call; tell them you're coming over.'

'I don't have any clothes with me.'

'That can wait till tomorrow. Let Jordan calm down, let him consider his actions. Call me if you want me to go and pick up anything. And if you want me to speak to your father . . .'

'I'll call him later.' April pushed the unopened water bottle away. 'I promise.'

Taking the cue, Flick said: 'I'd better go.'

Outside on the street, Flick stuck out her arm and a cab immediately pulled up beside them. She crouched at the window, while the driver was leaned away straightening the side mirror.

'Docklands, please, the lady will give you the address.'

Flick and April shared a long hug. The girl clung to her

tightly, reluctant to let go, and Flick was grateful for the physical contact. Then April climbed into the back of the cab. When it drove off, Flick answered a call from Eddie Upson's mobile.

'Eddie.' She heard the chatter of the Incident Room. 'What news?'

'I've been told to tell you to get back here,' he said. She sensed the anxiety in his voice and dread detonated in her gut. 'You're off the case.'

42

The road rushed towards him with a dizzy clarity. A time was coming soon when this life would be over and he could sleep, the boy sensed that very clearly. Good riddance to it, he was sick of it.

Glancing in the mirror at the girl speaking into her phone, he considered that it was at times like this when he felt most alive. All he'd ever wanted was to punish those people who had allowed the sickness to fester inside him, who had let him become – it wasn't too strong a word – a monster. When he was finally released from his life's work, when he had meted out justice to the guilty, he would step gratefully into oblivion.

His foot squeezed the accelerator of the stolen cab. He felt a quickening in his pulse. He would be at peace, reunited with his own family at last. Then, perhaps, he would know happiness. If not, if no one waited for him on the other side, as he suspected, he would at least know the comfort of the void.

When the girl finished her call, he took off his baseball cap, his appearance meant nothing to her so there was little point in wearing it, and ran a hand over his scalp.

He caught her eye in the mirror. 'You look sad.'

She smiled faintly, absorbed in her own thoughts. 'Family worries.'

'Oh, I know all about those,' he said, not without sympathy. Her phone lay on the seat beside her, he saw.

In years gone by, he had told himself that once his work was done, the rest of his days could be lived happily enough. But he realised long ago that there would be no happiness in this world for him. His adult life had consisted of three drives: to eat, to sleep and to kill, and he derived little pleasure from any of them.

The boy ate healthily because he had to keep physically and mentally able. His life was busy and demanding – with every new persona he was obliged to alter his body shape, which required a strict fitness and diet regime. His sleep was fitful because that was where his dreams and nightmares merged. Every night his sins soaked more heavily into his soul, like water into a sponge.

His mind only made room for the information that would allow him to complete his life's work. Years of study gave him a multitude of professional qualifications, the mastery of a skill or command of a new identity. Money, possessions, held no appeal. The exception was the small collection of mementoes he'd taken from his victims, every new trophy a reminder that he was a step closer to his own release. They sat on the top of the fridge in his rented house.

There was the tobacco tin he had taken only this morning from the flat of Deborah Willetts before he torched her. Beside it was the horseshoe he'd picked up when working as an animal feed salesman visiting the Australian stud farm where David Horner lived. Propped behind that was a torn coaster from the pub where he'd befriended Jason Burgess. Then there was a bicycle pump he'd borrowed from Ricky Hancock when he'd been his sponsor in Alcoholics Anonymous. And the china

301

figurine he'd slipped in his pocket before he gutted Kenny Overton's wife.

As Gavin, he'd stolen an air freshener shaped like a pine tree from Elliot Juniper's van. As well as all that money, which he passed on to third parties in pursuit of Juniper's ultimate humiliation. Juniper, of course, was unfinished business. The boy wanted him to suffer, wanted to take everything from him, so that in the end he would understand how contemptible he was, and had always been.

There were other objects, so many objects.

But from the policeman, when the time came, he'd take nothing. There was only one thing he required from him.

With his life's work almost complete, the boy would probably never go back to that house, never again touch those trophies, but he didn't care. That place was never a home, it was just one of a succession of temporary addresses where he slept and prepared and planned. He moved from place to place as required, had lived in so many cities as so many people, and soon his long journey would be over.

A car edged out of a junction and he politely gestured for the driver to pull out, *go ahead*.

All those lives he'd lived. All the people he had been. If you put all of his identities in a room together, if such a metaphysical act were possible, you wouldn't believe they were all the same person. They would bicker and take an immediate dislike to each other. He had no real sense of self, not any more, which is why perhaps it was so easy for him to become someone else.

His consciousness was as shattered as the bones of Kenny's brat when he fell to his death. It was always a relief to step into the skin of another person, and another, and then another.

Physically, he'd learned to alter every aspect of his appearance and personality: his gait, the very cadence of his speech. He'd mastered new accents and mannerisms, taken jobs up and down the country and abroad.

Say what you like about the boy, grind his reputation into the dirt, but he'd always been clever.

Years ago, he'd discovered it was easy to ingratiate yourself into other people's lives. Nobody remembered the child he'd been, nobody wanted to remember him or the home. Damaged and unhappy, those people smeared their fear and paranoia onto everybody who came into their orbit, so that it was easy for him insinuate himself into their lives. As a social worker, a well-heeled neighbour or work colleague, a friend in the pub. It was sickening the way they threw themselves at him, leeching comfort, love – and money, always money. He hardly had to do anything. These people, the kids who had let him kill his parents – caused him to stove in their skulls until the head of the hammer was matted in hair, gristle, splinters of bone – circled him like ravenous hyenas, darting in to greedily snatch what they wanted. Their lives were as useless as boneless limbs. When you thought about it, he was doing them a favour, putting them and their dismal kin out of their misery. It wasn't right that they were able to live their lives as if nothing had happened, and he had nothing. They were guilty, every single one of them.

It had been easy for him to find the people from the Longacre. They left a paper trail – of institutions, criminal records, benefit claims – and Amelia Troy lived a life in plain view. The boy looked long and hard, he never gave up, and eventually he found them all, with a single agonising exception.

303

There was only one person who had managed to evade him, and his absence left a massive, angry hole. The boy had come to the conclusion that he was dead – a bitter pill to swallow. And it was only by blind luck, or perhaps it was destiny, that the boy discovered him.

Short weeks after he'd driven Ricky and his family into the river, he'd been sitting in a café vacantly staring at a television. The news was on, a report about the completion of a criminal case. A high-ranking policeman was making a statement outside a court building. News cameras pressed forward, microphones jutted into the scene, flashes exploded.

We are pleased to get a conviction, blah, blah, blah, justice has been done. The policeman's chest puffed out. *The end of a long and difficult investigation, and so on, thanks to Detective Inspector Raymond Drake . . .*

Detective Inspector Drake looked none too pleased about being identified. He stood at the edge of the throng, trying to melt into the background. Physically shrinking from the attention. Mesmerised by that grim expression, the boy felt a surge of joy, a moment of rapture the likes of which he'd never dared to hope to experience.

And then the report ended. The boy tried to organise the euphoric feelings that ricocheted around inside him. There was no TV in the bedsit he lived in at that time, so that night he stood in the sheeting rain to watch a bank of televisions in the window of an electrical retailer. He was petrified that the story would be dropped for the evening bulletin. But there it was again, the same footage: the bustle outside the court, the high-ranking policeman droning on – and the man identified as Ray Drake trying to make himself invisible by the sheer force of his will.

The boy stood outside that shop and wept. He felt complete, even as his tears of happiness, tears of powerful rage, were washed away in the deluge.

Take my hand. Take it.

You're alive.

You can go home.

If the policeman had let the boy die that day, if he had let the flames consume him, then all those others would be alive. All those men, all those women, all those children.

This, then, was the endgame.

As he shifted up a gear to slip past a green light, he accepted his own imminent death. The Two O'Clock Boy was tired, he didn't want to live. If people believed he had sailed through life without a thought to what he had done, and what he had become, they were sorely mistaken.

He was ready.

'This isn't the way,' said a voice.

Blinking, he remembered the girl in the back – April Drake. She perched forward, reading the street signs. He smiled in the rear-view mirror.

The conclusion was near, and it would be sweet.

43

The call came from April's phone. It barely rang once before Drake snatched it up, expecting to hear her. Instead, the electronic voice said: 'I have your daughter.'

Drake's stomach churned. Phone clamped to his ear, he stumbled against his desk. 'Where is she?'

'Remember what I told you,' said the Two O'Clock Boy, his anger twisting and surging in the synthetic swirl. 'You are to blame.'

'Please, don't hurt her.' His own voice was faint, as if it were coming from the end of a long tunnel.

'I wanted to die. If you had let me go to sleep, those others would still be alive. Say it.'

'I'm to blame,' said Drake. 'I'm guilty. Let me talk to her, just let—'

The line went dead and his mind whirled. The gun Myra had given him was in the boot of his car – if he only knew where to go, how to find April. But when he turned, Flick Crowley was standing in the doorway, hands on her hips.

'Why have I been taken off the investigation?' she asked.

Drake scooped up his car keys. They scraped loudly along the desk in the quiet of his office.

'I don't have time for this,' he said.

But Flick blocked his way. 'I've a right to know.'

'Not now,' he said, stepping forward.

'You can't just—'

'April is gone,' Drake said. 'She's—' He stopped himself saying it, wanted to get out of there and find his daughter.

If *he* had her – *oh God*.

The fear, the anger, made his head swim.

'What are you talking about?'

'Never mind,' he said, but she wouldn't step aside.

'I was with her this afternoon.'

'Where?' Drake grabbed her upper arm.

Flick stared at his hand. 'We met at a café in Camden. Jordan's thrown her out. She needed to talk to someone but was too afraid to contact you; she thought you'd be angry with her.'

'Where?' His mouth was dry. 'Where did she go?'

'To a friend's.' Flick warily absorbed the alarm in his voice. 'I put her in a cab.'

I have your daughter.

He pushed her against the doorframe, fingers pressing into her shoulders. 'Do you know what you've done?'

Flick cringed in shock and disgust, and Drake's head dropped. He closed his eyes to stop the room spinning. April could be anywhere by now. Could be dead by now.

He killed all those others. Men, women, children. Didn't think twice about it.

'Who is Connor Laird?'

Flick's question jolted him back into the room. When he opened his eyes, she was looking straight at him.

'I think he's alive,' she said. 'I think Myra is afraid of him, and I believe you are, too.'

'No.' He wanted to tell her everything, but couldn't. For the first time in his life he had no idea what to do.

307

'Who is Connor Laird?' she repeated.

'The investigation is drifting.' He cleared his throat, tried to sound authoritative. 'Upson told me you led him on a wild goose chase around town. I'm taking over.'

'Who is Connor Laird? Why were you tampering with evidence?'

'I told you to leave Myra alone.'

'Who is Connor Laird?' She kept hammering him with that question. All he heard was that damned name in his head. He couldn't focus, couldn't concentrate. 'Why did you destroy that cutting?'

'You're not—'

'Why did you tear out that photograph?'

He needed to be out of there, looking for April, for his daughter. 'You're not making any progress.' It was all he could think to say. 'We need to get the investigation back on—'

'What was in that photo, Ray? What was in it that you don't want anybody to see?'

'Go home, Flick.'

'Or what?' She didn't look away. 'What will happen?'

Drake didn't have time for this, didn't—

'Who is Connor Laird?'

Drake stared.

'Is he alive?' she barked.

'He's *gone*,' whispered Drake, his fingers digging into her shoulders. 'Long gone.'

'I don't think so,' she said softly. 'He's out there, and he's very dangerous, and I think you know who he is. Tell me.'

'You don't understand . . . the Two O'Clock Boy . . .' Drake needed to find his daughter, had no time to spare, but he was weary – his life was fragmenting, shattering into a thousand pieces – and all the secrets, all the lies . . . it wasn't worth it any more.

He would tell her. 'Connor Laird is—'

'What's going on here?' asked a voice. Peter Holloway stood in the corridor. His gaze dropped to Drake's grip on Flick's shoulders. 'Take your hands off her, please.'

When Drake let go, Flick quickly slipped past Holloway and out of the room. He heard her slam through the fire door along the corridor.

'What on earth is going on?' asked Holloway.

'It's none of your concern.'

Drake moved to go, but Holloway held a hand to his chest. 'On the contrary, it looked to me very much that—'

There was a knock on the door and Holloway turned irritably to see Frank Wanderly, knuckles raised to the wood, a scrap of paper in his other hand.

'Sorry to barge in, gents. I was looking for DS Crowley.'

'Not now,' said Holloway.

'I've been asked to give her a message.'

'She's not here, Frank,' Holloway snapped.

Wanderly blinked, his gaze moving from the CSM to Drake, who pushed roughly past him.

'DI Drake, wait!' Drake swung open the fire door to drop into the stairwell, flew downstairs as fast as he could. But Holloway kept pace behind him. 'Ray! Is there anything I can do? Please stop and talk.'

Drake didn't look back. 'Mind your own business, Peter.'

'I heard how you spoke to DS Crowley, and you can be sure I'll be taking this further.'

At the landing Drake whirled. 'Do what you have to do.'

'You can speak to me, Ray, I'm a friend. And now Laura is gone . . .'

When Holloway attempted to place a hand on his shoulder, Drake jerked away.

'I appreciate your concern, Peter. But there's nothing you can do. My daughter, she . . . I wish I'd taken more care of her.'

'Let's go to the canteen,' Holloway said kindly. 'My shout.'

Drake ran down the rest of the stairs, leaving Holloway behind.

In the car park, he opened the boot and took out a plastic bag containing the gun, slipped it in his pocket. Climbing behind the wheel, he called April's phone again. It rang and rang and rang.

Drake smashed his hands again and again against the dashboard. When a pair of uniforms came through the gate, he fired up the engine and accelerated onto the High Road.

Flick said Jordan had thrown April out. Hours later, she'd been taken. Drake didn't believe in coincidences. Besides, he had a score to settle with the kid.

He drove to the Docklands, hands shaking on the wheel, willing the phone on the passenger seat to ring. The evening traffic was thick. Drake forced himself not to panic, to stay focused, as he edged forward, each slow yard of the commuter snarl pure torture.

44

The first thing she would do when she got home was get it all on paper. Ray Drake in the Property Room; his old mother's connection to the home; the way he pressured Flick to ignore the cuttings. And how he lost control in his office. Holloway had seen everything, so she had a witness – that episode, at least, wasn't a figment of her imagination. She would hand her report to DCI Harris and he could decide what action to take. Whatever happened to her, it was clear to Flick that Drake was losing the plot. He was still grieving for his wife, that much was clear; he was in no fit mental state. He needed to take compassionate leave, seek medical help.

Taking long, calming breaths, trying to get her head on straight, she just wanted to get out of the station as quickly as possible. But slamming through a fire door, her heart sunk when she heard Millie Steiner's voice behind her.

'Ma'am, wait up. Flick!'

Flick composed herself and forced a smile onto her face.

'I was hoping to catch you,' said Steiner. 'I'm so sorry. I feel like we just haven't been able to deliver for you.'

'It's nobody's fault,' said Flick. Her removal from the investigation was obviously big news by now. 'We haven't been looking in the right direction.'

If Steiner had asked her to elaborate, she would have

blurted it all out there and then, shared her concerns and suspicions, but instead the young detective said: 'DS Kendrick is going to take charge with DC Upson assisting, that's what we've been told, and DI Drake will give us more of a steer.'

Drake will take you in completely the wrong direction, thought Flick. He'll let the investigation go cold, let it fade away. Because there's something about the death of Kenny Overton and countless others at the hands of a remorseless predator that he doesn't want you, or any of us, to know about.

Drake had been ranting about April going missing and somebody called the Two O'Clock Boy, she remembered that now, and it made her uneasy.

'What are you going to do?' asked Steiner.

'Go home, take a bath, drink wine.' Too shocked after her encounter with Drake, she wasn't going to get anything done here. She wanted to talk to Nina. Her sister would know exactly what to do. 'I'll catch you later, Millie.'

Buzzing out of the exit, Flick took out her mobile to call her sister – it would also provide a useful human shield if anybody else tried to speak to her, but there was no answer on the home number – which was unusual. Nina was like an old person with her mobile, she regarded it strictly as something to be used in emergencies, if she broke down on the motorway or if there was some kind of alien apocalypse, but Flick tried it anyway.

The phone rang and rang. Flick was nearly at her car when the call connected. Nina spoke loudly, as she always did when she had a couple of drinks inside her.

'Hello, darling!'

'Are you in?'

'We're out tonight,' said Nina, over loud conversation in the background. 'Meeting bigwigs from Martin's new company. They're visiting from Down Under. Oh, Flick, I was really worried about moving to the other side of the world and knowing hardly anyone, but they seem really nice people.'

'Who's looking after the kids?'

'They're on a sleepover at Imogen's next door.'

'I can pick them up and stay over if it helps.'

'Oh, thank you, darling.' Nina's voice was almost lost against a burst of laughter at her end. 'But they've been so looking forward to it.'

Flick climbed into her car, slammed the door. The traffic noise from the High Road dulled.

'Dad said he saw you,' said Nina. 'Said you looked great. He was so happy, Flick, he was so excited.'

'Nina, we didn't—'

'You don't know how pleased I am, what a weight it is off my mind to know the pair of you are talking again. Thank you so much. I feel much better about everything. Oh Christ, someone's put *another* glass of champagne in my hand. The last thing I want to do is get pissed. Tell me to watch my step.'

'Three glasses and then you're on the water.'

'Got it. I want to see you as much as possible in the next month.'

'Month?'

'We're leaving in a month. Not much notice, is it? But they're keen for Martin to start work as soon as possible.' She hesitated. 'Is everything okay there, you sound . . . quiet.'

'I'm fine,' said Flick. 'You'd better go.'

313

'I'm sorry, I'll call tomorrow and we can talk properly. Love you.'

Flick threw the phone on the passenger seat and turned on the heater. It throbbed loudly. The gate rattled open and a patrol car pulled in.

She'd go home, change into her pyjamas and try to relax. Write up those notes. Then she'd message some people on Facebook, maybe even arrange a few catch-ups. There was a sudden rap on the window, and she flinched in momentary terror when she saw Frank Wanderly hunched there, bald head ghoulishly haloed against the sodium lamps in the car park. He spun his fist – *wind down the window*.

The glass lowered with a whine, and Wanderly stuck his head in. 'Glad I caught you. Someone's been trying to get in touch.'

He handed her the scrap of paper. Above a number was a name: Trevor Sutherland. She stared at it, expecting it to make some kind of sense. She'd no idea who it was.

'Thanks, Frank.'

'You're very welcome.' He waved over his shoulder as he headed towards the gate, and out of the station.

Flick dropped the paper beside the phone, started the engine, wincing again at the sudden, unwelcome memory of her confrontation with Drake in his office, and drove to the gate. As it trundled open, the penny dropped and she snatched up the note.

Trevor Sutherland, the photographer who took the image at the Longacre all those years back.

She called him straight back.

45

The Thames churned angrily, a speedboat bumping across the choppy water, as Drake arrived outside Jordan's apartment building. He flew into reception.

'You can't just . . .' The porter stepped forward, but Drake headed straight to the elevator.

On Jordan's floor he heard the throb of music inside. He knocked on the door, stepping aside to avoid being seen through the spyhole, and when it opened, Drake kicked at it, sending Jordan stumbling backwards.

Back-heeling the door shut, he yanked Jordan to his feet, gripped the back of his neck to push him into the living room. The kid wore a vest top and underpants. His spray tan glowed faintly in the winter glare of the tall windows and the impressive panorama of the broiling brown river below. On a table of white glass was a smear of pale dust, an open wrap of coke. Yanking a power cable from it socket, Drake killed the music. He forced Jordan's face to the table. A faint spurt of breath blossomed on the glass beneath his nose.

'What did I tell you would happen if I caught you with that stuff?'

The kid's fingers were splayed rigid on the surface. 'Mr Drake! Let me . . . let me . . .'

On top of everything else, April had been exposed to

drugs, had maybe even taken them with Jordan. The certainty of it ignited his fury. He jerked back the young man's head and smashed his nose down hard. Strings of blood spurted along the glass. Jordan cried out. Drake took gloves from his jacket pocket. The kid lifted himself from the table, cupping his bloody nose in his hands.

'And I haven't thanked you for the visit.'

'What you talking about?' Babbling now, terror and coke popping goosebumps on his skin. 'I've no idea what you're saying!'

'Those thugs you sent to beat me up. That was above and beyond the call of duty.' Drake stretched the left glove tight over his hand. 'I'm guessing that was your own idea.'

'My nose!' Blood poured through his fingers, pattering into the thick weave of the cream carpet. 'This is police brutality!'

'You don't realise how often I've dreamed of this moment, Jordan. How long I've wanted to go to work on someone. You were right; it's a relief to let it out. The fact that it's you I'm going to beat unconscious makes me very happy.'

When Drake balled his fists and moved forward, Jordan cowered. 'Woah, woah! All right! I hired a couple of guys to do you over! Thought I'd teach you a lesson. You were giving me grief!' He nodded at Drake's face. 'But no harm done, it don't look so bad.'

'I don't care about my face, Jordan, or that you paid men to kick me around. We'll let bygones be bygones about that. But I want to know about the *other* thing.'

'What other thing?' Jordan hopped from foot to foot. 'I don't know what you're talking about!'

'Someone paid you to keep my daughter from me.' Drake

cuffed the top of his peroxided head. Jordan was soft, snide, weak, no amount of gym time could compensate for that. 'This isn't a game. Someone's trying to kill April.'

Jordan flinched. 'I don't know what you're—'

'Shut up.' Drake slapped his cheek. 'My guess is that you were made an offer. This person came to you because they very much want to keep me apart from my daughter.' Drake nodded at the spectacular view from Jordan's apartment, the swell of the Thames, the skyline of skyscrapers and bridges and monuments at twilight; at the expensive furniture and decor, the biggest television screen he'd ever seen. 'I imagine the sports car and the horse, the drugs, all the rest of it, cost a fortune.'

Jordan gawped. 'Kill her?'

'Someone's trying to kill April, and kill me.' Drake clenched Jordan's throat, dragged him close. 'And when he's done that, I imagine he's going to want to tie up a few loose ends. You, for example. Because this man, he's killed many, many people, Jordan, and he won't think twice about offing a preening little squirt like you.'

Jordan's eyes bulged. Drake released his throat and he slumped on the table. Gingerly dabbed at the blood streaming from his nose.

'He said he'd help me out.' Jordan gulped down air. 'I got debts, Mr Drake. I made some bad investments. He said he'd look after me if I treated April nice, and kept her away from you. And I did, Mr Drake, I treated her very well.'

'Till you couldn't stand it any more, and threw her out.'

'I don't want to get tied down. I'm a young guy, my whole life ahead, and I don't need the grief.' Jordan looked up warily. 'I swear, Mr Drake, she hasn't done any drugs, not with me. She's not interested in anything like that.'

'She just wanted to be with you,' said Drake.

'Yeah.' Jordan swallowed. 'She loved me.'

'You told him where she was going when she left?'

'I told him I was through.' He wiped his nose along his arm, leaving a streak of blood. 'I let him know I was gonna do it this afternoon.'

'By phone?'

'I've got an email address.'

'Tell me about him.'

'I met him just after I'd started seeing April. I wasn't all that into her, to be honest.' He eyed Drake's clenched fists. 'She's too classy for the likes of me.'

'That's the first truthful thing you've said.'

'We got talking in a pub. I thought I was going to lose it all and he said he could help. He wanted me to get April away from you. It was a wind-up, he said. I presumed it was someone you'd banged up in the past. He offered a lot of money, no questions asked.'

Drake rubbed his temples. 'And you thought, yeah, it'll be easy getting this girl to fall for me, it'll be a laugh.'

'It weren't easy, Mr Drake. She liked me, yeah, but she weren't interested in . . . going further.' Mucus and blood strung between Jordan's lips. 'But when her mum died, and things weren't so good between you, it . . . got easier.'

'This man who came to you,' said Drake, tired, 'what's his name?'

'Mr Smith. Well, that was what he said.'

'Describe him.'

'I can do better than that.' Jordan stumbled to an android phone on a cabinet. 'I took a sneaky photo of him one night. Just in case, like.'

He swiped a thumb across it, smearing a blob of blood that had dropped from his nose onto the screen, just as Ray Drake's own phone rang. His stomach lurched when he saw the call was from his daughter's phone. Turning away from Jordan, he said: 'Please, don't hurt her.'

'Your daughter?' The electronic laugh howled in his ear. 'I don't have your daughter any more.'

The thought that she was already dead sent him staggering to the window to press his forehead against the cold glass, before his legs gave way. The room, the glow of the golden river and the city at twilight, melted away. Drake tried to focus, gripping the phone in both hands to keep it steady.

The thought of what he would hear next terrified him.

She was gone: killed, tortured.

He imagined April's screams of terror, her agonising last moments. His legs nearly buckled. If he fell, he didn't know how far he would drop. When Drake tried to respond, his lips moved but nothing came out.

'I'm visiting another old friend of ours,' the voice said triumphantly. 'And we're waiting for you.'

Drake heard screams in the background. 'Ray, oh God! Help me!'

The call disconnected and Drake flew towards Jordan.

'Show me!' he screamed.

46

When a couple of days went by and Sally didn't phone, Ray tried not to panic. She had things to do, he reasoned. She was a grown woman with responsibilities, and he had to respect that. She had made him a solemn promise that she would stay in contact, would call him when she was able. But more days passed, a week, and he knew something was wrong.

That home was the last place he wanted to go, but he had no choice. He would wait outside, he decided, until Sally came out and he would ask her why she hadn't called, why she had made him so worried. But when he arrived he saw her car was gone, and swallowed down the panic he felt.

He waited all day at the bottom of the street, and well into the evening, but he couldn't – wouldn't – wait any longer. A red sky was flattening across the slope on the other side of the train track when he hammered on the door of the Longacre.

'Can I help you, lad?' asked Gordon, when it opened.

'Where is she?' Ray tried to look over his shoulder into the home. 'Where's Sally?'

Gordon told Ray politely that he was very sorry but he

320

had no idea where she was. She was gone, he said, had decided to leave. It all happened very suddenly; Sally just got up and left. Somewhere up north, he said.

'No.' Ray felt the ground lurch beneath his feet. 'She wouldn't go without telling me. She wouldn't just leave.'

'I don't know what to tell you,' said Gordon sadly. 'If I knew any more . . .'

'You're lying.' Ray pushed past Gordon and into the office. When he didn't see her there, he opened the door to the small room at the back. The only light came from a dirty skylight above a mattress. Sheets lay tangled on top of the bedding, and a petrol canister, its pungent fumes overwhelming in the small space, was placed beside a green radiator.

'I'm going to have to ask you to leave,' said Gordon, the kids crowding behind him to watch the commotion.

'Amelia!' He saw the girl he had met on his last visit. 'Where's Sally?'

But the girl just stared. A band of steel coiled tighter around his chest.

'She left one morning,' said Gordon. 'Got a better offer, she said. You know how she is, Raymond, a free spirit.'

'I don't believe you.' Ray was on the verge of tears. 'You're lying.'

'I'm sorry, son. I don't claim to understand what goes on in that woman's head.'

'She wouldn't go away without telling me.'

Ray walked to the office door, thinking about bolting upstairs, but he saw Elliot stood with Connor and knew he wouldn't get far.

'Where is she?' Ray demanded, but Elliot wouldn't meet his eyes.

'I wouldn't ask Elliot,' said Gordon quietly. 'He'll not tell you anything. He's one of my pals, one of my Two O'Clock Boys.'

'Where is she?' Ray turned to Connor, and thought he saw something unfamiliar in the kid's defiant stare, something he didn't understand. Connor's fists were clenched, the skin of his knuckles stretched white.

'She left,' said Ronnie Dent, storming out of the kitchen with his wife, 'pissed off without telling anyone; and you can do the same.'

'I want to hear it from him.' Ray prodded Connor in the chest. 'I want to hear Connor say it.'

At Gordon's nod, the Dents moved to either side of Ray to lift him off the floor. He tried to escape, kicking his legs, screaming 'get off me' at the top of his voice, but they were too strong and Ray was hurled out the door. He fell down the steps, just managing to stick out his arms to break his fall. His stinging palms were red raw where the skin scraped on the pavement. Ronnie and Gerry laughed.

'I'm sorry for you, son, and for your loss,' said Gordon at the door, 'but stay away now. There's nothing for you here no more.'

Ray wasn't finished. He stood to force his way back inside, he wasn't going to leave until he discovered where she had gone – but Connor blocked his way.

'Go,' he said.

'Tell me where she is.'

'Get away from here or . . .'

'Or what?' Ray's cheeks were wet with tears. 'What will happen?'

'You don't want to mess with Connor, lad.' Gordon made

322

himself comfortable on the top step, like an emperor taking his seat at the Colosseum. 'He'll eat you for breakfast.'

Connor could smash him to bits, Ray had no doubt about that, but he didn't care, he wanted to know where Sally was. He had never in his life felt such anger.

'She wouldn't go!' he cried. 'She wouldn't leave me!'

The heel of his hand shot into Connor's chest. It felt good to lash out, but Ray expected to go down instantly, expected Connor to knock him to the floor and punch and kick him. But Connor didn't move – and Ray went in swinging.

Screaming in fury, he surged forward, hitting Connor again and again – in the chest and arms, in the face – making him stagger into the road. Connor hunched against Ray's blows – but he didn't hit back. Insensible with rage, Ray roared, and the other kids poured onto the street to watch.

And just as suddenly, Ray stopped. Exhausted, fists throbbing, head pounding. Connor's face was cut and bruised, his teeth blood red from a split lip. Ray covered his eyes and sobbed, right there in the middle of the street, in front of them all.

Because Sally was gone, and there was nothing he could do about it.

'I'm coming back.' Ray pointed a trembling finger at Gordon. 'And I'm going to bring my parents.'

And he would do it. Ray would make Leonard and Myra listen to him. They might not care about the poor kids in this place, or about Sally, but for first time in his life he would make them listen to what he had to say.

'You do that, lad.' The manager lifted himself off the step and went inside, taking most of the children with him.

Amelia remained, and Kenny and David and Elliot, and a small blond boy Ray had never seen before. And Connor was in front of him, eyes bulging with intense emotion.

'Where is she?' Ray asked, but he didn't expect a reply. His hands pulsed with pain, but he didn't care.

Connor shook his head.

'*Please*,' said Ray.

'Gone,' said Connor, in a voice barely louder than a whisper.

'Connor, come on, son,' called Gordon, at the door. All the others had already disappeared inside.

Ray nodded at the home. 'You can do something,' he told Connor. 'Why don't you do anything?'

'Let's go,' said Gordon, more loudly.

Just before Connor left, Ray saw it on the boy's face again, just for a second. That look of . . . what? Confusion, bewilderment, and something else – something that was both frightening and frightened.

And then Ray Drake was left alone in the street with the terrible certainty that he would never see Sally again, and that something inside of him had changed for ever.

47

The plan was to clean up. He would stash his mud-spattered clothes and the rucksack, and take a shower. Stand under the steaming hot spray and wash off the filth and the blood, scrub his skin till it was pink, maybe put on some aftershave.

It wasn't going to do him any good, because splashing on a bit of Paco Rabanne wouldn't conceal the stench of guilt and shame lifting off him, Elliot knew that. There was no going back from beating a man to death and stuffing his corpse in the boot of a car. But maybe he wouldn't frighten the life out of Rhonda when she got home.

And it would give him time to work out what to do next. He would convince her to leave with him – he'd make up some cock and bull story, if he could clear enough space in his head to think of one – and they would go far away, the three of them. Start all over again.

But what he wasn't banking on was Rhonda being home when he came in, covered in mud from head to toe, his fist red and raw and smeared with dried blood. Elliot stared in shock at the sight of her sitting on the sofa, and a voice spoke behind him.

'What the . . . ?'

When he turned, twisting his body at the waist so that he didn't suffer searing neck pain, he saw Dylan at the window.

'What's that?' Rhonda pointed at the rucksack. Elliot dropped it as if it was white hot.

'Why don't you leave me and your mum for a few minutes, Dylan, mate?' If he had intended to say it casually, like they had boring home insurance to discuss, he failed miserably. His terror instantly transmitted to the boy, whose eyes darted to Elliot's spattered clothes, his bloody hand, the bag pulsing at his feet.

Rhonda asked again: 'What's in the bag, Elliot?'

'Dylan,' Elliot said, 'do us a favour and—'

But the teenager rushed to the rucksack. Elliot stiffly tried to reach it first – 'Leave it!' – but Dylan whipped it away by the straps, and plunged his hand inside to lift out a fistful of money. An ornate necklace hung off his fingers.

'I said I'd get the money back,' Elliot explained, but Rhonda's face was set hard. And that was even before Dylan gasped and pulled the gun from the bag, lifting it gingerly between two fingers.

'Put it down,' whispered Rhonda. Dylan worked the weapon into his hand so that his finger rested on the trigger guard. 'I said put it down!'

Her son dropped the gun back into the rucksack. 'Is this why the police were here earlier?'

'The police?' asked Rhonda.

'No,' said Elliot. 'That . . . that's not . . .'

Rhonda stood. 'Dylan, go and pack a bag.'

Elliot's nose throbbed, his hand, his neck. 'I know what it looks like.'

'Will someone tell me what's going on?' Dylan's voice quivered with fear. For once, when his phone vibrated in his pocket he ignored it.

'Go upstairs, Dylan. Right now!'

The boy backed away, staring at Elliot, soaking up the desperation in his face, and ran up the stairs. They heard his heavy footfalls above, drawers slamming open.

Rhonda nodded at the bag. 'Where did you get it?'

He opened his mouth to answer, but nothing came out. Elliot couldn't tell her what he had done, because it would be the end if he confessed. After all, he had killed a man. Beaten him to death and left him to rot. And there was no going back from that. Not now, not ever.

So he just had to let the scene play out to its bitter conclusion.

Rhonda crouched over the bag. She touched the jewellery – some of it very old, inlaid with sparkling gemstones – and the money, and the personal items that Perry had swept from the safe, the deeds of property and other documents. 'This isn't our money, Elliot. This isn't our savings. Whose it is?'

He shook his head.

'Tell me,' she said. 'Tell me what you've done.'

He'd had plenty of opportunity to tell Rhonda all the things he'd done in the past, but never had. It occurred to him with a sinking heart that if he had told her what had happened to him as a boy, when he was a child and didn't have a choice, she would have forgiven him, supported him, because it was all so long ago. But all those secrets, all those lies, were nothing compared to murdering a man in cold blood.

She shouldn't be near him. Dylan shouldn't be near him. He was despicable, toxic, and deserved their contempt and hatred. His old man had made him that, and that creep

Tallis. Both of them long dead, but both still gleefully pulling his strings, making him dance to their tune.

All he could think to say, even though he knew it was the understatement of the century, was: 'I messed up.'

'Tell me what you did.' Her eyes dropped to his bloody fist, which throbbed on the end of his arm. He wished she wouldn't keep repeating it. 'Tell me what you did.'

'I can't,' he said, voice hoarse, because it would be the end.

'Tell me.'

Elliot shook his head.

Dylan clattered down the stairs with a bag, and Rhonda told him to get to his room. She needed to pack some things before they left.

'Where are we going?' asked the boy. 'What's going on with Elliot?'

'Go back upstairs.'

'I didn't mean what I said, about him being just some passing bloke.'

'It's not your fault.' Elliot's voiced cracked with emotion. 'And don't you ever think it is. None of it.'

'Go to your room!' snapped Rhonda, and the boy thumped back upstairs, a strangled little noise coming from his throat. 'We can work this out. Whatever you've done, or think you've done, we can get past it.'

'Not this.' His tongue felt swollen. 'We can't get past this.'

'Tell me what you've done.'

Wild horses couldn't drag it out of him. After a lifetime of lies, to himself and everybody else, they had become such a part of him that he barely knew where they ended and where the real Elliot Juniper began. The Two O'Clock Boy

328

had always known the truth about Elliot, had known the kind of man he was.

'You have to take responsibility for yourself,' Rhonda told him. 'If you can't do it for me or for Dylan, then do it for yourself. Because if you don't, you will never be happy.'

'I'll never be happy without you.'

'You should have thought about that earlier. Before you brought this, whatever this is,' she kicked the rucksack with her foot, 'into my home.' She didn't raise her voice, that wasn't Rhonda's style, but it was full of quiet contempt. 'Congratulations, Elliot, you've finally gone too far. You've brought it into our home, Elliot, *our* home, and you can't even be truthful with me.'

'That's me.' He laughed miserably. 'Elliot the idiot.'

'Ask yourself how you can make it stop, all the unhappiness you carry with you, because I don't think I'm enough. I hoped I would be, that Dylan would be, but we're not.'

'This isn't your fault.'

'No,' she said bitterly, 'it isn't. You're the only one who can stop reacting to the world like a bullied little boy and become a grown-up. And you can start by taking responsibility for this.' She nodded at the bag. 'Will you do that, Elliot?'

He whispered, 'I hope so.'

'Then tell me what you've done,' she said. 'Tell me why there's a gun in my home and I promise we will get through this.'

He wanted to tell her, but he had killed a man, and there were some things that could never be, *should* never be, forgiven.

She shouldn't be around him, neither of them should.

The one sliver of hope was that he would get them away from that maniac, and they would be safe.

And so he said: 'Just go.'

And Rhonda gave him a cold, reproachful look that obliterated all his hopes and dreams of a future, any kind of future, and climbed the stairs.

48

Ray Drake's car skidded to a stop outside Amelia Troy's warehouse. He killed the engine and lights.

Amelia's floor was dark. The steel door was ajar. Edging inside the building, he called the lift. The mechanism boomed into life high above him. He raised the handgun, but when the elevator arrived, its innards lit by the sallow bulb, it was empty.

Drake stepped inside, pulling the metal cage shut, and hit the button. In this tiny box he would be a sitting duck when it reached the top, but it was the only way up. Unscrewing the hot bulb above his head, Drake plunged the lift into darkness. He crunched the bulb beneath his foot. The upper floors passed dimly, infused faintly with an ambient glow.

The lift thunked to a halt at Amelia's floor. Inches of speckled floor were visible at his feet, and the lights of the city in the windows, but the space in between was a blank. Careful to keep his gun raised, he rattled open the cage and called: 'Amelia!'

Stepping out, Drake could just about make out the surface of the long table. The rectangular canvas frames loomed black against the sills, like portals into space. His careful steps scraped on the concrete floor as he swung round the side of the elevator, back pressed against the shaft. The furnished area of the space was smothered in gloom, the lamps switched off. Drake wished he'd brought a torch.

'Anyone here?' A rustle in the darkness. 'Amelia?'

He moved forward and bumped his knees against the sofa. Drake found the metal pole of the standing lamp and scrabbled with the switch – but it didn't come on.

There was a muffled sound of distress. Pistol raised, Drake took out his phone with his free hand and touched the screen to bathe the area in front of him – a foot, perhaps, no more – with a faint blue light. Gun pointed, phone light sprayed ahead, he rounded the sofa.

A figure was seated in the dark, just beyond the circle of light. He heard the shuffle of plastic, a muffled cry. Drake stepped forward, stumbling over the lip of a rug, and the figure in the chair was revealed.

Amelia bound in layers of clinging plastic.

As soon as she saw him, she strained in the chair. Drake moved forward. And the phone light whipped across someone rushing towards him in the darkness.

Drake lifted the weapon, bracing with both hands against the recoil, and fired. Once, twice.

The explosions were deafening in the dark. The windows vibrated in their frames, a toneless buzz, and the figure was flung backwards. Drake lifted the phone and edged forward, small pigeon steps in the dark, to see the featureless face of the tailor's dummy on the floor. Jagged splinters splayed from its wooden chest. The upended wheels spun on their stand.

Drake retreated to Amelia and tore at the plastic over her mouth. Her eyes stared at him in terror. He was getting nowhere fast with the gun in his hand, and shoved it beneath his armpit to fumble in his pocket for his keys, using a serrated edge to cut the material. It tore away, shreds of it corkscrewing around her cheek.

'It's going to be okay,' he told her, 'just stay still.'

When her mouth was free, Amelia was almost hysterical. 'He's . . . he's—'

Then she screamed.

A blur of movement at the edge of the tiny circle of light.

A metal bar swung out of the darkness. Instinctively, Drake lifted his arm high to protect his head. His shoulder went dead. The gun dropped to the floor. Another stinging blow to the thigh dropped him to his knees. Reaching for the gun he swung it up, but the weapon was knocked from his hand and skittered into the darkness. Drake's arms and legs propelled him backwards. He scuttled like a crab as a shape – a mass, a weight barely heavier than the blackness surrounding it – moved with him, bringing down the steel rod. Sparks flew up from the concrete floor in the space between his legs.

At any moment, one of those blows would find his skull and it would be game over. Drake kicked blindly with his leg into the dark, and the mass stumbled. He heard the metal bar clatter on the concrete.

A faint rectangle of light lay behind him, the phone upside down on the rough floor. Drake rolled on his side, scrabbling the last few inches to snatch it. Holding the phone to the floor, its glow revealing an inch of racing blue concrete, he scrambled to where the gun had disappeared.

Behind him, he heard the metal rod scrape as it was picked up. The gun appeared in the phone's scant light and Drake lunged for it, rolling onto his back and pulling the trigger.

The gun discharged three times. He heard the rod hit the floor with a discordant clang.

When the echo of the shots had died, he lay there – trying not to pass out from the juddering pain that rippled through his already beaten body. The rod rolled out of the blackness and touched his foot. Drake listened to his own rapid breath, heard the elevator cage open.

'Not yet!' that familiar voice echoed. 'Soon, though. Very soon.'

The cage door shut. The elevator chuntered into life and descended.

Amelia screamed in the chair, rocking from side to side in a frenzy.

'I'm here,' said Drake, climbing wearily to his feet. 'I'm here.'

49

There it was again, that noise, barely louder than the squeak of a mouse.

Myra Drake had lived in this house all her life and was familiar with its every wheeze and sigh. People presumed that the older you got, the more your senses degraded, but she had always had excellent hearing. Her eyes weren't what they once were, and these days everything tasted the same, but her ears were as sharp as ever.

Raymond insisted that she leave, but she had always intended to stay, despite her promise to him. This was her home, and she was not going to let anybody scare her away. Besides, she didn't even know if she still had a suitcase. At Myra's age it was sensible to assume your next trip would not require luggage.

A few months ago, Raymond had given her a mobile phone with his number programmed into it, in case of an accident. She held it now. The small plastic rectangle felt insubstantial in her palm. Raymond had told her how to operate it, explaining the buttons in a loud and condescending manner. She was a pensioner, she had told him, not an imbecile. But no matter how many times she pressed the *On* button, the screen remained blank. The battery on the device had died. She had never recharged it. So she sat on the sofa and listened. Seconds later, a loose tile on the parquet rattled outside the door.

'Stop that creeping around, I can hear you.' It was a big house, and easy to get lost. 'In here.'

A man walked in, dressed in black from head to toe, and wearing a balaclava. He held a long knife in his hand.

'Take that off,' she said. 'You look ridiculous.'

The intruder's eyes bulged. Then he pulled off the woollen garment, brushing a hand over his scalp to remove any clinging fibres.

'Careful.' Myra's smile was brittle. 'You don't want to leave any DNA around the place.'

'It's too late to worry about that,' said the boy. He walked around the room, hands clasped behind his back. Perusing the bookcase, the items on the mantelpiece, taking a great interest in everything, as if he were a tourist at a stately home. 'Do you remember me?'

Myra considered him. 'You appear to be an eminently forgettable person. Should I?'

For so many years he had strived to be invisible to others, as insubstantial as vapour – that was how he was able to go about his business so successfully – and yet her response made his blood boil. He perched on the arm of a chair, sensing it would irritate her, even as she was facing death.

'We met a long time ago.'

'And you are here to kill me.'

'Yes. And then your granddaughter will die. And, of course . . .' His grin was sarcastic. '*Your boy.*'

Myra Drake's thumbs spun restlessly in her lap. 'I doubt that. Raymond is a better man than you in every way. He has more intelligence and more guile. He will not allow himself to be murdered, by you or any other person.'

What the boy could tell her, the supercilious old crone,

was how he could have killed him twice already; how he had placed a knife to his throat only this morning, was so close he could see the tendons in his neck glide beneath the skin; how he had toyed with him in the warehouse only this evening. He could also tell her just how many people had died at his hands. That would wipe the sneer off her face. 'After everything you have done for him, and he's allowed you to die.'

'It is not his place to allow me to do anything. Besides, it's something of a relief. Since the death of my husband, I confess I've found life somewhat trying.'

'I can understand that. My time is also coming to an end.'

'Well,' the corners of her mouth twitched, 'that's something, I suppose. And how do you intend to kill me?' He placed the long blade, its polished edge gleaming, across his knees. Myra pulled her cardigan around her shoulders. 'Will it be quick?'

'I'm afraid not. I'll take my time and you will die in agony. I harbour a lifetime's resentment against your family.'

Myra's stare glittered with contempt. 'I remember you now. There was something off about you even then. It was those dead eyes.'

'I was just a boy!' he shouted.

'And you are now a dismal little man.'

A tear ran down his cheek. He wiped it away with the back of his hand. 'I'm not the man I should be, that's true enough.'

'Well, if nothing else, you're not self-deceiving.'

The man checked his watch and jumped up. 'Well, let's get on.'

Myra nodded bleakly. When he stepped forward, lifting the knife, she raised a shaking hand.

'Please,' she said, and he stopped.

Myra Drake took off her glasses and folded them neatly on the occasional table, beneath the ornate lamp and beside her copy of Trollope, as she had done every night for fifty, sixty years.

Routine was important to Myra Drake and, looking back, considering all the turbulent events she had experienced, the people she had lost . . . well, it hadn't been a bad sort of life. She clicked open the locket to look one last time at the photograph inside. Running a trembling thumb over it, she thought of her boy, Raymond. Then she folded her hands in her lap and shut her eyes. Whatever happened in the next few seconds, she would not open them again. She nodded.

Myra felt a faint breeze as her murderer swung the blade high above his head. She clenched her teeth, determined not to cry out . . .

And then there was a knock on the front door. Her eyes snapped open. Myra was ready to shout, but the man lifted the tip of the blade to her jaw.

Another knock, and someone called. The man's eyes slid towards the hallway, and the smile that lit up his face was ghastly.

'I'm going to enjoy this.'

50

Leonard and Myra Drake arrived unexpectedly on the door-step of the Longacre with Ray and a photographer from the local newspaper.

'I hope we haven't come at an inopportune time.' Myra's faint smile to Gordon Tallis suggested that she didn't much care one way or the other what he thought. 'My son was keen for us to see the work you do here. And Mr Sutherland from the local newspaper has agreed to record the occasion.'

'Of course,' said Gordon, biting down on his panic. 'It will be my pleasure to talk to you, and perhaps give you a tour. However,' he said, eyeing Ray, 'your son can't come in. I'm afraid he attacked one of our children. I don't know what he's told you—'

'He's told us enough,' said Leonard, looking unhappy about leaving his car in such an unsavoury area.

'I will vouch for my son's behaviour,' Myra said.

'I'm afraid I'm going to have to insist that he remains outside. The rest of you are welcome to come in.'

Myra Drake considered Gordon. 'Very well,' she said eventually.

'I want to come in,' said Ray, annoyed. 'I want to hear what he says.'

339

'Wait in the car,' his mother told him. 'And we'll talk afterwards.'

Ray pressed forward. 'I'm not staying outside.'

'Raymond,' said Myra Drake quietly. A single look from her silenced him. And no wonder, Gordon decided. It was a look that could fell a charging elephant. 'Go to the car.'

The boy threw an angry glance at Gordon, and pushed past the photographer down the steps, throwing himself against the Daimler parked below.

'Come in.' Gordon led them into the office, Myra taking her older husband's free arm – he leaned heavily on a cane with the other – to help him inside.

Gordon was panicking. There had been no warning, no time to make the home look halfway presentable. All he could do was command the Dents to tidy the place as best they could in the time available. But Ronnie and Gerry had never had a talent for moving quickly, and to his frustration he knew the house wasn't going to be miraculously transformed in a few, short minutes.

'Which of the little bastards look presentable enough to meet them?' He surveyed the kids roaming the garden.

'There's the new one,' said Gerry. 'The little fella's going home soon, so he'll be in a good mood.'

Toby Turrell sat cross-legged, staring at the ground. Listening nearby, Connor saw Gordon tense at the thought of the boy returning home, and knew he wouldn't – couldn't – allow that, not after what the kid had seen. Someone like Sally, estranged from her family and with few ties to the world, could disappear, but not a boy with devoted parents. Gordon must see that no more harm could come to him. Trouble was, these days his thinking was all over the place.

340

The manager grabbed Connor. 'Round up some of the ones you trust to keep their mouths shut and come to my office.' When Connor turned to leave, Gordon pulled him back. 'But not the boy.'

Connor found Amelia, and Jason and Kenny, and Elliot. And, despite Gordon's strict instructions, he went to get Toby.

'Please go away,' pleaded the kid.

'You're coming with me.' Connor hauled him to his feet. If Toby was going to get out of this place alive, the more people who knew about him the better. He needed to be seen by adults, important people – and they were taking a photo for the local newspaper.

'Please!'

'Listen to me.' Connor shook his arm. 'You're gonna go in there and talk to the judge and tell him you're going home.'

He pushed Toby to the office. Gordon scowled when he saw the boy, but bit down on his anger in front of the visitors. He'd made an effort with his appearance, but the long hair slicked neatly inside his collar jarred with the clammy sheen on his forehead.

Connor had never met anyone like Leonard Drake. A giant of a man in a three-piece suit, he dominated the room, towering over the other adults despite a stoop. A thick mane of hair surged back from his heavy brow, as he looked around him in barely concealed disgust. Myra Drake was scarcely shorter than her husband and stood stiffly, looking down the slope of her nose at the children.

'Raymond is very attached to his cousin,' she said, 'and he's concerned about her whereabouts.'

'As we all are.' Gordon pressed his hands together, as if in prayer. 'I'm afraid Sally stole money from me, so I would very much like to know where she is.'

'Have you told the police?'

'I'm very fond of Sal and would rather not get the local constabulary involved. Despite everything, she's always welcome here. Ain't that right, kids?' He wiped his slick forehead with a sleeve. 'But she's a handful, that lass, so who knows where she's got herself off to.'

'What is your name?' Myra asked each of the children in turn. When she came to Connor, she eyed him curiously, perhaps because he brazenly stared right back. 'And who are you?'

'Connor Laird,' he said, and her attention lingered on him.

Gordon gestured at the photographer's camera. 'Many of our children lack confidence, and you'll give them a fright with that thing, Mr ... ?'

'Sutherland,' said the man, cleaning the camera lens. 'Trevor.'

'Why don't you stay here, Trevor, and relax. We'll be back soon.'

Leaving Sutherland in the office, the group walked around the house. The kids trailed behind the adults as Gordon stammered his excuses about the state of the home. The judge and his wife listened solemnly as he explained that, despite the homely nature of the place – 'it could do with the odd nail here and there!' – the children adored the Longacre.

But even Connor could see there was a huge gulf between the praise Gordon heaped on the home and the reality of the squalid, characterless rooms. Children were positioned carefully in front of some of the worst patches of damp, or sat on beds to hide ripped mattresses. All the best furniture had been moved hastily to the two or three bedrooms Gordon allowed Myra to see inside. Unable to climb the stairs, her husband waited at the bottom with the Dents, who watched beneath the banisters like trolls beneath a bridge.

The judge took the time to survey each ground-floor room carefully, despite Gordon's desperate efforts to hurry him. Aside from asking a few terse questions, he said little. Every now and then, Connor would catch Myra looking at him.

'Why are there no doors?' asked Leonard Drake.

'The children get scared when they bang in the night.' Gordon smiled. 'So we thought it best to remove them.'

The tour lasted less than fifteen minutes. When they returned to the office, the photographer jumped up, asking to get some quick shots before he rushed to another job. He was in a hurry, he said, because the paper was going to press that evening. He placed them in a line, the kids and the adults, on the very spot where Sally had died.

Connor didn't want to be photographed. Call it instinct, call it some innate protective urge, he positioned himself at the very edge of the group.

As the camera flash whined and popped, and the room was soaked in a fluttering light – 'Let's have some big smiles from the little ones!' – he swung away from the others. The photographer frowned, disappointed with the framing of his shots. But he was late for his next job, he said, and after getting brief quotes from Gordon and Leonard Drake, and jotting down everyone's name, he left.

'A glass of wine, perhaps?' Gordon asked the judge.

Leonard Drake leaned grimly on his cane. 'Of course not, it's midday.'

'You must understand, my son was very insistent that we come here, Mr Tallis,' said Myra Drake. 'To see . . . the work that you do.'

'And what about you children?' The judge's eyes swept around the room. 'Are you happy here?'

Seeing Gordon's expression, Jason, Amelia and Kenny nodded.

'Don't look at him,' Myra told Jason. 'My husband asked *you* the question.'

'I just want to go home,' whined Toby. Tears fell down his cheeks.

Myra turned to him. 'You have a home, child?'

Gordon stepped between them. 'Connor! Toby's not feeling well, why don't you take the poor mite up to bed?'

Toby wrung his hands together. 'We dug in the garden.'

'Why don't—'

'Wait.' Myra Drake spoke over Gordon. 'You've a home, child?'

The other kids became agitated at Toby's weeping. Kenny and Jason looked like they would do anything to get away. Elliot couldn't tear his eyes from the spot where Sally had laid, blood blooming from the crown of her head across the floorboards.

'He's upset, aren't you Toby, lad?' Gordon tousled the boy's hair. 'I think this momentous occasion has been too much for him.'

'We dug a hole,' said Toby, between sobs.

'Connor, take—'

'Be quiet,' Myra told Gordon. 'And why did you do that, boy?'

Toby stared at her, dismally. 'We buried a rug.'

'What a curious thing to say.'

'Take him away,' Gordon hissed at Connor, but the boy didn't move.

'He's going home soon, ain't that right, Gordon?' Connor said. 'You promised him he'd be going home to his folks.'

'The boy doesn't belong here?' asked Myra Drake.

Gordon pressed a handkerchief to his forehead. 'He's staying with us, temporarily.'

'Toby wants to see his people again,' said Connor. 'His parents.'

'Temporarily?' Leonard Drake scowled. 'That sounds very unorthodox.'

Connor met Gordon's stare. 'He's going home.'

'That's right; the lad's soon to go home.' Gordon swallowed. 'To his folks. And we'll miss him, because we're a happy family here.'

'I doubt that very much.' The rubber tip of Leonard Drake's cane squeaked on the floor as he bore down on Gordon. 'I think we've seen enough. This home is a disgrace.'

'Let me—'

'*You* are an absolute disgrace. I shall ensure that this cesspit is closed.'

'Your Honour . . .'

The judge stood close to Gordon, who cringed beneath his steady gaze. 'And you will inform us where Sally is as soon as you hear from her.'

Gordon frantically followed Leonard Drake outside.

'You're a spirited one,' said Myra to Connor. Something

caught her eye at the skirting as she turned to leave, and she bent to pick up the paperweight. She placed it on the desk, chipping at a stain on its glass surface with a thumbnail. Then she plucked at his T-shirt to pull him closer.

He felt her hot breath on his ear when she whispered: 'This place deserves to burn.'

When she left, Connor joined the others at the window to watch the manager circle the judge as he reached the pavement, while Myra went to her son. Ray Drake listened while his mother spoke to him, slowly, firmly. His face was red with rage, but she wouldn't allow him to speak, and when she finished, he flung up his arms in impotent fury and ran off down the street. His mother watched him go, impassive. A chauffeur jumped out of the car to open the rear doors. Leonard and Myra climbed in, ignoring Gordon's panicked protestations.

Connor dropped the curtain and turned to see the others – Kenny, Jason, Elliot, Amelia and Toby – staring tensely at him.

Moments later, Gordon stepped back in the room. Hoping to disappear back amongst all the other kids, Kenny went to leave, but the manager blocked his way.

'Where do you think you're going?' Eyes jerking in their sockets, Gordon slammed the door. 'Let's not break up the party, not while the day's still young!'

51

Flick had never seen anything like it. She always presumed gardens were drab places in the winter but the grass was lush and green. The plants packed in the borders were colourful and vibrant in the dusk, and water trickled in a pretty pond. The wind was blowing hard now, but she couldn't spot a single leaf on the lawn, or on the rippling surface of the water.

'The wife's the gardener.' Trevor Sutherland stepped carefully across the neat paving embedded in the lawn towards a garden shed. 'I hardly set foot out here if I can help it. My life wouldn't be worth living if I damaged the grass.'

He was a sprightly man, with one shoulder hunched lower than the other. From carrying a heavy camera bag for half his life, he said. Keys of all shapes and sizes jangled at his waist, hanging from a solid brass ring a medieval jailer might fear too sinister. He lived in a quiet street in Barnet, in a modest two-up, two-down, with his wife and a pair of yapping dogs. Reaching the shed he considered the keys beneath tangled eyebrows, while Flick waited impatiently.

In the circumstances, this was the last place she should be. She should have washed her hands of the whole thing, should be at home with her feet up, writing notes about Ray Drake's conduct, not standing outside a stranger's shed in the suburbs.

'This used to be my darkroom,' he said. 'Now it's Shirley's Gardening HQ.'

'Do you miss it?' asked Flick. 'The job?'

'Not much, but these days it's a lot easier. You take a picture, and bang, the images are sent electronically to the news desk.' Trevor's fingers slipped from the key he'd finally located on the ring, and to Flick's frustration he began his search all over again. 'In my day you spent hours in the dark fiddling with chemicals – what a palaver! But it weren't all bad, back then all the journalists loved to drink and swap stories.' He winked. 'So it was a good excuse to snatch a few hours down the pub.'

'I'm amazed you remember the Longacre,' she said, fishing for detail.

'I didn't work local papers for long. I had a talent, you see. Not for photography, any monkey can point a camera, but for getting in people's faces. Lizzie Taylor, Princess Margaret, Stallone.' His eyes twinkled. 'They all knew me. I've always kept scrapbooks of my work. So when Diane from the *Argent* rang and said you were looking for something, I knew I could help.'

Her phone rang and she checked the screen: Peter Holloway. Wanting to discuss what happened in Ray Drake's office, no doubt. It could wait.

'I could have gone to Iraq and Afghanistan, trotted the globe winning awards.' Trevor fumbled keys against the padlock. 'But I don't care for crocodiles or war zones.'

Flick waited, anxious to intervene. 'Can I help you?'

'I can manage, luv, it's one of these little ones, and my motor skills ain't what they used to be.' He peered for a long time at a small silver key and then inserted it. The padlock bar pinged open. 'Been a while since I've been in here.'

When Trevor snapped a switch inside the door, the shed was bathed in red light. Gardening equipment was stacked against the walls, a lawnmower, a shovel and hoe. Bottles of weed killer and lawn feed sat on a shelf. At the back was a makeshift darkroom. Two sinks set into a counter, trays piled with brushes and stained Marigolds and plastic tubs.

Trevor looked around in wonder, as if he'd found the Holy Grail. 'You wouldn't believe how many hours I spent in here.' He picked up a chipped mug. 'I wondered where that'd got to.'

Flick's attention was grabbed by box files piled on top of a filing cabinet. 'In one of these?'

'Nah. That far back, it'll be in the cabinet.'

Flick tugged at the cabinet's handle but it was locked, and she had to stifle a groan when Trevor frowned at the key ring.

'Here we go again.' He held the keys close to his face beneath the soft red light, and by some miracle managed to quickly find a tiny key, turn it in the slot. The top drawer opened with a metallic shiver.

'When I was younger, I'd cut out my photos from the paper, stick 'em in a book. Let's take a look.'

He took out an old scrapbook, bloated by damp, the thick reams of paper stuck into it decades ago. Licking a forefinger, Trevor turned the pages, lingering nostalgically over articles and images. School fêtes; the opening of municipal buildings; long-dead authors giving talks in long-closed libraries.

'There you are.' He tapped at a page and handed the book to Flick. She read: JUDGE VISITS LOCAL CHILDREN'S HOME.

Noted High Court judge Leonard Drake dropped in to meet the kids at the Longacre Children's Home, this week.

Mr Drake and his wife Myra visited in his role as Chairman of the Hackney Children's Protection League to meet manager Gordon Tallis and his dedicated staff.

349

Her eyes dropped to the photograph beneath, and she grabbed the cabinet.

'You all right, love?'

She barely heard him, as she matched faces to names from the caption.

A tall man stood in the middle of the group lined up in a nondescript office, a thick mane of hair swept back over his head. Leonard Drake. Died of natural causes years ago.

Beside him stood a snooty-looking woman, Myra Drake, tall and rigid, dressed in a frumpy frock. But no locket around her neck, Flick noticed. That penetrating gaze was unmistakable.

At the far left was a man with a lopsided smile, Gordon Tallis. Fists clenched in a threadbare corduroy suit and flared-collared shirt, lank hair sliding to his shoulders. His face, hidden behind a scruffy beard, was bloated and shifty. Tallis died hours after this photo was taken.

The smiles of the children between them were strained. Kenny Overton, a plump, red-headed boy with an awkward smile. Tied to a chair and slaughtered with his family only days ago.

Next to him was another small boy, Toby Turrell, his expression blank, and then came Jason Burgess, who stared aggressively into the camera lens. He was murdered decades later with his family, the deaths recorded as a murder–suicide.

Beside Jason was Elliot Juniper, a sullen boy with surly, reproachful eyes, and then Amelia Troy, her fingers tugging at his sleeve.

And – finally – there was the last boy, rearing back at the edge of the shot. Caught in swift movement. A single pixelated eye, angry and intense, flashing at the camera. That night he would use the chaos caused by the blaze to disappear into the night.

The one that got away.

She knew now, with gut-wrenching certainty, that Connor Laird was very much alive.

Jason, Ricky, David, Karen, God knows how many others, dead . . .

'Yeah, you see, that's the kind of mistake an inexperienced photographer makes.' Trevor pointed at the shadows edging the image. 'But I ain't done so badly in the years, considering.'

Flick pushed past him to stumble into the garden. The red light still pulsed in her vision when she propped her hands on her knees to vomit into a flowerbed.

'I'm not going to enjoy explaining this to the wife,' said Trevor, watching. 'But at least you didn't do it over the koi. Would you like a glass of water?'

She nodded. 'Please.'

Trevor hopped back up the pathway while Flick felt hot needles of sweat on her forehead cool in the wind.

Connor Laird was alive.

Men, women and children. Burned, shot, drowned, stabbed.

Her mobile rang and she fumbled it from her pocket. Holloway again. When she hit the button she did her best to sound alert and engaged.

'Peter, what can I do for you?'

'I'm outside Ray Drake's house,' he said. 'I was worried about him after your . . . altercation tonight. But, DS Crowley . . . I think there's something terribly wrong.'

52

Emotion scraped in Ray Drake's chest like a nail. He had his daughter back. He didn't understand how, he didn't understand why, but she was with him and that was all that mattered. April gripped his hand as staff stacked tables and chairs in the café on the cavernous concourse of St Pancras train station, preparing to close for the night.

'Tell me again.'

Bewildered, April looked from her father to Amelia, who stared at the table. 'He dropped me off at Susie's house.'

'And he never touched you?'

'He helped me out of the cab. I thought it was a bit weird,' she said. 'That's when he must have taken my mobile.'

'Did he talk to you?'

'He asked me in the car why I was sad.' April glanced at Amelia again. 'I was upset, I'd just been talking to Flick about . . . Jordan.'

Drake saw the engagement ring was gone from her finger. 'Did you tell him anything about yourself?'

'No.'

She was going to call him, until she realised her phone was gone. Drake had received her call, from her friend's number, at Amelia's warehouse. April put a finger to her cheek. Her face was puffy with tears. She was more beautiful, more precious, to him than ever.

352

The girl looked at Amelia, confused as to why her father was with this strange woman. 'Why are you asking me about the cab driver?'

Drake's gaze restlessly swept the concourse. A steady flow of people passed, even at this late hour. He'd have liked to spend time with April, but time was the one thing neither of them had. Both women were lucky to be alive. Their safety was paramount. His reconciliation with his daughter, all the things he wanted to say, would have to wait.

'I think he may be linked to an investigation I'm working on.'

'An investigation?' April shook her head, uncomprehending.

The less she knew about the situation the better. 'It's . . . complicated. Threats have been made to officers involved in the case.'

She looked at the cuts on Amelia's face. 'What happened to you?'

'It's nothing.' Amelia's face was pale and strained. She wore a yellow windbreaker and red jeans, dirty white trainers. An overnight bag sat at her feet. 'It looks worse than it is.'

'Amelia is a witness in the case.'

'You're not telling me everything.' April frowned. 'What's going on, Dad?'

That word, *Dad*. He couldn't remember the last time she'd called him that. It filled him with gratitude, relief – and hope for the future.

'I want you to go away for a couple of days,' he said.

'What does any of this have to do with me?'

'April . . .' Amelia took a deep breath. 'Someone very dangerous attacked me tonight, and your father saved my

353

life. I have absolutely every reason to trust his judgement. I'm as much in the dark about what's happening as you are, but as I understand it, there's a slim chance that this person may try to get revenge against your father. The last thing he wants is for you to be placed in any danger.'

'I know somewhere you can go, out of the city,' said Drake. 'You'll be comfortable there. You'll have space to think about what you want to do next, whether you want to come back to live with me and your gran, or . . .' He didn't want to consider other possibilities. 'Whatever you decide, I'll support you.'

'So I am in danger.'

'Probably not, but it's better to be safe than sorry.' Amelia smiled. 'Believe me, I know.'

'I can't, there's Jordan – what if he tries to make contact?'

'Forget Jordan,' Drake said shortly.

'There you go again.' April removed her hand.

Drake rubbed his face. 'I'm sorry, I—'

'I loved him, Dad.'

'I know,' he said, and she slipped her hand back into his.

For the first time he imagined a scenario where everything would be okay. Now he knew the assumed identity of the Two O'Clock Boy. One look at Jordan's phone and he saw, with shock, who it was. All this time the murderer had been close, *too* close. But now Drake knew where to start looking for him. April was here with him, safe and sound. His daughter was back, and it was a start.

'And what about Gran, isn't she coming?' she asked.

'She's away, visiting relatives.'

When she blinked, Drake sensed the enormity of the situation hitting home to her. April knew that Hell would have to freeze over before Myra agreed to leave her precious house.

'We can look after each other,' said Amelia warmly. 'Trust me, I've plenty of experience of unsuitable men, and I'm a good listener. And like you, I could really do with a friend.' She turned to him. 'Give us a moment, Ray.'

Drake scraped back his chair and walked onto the concourse. Someone was playing one of the upright pianos placed along the crowded precinct. Drake watched April and Amelia talk, heads bowed across the table, and scanned the jostling crowd of commuters who marched past him. When he returned to the two women, Amelia threw him a reassuring glance.

'So I'll be under police protection?' asked April.

'No,' he said. 'I'm the only person who'll know where you are.'

Amelia nodded encouragingly. Drake wished he could tell April more, but it was impossible. Well, when all this was over, that would change. He would do everything in his power to make things better between them. She would be his main, his only, priority in life.

'When do we leave?'

Amelia stood. 'No time like the present, my car's around the corner.'

'Can I go to the toilet first?' asked April.

'Rather now than in my car.' Amelia laughed. 'I've just had it valeted.'

Drake wanted to escort his daughter to the toilet at the rear of the café, but Amelia touched his arm, *leave her.* He watched April all the way to the door.

'I haven't had the chance to say thank you,' said Amelia.

355

'If you hadn't got there in time . . . I still don't know why he didn't kill me.'

'He wanted me there.' Drake reluctantly tore his eyes from the door. 'He wanted us to watch each other die. It's what he did with the Overtons, I think, and probably the others.'

'I don't understand,' she asked, bewildered. 'Why does he want to kill us?'

'His experiences at the Longacre unhinged him. He . . . went through things.'

'But why target us?'

'He blames the kids he knew back then for what happened to him.'

To his surprise she slipped her fingers into his. 'And am I to blame?'

'None of this is your fault. He's sick, deranged.'

'And what about you? Are you to blame for what happened to him?'

Drake thought about that last catastrophic night at the Longacre, a night that changed the lives of those who survived it for ever. 'Yes, I am.'

'I doubt it. I married a violent man, but I'm not to blame for that. If Ned hadn't died when he did I'm sure he would have ended up killing me eventually. Well . . . my husband will never touch me again. I'm sorry I freaked out on you at the pub, I was scared. Were we . . . friends, back then?'

'Yes.' Drake decided that, whatever happened, he wanted to see Amelia Troy again. He looked away. 'We were friends.'

'Where did you get that gun?' she asked. 'I didn't think the police . . .'

'When all this is over, I'll explain it to you.'

She smiled. 'And what if I don't want to know?'

'Then I won't.'

She smiled. 'Decisions, decisions.'

She was a tough lady, Amelia, thought Drake. The vulnerable young girl with the precocious artistic talent had been knocked down so many times in life, and yet she kept going. 'You're a survivor.'

'Yes, I am.' She nodded, as if it had only just occurred to her. 'Hooray for me. But I'm not sure I want to know anything about the Longacre. When this whole nightmare is finally over, I just want to enjoy the rest of my life; I don't want to look back.'

'It'll all be over soon.'

Amelia squeezed his hand. 'Yes, it will.'

He wondered if that meant she wouldn't want to see him again, and the idea jolted him. Drake felt an unexpected affinity with Amelia. She was a survivor, but he was too.

When he blushed, she smiled wryly. 'Let's just see what happens?'

'Let's do that.'

'Where are we going?'

'There's someone who knows what's going on, he was at the home.' Drake didn't want to send them there, it was difficult to know how far to trust the weak-minded, anxious man he once knew, but he didn't know what else to do. At least now the so-called Two O'Clock Boy was in his sights. 'You'll have safety in numbers there.'

The toilet door opened and their hands separated.

'Right, then,' Amelia said to Drake and April. 'What now?'

'We're going to get you out of the city,' he said, 'and when you come back, I promise it'll all be over.'

He was about to take his phone out of his pocket when his daughter threw her arms around his neck. She held him tight, clung to him, sending shooting pains through his battered body that he barely noticed.

53

What nobody had expected, least of all Elliot, was that he would be left all on his lonesome with a gun at his disposal. Slumped on the sofa, the ugly thing rising and falling on the crest of his stomach, he thought about what to do next.

One thing came to mind.

He couldn't understand how everything had spiralled out of control so quickly. Just a few days ago he was letting that madman smooth talk him into handing over thirty grand. Just a deposit, the man calling himself Gavin had cheerfully explained. Elliot had never been so excited about anything, had believed it was a beginning for him, a successful new phase, which would prove, once and for all, that he was marching triumphantly forward in life.

But Elliot shouldn't be allowed to tie his own shoelaces, let alone make his own decisions. He had always hidden behind other people – Rhonda was just the latest – because he couldn't be trusted to do the right thing. Everything had been looking up – he had a home, a family, everything he needed – but then he had to cozy up to a multiple murderer, a man who wished him dead. Now, here he was, days later, and Rhonda was gone, Dylan was gone. He had killed a man. It would have been better if Perry had put him out of his misery.

There was no future that he could see.

She'll know the kind of man you are.

But at least he had a way out. The gun was not at all like the muscular-looking things in the movies, but it would do a job. So, sprawled there, smoking a last cigarette – because smoking inside the house was the least of his worries – Elliot decided that if the Two O'Clock Boy was so keen to kill him . . . well, he would save him the trouble.

All he had to do was flick off the safety; he wasn't going to repeat the same mistake that Perry had made. The trick was to stick the gun in his mouth, not to press it against the side of his head where it could slip. He'd heard the horror stories of the poor souls who botched it. Blown half their brains out and spent the rest of their days drooling vegetables hooked up to beeping machines. That would be typical of Elliot.

He had to focus on the tension of his finger against the trigger, concentrate on that, and nothing else, and then . . .

It would all be over.

All his memories of the Longacre would be gone. Of those summer days delivering Gordon's drugs; of a tearful Turrell gagging on the cockroach, the crunch of its shell in his mouth, the brown juices dribbling down his chin; of Tallis dashing the paperweight on Sally's head; of him and Connor burning her body, the smell of soil and petrol and burning flesh filling his nostrils, to this day as vivid a memory to Elliot as anything else in his life.

And that final, terrifying night in Gordon's office when he held them prisoner—

His phone rang.

Owen's number. Elliot killed the call.

His fist throbbed from pounding it into Perry's face. He

would never truly accept that the Two O'Clock Boy was right about him. That wasn't the kind of man he was – he couldn't be. He wasn't a bully, or a murderer.

Except he was.

The phone rang again, and he was going to turn it off, because he was sick and tired of the endless calls from Owen. But when he saw who was calling – and although it didn't matter now, nothing could make Rhonda come home, or Perry return from the dead – something, a faint glimmer of responsibility, made him answer.

'I need you to look after my daughter,' said the cop.

'Still ain't got this thing done?' Elliot had at least hoped that lunatic would be taken out of the equation.

'I'm working on it. But I need to think of my daughter's safety. Get her out of town till it's over. I'd be grateful if you could put her up for the night, maybe two. You'll be safer together.'

'Sure.' Elliot massaged his temples. 'Why not?'

'Unless explaining to your family—'

'That's not going to be a problem. They're gone, I sent them away.' One more night on Earth wouldn't make a difference. He touched the gun. 'She'll be safe here.'

'She'll be coming with Amelia Troy.'

'Amelia,' Elliot grunted. It was turning out to be something of a reunion. 'Be nice to see her after all these years.'

'Everything okay, Elliot?' Maybe the policeman could detect the weariness in his voice, the exhaustion.

'Yeah,' he said quickly. He didn't want to let him down, didn't want to get on his wrong side, not him, not on top of everything else. 'I'm good.'

Elliot scrambled off the sofa. He'd have to tidy the place,

get a fire going. He should shower, spray on some Lynx. That would be a start.

'And, Elliot . . . She doesn't know about *me*; she can never know.'

'I got that.'

'Make sure you do. He's coming for us, Elliot. If we let our guard down, he'll kill us all. Me, you, Amelia, the people we love.'

'If he dares to show his face here,' he said, trying to sound confident, 'I'll finish it.'

Elliot had killed a man already, had beaten him to death. But if it came to it, if he was forced to protect April Drake and Amelia Troy, he hoped to God that he could find the strength in himself to do it again.

54

Peter Holloway was sitting on the front steps of Ray Drake's house when Flick arrived. The side-panel lights on her vehicle winked when she locked it.

'What are you doing here, Peter?'

He stood. 'Since your . . . episode, DI Drake has been ignoring my calls. He's usually very prompt in getting back, and I'm concerned. He's my friend, DS Crowley.'

For the first time Flick detected a tension, an edge of vulnerability to the man. Maybe the officious Holloway was more human than she'd given him credit for. 'You old softy.'

'Myra Drake rarely leaves the house,' he said. 'I rang and rang on the doorbell but there was no answer.'

'When I knocked yesterday she came to the door pretty sharpish.'

Holloway regarded her curiously as they approached the door. 'You were here?'

'Long story,' she said. 'Perhaps she's gone out.'

'I could have sworn I heard somebody moving about inside, and . . . you should take a look around the back.'

'Stay here,' she told him, and walked down the alley at the side of the house. The glass in the patio doors at the rear had been smashed, the door forced.

'You understand now?'

Jumping in terror at the voice, she turned to see Holloway behind her. 'I told you to wait, Peter.'

'I would never let a lady go in alone. It's not in my nature.'

'Have you been inside?'

He held up his hands and Flick saw he was wearing nitrile gloves. 'I'm a very good boy, DS Crowley, and decided it best to wait for you.'

She'd left her own gloves in the car, but Holloway took out a spare pair and she snapped them on. 'This time, stay where you are.'

'Not a chance,' he said.

She led them into the big kitchen, which was more sleek and modern than she expected, and spotlessly clean, calling as she went, 'Myra! Myra, are you there?'

A door led into a long central hallway. More doors led off either side Flick knew the old woman lived in a basement flat below the main house. The internal connecting door was sure to be one of those. Holloway drifted ahead. Flick recalled his comment about hearing somebody in the house and was about to call him back, when he shouted her name.

When she followed him into a spacious reception room, she saw Myra Drake on a sofa, hands folded in her lap.

'Myra?'

The old woman didn't answer. When Flick came closer, she saw she was trembling. 'Myra, speak to me.'

Myra's hooded eyes were wide and round. Her lips moved, but nothing came out. Holloway crouched to check her pulse. 'She's in shock,' he said. 'Lay her down.'

'No,' croaked the old woman. Her arms fluttered as Flick tried to ease her shoulders down.

'Make her comfortable, I'll get a blanket.' Holloway left

the room. Flick heard his shoes clip across the parquet floor in the hallway and up the stairs.

'Peter,' said Flick, alarmed. 'Wait!'

Myra resisted Flick's attempts to lay her down and snatched at Flick's wrist, pulling her close. 'Listen to me, you must—'

'Is Ray here?' Flick tried to free her hand, but Myra's grip was surprisingly firm.

'It's not safe.' The old woman's eyes bored into hers. 'He's here!'

'Who's here, Myra? Ray?' Flick barked over her shoulder, urgently, 'Peter!'

Myra's fingers rubbed anxiously at her locket. 'You must go!'

'Let's get you out of here.'

Her bag, with her phone, was at her feet. She'd leave it. The priority was to get Myra outside. Myra swayed unsteadily when Flick helped her up. They moved slowly, taking small, hesitant steps into the gloomy hallway. The front door was just ahead. Something creaked on the floor above.

'Keep going, almost there,' said Flick in as calm a voice as she could manage.

Crossing the parquet, she peered up the stairs, which doubled back out of sight. A vase surrounded by photo frames stood in an alcove on the half-landing.

Flick rattled the handle of the door, but it was locked. 'The key.'

'The key?'

'Where do you keep it?'

The old woman blinked. 'He's here.'

'The key, Myra . . . Never mind.' She turned, intending

to lead Myra out the back, when a shadow moved across the half-landing. Making sure the old woman was upright against the door, Flick went to the bottom step. 'Peter!'

Gripping the banister, trying to avoid looking at the happy family photos of Drake, Laura and April on the wall, she called again. But there was no answer. The shadow shifted. Flick planted a foot on the bottom step, but thought better of going up. Myra stood, ashen, against the door.

What was that she heard above her – a voice?

'Peter, what is it?'

Against her better judgement, heart clattering in her chest, Flick climbed a couple of steps.

'Peter, is that you?'

Footsteps stumbled along the landing hidden above, and she edged back down.

Moments later, Holloway appeared at the turning, standing very tall and straight, his features hidden in the gloom.

'Peter!' She let out a sigh of relief at the sight of him, but when he didn't respond, she asked angrily: 'Have you called the Incident Room?' Holloway swayed gently, snorting loudly through his nose. 'Peter, don't play silly buggers!'

Holloway lifted his arms and stumbled to the edge of the landing. Knees buckling, he tipped down the stairs, fell forward onto her. His forehead slammed into hers, and she crumpled beneath him. Her spine jarred painfully against the parquet beneath Holloway's dead weight. Too stunned to feel the impact, stars bursting in her eyes, Flick scrambled from under him, scrabbling away on her hands and heels, sliding in the blood seeping from him, smearing it into the tile. Holloway lay face down, unmoving.

And when she looked up, there was somebody else standing in his place on the landing, face obscured in the dark.

'Ray?' she said.

'No, not him.' The figure stepped slowly downstairs, the shape of his bald head, the features of his face, that shy smile, solidifying as he moved into the light.

'Frank?' said Flick. Her limbs began to shake at the sight of the blood-smeared knife that Frank Wanderly clenched in his fist.

'Not Frank. That's not my name.'

Tap.

His upper lip trembled like a snarling wolf's and she glimpsed his white teeth, as he trod lightly down the stairs towards her, gently tapping the blade along the banister.

Tap, tap.

'Let me come down and I'll introduce myself properly.'

55

The skeletal trees lining the pavement shivered in the wind as Drake stuffed the gun into his belt at the small of his back and climbed from his car, walked to the address where the Two O'Clock Boy, or so he called himself, had lived under the name of Frank Wanderly.

He considered phoning Myra, but if she had any sense she would already be in the sticks, settling a few ancient scores with unlucky relatives. Just as April and Amelia would be en route to the safety of Elliot's home.

The address in Hornsey had been easy enough to find. The small, terraced house sat in the middle of an anonymous row, nothing to distinguish it from the houses on either side except the number embossed in bulging red tile above the door. The curtains on the ground floor were drawn. A security alarm was fixed beneath the bedroom window, but the dummy box was old, the telephone number on it prefixed with the long redundant 0171. Ray Drake glanced along the street to make sure nobody was about and then slipped round the back into a neglected garden.

At the kitchen window, he cupped his eyes against the glass to see a kitchen furnished with beige Formica units. The door was locked, but the frame was rotten. Drake leaned hard into it and the wood splintered. Inside, the kitchen was bare, nondescript, except for a curious collection of objects on top of the fridge. Among them, a horseshoe, a beer mat, an egg timer with mauve sand. There was a replica of Blackpool Tower, a bicycle pump and a china figurine of a maid with a bonnet and a milk pail, similar to the ones in the Overtons' bedroom.

Drake opened the door to the living room, which was dark behind the closed curtains, and flicked on the light. Dust burned on the bulb beneath a wicker shade. Everything in the room was impersonal, second hand, the atmosphere musty. There was an old sofa and a sideboard. Inside were textbooks, a single, upturned wine glass on a doily, a neat pile of newspapers, a box of matches.

Drake pocketed the matches and was climbing the stairs when his phone vibrated. One eye on the landing, he checked the Caller ID. Flick. She'd already left several messages, he saw, and there were others from Peter Holloway. Upstairs, the bathroom was empty except for a bar of soap, a deodorant, a toothbrush and towel. Strings of dust trembled along the skirting of an empty rear bedroom, below cartoon animals parading on faded wallpaper. No effort had been made to make this house anything resembling a home.

Walking into the main bedroom, he saw a single bed, diminished in a sea of carpet. The duvet was a perfect rectangle, the crisp white sheet beneath tucked with precision. On a bedside cabinet was a lamp and an encyclopedia.

Drake turned to the wall opposite, which was covered its entire length, from ceiling to floor, with photographs and newspaper clippings and documents. Sheets of information detailing victims clustered in groups; images of men and women, photographed going about their daily business; floor plans of properties; street maps; social-media screen grabs;

work schedules; diary excerpts. Keys labelled with passcodes hung from pins. Lengths of string raced across the wall, tacking in every direction, mysteriously linking clusters of pages.

Many of the names and some of the faces were familiar to Drake, others he didn't recognise. Maybe they had all been at the home, or perhaps in his murderous obsession, the Two O'Clock Boy had given innocent men and women an obscure, fatal relationship to the Longacre that they didn't deserve.

His eyes flitted from one newspaper cutting to another:

> . . . twins were last night killed in a blaze that ripped through a sheltered housing . . .
> . . . attached a rubber hose to the exhaust of their car on 12 November last year, and died of carbon . . .

Lifting the cuttings, he found others beneath.

> . . . blamed faulty brakes for the fatal crash, which killed a family of . . .
> . . . impaled on railings, causing massive internal . . .

Drake followed the trail of paper until he found his own name contained in a satellite of clippings isolated at the edge of the wall, along with Elliot Juniper and Amelia Troy.

There were photos of Elliot, sitting in the snug of a pub, and walking along a country lane with his stepson. A black-and-white image of Amelia – pale, sad – in a hospital bed after her overdose. And he himself was photographed from a window overlooking the car park at the station, and with

370

his daughter exiting from a restaurant. There he was again with Laura, helping her into the car, probably taking her to a hospital appointment in the weeks before she died. He tugged the photo off the wall – the tack popped out and flew over his head – and pocketed it. Finally, there was a photo of him with the man he had known as Frank Wanderly at some police function.

Drake stepped back to take in the elaborate design in its entirety, its sheer scale. The last thing the Two O'Clock Boy saw before he closed his eyes, and the first thing he saw when he opened them, was this macabre montage of death and conspiracy. Its mass loomed over him as he slept, imprinting itself into his dreams and nightmares. The conspiracy was overwhelming. All the people he had killed, men, women and children – and all the people he was going to kill. He would stare at it, absorbing it, his plans shifting and sliding in the dark, slotting together in his head like elaborate pieces of machinery.

Dead centre on the wall, separated from the other clusters of information by a thin moat of space, was a photograph: Toby Turrell as a small boy, taken at the coast. Wrapped in a windcheater, a big smile on his face, hair plastered to his head by rain. The boy held the hands of his happy parents. In the distance, a rainbow speared the horizon.

Drake looked one last time at the sprawling design, an insane representation of the inside of the Two O'Clock Boy's head, and went downstairs.

He opened the front door and walked to his car, checking he was alone in the street, and took from the boot a petrol canister. Back inside, he set to work, pouring the liquid across the bedroom, staining the perfect white duvet, and sloshing it on the wall, careful not to splash any on his shoes.

The cold canister ignited memories of that last horrific night at the home – and the lonely death of the boy who had saved him from Gordon, and whom he barely knew. A boy from whom he had taken so much.

For decades he had hidden behind a façade, the smiling face of a man few people really knew. Laura knew him and loved him, despite everything. He missed his wife, but she was gone and he was afraid that Ray Drake, too, would soon slip away.

When the canister was empty, its contents splashed in the kitchen and living room, he took out the matches at the front door.

Drake's phone rang again – his home number – and some instinct made him answer the call. 'Yes.'

'I'm ready now,' said the voice, this time undisguised by any electronic filter. 'I'm ready for you to finish what you started.'

Propping the phone between his ear and his shoulder, Drake pinched three matches together.

'You tell me when you want me to kill you,' said Drake, 'and I'll happily oblige.'

'It's time now, I think. Yes, I think so. We're waiting for you.'

Drake cut the call. He struck the matches and tossed them, watched fire blossom in an orange inferno at his feet, Gordon Tallis's agonising last moments flickering momentarily on the wall like a shadow play.

He considered how he was right back where he had started. How everything he had strived for would soon come to an end.

'See you soon, Toby,' he said.

56

Here they were, Amelia Troy and April Drake, pulling up the drive in a fancy sports car. He didn't want them here – couldn't stop thinking about what he had done, what he was going to do – but Elliot had made a promise. One more night wasn't going to make a difference when you were staring eternity in the face.

The wind chime was going nine to the dozen. Elliot loved its gentle tinkle in a soft breeze, but tonight the fierce wind was blowing the tops of the trees sideways – the gales were steadily picking up strength – and its incessant clinking, like a furious warning, made him want to rip it down.

'Ladies,' he said, forcing a smile, 'welcome.'

Elliot felt strangely emotional at the sight of Amelia Troy. He'd expected some butch old painter in dungarees, but when she climbed from the car he saw she was slim and pretty. She hugged him, and he smelled cigarettes on her, which made him like her all the more.

'Thanks for having us, Elliot.'

They'd gone through the wars together years ago, him and Amelia, but she looked like she'd come out the other side in better shape. She was worth more money than he could imagine – with millions in the bank! – all because she chucked paint at a canvas. Once, Elliot had gone to a gallery to see her paintings, had found them too . . .

373

disturbing. Elliot preferred more uplifting pictures, like that dancing couple with the butler. Life was hard enough without hanging depressing stuff on your walls.

When Amelia looked up at the cottage, with its peeling paint and rotting frames, Elliot grimaced. 'Not up to your usual standards; it ain't exactly a mansion.'

'It's comfortable.' She touched his arm. 'And, believe me, my place isn't exactly a palace. This is April, Ray Drake's daughter.'

He nodded, hanging back, not wanting to frighten the girl. She was a beauty in all her designer gear. Her dad's princess, no doubt. It couldn't be easy for her to be here, cowering from a deranged killer in a ramshackle cottage in the middle of nowhere, alongside an oaf.

'I've a son myself,' said Elliot. 'Well, a stepson, sort of thing.' A lump formed in his throat when he realised he'd never see Dylan again. 'Shall we get inside?'

April smiled, flatly. 'Do you have a . . . ?'

Elliot blinked, and Amelia prompted: 'We drank a *lot* of water on the way.'

'Of course! Bathroom's upstairs, first door.'

They watched the girl climb the stairs, disappearing out of sight. Elliot had made a fire, which crackled and hissed, throwing warmth into the small room.

'I hope it's not too much of an inconvenience to have us here. Your family aren't going to be put out?'

'They're away,' said Elliot quickly. 'Staying with friends. Thought it would be best, you know, in the circumstances.'

Amelia nodded thoughtfully, her gaze dropping to his injured hand. 'I'm sure we were good friends back at the home, but I don't remember much about back then.'

'Yeah,' said Elliot, uncomfortable. 'We were pals.'

'Then it's good to meet again, even if the circumstances aren't so jolly.'

He caught sight of himself in the mirror. He'd never been a handsome man, what with the nose smeared across his face like gravy across a plate, and he was carrying a few more pounds than he should, but he looked wretched right now. Dark rings cupped his eyes, his skin was grey. Emotion pressed against his ribs. He had given her hell back in the home, her and those others – particularly Turrell, who was now going about murdering all and sundry – and she had every right to hate him. 'This is my fault.'

'What are you talking about?'

'I just want you to know that I'm not the same person you knew back then.' He gripped her arm. 'I treated you wrong, I'm sorry. I was scared, I was . . . That's not me any more. I got a partner who loves me, and a son. That's me now, that's who I am.'

A look fell down her face – discomfort, maybe even fear. He realised his fingers were digging into her skin, and let go.

'It sounds like you love them very much.'

He closed his eyes, overwhelmed by his own stupidity. Rhonda and Dylan were the only good things that had ever happened to him.

'Yes.' His voice was barely a whisper. 'I do.'

'Whatever you're thinking,' said Amelia, 'I promise you it's not that bad.'

But it is, he thought. He couldn't tell her about the dead man hidden in a car boot, and the stolen money, an old couple's savings, stashed in his wardrobe. He just had to get through this night. Stay focused. He was expected to protect these girls. 'Look at me, this ain't no way to welcome an old friend. Let's have some tea . . . something stronger.'

'Tea would be good.' Amelia smiled. 'I mean it, Elliot. It's good to see you. One last time.'

'You're safe until our friend—' He checked himself. It didn't feel right saying the policeman's name, he would have to be careful about what he said in front of the girl. 'Until everything's good for you to go home.'

'I just . . .' Amelia nodded, her cheerful façade cracking. 'I just want it to be over.'

'Do you trust him?' he asked quietly, nodding up the stairs to where April had disappeared. Her father had changed a lot since Elliot had last seen him, on the night of that fatal fire more than three decades ago.

'Yes, I do.'

The way she said it, with a quiet confidence, made him feel slightly better about the whole fucked-up situation. He heard the toilet flush and the tap running. The pipes shuddered. An old cottage like this, you heard everything that went on in every room. Then April stepped downstairs.

'There's plenty in the fridge,' Elliot said, 'but we're out of foie gras.'

'I'm afraid that's utterly unacceptable.' Amelia tapped a finger on his chest. 'And I promise there will be serious consequences for you.'

It was dark now, they were a long way from street lamps and the evening dropped like a blackout curtain. The night sky was filled with lumbering cloud. He didn't like the idea that the poor, insane Toby Turrell was out there somewhere watching, waiting for his moment.

The women sat at the kitchen table while Elliot brewed tea, but the conversation was stilted. The girl, in particular, was subdued. Amelia did her best to put everybody at ease, asking Elliot about his family and his life. But he was nervous in front of April, unsure of how much he could say to her. He didn't want to tell them Rhonda had left him, and the information that he intended to kill himself just as soon as they were safe would add the finishing touch to an already strained atmosphere.

'I know you're frightened.' He placed a steaming mug in front of April. 'But your dad – he'll fix this. He'll, er, arrest this guy.'

April cocked her head. 'How do you know him?'

'An old investigation he worked on,' said Amelia quickly. 'Isn't that right, Elliot?'

'Correct.' Elliot cleared his throat. 'Way back in the mists of time.'

The girl stared doubtfully, looked like she was about to say something, when the doorbell rang. Two angry bursts. April's hand immediately searched for Amelia's across the table.

'Are you expecting anyone?'

'A salesman, probably.' Elliot smothered his anxiety with a grin. 'Get a lot of them around here. You girls stay here, relax.' He placed a biscuit barrel on the table. 'Help yourself.'

At the door, Elliot stifled a groan when he saw the shape on the other side of the patterned glass. Slipping his grazed fist into his pocket, he opened the door.

'Owen!' he said loudly. 'What a pleasure!'

The old man was watching leaves blow across the bonnet of Amelia's sports car. 'Evening, Elliot.' He nodded at the vehicle. 'Been splashing the cash already?'

'Good one,' said Elliot tensely.

Amelia called from the kitchen doorway: 'Who is it?'

'Just a mate,' said Elliot, over his shoulder. 'Nothing to worry about, I'll be back in a minute.'

Owen tried to look inside but Elliot stepped out, closing the door behind him. The black wall of trees across the lane hunkered against the relentless wind. The barn creaked and cracked.

'Nice to see you, Owen.'

'Is it?' asked Owen, dabbing at one of his watery eyes with a knuckle. 'Is it nice to see me, Elliot?'

'Course it is.' Elliot's laugh was brittle.

Owen nodded at the closed door. 'A bad time, then?'

'Got some friends round, that's all.' Looking down, he saw the old man's trousers were neatly tucked into a pair of wellingtons. 'What can I do for you?'

'Sorry for the inconvenience, Elliot, but I want to know where he is.'

'Where who is?'

'I haven't heard from Perry since he left to pick you up. Everything go as planned?'

'Yeah.' That bloody chime clanging in his ears. 'Like clockwork.'

'Then where is he?'

'Please, Owen. I've people here.'

'Well, we don't want to spoil the party. Why don't we head to the barn? We can talk about it there.'

'Sure.'

Elliot followed Owen down the drive.

'Thing is, Elliot, I'm worried.' Owen's small frame braced against the wind as they walked. 'It's odd for Perry not to get in touch. He usually sticks to me like glue.'

'He dropped me off and then sped away,' Elliot said quickly. 'That was the last I saw of him.'

'You don't think he's trying to pull a fast one, do you, and taken all the money for himself?'

Elliot let out a long breath. 'He seemed pretty fired up. Angry, you know, volatile. And . . .'

Owen stopped outside the barn. 'And what?'

'Well, he had a few choice things to say about you.'

'What did he say?' Owen blinked. 'Tell me.'

'Nothing.' Elliot folded his arms. 'It's not stuff you would want me to repeat.'

'Son of a bitch,' said Owen quietly. 'How could he do it, Elliot? He's worked for me for years. Perry has been like a son to me.'

'Last I saw, he was driving off with the rucksack.' Elliot sighed. 'Sorry, Owen, it looks like he's done a runner.'

A branch cracked in the darkness. They heard it crash to the floor.

'Can't trust anyone, these days,' said Owen sadly. 'You really can't.'

'No,' agreed Elliot, 'you can't.'

'If only Perry were here to put his side of this.' Eyes fixed sourly on Elliot, the old man prodded open the barn door with his foot.

When Elliot looked into the gloom, he saw a figure standing in the empty space: Perry. The man's eyes, those small, hard pellets, almost hidden in his swollen face, glittered with hatred.

Owen placed a hand on the small of Elliot's back and guided him inside.

57

The first thing Drake saw when he entered his house was Toby Turrell, the man he knew as Frank Wanderly, waiting in the hallway, a long knife down at his side.

Flick Crowley sat tensely on the bottom step of the staircase. On the floor in front of them both, face down in a pool of blood, was a body.

'It's Peter Holloway,' said Turrell helpfully.

Closing the door, Drake saw the old woman against the wall, her arms crossed over her chest as if she had already been entombed. 'Myra?'

Lips pursed tightly, she nodded.

'We thought you'd never get here.' The way Turrell listlessly rubbed his scalp made Drake lower his gun. 'Don't do that,' Toby snapped. 'You'll need it in a moment.'

Drake took a good look at the man. In all the time that Frank Wanderly had worked at the station – several years now – Drake had never recognised him. Turrell's features from that chaotic time had always been muddy in his memory, and there was little to connect Wanderly to the boy from the Longacre. Wanderly was tall and bland, a happy, amiable man who Drake saw for a few seconds each day. Toby Turrell had been small and slight, with a mop of thick, blond hair. All he remembered about him was the misery and terror etched onto his face that last night at the home. The forgettable child had grown up to be a forgettable adult, the kind of man who slipped from your memory the moment you turned your back on him. Which, of course, was exactly how he went about his murderous business.

'All those people, Toby, all those families.'

'And why should they have people to love?' Turrell made a face. 'Sons, daughters, wives, husbands – and I have nothing! I worshipped Mary and Bernard, I adored them. None of you stopped me, and I have had to live with the consequences of what . . . I did.'

'You killed your parents,' said Drake quietly.

'You should have let me die at that home,' said Turrell. 'If you had, I wouldn't have done it, or killed any of those other people. In a way, all this is entirely because of you.'

'It's always someone else's fault with you, isn't it?' said Myra, from the corner.

'But I'm going to give you the opportunity to do the right thing. Kill me now, put right what was made wrong all those years ago, and I promise I'll let your daughter live.'

'She's out of your grasp now, Toby.'

Turrell smirked. 'You tried to run me down in your car; you came to kill me at Amelia's.'

Drake paced the hallway, trying to think of one good reason to blow his head off, in spite of Flick. 'Why didn't you kill me when you had the chance, Toby? Why didn't you kill Amelia or April?'

'Because I've been waiting for this moment,' said Turrell. 'Waiting for you and me to meet, face to face. You set all this bloodshed into motion, and it's your responsibility to finish it.' He pointed with the knife. 'I have chosen *you* to do it.'

In any other circumstances Drake would be happy to oblige Toby Turrell. But with Flick Crowley present, killing him in cold blood was out of the question. 'I'm not going to kill you, Toby.'

'You must! I want to be with Mary and Bernard. Go on, right here.' He pulled back his arms and puffed out his chest. 'Shoot me in the heart.'

When Drake didn't move, Turrell grabbed Flick's hair, dragging her to her feet. She cried out, and Drake snapped his gun towards him.

'That's more like it.' Turrell's eyes flashed. 'That's more like the old *you*. I really thought I'd lost you, so you can imagine my joy when I found you – hiding in plain sight! It's all so perfect. I want to die, and you want to kill me. Look, I'll show you how.'

Pulling Flick to him, he traced the knife in a slow panto-mime from her throat to her stomach, the tip snagging on the cotton of her shirt, to show Ray Drake the bloody journey of the blade if he chose to slice her open.

'I discovered a long time ago that killing is easy. Believe me, I'm very good at it, I've had a *lot* of practice. I've always been good at things.' He laughed in delight. 'Mummy and Daddy always said I was a clever little boy.'

'Your parents left you in the Longacre, Toby,' said Drake.

'My parents loved me!'

'They left you there.'

'They didn't know what went on at that place!' Spittle flew from Turrell's mouth.

'Are you absolutely sure about that?' asked Drake. 'Because they didn't hurry to take you away, they took their own good time about it. They left you there as long as possible, with

Gordon, with all those kids, and let those things happen to you. They were terrible people, Mary and Bernard, selfish and cruel and thoughtless, and they deserved to die.'

'Shut up!'

'They hated you so much they sent you to that place.'

'Shut your fucking mouth!' Turrell screamed. 'They loved me!' He covered his face with his knife hand and howled. His shoulders heaved, snot bubbled from his nose. 'They weren't like that!'

'But that's what you've always suspected, isn't it?' Drake tapped his chest. 'In here, Toby, you've never been able to rid yourself of the nagging feeling that they hated you so much that they left you there on purpose.'

'Call it in, Ray,' said Flick, through gritted teeth.

'That's a cruel thing to say!' whined Toby. 'They loved me, and they made a mistake! You're just like all the rest. No fancy home, no snooty mother or spoilt brat of a daughter makes you any different. You're just the same as Elliot and Kenny and Jason and that other scum.'

Drake stepped forward. He was no marksman, and Flick was too close to Turrell. 'You killed your parents. No one else is responsible.'

'But I didn't want to.' The hallway echoed with Turrell's sobs. 'I miss them so much!'

'Call it in, Ray.'

'I know you do, Toby,' said Drake. 'But it's over. April is safe, Amelia is safe, it's just you and me now.'

'No, it's not over.' A nasty smiled twisted on his face. 'It's all worked out just the way I planned it. Elliot, your daughter—'

'Are safe,' said Drake.

'Make the call, Ray,' said Flick, her voice cracking.

Pushing Flick away, Turrell clamped his eyes shut. 'I'm ready now, you can shoot me.' But Drake didn't move. 'I said I'm ready!'

'I'm not going to kill you, Toby,' said Drake. His free hand tapped rapidly against his thigh as he tried to fit together the sequence of events. Turrell took his daughter, and attacked Amelia. But they both survived. All those others died.

'Why didn't you kill April? Why didn't you kill Amelia when you had the chance?'

Turrell leered. 'Kill me and I'll tell you.'

'It doesn't make sense, Toby.'

'So you're not going to kill me?'

'You're going to prison. It's over,' Drake said. 'For both of us.'

'I understand,' said Toby bitterly. 'But there's one thing I have to do first.'

And then, shrieking at the top of his voice, Turrell lunged towards Drake with the knife raised above his head.

Ray Drake lifted the gun in a precise, fluid movement and fired at point-blank range into his chest. Turrell's feet lifted into the air and he flew back against the stairs and slid to the floor.

Drake dropped the weapon and went to Flick, who was crying and shaking. He took her in his arms and she clung to him.

'It's over,' he told her, desperately wanting to believe it. 'It's all over.'

Myra stepped away from the wall to nudge Turrell's body with her foot. 'He's dead, Raymond.'

Flick pushed Drake away and staggered to the old woman, her face full of rage.

'Don't call him that!' She swung to face him. 'That's not who he is!'

58

1984

Ranting and swigging from a bottle, Gordon Tallis worked himself into a fury.

Forced to listen to his bitter tirade, they sat in the room – Connor and Elliot, Kenny and Jason, Amelia and Toby – anxious and fearful. Each of them was accused of trying to destroy him. But mostly it was the Turrell boy who bore the brunt of his drunken anger. Toby sat with his face pressed into his knees, unresponsive to Gordon's threats.

Huddled against the wall, Amelia reached for Connor's hand, and he took it. Her grip was hot and clammy. Elliot darted glances in his direction, as if expecting him to do something, anything.

Life at the home carried on as usual outside the room. Connor heard the Dents shout commands in the kitchen; the chirp and chatter of conversation over the evening meal; the bedtime stampede, feet thundering on the floorboards above.

'It's all over for me.' Gordon paced, flinging out his arms. 'I've associates breathing down my neck, and a high court judge on my back. It's all right for you people, you've your whole lives ahead, but who's looking out for Gordon? All the effort I put into this place, the commitment. All that good work ruined because of a stupid bitch.'

He stopped in front of Connor. Liquid plinked in the bottle as it dropped from his fist and rolled on the floor. 'What do you think, lad? What should Gordon do next?'

'You should let us go, Gordon. We just want to sleep.'

'But where's the fun in that?' Gordon's lips curled back, revealing his jumble of teeth. 'After everything I've done for you, and you let me down!' Lurching forward, he grabbed Toby. The boy hung limply in his grip, his eyes had lost all focus. 'And this is the one who's caused it all. I do people a favour out of the goodness of my heart, and this is what happens.'

'Put him down.' Connor jumped to his feet.

'Yes.' The manager threw Toby down, wiped his palms down his sides. 'Let's get this over with.'

He pushed Connor, who nearly fell over Jason's outstretched legs, stumbling into the room at the back. Connor saw the threadbare mattress, the petrol canister beside it, and the green ribbed radiator.

'I've been waiting for this, boy.' Gordon slammed the door shut. 'It's time for us to settle our differences, one way or the other.'

Connor was pinned against the radiator. 'Promise you won't hurt them.'

'I can't do that.' Gordon giggled. 'This anger inside me has been building, building. I've nothing to lose no more. The boy ain't going home, I'll tell you that much.' He ran his fingers through Connor's hair, and his face was pressed so close that the boy could smell his fetid breath. 'You've been a big disappointment to me, lad. I thought we were chums, partners. I thought we shared something special.'

Connor reached for the manager's hand, felt his calloused fingers, and whispered: 'I've been waiting for this moment.'

Gordon stared, as if in a trance. 'You and me both, boy.'

Then Connor let go of his hand, and slid out from against the radiator. Gordon's hand snapped towards him angrily – and jerked to a stop. He was handcuffed to the radiator piping. Gordon yanked at the cuff, then lunged at Connor, clawing with his free hand, but the boy stepped out of his reach.

'Get these off!' Straining against the radiator, the cuffs jangling against the metal strut, Gordon's face twisted with rage. 'Sooner or later I'm going to get free. You may be long gone, I don't expect you to stick around, but the others will be here.' His laugh was laced with bile. 'And, believe me, boy, I'm going to make those cunts pay.'

And it was at that moment Connor knew what he had to do. Knew why he had stayed in this place. Maybe he had always known why. With shaking hands, he picked up the canister and unscrewed the cap.

Gordon sneered. 'Oh, come on now, you're not going to—'

He reared back as Connor lifted the canister and slopped the contents all over him.

'What do you think you're doing?' The petrol soaked his chest and legs; Connor threw it into his face and he spluttered. 'What the fuck are you doing?'

The pungent liquid spattered onto the diamond-patterned carpet. Connor splashed it over the walls, and it soaked into the mattress as Gordon hurled threats, obscenities, working himself into a frenzy. Then he threw down the canister. Its contents gulped onto the manager's feet.

Connor's head pulsed with cold, hard contempt.

He took out the lighter he'd kept from the night before. Thumbed the flint. Sparks flew off it.

'You ain't gonna do it!' snarled Gordon. 'You wouldn't dare! You and me are pals!'

Connor swayed on his heels, the fumes making him light-headed, and lost his balance. Stumbling too close, Gordon grabbed his wrist. Connor screamed as his arm was wrenched behind his back, and he was pulled close against Gordon, who lifted his arm around the boy's neck.

'Drop it!' screamed Gordon, who couldn't snatch the lighter with his free arm and instead tightened the crook of his elbow around the boy's throat and squeezed with all his might. Connor felt air trap in his lungs, blood bulge in his head, as he struggled to keep the lighter at arm's length. He plucked ineffectually at Gordon's arm with his free hand. The lack of oxygen, the stench of petrol in his nostrils, made the room warp and bend and his thoughts became sluggish.

And just as his outstretched arm ached and he was afraid that he would drop the lighter, he had a fleeting sense of glass shattering in the skylight and a figure dropping into the room.

And then Ray Drake was pulling at Gordon's arm, digging his fingers into his flesh. The lighter fell from Connor's hand and bounced across the floor. Gordon released his arm from Connor's throat to punch Ray in the side of his head, sending the boy flying into a corner.

Connor fell to his knees and crawled to the lighter – gulping for air, colour and shapes rolling in his vision – to spark the flint. The flame took, and as the manager struggled in panic, Connor lunged towards him – pressed it into his face.

Flame crackled across Gordon's skin, sizzling greedily into his hair and collar.

Connor stood back and saw him burn. Watched his body erupt into flame. Fire leapt from Gordon, igniting the curtains, and racing across the floor to the mattress.

Gordon screamed and thrashed in agony, frenzied hands clawed in submission, his skin cooking. Then Connor snapped out of his trance – knew they had to get out of there. He shouted to Ray in the corner, who climbed unsteadily to his feet. But his path was blocked by the burning mattress on one side and Gordon's flaming body on the other.

'Quick!' Connor held out his arm, and Ray moved forward, cringing against the heat, to pass close to Gordon—

Whose hand thrashed out, knocking Ray behind the rising wall of fire.

'No!' Connor tried to get to him, but was forced back. Flames rippled to the ceiling. Smoke rolled into every corner. When he tried again to get to Ray a hand held him back.

'No!' Connor wept tears of rage and frustration. 'No! No! No!'

'You can't,' shouted Elliot, as Ray Drake disappeared behind the thickening fire and smoke. Connor angrily shrugged off Elliot and surged forward, but couldn't find a way through the intense heat.

Connor's last memory, as he was dragged from the room, was of Gordon, a fireball shaped like a man, on his knees, his last agonising screams lost in the snap of the fire.

And Ray Drake's eyes, imploring, terrified, vanishing behind a black curtain of smoke.

Back in the office, Kenny and Jason pounded desperately

at the locked door to the hallway. Toby was still slumped against the wall.

'Help us!' screamed Elliot, but Connor stood dazed in the middle of the room.

The two biggest boys, Elliot and Jason, picked up the desk chair and threw it at the window, smashing the glass. Cold night air sucked inside. Flame and smoke billowed greedily from the back room. Elliot kicked out the shards of glass around the frame, and one by one the children climbed onto the sill and jumped to the pavement.

'Connor!' Elliot shouted, and Connor lifted Amelia in his arms. The children from upstairs poured onto the street from the front door. People from the squat opposite came to watch. Connor swung Amelia out of the window and climbed out after her, falling to the pavement. He sat on his haunches in the road to watch the fire take hold of the building.

'Where's Gordon?' Ronnie Dent stumbled through the crowd of kids. He angrily hauled Connor to his feet. 'Where is he?'

'He's dead,' Connor said softly. 'I killed him.'

Dent flinched from the boy's calm stare and disappeared quickly back into the crowd.

Elliot came up behind him. 'Where's Toby?'

Connor looked everywhere, but couldn't see him. When he moved towards the house, Elliot grabbed at him. 'You can't—'

But Connor shrugged him off and ran up the steps. Smoke poured from the window, clawing at his eyeballs. He covered his mouth and pressed inside, the image of Ray Drake's final, terrified look as he disappeared behind the whirling flame and smoke repeating in his mind's eye. In the hallway

Connor kicked at the office door, pumping his leg against the lock.

The door splintered. Smoke and heat rolled towards him, forcing him back. He dropped to his hands and knees and crawled inside. Orange flame climbed every wall. The desk was alight on one side, the sofa on the other. Toby was curled into a ball when Connor reached him. He tugged at the kid's arm, barely able to open his stinging eyes, or to breathe.

'No,' mumbled Toby.

'Take my hand,' Connor said. 'Take it.'

He bunched the kid's jumper in his fist, tugging him towards the door, blind from the smoke, which burned his lungs and throat. Connor's limbs became sluggish, heavy. Toby's body was limp, his feet dragged. The kid made no effort to escape or even move. The door was so close – but Connor collapsed, hardly able to breathe.

And then he felt the boy rise out of his grip, the weight lifted. Squinting up, he glimpsed Elliot stumble to the door with Toby over his shoulder. Connor crawled out after them, tumbling down the steps, rolling onto the pavement just as the upstairs windows exploded from the intense heat. Connor fell across Toby as glass rained down around them. All the children screamed in terror.

'You're alive,' Connor gasped. 'You can go home.'

The boy lay on the road, staring at the sky.

In the distance they heard sirens. Connor pushed his way through the crowd, the screams and shouts and distant sirens muffled in his head, as if he were underwater. Amelia and Kenny, all the other children, sat on the pavement watching the house burn.

Elliot stared when Connor told him: 'You'll never see me again.'

At the dead end of the road he used his last vestiges of strength to scrabble over the wall and into the cool darkness. The burble of excited voices faded as he stumbled across the train track, and up the verge on the other side.

Connor collapsed on the grass to watch the night sky consume the smoke pumping from the windows. A wave of flashing blue light, police cars and fire engines, poured towards the home. Flame threw flickering shadow over the uniformed men moving urgently among the kids.

He had killed a man.

He'd poured petrol over Gordon Tallis and set him alight. Watched him burn.

The truth was, once he had decided to do it, it had felt right.

But Ray Drake had also died. Connor told himself it wasn't his fault. Ray had tried to save him, and instead had been killed. He shouldn't have been there.

Connor's anger had gone now, but he knew with a sickening certainty it would return. The whirling chaos inside of him would eat him alive him if he allowed it.

He needed to tell them, the judge and his wife, that it wasn't his fault. Tell them Ray had saved him. And now he was dead. Their son was dead.

When Elliot saw him on the other side of the tracks, barely a shadow against the night, Connor turned and walked into the night.

They wouldn't meet again for another thirty years.

59

'The decades since my boy died have seemed like a dream. We waited for Raymond to come home, we waited for days, but he never did. And then Connor found his way here and told us what happened, and it was the most terrible, the most awful, thing to know our son was dead.' Myra Drake swallowed. 'And that I was in some way responsible. He died because he cared too much and his parents cared too little.' She lifted the wisps of fine hair drifting down the back of her neck. 'Do you mind?'

Drake stepped behind her to undo the tiny clasp, and Myra offered the locket to Flick, who took it. Inside was a small photograph of her dead son, its edges clipped in a rough hexagonal. In the photo he was seven or eight years old, and he straddled a turnstile in the countryside, smiling easily, eyes burning with a fierce intelligence.

'It's the only photo I have here,' said Myra. 'There are one or two in a safety deposit box, but the others were destroyed. Ray was a good boy, a popular child. I wish I had got to know him better, I wish Leonard and I had taken more time to listen to him before he . . .'

Myra shook her head, as if she had said enough. Stunned, Flick sat back in her chair. The boy who had been Connor Laird and was now called Ray Drake paced the kitchen, willing his mobile to ring. The bodies of Peter Holloway and Toby Turrell lay undisturbed in the hallway.

'And when Connor came to you . . .?' prompted Flick.

'Everybody believed him dead, so when he turned up on our doorstep, Leonard and I . . . well, we took him in. We understood the consequences of what we did. The boy had a fire in him, an anger, and we knew it wouldn't be easy, but we felt such anguish, such guilt, you see, so it was a kind of penance. There's no doubt in my mind it is what Raymond would have wanted. If he had lived, he would have helped people, in the same way he was desperate to help that wretched cousin of his.' The old woman's hooded eyes followed Drake around the room. 'We cut family ties, and, of course, he couldn't go to school, so he was taught here. We lost quite a few tutors along the way, I can tell you, he was a difficult young man, to say the least. Life was a challenge for a number of years. But also . . . oddly exhilarating.'

And it hadn't been easy for Myra, thought Drake. But she'd never compromised, never backed down. When he was young, when the anger blasted off Connor Laird like heat off a furnace, she never flinched. She stood her ground. His guilt and rage threatened to engulf them all but she never showed any weakness, any fear.

'He'll never be my son, he'll never be my boy, he understands that. But I'm proud of him, and proud of what he has achieved.' Myra turned to Flick. 'He's come so very far in life. He's a different person now, I think, to the youth we took in.'

When Drake had tried to call April's phone it was switched off, the same with Amelia's phone. When he tried Elliot's number the call went to voicemail.

Myra reached for the locket, the thin chain slithering across the table, to click shut the image of the son she lost many years ago. She closed her fist around it.

'I thought it was you,' Flick told Drake. 'I thought you killed all those people.' She took out the cutting with the photo of Connor Laird cringing from the camera and placed it on the table.

'Yes, that was Connor.' Myra tapped the image as if it was a different person entirely from the man she raised. But Drake didn't look, his eyes remained fixed on his phone, a nameless anxiety seeping through him.

'Look at the photo,' Flick told him, and when he ignored her, she said it again. '*Look at it.*'

Finally, he picked up the cutting to gaze for a long moment into the flashing eye of Connor Laird. Then he dropped it and tried Elliot's number again. It went to voicemail, so he called Amelia's number. He would keep calling for as long as it took.

'Tell me,' Flick said to Drake.

Myra sighed. 'I've told you everything you need to—'

'Shut up, Myra,' snapped Flick. The old woman blinked. 'I want to hear it from him.'

So Ray Drake told her about his life as Connor Laird, and about the Longacre home. It all tumbled from him. He told her of Gordon's murder of Sally, and how Connor and Elliot and Toby Turrell had been forced to bury her, something inside of Turrell becoming corrupted in the process. He recounted Leonard and Myra Drake's visit, and said that a fire broke out later that night; told her how he stumbled, filthy and feverish, across the city, and found his way, days later, to Myra and Leonard, who took him in; and how the judge used his wealth and influence to ensure Connor Laird took the identity of their dead child, Raymond Drake.

He explained how he had long ago destroyed any evidence

– every file and photo – that linked Connor Laird to that place, burying the past, his former identity, as best he could; removing files and destroying documents about the Longacre. He took every copy of the article about Leonard and Myra's visit from newspaper offices and libraries and destroyed it. Or so he had thought. God only knows where Kenny had found that article about the visit of the Drakes to the Longacre.

Finally, he told her about Turrell's manipulation of Jordan, and how he himself had saved Amelia's life earlier in the evening, and sent her and April to Elliot's cottage in the middle of nowhere, where they would be safe, or so he hoped.

He told her everything that happened at the Longacre on that last night.

Or almost everything . . .

What he didn't say was how he had cuffed Gordon Tallis to the radiator and soaked him in petrol and burned him alive. Myra knew, and she would take that secret to her grave. Laura had known, but she accepted the person he had been because she loved the man he had become. But Laura was gone now, as the real Ray Drake had died decades ago, and Sally Raynor, and so many others.

'What will you do?' Myra asked Flick.

'Peter Holloway is dead.'

'Killed by Turrell.'

'And Toby Turrell is dead.'

This is where Drake expected it to end. The lie he had been living since he arrived on her doorstep had been blown wide apart. But he had much to be thankful for in his life. He had been given an education, a career. And he had a family of his own, a loving wife and daughter. April might never understand why her father kept the truth from her, but the most important thing was that she was safe. Turrell was dead.

She was safe. He kept telling himself that, but the sudden nature of Turrell's death nagged at him.

'You helped Toby get out alive from that place,' Flick said.

'And if I had let him burn,' Drake said, 'all those people would be alive.'

'Give me the gun.'

He placed it on the table.

'We'll call the office.' Flick ran a hand down her face. 'And you can make a statement.'

'*I* killed Turrell,' said Myra tersely. 'In self-defence. This has nothing to do with Ray, and everything to do with me. He has already lost his wife, and if you take this further, he will lose his daughter, his livelihood and his reputation. I am asking you to consider very carefully what you do next. If you feel any compassion for him at all do not destroy his life for something that has absolutely nothing to do with him.'

Flick scraped back her chair. 'I need to think about this.'

'Of course.' Myra smiled sourly. 'You must do what you believe is right.'

Drake lifted himself from the wall, agitated. An image churned in his head: a jaunty red hoodie disappearing at the corner at Ryan Overton's estate. He heard Amelia's voice.

My husband will never touch me again.

When he came to the table, his fingers dabbed anxiously at the surface.

'What?' asked Flick.

398

'It doesn't make sense,' he said. 'Turrell had the opportunity to kill me more than once. He could have killed Amelia and taken April anywhere, knowing how important she is to me, and yet he let her go. At one time or the other, he could have killed us all. Why?'

'Turrell had a death wish. He was obsessed with you killing him.'

'He spent many years murdering those people, and he hated me and Elliot more than any of them.' Drake winced. 'All that intricate planning, and yet he chooses to die before his task is finished?'

He tried Elliot's number again, his stomach tightening with every unanswered ring.

'Where did he get the money for the endless changes of identity and location?' he said. 'Or the money to pay Jordan? He's been saving something special for us both, he – oh, God . . . He's got everyone just where he wants them.'

She's out of your grasp now, Drake had said, and Turrell had smirked.

Drake scooped up the gun.

Flick jumped to her feet. 'Ray, you have to stay here. We'll call—'

His face drained of colour. It wasn't over; he was a fool for ever believing it was.

'Turrell was content to die in the knowledge that his work would be completed after his death. The intention was always for Elliot and me to die together. We were the other Two O'Clock Boys; we were always together at the home, that's how he remembered us. And April . . .'

'An armed response unit will get there quicker than we can,' said Flick.

'No, if police approach the house, April will die.' His voice was a whisper. 'Please help me.'

Flick looked at him impassively, and then stormed into the hallway, stepping around the corpses. As Drake followed her, Myra hooked a finger around his wrist.

'Do you trust her to do the right thing?'

'Whatever happens, happens,' said Ray shortly.

'We have come too far to allow our lives to fall apart. Do whatever you must to safeguard your daughter's future, and your own reputation.'

'Myra—'

'Wake up, boy!' She slapped him hard across the face. 'Wake up!'

His bruised cheek stung, but the blow crashed through his body like a shockwave. All these years, the old woman had never raised a hand to him, not once. She hadn't needed to. She could chill the blood in his veins with a single contemptuous look.

'There are times when I miss our friend Connor, his vitality and passion. Connor would never let events unravel like this.' Moisture shone in her eyes, a greasy film that could be no more than another sign of her failing eyesight. He had never seen her cry, and knew he never would. 'I have lost one child, and I will not lose another. Come home, Raymond.'

When he left, she went to the cutting to look at the image of Connor Laird one last time. And then, igniting the hob, she set fire to the paper, let it blacken and burn to the tips of her fingers.

60

'Whatever happens next,' said Owen, voice low against the wind moaning through the warped planks of the barn, 'is entirely up to you. Because the fact is, son, you're in big trouble. Perry here is keen to beat the shit out of you, and I can't say I blame him. He's very unhappy at being locked in the boot of a car, particularly as he gets very claustrophobic. Ain't that right, Perry?'

Perry, leaning on a cricket bat, his swollen face almost unrecognisable in the dark, muttered something.

'It's lucky he had his mobile with him,' continued Owen. 'Or he'd still be in there. It's not going to be good for you. You understand that, don't you?'

'Yes,' said Elliot, pale with shock. He lurched forward on the muddy ground; wanted to touch Perry, to make sure he was real. The flatulent crack of Perry's grip tightening on the rubber handle of the bat made him snort. His stomach convulsed, his heart raced. He felt . . .

Joy.

Elliot experienced such a grateful release of tension that despite the danger of the situation – there was no doubt Perry and Owen would make him pay for what he had done – he couldn't help burst out laughing.

The truth was, Elliot wanted to plant a smacker on Perry's lips and hug him. Tell him how happy he was. He propped his hands on his knees and laughed and laughed till his sides ached. Tears of relief dropped from his cheeks, spotting the hard floor.

'I don't think you've got much to laugh about,' said Owen angrily. 'You're in big trouble.'

And then just as quickly, Elliot fell to his knees and wept. The sobs came so hard that he was barely able to breathe. All the guilt and dread, all that toxic shit locked inside him for so long, poured out.

'That's more like it,' said Owen, not understanding.

Because Elliot felt blessed. Everything was going to work out. The worst hadn't happened. Perry was alive. He was flesh and blood, standing in front of Elliot. Angry, dangerous, as ugly as sin, but alive and kicking. And Elliot knew that whatever they did to him, Perry and Owen – and it would be very bad indeed – it didn't matter.

None of it mattered, because now he could look Rhonda in the eye, hug Dylan to him, and ask for their forgiveness. It wasn't too late. He could put it all behind him, this whole nightmare scenario, and start again.

The worst hadn't happened. His mind whirled with new beginnings and possibilities. He was friends with Amelia now, and she had money, plenty of it. And that copper Drake – his mad, bad old mate Connor Laird – owed him *big time* now.

He picked himself up. Owen's face was twisted with revulsion, as if Elliot had revealed something about himself, something unsavoury.

'Just let me do him,' Perry growled.

'We'll get the money first, and then you can set to work on him. I'm looking forward to giving you a hand,' said Owen, rolling up the sleeves of his jumper with great care.

'You know what, Elliot, I can see a pattern emerging here.'

'Yeah?' Elliot wasn't bothered by what Owen had to say. He was only thinking about Rhonda and Dylan. He would fall on their mercy. Tell them about what happened at the Longacre – Connor Laird be damned. If he had to do time for the robbery, or the assault, he would do it willingly, wipe the slate clean and start all over again.

'Bloke called Gavin came to me a few days ago.' Owen circled him. 'Bren brought him to me. Said he'd taken your money. Gave half to me, half to Bren, your *good mate*.' Owen mimed reeling in a fish. 'He told us to hook you in, get you on a job. Scratch the surface, he said, and you were a rotter, a scumbag, said you're a thief and a bully. I've never heard the like of it. He really despises you, Elliot. You always struck me as strictly pound shop, a little man, but he was quite insistent. I don't know what you did to Gavin, son, but he's got it in for you real bad.'

'His name's not Gavin,' said Elliot, wiping the tears from his eyes. 'It's Toby.'

Gavin – Turrell – was wrong about him. He wanted to get on with the rest of his life now, was impatient to be with Rhonda and Dylan, and he just had to get through this night.

'Where's the money, Elliot?'

'In my bedroom.'

When Owen moved towards the door, Elliot stepped in front of him.

'Please – my guests. Let me go get it. I swear I'm not going to make any trouble, or try to leave. I'll come right back, you have my word.'

'Your word.' Owen rubbed his chin thoughtfully. 'Five

minutes, then. Any later and Perry will introduce his cricket bat to your lady friends.'

Perry rested the bat on his shoulder, as if in readiness for a long night's work.

Elliot ran into the howling wind, the gale lifting his heels. Cloud raced across the moon. Leaves flew around his head like demented bats. He sensed Owen watching at the barn door. The wind chime was turned sideways, its metal threads thrashing, white noise in his head.

Inside the cottage, the final embers of the fire clung to blackened logs. The kitchen door was closed. Elliot took the stairs two, three, at a time, and slipped into his bedroom.

Grabbing the rucksack from the wardrobe, he unzipped it, took out the gun. Part of him wondered whether he should hold Owen and Perry at gunpoint and call the police – give himself up, then and there – but he didn't want anything to do with the weapon. Just wanted it gone, and them gone. Elliot dropped it into the bag with disgust and zipped it up.

He was about to go back downstairs – five minutes, Owen had said – but couldn't help himself. He took out his phone and called Rhonda's number. It rang and rang and dropped to voicemail. Elliot wanted to assure her that the worst hadn't happened. Everything was going to be all right, he was free now, and they could be together.

'I've done a terrible thing,' he said, 'some terrible things, and I want to tell you about them. From now on I'm going to tell you *everything*.' At the window he lifted the net curtain, thought he saw a figure slip into the barn. 'I'll never keep anything from you or Dylan again, that's a promise. If you decide it's all over between us, I will accept it. But—' He pressed his fingers into his eyes. 'If you can find it in your heart to forgive me, I will do everything in my power to make you both happy. That's a promise, Rhonda. I've never felt as sure about anything in my whole life. I will do *anything*. I love you both. Please call me back, let me make things better.'

He cut the call. The phone rang immediately and his heart leapt. But when he looked he saw a string of miscalls from Connor. Not now, he thought, let's deal with one fucking problem at a time, and threw it on the bed.

The kitchen door was still closed when he crept downstairs. Elliot crunched down the drive. The trees swayed and creaked above him. His spine chilled where sweat popped on his back and froze.

'Take it.' He strode into the barn and threw the bag on the dirty floor. 'The gun is in there, too.'

No one replied.

For one brief moment, Elliot thought Owen and Perry had gone. But above the moaning wind he heard a curious gurgling sound. Stepping carefully through the shards of silver light pouring in through loose planks in the roof, his foot hit something.

Perry was sprawled on the ground, perfectly still. Face pale, almost luminous, a final glimmer of light fading from his swollen eyes. Blood, jet black in the moonlight, ticked gently from his gaping throat, like a water feature in a rockery, pooling around his shoulders. A hiss of escaping air whispered from the exposed piping in his neck.

'Christ almighty.' Elliot's legs buckled, and he fell to his hands and knees into the warm, sticky blood. He smothered a cry, smearing his face in Perry's blood, frantically wiped his hands down his jeans.

He found Owen a few moments later, behind hardened

sacks of clay. The old man's hands loosely cupped the remains of his throat, the meat of it bulged between his fingers, strings of blood and tissue hanging from the yawning wound. His wellington boot jerked, and went still.

The barn door banged against the frame, and Elliot turned quickly.

'Hello?'

A cloud passed in front of the moon and the barn was plunged into darkness. Elliot listened to the wind howl through the rotten planks, then rushed forward.

Stumbling over Perry's leg, he fell, throwing his arms forward to protect himself, jarring his elbows on the cold, hard mud. He had no idea if he was alone or – oh God, if Turrell was still in the barn.

He could be in here, could be standing right over him.

Elliot swept a hand in front of him, scrabbling for the rucksack, desperate for it. Finding fabric, grabbing it. He unzipped it with shaking hands, shoulders cringing against a sudden blow to the head, or a knife slicing out of the darkness. Elliot tipped out the contents and snatched up the gun, flicked off the safety, and pointed it at the banging door.

He edged towards it, swinging the gun wildly, not knowing from which direction he would be attacked. Waiting for any movement, any tiny change in the density of the dark. Then he barged through the door to run towards the cottage, trying to keep his balance on the uneven ground.

'Amelia! April! Get out,' he called, but his shouts were lost in the blast of the wind. 'Get outside!'

Elliot ran inside and shouldered open the kitchen door. Cups of tea sat on the table, untouched. He stomped upstairs, shouting hoarsely, 'Amelia! April!'

He raced into every room, one after the other, and then into the front bedroom. Empty. He looked out of the window. With that sick maniac Turrell roaming about the place, he hoped desperately that the two women had got away into the woods.

Owen dead, Perry dead. He struggled to think. Focused on the fact that his family was waiting for him. Everything was going to work out fine, he felt it in his bones. He wasn't going to die now, not now.

Emboldened by the heft of the weapon in his fist, he felt a surge of fury and chambered a bullet.

'Elliot?'

He whirled, his finger squeezing the trigger. Amelia Troy let out a frightened whimper in the doorway, lifted her hands above her head.

'Jesus! You scared the shit out of me!' Elliot took her wrist and lowered her to the bed. 'Where've you been?'

'We've been looking for you,' she said, gawping at the weapon. 'You went outside and didn't come back.'

'He's here!' he hissed.

Amelia stared. 'Who?'

'Turrell – he's in the house!'

'Oh my God!' Her hand flew to her mouth.

The last thing he needed was for her to start screaming the place down. He had to take the heat out of the situation, asked quietly, 'Where's the girl?'

'Downstairs,' she said. 'In the living room.'

'She's not,' Elliot whispered urgently. 'I was just there.'

The idea that April was alone somewhere frightened him. Christ, if Connor's girl disappeared . . . he didn't want to think of the consequences. All he had to do was get through this.

Rhonda was waiting for him, Dylan was waiting.

'We've been everywhere looking for you!' Tears filled Amelia's eyes; she was starting to get hysterical.

He pulled her off the bed, waved the gun in front of her face. 'We're going to get out of this. We find April and get in the car and drive away, do you understand?'

She nodded.

'Do you have your keys?'

'Yes.' Her voice trembled.

'All you've got to do is stay behind me, okay?' He squeezed her arm. 'Good girl, you're doing great,' and added: 'We both are.'

He led her out of the bedroom and onto the landing, pointing the gun ahead, holding a protective arm in front of Amelia. At the bottom of the stairs, the front door shuddered. He leaned over the banister, but couldn't see anything.

Elliot called down: 'April, you there?' There was no response. A log shifted in the grate, sending up a billowing cloud of sparks.

'Elliot,' Amelia spoke low behind him.

He needed to listen, needed all his wits about him, put a finger to his lips: 'Quiet!'

She said it again: 'Elliot.'

'What?' He turned to face her, and Amelia pressed a knife into his gut and twisted it, this way and that, her face straining with concentration.

And when she calmly lifted her gaze to his, all Elliot had time to do was stare in shock, let out a brief grunt, and feel his legs give way, sending him toppling backwards down the stairs.

61

They drove in silence, threading slowly through the late-night traffic and accelerating at the edge of the city, both lost in their own thoughts. Drake stared ahead, reflected street lights pulling silently down his face, focused on his daughter's safety. When they left the motorway and drove deeper into the countryside, the tall trees a blank wall on either side, the car scythed a knife of light on the black road. Something with shining eyes skittered across the headlights and plunged into the verge.

'You didn't have to come,' he said, as they approached Elliot's cottage.

'No, I didn't.'

'Then why did you?'

Flick watched the canopy of trees fold above them, as if the car was going down a tunnel beneath the earth. When the branches parted, they saw the silhouette of the barn. Elliot's cottage, its lights off, was barely an outline beneath the cloud. Drake eased the car to a stop and killed the engine, the lamps. They sat in silence.

'Why was Gordon Tallis handcuffed to a radiator?'

'Tallis was unstable, unpredictable. He killed himself in front of us.'

'Hell of a way to do it,' said Flick.

'Yes.'

'He was trapped by handcuffs *you* took from my father.'

Drake grunted in surprise. She saw the harsh plummet of his cheeks in profile and a pinprick of light in one eye, and it reminded her of the image of Connor Laird cringing from the flash of the camera. 'I'm different now, I'm a different person.'

'Are you?' she asked. When he didn't answer, she held his hand. Badly needed the reassurance of his touch. 'You asked why I'm here. It's because right now you're the only person I have left. Because I can't bear to lose anybody else from my life.'

'Thank you,' he said, 'for—'

She dropped his hand, snapped off her seat belt. 'Let's just do this.'

'No, stay here.' Drake reached for the door release. 'Lock the door. I'm going to look around. If I'm not back in ten minutes, call for back-up.'

And then he climbed out, slamming the door behind him. Flick watched him trot up the drive.

As soon as he was gone, nausea washed over her in the silent compartment, turning her stomach, slipping along her skin like a clammy chill, as all the terror of the night hit her. She had watched Peter Holloway and Toby Turrell die; had been convinced she was going to be killed. And now, here she was, sitting alone in the middle of nowhere in the dark, every muffled sound making her tense with fear. A minute passed, and then another, and the longer she sat there, the more she realised how wrong it all was. She was scared – and confused. Well, enough was enough.

Flick scrambled for her phone. Its blue light bathed the

interior. Out here, the signal was weak, a single flat bar – if the call even connected it would be a miracle. But the device managed to find a mast somewhere, and the call was blasted to a satellite thousands of miles above the woodland. After a few moments a phone rang somewhere in the city.

'Fli –' Eddie Upson's voice dropped out almost immediately.

'Eddie, I'm at Elliot Juniper's.'

'Wha –' Upson's voice kept disappearing. '– ick, is tha –'

She clamped the phone tightly to her ear, said: 'I need a response unit, Eddie . . .'

'A what? I can't – you, Fli – ere are – ?'

'A response unit, Eddie! Now! Elliot Juniper!' she cried.

'Ell –'

'It's Ray Drake, Eddie.' She gripped the dash. 'He's – '

'Eddie's voice said: '—per,' and the line went dead.

Flick threw the phone down in frustration. She cracked the window. Wind howled into the gap. Somewhere, an owl hooted. She'd try Steiner next, was bending over to pick up the mobile when the bushes quivered on the verge ahead, and a figure stepped onto the road.

Flick held her breath, leaned forward to see who it was – and was relieved to see Drake approach beneath the moonlight, a silver ghost. He came along the passenger side and rapped on the glass.

'It's difficult to see inside,' he said. 'All the lights are off. And in the barn . . .'

She stepped unsteadily from the car. 'In the barn, what?'

'Never mind.' He hesitated. 'The cottage looks empty, but—'

Flick's hands flew to her face. When she pulled them

411

away, her palms were wet with tears. 'Jesus Christ, Ray!' she said bitterly.

Ray Drake nodded. 'I understand. You don't have to come inside.'

'No.' Her hands clapped her sides. 'Let's get this over with.'

If anything happened to April she would never forgive herself. All she hoped was that Upson had heard her, and help was on its way.

Drake reached into his pocket and took out the pistol. He snapped the magazine from the grip and slapped it in again.

'You can't use it,' she told him.

His eyes flashed. 'My daughter is in there, Flick.'

She held out her hand. 'Leave it here or I call this in right now.'

Drake handed her the weapon. She opened the door and threw it under the seat.

'When you get April out of there, drive away and keep going.' He pressed the car key into her palm. 'If I'm not with you, don't wait. Just get to safety.' He touched her arm. 'Are you ready?'

Flick nodded, but barely heard him. She strained to hear sirens, the sound of distant engines, but the wind crashing through the trees obliterated every noise.

Staying close to the verge, they walked along the lane, leaves churning around them. A hundred yards ahead, the drive rose steeply.

62

The windows of the cottage reflected the swaying wall of
trees. A saucer of moonlight struck the glass and vanished.
A wind chime lifted sideways in the wind, clinking like
crazy.

'Go round the back and keep your head down. And be
careful.'

Flick nodded, and disappeared around the side. There
was little point in creeping around, Drake decided. He stood
tall, crunching up the drive, his tie dancing in the wind like
an angry viper.

The front door was unlocked. When he walked into the
dark and closed the door, the sound of the chime, the whistling wind, was muffled. The window frames shuddered.
Definition bleeding into his vision, the layout of the room
slowly emerged. He could make out the fireplace, its final
embers fading. LED lights glowed on a television, a Wi-Fi
router and stereo. He heard the loud thrum of a boiler, and
something else . . . a rasping breath on the floor.

'April?' he called. 'Elliot?'

A voice rattled wetly in reply. Somebody lay at the bottom
of the stairs. Elliot. His shirt – and the carpet around him
– was jet black and sticky.

'Lights?' asked Drake.

'By . . . the door.'

Drake pressed the switch. Light illuminated the space. Elliot's face was drained of colour and soaked in oily sweat. Black rings circled his eyes, which were swollen blood red by broken capillaries. His body was drenched in the blood ticking patiently from the gaping wound in his guts.

'Finally.' His lips smacked together. 'The cavalry.'

'Where is she?' Drake leaned close to Elliot. 'Where's April?'

Elliot's eyelids fluttered. Two figures appeared at the top of the stairs. Drake's heart leapt when he saw the gun held at his daughter's throat. Amelia jammed the muzzle into April's windpipe as they moved together down the steps.

'It's a crying shame Toby isn't here,' said Amelia brightly. 'He would have enjoyed seeing this. But the poor man was desperately tired, and so eager to be gone. I assured him that he could leave it all to me, that I would complete his magnificent obsession. I presume he's . . . ?'

Drake focused on his daughter, who trembled violently in Amelia's grip, and her stricken eyes were fastened on his. 'He's dead,' he said.

'I'll miss him, but it's what he wanted.' Amelia sighed. 'There was no talking him out of it. The truth is Toby was too sensitive a soul to survive in this stinking world.'

Elliot's throat hacked a wet laugh.

'Why?' asked Drake. 'Why are you doing this?'

'I loved him.' Amelia's eyes filled with tears. 'He saved me. He taught me how to live my life without pain, without torment, and you can't imagine how much of a release that was, how much of a revelation.'

'He killed your husband, and very nearly killed you.'

414

'He meant to kill us both, of course he did. I was never meant to survive that overdose. We discussed it like grown-ups. When I woke up in hospital my memories of the Longacre were gone and I felt free. For the first time I could begin to enjoy life. They came back eventually, of course they did, in bits and pieces, but they held no power over me. The death of my hateful husband, the abusive man who made my life a perfect misery, gave me hope that I could finally live. And Toby assured me that when it's all over, when I leave here tonight, I will be reborn. I will live without fear, somewhere far away.' Tears slid down her cheeks. 'I'm for ever in his debt for what he's done for me. In another life I believe he would have achieved many great things, and I'm grateful to have been at his service. To be honest, I believe he was happy for the company on his difficult journey.' The corners of her mouth lifted in a repugnant smile. 'Not all of us can do the Lone Wolf thing, Connor.'

'By killing all of those people?'

'Well,' she said modestly, 'I helped, just a little bit.'

'Ryan Overton.' Drake sensed movement in the corner of his eye, Flick edging through the kitchen door.

'Yes, that was me,' said Amelia. 'I've always been super supple, I used to love climbing the trees in the garden at the home, and Toby had to work that evening. But mostly I financed his work. Provided documentation, identities, forged qualifications, that kind of thing. None of that stuff is cheap, believe me. I like to think of myself as more of a facilitator, a sponsor. It was actually kind of fun.'

'I can help you,' said Drake, edging forward.

'You could have helped me at the home,' she spat. 'But you never did. Ray was the only one to make any effort, the

415

only one who ever took an interest in my welfare. But you killed him, and took his future for yourself.'

'Whatever Turrell told you, it's wrong.'

'That poor, sweet boy burned to death, and you didn't save him. You forget, Connor, I was there.'

'Toby said he'd let April go if I killed him.'

Amelia gave him a sympathetic look. 'I'm afraid I didn't get that memo. But I tell you what . . .' She took a knife from her belt and threw it at his feet. 'I'll consider letting your precious little girl live if you save me the trouble and kill yourself right now.'

'How do I know you'll let her go?'

'Oh, you don't! I could just kill her anyway, but you're going to have to trust me. I'm a very trustworthy person, and trusting in return. Ask Toby, ask my beautiful, brutal husband, may he rot in hell.' She nodded. 'Don't be coy, Connor. Pick up the knife and gut yourself. I've seen the things you can do when you put your mind to it.'

Flick moved closer behind Amelia as Drake crouched over the knife.

'Don't do this, Amelia.'

'I'm waiting.' She shuffled backwards, April whimpering in her grip.

He flipped the knife in his hand so that the tip of the blade was pressed to his stomach. 'We'll get you help,' he said.

'But I don't want help.' Amelia's eyes bulged. 'I've never felt better!'

When he stepped forward again, Amelia jammed the barrel of the gun up into the soft flesh beneath April's jaw. 'Just do it!'

Drake stood hunched over the knife as if to disembowel himself, and Amelia shivered with expectation.

He shouted: 'Now!'

Flick lunged to grab Amelia's gun hand, wrenching it away from April. Plaster exploded in the ceiling when Amelia squeezed off a shot, but Drake flew forward, sending them both to the floor.

'Get out!' he shouted, and April ran screaming out the door. Drake slammed Amelia's gun hand against the floor and the weapon went off again, splintering the wooden stairs above Elliot's head. Drake crunched her wrist again, and the gun leapt from her hand.

A furious wind blew in through the open door. Amelia and Drake rolled towards the fireplace, tumbling over each other, her nails clawing at his face, his eyes, as she scrabbled on top of him. Screaming, clawing, slapping and punching his temples and cheeks. A riot of colour swam in his vision.

Flick flew at her, but Amelia stretched to pump the knife into her left side in three quick stabs, *in, in, in,* and when Flick's body stiffened in shock, she swung her against the fireplace. Flick's head cracked against the mantelpiece and she slumped against the wall.

Amelia dropped back onto Drake, and he glimpsed the flash of the blade – a searing pain ripped through his shoulder. She pressed down on it with a banshee shriek, wrenching the knife around in his flesh, leaning on it with both hands, opening the wound. Arching so low that her lips brushed against his, and he thought he was going to black out. Then he felt the knife suck from the wound and Amelia sat bolt upright, holding the blade high, ready to bring it down into his face.

417

She stroked his cheek tenderly, said: 'Goodbye, Connor.'

Then there was an explosion, and chips of stone flew from the fireplace. Amelia flinched at the gunshot, giving Drake the moment he needed. He twisted his fingers into her hair and smashed her head down into the stone surround with all the force he could muster. He heard a crack as her skull splintered, and Amelia went slack on top of him.

Trying to avoid the weight of her lifeless body pressing on his wound, he pushed her aside and lay against the warm edge of the fireplace. Elliot made a feeble smacking sound in his throat. Drake climbed to his feet.

'Shit,' Elliot mumbled. The gun dropped from his hand. 'Missed.'

When Drake crouched beside him, Elliot said: 'You get him?'

Drake nodded, gingerly pulling the jacket from the wound in his shoulder. The slick dome of Elliot's scalp was sallow, and his breath rattled, as if his lungs were flapping loose inside.

'Ain't lost your touch, have you? Turrell, the girl . . . and Gordon. I remember your first one.' Elliot winced at a shooting pain. His pupils were almost obliterated behind a sea of clotted red. 'You ever think about it, Connor . . . what you did to Tallis?'

Drake said: 'He deserved to die.'

'You did him good. In cold blood. The look in your eyes, the way you torched him, it was ice cold. I ain't ever forgotten it. But it's got to stop now. All these lies, all these secrets.' He attempted a slack smile. 'They'll be the death of me.'

Drake glanced at Flick, unconscious against the wall, blood seeping from the ragged wounds in her side.

418

Faintly in the distance, the sound of sirens.

'She's coming back to me, my Rhonda,' said Elliot. 'I know she is – and the boy. I'm getting a second chance . . . and I'm going to tell her everything. Get it all out where it can't hurt me any more.'

Blood spurted from his mouth. Chances are, Elliot wasn't going to last much longer, he had lost too much blood. But stranger things had happened. Drake reached into his pocket, took out a pair of disposable gloves.

'They're probably on the way back now, and I'm gonna tell 'em everything. About the home, and what happened there . . . and what became of us. It's the only way. Me and you, we'll tell the truth for the first time in our lives, and the lies won't hurt us no more. And then . . . we'll be free, at last.' Drake crouched, snapping the gloves over his fingers. 'What do you say, Connor? A new start for the both of us.'

'I think it's a fine idea, Elliot,' said Drake, and he pinched Elliot's nostrils together, cupping the hand over his mouth. Elliot tried to struggle, his hands scrabbled weakly at Drake's wrist for a few moments as his mouth filled with blood. Eyes fastened on Drake, his arms swayed slowly like reeds in a gentle stream, then fell to his sides. A short time after that he stopped moving – and his dead eyes stared blankly.

Drake stood, pulling the gloves off his fingers, and when he turned, Flick was staring at him.

Right at him.

63

What did you see?

Drake was leaning over her when she came to, pressing a towel into the wounds in her side. Flick's head swam; she was ice cold and shook uncontrollably: her muscles, her nerves, her whole body. 'Am I . . .?'

'Easy,' he said, glancing towards the door. 'They're here.'

The sound of vehicles outside. Doors slamming and shouts. Lights, blue and yellow, refracted off the windows and whirled across the ceiling.

'What did you see, Flick?' he asked. Her mouth was dry, despite the icy sweat dripping into her lips. She tried to speak, but couldn't. She felt pain, but didn't know where it was coming from. He smeared her sopping fringe away from her eyes. Drake's face was close to hers, and he spoke quickly. 'What did you see?'

There was blood everywhere. His own suit jacket was sodden. Amelia Troy was face down beside the fire, Elliot Juniper's body by the stairs.

'We're good, aren't we, Flick? We're going to get through this, me and you together.' Drake smiled gently. 'What did you see?'

Then the bodies were surrounded by uniformed men and women as paramedics and police poured inside. Drake called: 'Over here!'

She heard shouts, urgent commands, and then Eddie Upson was standing over her. She heard him ask Drake if there was anything he could do. His voice echoed, as if from the far end of a long pipe.

'Let us through, please!'

A pair of paramedics kneeled beside her and started barking questions. Talking in slow, loud voices as they unpacked equipment. One of them moved Drake aside to press hard on the sopping wound – Flick's body couldn't stop juddering – and fired questions at her.

'Are you cold?'

'Can you breathe properly?'

'Tell me your name.'

'She's in shock,' said Drake.

One of them held up a hand, irritably. 'Move away, please. Let us work.'

Drake stepped back, and Flick dimly registered some kind of dispute as more paramedics surrounded him. He didn't want treatment, didn't want to leave her.

And minutes later, when an oxygen mask had been placed over her face, and a clotting agent applied to her wounds and bandaged, she was lifted onto a trolley and brought out of the cottage. The breeze cooled her burning face. The furious winds of the night before had subsided and the wall of trees on the other side of the lane had emerged from the dark. She sensed Drake keeping pace with the trolley.

He had asked: *What did you see?*

And the question kept going round in her head, but she didn't understand it. Her head was groggy with the throbbing pain and the cold that coated her bones. Images repeated in her mind, each one layered transparently on top of the other like a double exposure. She saw Amelia Troy's twisted leer as she gleefully stabbed at her; Peter Holloway falling on the stairs, arms outstretched; and Ray Drake crouched over Elliot, doing something with his mouth, as Juniper's hand plucked ineffectually at his sleeve.

'We're taking you to a trauma centre.' She barely heard the paramedic as she was secured on the ambulance. 'You'll go straight into surgery.'

She tried to speak, wanted to say goodbye to Nina and Martin and the kids. Needed them close, now more than ever, but knew she had to let them go.

'Do you want someone with you?' asked the woman.

Eddie Upson and Millie Steiner and Vix Moore crowded at the back door of the vehicle. 'Is she going to be okay?' Steiner asked.

'We'll need one of you with her,' the woman said.

And she heard Drake say: 'Let me go.'

Flick said, *No*. She didn't know why, but she didn't want him near. Needed time to order the images in her head. *No, please*. But nobody heard her, because her voice was muffled and weak beneath the mask, and her head swam, and she had no idea if she'd even spoken.

Millie Steiner climbed on board and took Flick's hand. The throb of the engine pulsed through her. Beyond the doors, she glimpsed the patrol cars and ambulances, the uniforms scattering across the drive, and saw the boy called Connor Laird staring at her, oblivious of all the commotion around him.

And she had no idea what he was thinking.

A last glimpse of racing cloud, a whirl of flashing blue light across the gravel, and the ambulance doors slammed shut.

422

Acknowledgements

But, wait – before you bung this book back on the shelf, there are people to thank. For no man is an island, not even Ray Drake, and without the help and encouragement of certain people The Two O'Clock Boy would never have gotten up to no good. I'll keep it brief because I know you have things to do.

There's my agent, Jamie Cowen. Jamie's passion for *His First Lie* was a game-changer, and I'm hugely grateful for his belief in the novel and my writing. The same goes for Rosie and Jessica Buckman, and the other lovely people at The Ampersand and Buckman Agencies.

My editor at Sphere, Ed Wood, worked his astonishing magic on the story, and has gently challenged me to raise my game as a writer at every turn. And, gosh, there are so many others at Little, Brown to thank. It's been a joy to work with Thalia Proctor and Alison Tulett, Tom Webster, Emma Williams, Ella Bowman, the wonderful Sales gang – and my thanks to Sean Garrehy and Bekki Guyatt for their eye-popping covers.

I'd like to thank everyone who has read part or all of the manuscript along the way and taken time to comment. Debi

Alper – who made me cry with relief – Isabelle Grey, Claire McGowan, Laura Wilson, Rod Reynolds, Steph Broadribb, David Scullion, Charles Harris and Lisa Thompson.

There are patient and helpful people to whom I ran for professional expertise: Mick Gradwell, Jason Eddings, Bob Cummings, Bob Eastwood and Ian Sales. Anything I got wrong is down to my own pig-headedness.

And finally I'd like to thank Fiona Eastwood for her inexhaustible love and patience. Without Fiona I would never have been able to fulfil a lifelong dream. Ever since I started writing *His First Lie* one snowy winter's afternoon in midtown Manhattan, she has supported and encouraged me.

My debt to her – for this book, and for just about anything else worth a damn in this life – is incalculable.

Now read on for the beginning of the next
Ray Drake thriller

THE THRILLER WHERE NOTHING IS AS IT SEEMS

Did she
kill him?

Was he the
only one?

It

Was

Her

MARK HILL

1

After Will:

One moment Will was there, and the next – he was gone.

Clumps of grass trembled on the lip of the chalk cliff. An armada of cloud scudded across the thick line of the horizon where the sky met the ocean. But all that was left of Will was a ghost of a movement. An absence in the empty space where he had been, above the quivering tufts of grass and the white stone, and now – in the blink of an eye – wasn't.

Joel's parents ran down the slope. Their screams and shouts were muffled in the rattle of the wind in his ears. His mum's eyes bulged with terror as she stumbled over the uneven ground. His father roared for them to get back, step away from the edge, for god's sake, get back. Joel saw Poppy run back towards them, in floods of tears.

But Sarah was leaning over the edge, where the cliff dropped away to the waves lashing angrily against the jagged rock hundreds of feet below. Hands planted hard on her knees to stop her toppling, the fierce gale making her hair twist and tumble around her pretty face.

His dad's voice was hoarse: 'Get away, get back!'

'Will! Will!' shrieked his mum.

And then Sarah glanced over her shoulder at all the commotion, and her eyes fell on Joel.

And she was smiling.

This big smile on her face.

One moment Will was there, and the next—

2

Now:

This, she decided, was her favourite room in all the world.

There were so many beautiful things. Sitting at the antique dressing table, she touched the bottles and containers of all shapes and sizes – magenta, turquoise, jade, every colour of the rainbow – which glimmered in the gentle light of the bulbs decorating the mirror. The bed was the biggest she'd ever seen, and piled high with pillows and cushions and throws. It was a delight to scrunch her toes into the delicate weave of the soft carpet.

The woman walked to the wardrobe, which was set into a wall so that you hardly noticed it was there. And when the door slid open – with a sound as faint as a whisper – neat rows of dresses and skirts and blouses were revealed, and neatly stacked racks of pretty shoes: heels, flats, pumps, sandals. Hangers clacked when she took out a summer dress imprinted with pale blue flowers.

Holding it to her body, she twirled before the dappled rocking horse in the bay window. The creature's silver mane fell across one ear. Polished stirrups and buckles sparkled on its leather saddle. She saw approval in its painted eye.

Yes, that one.

If anything, this room with its gleaming walls and silver trinkets spilling from the jewellery box on the dressing table, the sparkling chandelier, and the heavy antique wall mirror with aged black spots on its faded surface, was even more lovely than the others.

Earlier, she had soaked in the oval tub in the bathroom, relaxed in flickering candlelight, enjoying the scent of pomegranate and blueberry and winter spices from the salts and soaps and creams. Let the steaming heat lift the cares and worries from her muscle and bone.

But then a sudden, terrible image of that *poor man* came out of nowhere, making her gasp and jerk upright. Water surged over the side of the bath to slap angrily on the chequered tiles.

And just like that, her composure was shattered.

Tension knotting her shoulders, the woman reached for the plump towel of Egyptian cotton warming on the heated handrail, avoiding her nakedness in the mirror – the pendulous breasts and heavy thighs, the sagging stomach, the thick threads of scar tissue snaking down her shoulders and back – and wrapping it around her, opened the cabinet to choose from all the lotions. The face cream she selected was cool against her flushed cheeks.

Now, she placed the dress on the bed, careful not to crease it, to apply make-up from golden tubes and black compacts which snapped closed between her fingers. Her face, usually pale and careworn, burst into colour. Finally, there was just a lipstick to choose. Her fingers hesitated over the different shades and settled on a bright red infused with a faint sparkle, to the admiration of the rocking horse.

Yes, it said. *That one.*

The woman picked up an ivory hairbrush, its milky surface inlaid with pretty curlicues and loops, and pulled it through her hair. The brush crackled against her scalp, the static charge kinking her tangle of curls.

'It's ready,' called a voice.

She winced again at the thought of that *man*, just left there like that. It was no good, the whole night would be ruined if she didn't do something about it, so she went to her cargo shorts balled on the floor and took out a phone with a screen as big as her hand.

The woman hesitated. What she was about to do was a dangerous thing. But when she pressed the power button and the keypad appeared, she had no idea of the passcode.

'Come on down!'

The voice flustered her and she pressed random numbers on the screen. The phone buzzed tersely. She tried again, but it was pointless. The woman turned it off, replaced it in the pocket of the shorts.

Walking past the horse on its bow rocker, she inched the curtain aside. In the early hours of the morning the road seemed abandoned beneath the wash of streetlight. And yet inside all those big, handsome houses, she knew, people were safely tucked up in bed, and the thought comforted her. The roar of a car receded into the distance. She wished the driver god speed and hoped they would be reunited soon with family, with the people they loved.

'It'll get cold!' shouted the voice.

The dress she had chosen was too tight – she'd never be able to zip it up – but there was no time to choose another, and she went downstairs.

The kitchen at the rear of the house was vast. A skylight ran its entire length. This room, like all the others, was a bright, happy place in daylight, and at night was infused with a cosy glow from all the hidden lighting. Sleek appliances covered every surface. A silver range cooker was set into a converted fireplace. The cabinets were the type that popped open at a touch, and the long island unit was topped with a shining granite surface. But pots and pans had been dumped in the sink, and the tap, its neck as long and graceful as a swan's, seemed to recoil from the mess.

Her companion was hunched over a table, forking food into his mouth, and when she sat he squeezed her hand, gazing at her in adoration.

It was late; they were both weary, both hungry.

'Eat,' she told him.

The prongs of his fork rang against the china whenever he speared a shell of pasta on his plate. She prodded at it, but the food was burned, rubbery. Popping a piece into her mouth, the woman tried to enjoy the ambience of the lovely kitchen, and ignore the ugly chewing sounds of her companion.

She considered once again the twisted path that had brought her to this man, to this place.

And then a noise made them both look up sharply . . .

The door opening at the front of the house.

They heard anxious voices in the hallway. The front door slammed. A fragment of urgent conversation. Wheels fluttered along the floorboards.

Seconds later, the kitchen door swung open and a tanned woman in bright, loose-fitting clothes stood in the doorway. She cried out, and then a man pushed past her, dropping the handle of his case. His face was bronzed beneath steel-grey hair, but his arms, the skin on his neck, were sunburned.

For one stunned moment, the two couples looked at each other, and then the man in the doorway demanded angrily: 'What are you doing in our house?'

The woman at the table felt a terrible sadness.

She scraped back her chair to stand, its legs screeching on the tiles in the fierce silence. Beside her, the man's fork clattered to the plate. His chair tipped backwards. He jumped to his feet, the tendons in his wrists jerking taut.

The woman thought of this house, made into a wonderful home thanks to the care and attention, the *love*, of the couple in front of them.

Tatia wished it didn't have to end this way.

Stepping over the body was out of the question. It stretched along the hallway, one arm flung over the face, the other reaching for the stairs, fingertips pressed against the bottom step like a swimmer grasping for the edge of a pool. Simon Harrow's pink shirt rode up over his belly, which was mottled purple. His shock of grey hair was plastered by blood to the tiled floor. One leg, the bone snapped, rested heel-up against the wall. Teeth were scattered like dice along the skirting.

Harrow's body caused a bottleneck. If police and crime scene examiners wanted to reach the dining room at the rear of the house, where Melinda Harrow's body lay curled beneath the baby grand, they had to go through the living room to the left.

'I don't want to pre-empt the autopsy,' said Detective Constable Millie Steiner. The young black officer stepped back to consider the fire poker, matted with hair and gristle, and sticky with blood, dropped at the victim's feet. 'But I'm guessing they were beaten to death.'

Eddie Upson winked. 'Top-notch detective work, Millie.'

She shoved a bony elbow into Eddie's ribs just as Detective Inspector Ray Drake stooped over the body.

The skin on Harrow's leg was ruptured, torn apart beneath the force of the poker like the flesh of a dropped peach. Muscle and tendon bulged from the tear; there was a glimpse of arcing white bone. Bruises, imprinted from the killer's footwear, crisscrossed the edge of the wound.

'He was brought down hard with a stamp on the lower leg.' Tugging at the knees of his scene suit, Drake crouched to look at the victim's crooked fingers, the lacerations and lesions across his arms and shoulders. Most likely defensive wounds from where he lay on the floor trying to protect himself. 'And hit repeatedly with the poker.'

Millie Steiner watched Drake examine the corpse, fascinated by his hard face, the sharp, jagged cheeks, the straight nose and tapered jaw, those pale blue eyes from which the colour seemed to drain the longer you gazed into them. Not that Ray Drake ever let you meet his eye for very long. He was a shy man, it seemed to Millie, who kept a healthy distance from his team.

'The crime scene people are happy bunnies,' she said. 'They're picking up plenty of fingerprints all over the house, forensic samples galore, and some new words, too. One of them told me there's a *cornucopia* of evidence.'

'I went to a restaurant called Cornucopia,' said Eddie. 'It was very pricey.'

'And plenty of footprints.'

A faint footprint yielded the best results. Bloody prints were often difficult to read. The liquid poured into the pattern, obliterating the unique signature of the tread caused by wear and tear. Every sole on every shoe was different, in the same way as every fingerprint was unique, or every gun barrel.

'It's good to have you back, boss,' she said.

'Thank you.' Drake smiled, but his eyes didn't lift from Simon Harrow's cruel injuries. 'This . . . is not your usual.'

'No,' agreed Millie. 'Not your usual.'

Drake considered the victim's cotton shirt, his quarter-length trousers and the boating shoes flung across the hallway. Next door, Melinda Harrow's body was barely a foot from the phone, sat in its cradle on a cabinet shelf. Like her husband, she had almost certainly been bludgeoned to death, suffering fatal blunt force trauma, multiple blows to the head and body. Melinda was dressed in a fitted shirt and silk skirt. A single espadrille hung off one tanned foot – sky-blue nails glistened in the light – and the other was kicked against a piano leg.

A trolley-case was on its side in the kitchen doorway, a baggage claim tag tied to the handle. A larger case – the companion part of a matching set – stood inside the front door, along with Mrs Harrow's Hermes handbag. Two passports were tucked into a pocket, and a pair of airline boarding passes.

Everyone knew the relief of getting home from holiday. It was good to go away, but there was a special kind of pleasure in returning home. Boiling water in your own kettle, brushing your teeth at your sink. Curling up beneath a crisp duvet, surrounded by beloved things accrued over a lifetime. But the Harrows had instead arrived home to find themselves plunged into a life or death struggle.

The confrontation was swift, catastrophic.

Two plates on the kitchen table contained half-eaten pasta. The lights were on upstairs. A dress was dumped on the floor in the bedroom. A tideline in the bathtub and a damp towel suggested someone had used it.

Someone was here, in the Harrows' comfortable home. Someone they knew, perhaps, minding the house. Friends, neighbours, or people they had found on Airbnb. But that didn't explain the forced window at the side of the house.

'How much do you think a place like this is worth?' asked Millie. This was a four-floor, six-bedroomed detached home in a sought-after area in Tottenham. All the rooms were bright, spacious and immaculately decorated.

Eddie Upson scratched at the collar of his scene suit. Sweat filmed his forehead. The spring morning was warming up. The bodies would have to be moved soon.

'A pretty penny, although the asking price is plummeting by the second.'

'I never thought I'd say it, Eddie,' said Drake. 'But I've missed your repartee.'

Eddie winked at Millie. Loud voices disturbed Drake. A pair of officers stood at the front door in animated conversation about rugby with the arriving pathologist. Then the fabric of the tent erected outside lifted – Drake glimpsed squad cars and support vans parked in the street – and a small woman pushed through the men. The protective hood that framed her wide face rose unnaturally high around her head and her foot coverings were stretched tight over heavy boots. Deeply engrossed in her phone, thumbs dabbing at the screen, she barely noticed the body sprawled in the hallway, and walked upstairs.

'Who is that?' said Drake.

She wore a lanyard, at least. A lot of people came and went from a crime scene. It would be nigh-on impossible for anyone unauthorised to breach two cordons, but he didn't like the idea of people wandering about checking their lottery numbers.

'Who's what?' Eddie looked up, but she had already gone.

'Never mind.' Drake was irritated by the men's braying laughter. 'Do me a favour, Eddie. Tell them to take the conversation outside.'

'Sure thing.'

Drake stood, rolling his shoulder. The wound he had sustained several months ago had healed, but the muscle stiffened easily.

'Where's DS Crowley?' he asked the young black officer.

Millie gestured over Drake's shoulder. 'In the garden.'

Through the kitchen window, he saw Flick Crowley on the lawn with a police search advisor. He watched her for a moment, his anxiety building. When he turned back to the body, DC Vix Moore was standing beside him.

'I spoke to the cab driver,' she said.

'Hold on.' Eddie had joined the conversation at the front and it was even louder than before. Drake could hardly hear himself think. 'Next door.'

In the living room, tasteful abstract art provided splashes of colour on the brilliant white walls. A charcoal grey sofa and matching chair sat at right angles to an antique fireplace. The long neck of a floor lamp reached across the room.

Pride of place on the mantelpiece was a framed photo of Simon and Melinda Harrow on a beach of white sand. A handsome couple in their fifties, they looked relaxed and happy at a table in the surf, silver water lapping over their feet. A glorious sunset flared off the rims of their lifted champagne flutes. Simon was tanned and trim in tennis linens. Melinda's white teeth flashed between full lips. Her scooped top was edged with sequins which glimmered in the red dusk.

The circular mirror above the fireplace gave the room a

sense of space and light, despite the tent erected across the front of the house. A rattan rug was rolled up on the painted floorboards so that Crime Scene Examiners could collect samples – prints, fluids, stains. In the dining room next door Melinda Harrow's body was partially hidden beneath the legs of the piano.

'I spoke to the cab driver,' repeated Vix. 'He picked up Mr and Mrs Harrow from Gatwick at 12.45 a.m.'

'And they were alone?' asked Drake.

'Yes, they chatted with him about their holiday – the food and the weather.'

'Neither of them made any calls, or sent texts?' asked Drake. 'Or mentioned anyone would be here when they got back?'

'They were tired, but in good spirits,' said Vix. 'Mr Harrow told him they had come home because of a work emergency.'

'They speak to anyone on the phone?' Drake asked again, and Vix blinked. 'You didn't ask.'

Her cheeks reddened. 'No.'

Drake stepped back into the kitchen, careful to keep to the transparent footplates laid on the floor. The atmosphere was stuffy as the sun pulled across the roof of the house.

The fridge was a giant Smeg. Using a single finger of his gloved hand, he tugged open the door. The chill air cooled his face. Inside, it was mostly empty. The Harrows had binned most perishables before their holiday. There were jars of pickles and olives on a top shelf; a tub of butter; a lonely bulb of garlic. A carton of milk from Quartley's Supermarket was forgotten on a shelf in the door. The curdled contents slopped lazily when Drake tilted it.

'I've the driver's details,' Vix said. 'I'll get back onto him, and do a background check.'

'Thanks, Vix,' said Drake. 'We'll go over the rest later.'

'Yes.' The tips of the young detective's fierce blonde bob twitched like the antennae of an anxious insect. 'I'm so glad you're back, sir, I've already learned so much from you.'

Fishing for compliments, she waited for his reply. But Drake's attention kept returning to the garden, and to Flick.

It was good to be back on the job, doing what he did best. This was his life. But it could all be ripped from him at any moment. And not just his career – everything. His family, his good name – maybe his freedom.

It was all in Flick's hands now.

Ray Drake took a deep breath and stepped outside.